Hellsucks

Hellsucks

Noël Sweeney

ALIBI

This edition first published in Great Britain in 2009 by Alibi
PO Box 1615 Bristol BS40 5WF

A catalogue record for this book is available from the British Library.

ISBN 978-1-872724-06-5

Printed in Great Britain by CPI Antony Rowe, Chippenham, Wiltshire

For Gertrude Ansell

Women are inferior animals. We must make them afraid of us. Otherwise we'll be governed by the brutes.

Balzac: The Black Sheep

Because the Night

"Gotta guillotine the Queen. Gotta guillotine the Queen. Gonna guillotine the Queen. That's my last life-time dream", Qualm sang in a drunken caterwaul. He sang it along with the bootleg, making a keen song, Guillotine the Queen, sound dull. Kevin Qualm was sat in the middle. Qualm glanced left at Dean Canker and right at Lee Hornet, who both cackled and then joined in on the chorus. Their noise became louder as they added their own version, "Maroon the bitch on my muscle machine". They repeated the chorus and ended with their own favourite mantra, "Let's stick it to 'em tonight".

The three sang as the grimy green van rumbled through the country lanes. Canker clapped his hands and Hornet banged his palms on the steering wheel. Qualm slapped his heavy thighs while his mouth moved with the motion of a hungry hippo. As usual, they were all out-of-tune. They had a way of strangling a song as to make it their own and so unrecognisable.

It was a clear night near the end of summer as their van shot through the lanes, Hornet cutting corners and hammering on the horn. Far from being tired, they were all wired. The trio were still tense from a small argument that led to a big fight in the saloon bar of the 'Half-Empty Glass' earlier in the evening.

As the trio were passing Cedar Field the red-yellow moon was high and bright, here and there concealed by a wispy, passing cloud. A crisp tinge in the late night air would make someone with ordinary blood feel cold. What you really needed to keep warm was to have your blood mixed with alcohol. That was no problem for the trio. Their blood was distilled with booze every night and day.

1

For Qualm and his two mates it was just another lousy night littered with the splinters of other people's lives. Their nights were filled with varying degrees of violence, depending on the victim's response. Usually they sucked the unwitting victim into the vacuum of his pride and their aggression. Though the booze and blood often flowed in tandem, none of them needed an excuse to batter someone.

An American baseball bat was always at hand. It was secreted beneath the driver's seat in case the chance came to swing it to cave in some stranger's skull. Qualm loved touching it, holding it, feeling the power as he imagined wielding it. For him it was like an extra limb. When he first filched it from the local sports club storeroom, Qualm said to them, "Hold it. Feel it. Pure maple. See how it balances?" He held it in his outstretched right palm. "We could do some serious damage with this. Here, have a go. Swing it."

"Sweet, man," Canker said as he swung it like Babe Ruth.

"Let's have a go," Hornet said, grabbing it from Canker. He swung it avidly, imagining someone's head cracked open by a single blow.

For Qualm the balance of the bat when he held it with both hands was perfect, as if it was made for that purpose. A tool to maim and maybe mutilate.

Tonight was no different. When the rough cider kicked in, just like any fash-seeking vandal, they always needed another kick to end the evening. The trio still had energy to burn. Some surplus anger too. They were angry about everything and nothing. The night would grow old before they were cold. Besides, a spot of mayhem always seemed to help them sleep.

Qualm was fashionably fat, his clothes stretched in

2

every direction to fit his flabby frame. A number one haircut emphasised his double chin and black-ringed eyes. He was big all over, but especially his wedge-shaped head, which sat on his gnarled neck like an upturned galvanised bucket on set concrete. Even when he wasn't hot he stank of stale sweat. Though now thirty-three years old, in mind and manners he remained an ageing juvenile.

Hornet was similar in build, but shorter and squatty. An eruption of fat. He always wore the uniform of the unfit: the scuffed trainers, the baggy elastic-waisted tracksuit and a shapeless T-shirt tent to cover his growing gut. That started at his chest and ended on his crotch. In a bad light he resembled a defeated Sumo wrestler. In a good light he looked the same. Mentally he matched Qualm.

Canker was tall and thin, but blessed with a big beer belly. His bump was a badge for his generation. Long greasy hair fell across his high-domed forehead as strands of tarred seaweed. At the back it was bunched in a lank ponytail, held by a postman's discarded red elastic band. His bony physique and sunken eyes gave him a scared, sly look. In profile he was S-shaped, his heavy gut supported by spindly flamingo legs. He hung his clothes wherever they fell. Gravity was the hook. Routinely he woke and grabbed his stained jeans and creased fleece from the floor, then wore them all day and night. At night he dropped them on the floor again ready for the next day. He didn't mind the smell from Qualm. He didn't notice it too much as he smelt worse himself.

None of the trio favoured shaving as a habit. Even when they shaved, evidently they used blunt blades. Canker and Hornet always seemed to have at least three days stubble, but never a beard. Qualm had a face as pocked as an old golf ball.

They were all around the same age, having grown up and out together. The trio shared their days and nights. Whatever nerves they each had disappeared when they talked and walked as a gang. Then they were as one. Wherever Qualm led, Hornet and Canker followed close behind. If you crossed one you crossed them all. Then you had to contend with their friends too, who, like them, had short tempers and long memories. Together they spoke the street poetry of violence using the bat and steel-capped boots to deliver their message. The baseball bat was a symbol of their lives.

Hornet continued to career around the country lanes. His driving was always dangerous as he hurtled towards every destination as if on a racetrack without a thought to any traffic coming the other way. He drove at two speeds, reckless and crazy.

"Stop. Stop the motor!" Qualm shouted, between laughing and singing, "Let's stick it to 'em tonight." Laughing, he flashed his gummy mouth and near-toothless grin. Those teeth he still had were puny black and pale tan pegs.

"What, here?" Hornet asked. He braked, sharply turned the steering wheel and barely missed the ditch. As the tyres skidded on the gravel he asked, "Why here?"

"Look. Over there." Qualm pointed to a group of dark shapes huddling under a huge oak tree near the left hedgerow in Cedar Field. "Pull in. Now." He rubbed his hands together. He was not cold, just on heat.

"I'm with you," Hornet said.

Canker strained his head to see what Qualm saw. "Oh, yeah," he said, looking at Qualm. Canker's face began to brighten. Hornet moved the van forward, braking harder right in front of the six-bar farmhouse gate. As the van stopped, Qualm scrambled over Canker and got out. In less than two minutes he unhooked the cast-iron clasp, grasped the crossbar of the beech gate and using his bulk, forced it open across the worn cobbled stones.

As the bootleg finished they stopped singing and Hornet turned the radio on. "Hey. Listen up. Stitch The Witch Down. Great sound." He twisted the wonky knob, turning the volume to the maximum. A rap rant rang from the cab. "Brilliant." He banged on the steering wheel, still out-of-time. The rusty hinges creaked as the gate swung on the cobbles. The creaking was drowned by the sound of the revving engine and the rap that split the silent night sky.

Although it was pure chance, the trio found what they were looking for in Cedar Field. It was just luck they were there, good luck for them and bad luck for everyone else. Cedar Field was a desolate area on the outskirts of Chantilly Village in deepest Wintersett. There were various ash and cherry and oak trees. The trio looked towards the biggest oak tree and saw a group of animals under it taking shelter from the cold late night air. It was mainly horses and a few cows. The moonlight mirrored the lonesome animals for there was no one else there, but the trio. The farmer, Wylie McTell, lived a considerable distance away. The nearest neighbours, the Stent family, were even further, near the Mozz Quarry on the way to Swinestone, the next village. All the horses except one and the few cattle were free to move. Among the horses, one pony was tethered for her own safety.

Louise Rowe, an early-retired infant school teacher, owned Molly. She had little interest in people anymore. She never married and now lived for her animals. In her absence, her friend from the village, Lily Mernaugh, tended to the pony daily. Molly was a chestnut brown

5

Shetland pony, about twelve hands high. She was six years old. Everyday Louise called Lily to ask about Molly. Everyday Lily lied. She said, "Molly is doing fine and in fantastic form." Later she told her, "Molly is eating well and galloping around the field. You should see her, Louise. She's really missing you and just waiting for your return." Lily knew now was not the time for truth, diluted or otherwise.

Qualm, eager as ever, was first in the field. Canker jumped out of the van and joined him. Canker and Qualm smiled and nodded to each other. They both rubbed their hands together in harmony. Their eyes flickered with intent. Both opened the gate a bit wider. Hornet drove straight towards the animals, shining the full beam into their frightened faces. When they first heard the music and the drunken grunts of Qualm's singing, the cows were startled and scurried away to the far end of the field. A few of the horses moved too, seeking sanctuary in the distance. The rest shuffled uneasily under the oak tree. Now they scattered when the revving van shot through the gap and skidded on the grass and shattered the country skyline silence.

That left only one, Molly.

All the animals had antennae for impending trouble that served as an internal alarm. For Molly there was a vibration, a sense of the smell from the strangers. She tried to run. She failed. In vain she tried again. She was tied to the cherry tree. She was at the end of her tether. The virus in her swollen colon had sharply sapped her strength.

"Well, what have we got here?" Canker asked, looking at Molly. Grinning, his tawny teeth were as brown as a mouldy owl.

"Quick, Lee, get the gear," Qualm shouted. "It's in the back."

They looked a little too long at Molly. Smiles slowly formed on each of their faces. No one said a word. They all looked happy as the moon reflected their eyes shining with hate.

Hornet ran to the back of the van and pulled the doors wide open. In his rush he threw the breakdown tools and the jack and the socket set aside. He couldn't find the gear. "I know they're here somewhere," he said aloud. He rummaged among old tyres and stiff rags, "where are they?" He clumsily climbed inside. Finding what he was looking for, he put one on each arm, sat on the edge of the van and jumped down. Stumbling, he almost fell over, saved by his gut's low centre of gravity. He ran from the van with the ropes. Using both ropes, Hornet lassoed Molly.

"Dean, take this." Hornet held one and Canker held the other. Qualm untied the one that tethered her, each holding a rope and keeping Molly in a tension of terror. Her eyes began to glisten with a glassy fear. Her ears were dead straight and angled backwards as the fear filtered through her body. Molly was held tight between the three ropes as the trio moved awkwardly around her.

As the others held her tighter, Canker struck a well-aimed boot, storm trooper-style, in her belly. Hard. Hard as a hammer on an anvil. Molly writhed in pain, tried to move away. They laughed. Her hoarse shriek pierced the night, then faded and died. Their echoing laughter drowned her doleful sound.

Qualm went over and with his right hand gently stroked her head and said, "Oh, what a good girl. What a lovely pony." He whispered to her, "Sweet girl. Don't worry. You'll be all right. That's better. Calm down." He had a way with all kinds of animals, especially equines. "Trust me." Molly was suckered. Even in the state she was Qualm's act momentarily soothed Molly. His slick touch and oily words pacified her. He patted and stroked her. Qualm moved closer and whispered more calming lies in her ear. His soft stroke got heavier, in time with his breathing. He shifted his arm and slid a stiletto from his soiled sleeve into his palm; with a flick of his wrist, his right thumb pressed the button and released the blade. He stugged her right in her right eye. He swiftly twisted the blade and slowly withdrew it.

"Wow, look at that," he said as a fountain of blood spurted from Molly's eye.

"Yeah, yeah," Canker and Hornet shouted in unison. "Fanbloodytastic," Canker shouted. Qualm's excitement was contagious.

Qualm grabbed the lasso and held it tight in his left fist. He gently patted her head even as she tried to pull away. He spoke in a lower whisper than before. While he whispered he moved forward slightly and slashed at her jugular, cutting just deep enough to damage her voice box. Several times she attempted to scream. Her attempts came out as low moans with intermittent gurgling of the blood-bubbles trapped in her throat. Qualm turned the knife through his hand and gripped it hard. He forced it through the cold mist-forming air ending the arc at Molly's left eye. The second blow blinded her.

"Who wants it?" Qualm asked. He tossed the knife in their direction. Hornet caught it.

"Kev, look. Watch me." Canker got down on all fours and lurched from side-to-side in front of Molly. He mocked her by acting like an ass. His mockery spread. She stood motionless as the trio mimicked her misery, 'neighing' in a repeated coxy cry. The fresh gaping wound nearly severed her throat. Molly looked as sad and lonely as life itself.

"Let's have some fun tonight," Hornet shouted, as he wrenched the rope, almost strangling her. "Are you ready? I said are you ready?" Holding his left hand high, he threw a shape and posed. He looked like a fat roadie acting like a fat roadie.

"Yeah," Qualm shouted, "let's stick it to 'em tonight." Canker joined in.

They dragged her to the van and tied the ropes to the back bumper. As Hornet revved the tyres span on the grass, the van jolted and jerked Molly off her feet. He bounced her around the field, the ropes forming a tourniquet.

"Hey-Hey-Hey," Canker shouted, as the one-beat techno rap blasted from the battered speakers.

"That's what I say," Hornet bawled and banged the steering wheel, almost in time with the bass drum.

Hornet kept revving, his itchy foot forcing the worn steel pedal to the crisp-packet-piled, lager-can-littered, butt-strewn floor. Qualm, hanging out of the driver's door, urged Hornet to, "Pump it, pump the bitch!" Canker, hanging from the other door, was screaming at fever pitch.

"Whoa! Whoa!" shouted Qualm. They took no notice. He banged his right fist on the dashboard. They ignored him, fired with their own frenzy. He banged the steering wheel. Hornet looked at him. "Stop. Stop!" screamed Qualm. As Hornet eased his sticky boot off the pedal, the van juddered to a halt.

"That's enough," said Qualm, adding under his breath, "for the moment." His thighs rubbed as he jumped down onto the grass. He took another lingering look at Molly. She lay on the hard ground. Her misery, though visible, was not the first or last thing on his mind. It was absent from it. She was his property. Qualm moved towards Molly as a Catholic priest moves in on a choirboy, ready to rob him of his innocence. The buccaneer moon caught the sheen on his bulbous spotty cheeks. Molly became just another notch on his loose belt, one more statistic of misery. With his lust spent, Qualm moved slowly backwards and slunk away, his fat hot face mirroring his pleasure. The moon caught the sheen on his red, pitted cheeks.

"Nothing like it!" he shouted to the night, his right fist clenched in triumph. "A different kind of meat, 'eh boys." His cohorts forced a short laugh. "Fill your boots boys. Who's next?"

Canker and Hornet untied the ropes and held her. They dragged her to her feet, but she couldn't stand unaided. They let her fall. She stayed where she lay in a gathering pool of fresh spreading blood. The trio glanced at Molly and then each other. Each one traded a nervous smile. Content to speak with their eyes in the way of lovers and liars.

Qualm turned away and sauntered to the back of the van. He grabbed a can, ripped it open and gulped the scrumpy in one long guzzle. "I needed that." He tossed the can, kicked it, watching its trajectory as it ascended and landed and spilled foam bubbles on her bloody belly. "What a shot." He laughed, the others clapped. He grabbed another can, burst it open and swigged it greedily, his lips glued to the top. He gulped it as if his mouth was on fire. "Ah, that's better."

"Hey, let's have a swig. You greedy bugger," said Hornet.

Canker seeing him, said, "Yeah. C'mon. You fat bastard. Sling one over here. After all, I nicked 'em too."

"There you go, my man," Qualm said and threw Hornet a can. "Here's one for you, Dino. You deserve it." Qualm smiled at Canker's claim. He always approved of attitude. "You know me, I'm happy to seal a deal by breaking a few thumbs. But stealing is always the best deal 'cos then it comes with some danger and for free."

Qualm reached into his ripped back pocket, pulled out a dented, painted tin and rolled the dark Virginia tobacco into a thin cigarette. Neat and round, a little thicker than a match, the kind of fag liked by old lags. His habit was a relic from his time inside. He threw the oblong tin to Hornet, who used the shag to make a squashed fag. It was poor even as a roll-up. Hornet threw it down and ground it into the grass with his left heel. He made another one much the same. He just lit it, striking the red top match on his left thumbnail. He handed the scratched tin to Canker who made a raggedy roll-up with strands of tobacco hanging from each end, matching the stray hairs poking from his arrowhead Who nose and Windsor ears. Qualm held a fluorescent yellow beretta with a chrome handle and pointed it directly at Canker's nose. He clicked the trigger twice in rapid succession, lit the cigarette and gave him a nasal singe.

Hornet held the cigarette between his teak-stained teeth and sucked on it as if it was a teat. Canker's cheeks became concave as he cupped his between his right thumb and index finger and deeply inhaled every last strain of nicotine. Qualm formed and blew a smoke-ring and followed through by blowing the rest of the smoke through it. Qualm stretched his tongue to lick the tip of his glans-shaped nose. He stared into the darkness. He pondered on what more he could do and should do and would do.

Molly lay where she fell. Her bloody pool was slowly

11

spreading. Her breathing became more laboured. Bubbles of blood continued to burble and lock in her throat. The trio stood over her, drinking and smoking, cider and tobacco mixed with the reek of their fresh and stale sweat. A sense of menace still hung in the starless night.

"Who's got my shiv?" Qualm asked.

"Here it is," said Hornet. He'd used it to flick the muck from under his fingernails. He used the tip to scratch his hairy nostrils and the blade for his itchy crotch. He went to wipe it on his grease-encrusted jeans, but couldn't be bothered, so passed it to Qualm who didn't even look behind. Qualm was busy thinking about her. He looked at her and then into the black distance. He mused about Molly. As the moment passed, Qualm got his stiletto and cut Molly cleanly from her throat to her tail and beyond.

He held the knife in his open right palm. Its shiny blade dripped with bright, rich blood. The tip was pointed at Hornet. He took it and carved his initials on Molly's body. "Give it here, Lee." Hornet passed it to Canker who cut 'DC' on her flank. Canker then casually and carelessly cut through part of her tail. "Just what I need for my collection." He'd add it to his other victims' knick-knacks and knickers. A trophy. Give him something to brag about down the pub.

"Don't," said Qualm. He grabbed Canker's wrist before he could complete the cut and took his knife back. He held it at Canker's chest, pressing the point on his breastbone. "I've got a better idea."

Unnoticed by the others, Hornet wandered back to the van and rifled through the toolbox. Having found what he wanted, he made a beeline for Molly. He bent over her to get a good position, almost kneeling. He held her throat, stretching it, opening the wound. He got in position ready

12

to hack her head off with the honed handsaw. As Hornet was poised to make the first stroke, Qualm saw him. Qualm rushed over, kicked his right hand so hard the saw flipped through the air and cut Hornet's left jaw. He roughly pushed Hornet over, placed his boot on Hornet's ribs and said, "You deaf, gobshite?"

Hornet struggled to his feet and looked at Qualm. Both were grinding their teeth. Qualm stared at him, brought up a ball of phlegm, rolled it for volume and spat it at Hornet. It landed on Hornet's right cheek. "Something wrong?" Qualm asked, breathing fast, standing with both fists clenched, ready to rumble. Hornet appeared about to rush him, moving forward a few feet. "Try me. C'mon." Qualm hooked his forefinger. Hornet saw the stiletto flash in Qualm's tight right fist and froze. Hornet shrugged, wiped his face, moved back and looked towards and through Molly.

Qualm threw the saw in the back of the van. He returned with a red gallon can. He sprinkled the diesel on her hacked tail-stump, all over her body and ears. The diesel seeped through the wounds to her bones. Qualm pulled the trigger of the beretta twice. Ever so slowly, he lit her at each end. He winked and said, "Always destroy the evidence."

Qualm stood in front of her. Canker and Hornet loomed behind her head. As they admired the fire, in the red spark-filled glow, their faces perspired. Spontaneously, one-by-one, they unzipped their shrivelled Clintons and diluted her hot crimson blood, as each let a steaming jet of scrumpy gush into Molly's bleeding eyes.

About sixty seconds later, the trio strolled nonchalantly to the van.

Qualm stopped. He turned around and walked back

towards Molly. Canker and Hornet strolled to the van. Qualm held his mobile phone high and took a series of colour photographs from different angles. As he viewed her, he laughed and sang in a Cockney accent, "What a picture, what a photograph." He took twelve of her, removed the SIM card and walked away. Half turning as he walked, he lobbed the lighter towards the fire. It landed near Molly's blind eyes.

Canker went to get in the van, hesitated, waited and let Qualm clamber in first. Canker pulled the passenger door shut. Hornet climbed in and drove off. After a few seconds he crashed into the gate, causing it to jam up against the front wheel arch. Hornet sat there. Qualm put his right hand on Hornet's left shoulder, grasped it, forcing Hornet towards him. Qualm glared hard at him. The left side of Qualm's top lip curled, baring his black teeth. Nothing was said. There was no need. Hornet jumped out and manhandled the gate, freeing the wheel from the bent metal. He kicked the gate across the cobbles and noisily got back in the van, mouthing off as he did so. Though not loud enough for Qualm to hear, the message was clear.

"You got a problem?" Qualm asked Hornet.

"No. I was only-..."

"Only what? You're a pussy. Just drive."

Canker shrunk in his seat. He could hear Qualm's time bomb ticking. Canker was praying the fall-out wouldn't land on him. The temperature in the clammy cab made the smell rise.

Hornet raced off, letting the gate swing unevenly, to-and-fro, on its loose hinges. As he left, the weight of the gate caught the back bumper and buckled it at right angles. He accelerated. Hornet, panicky, kept pressing the pedal and struggled with the steering wheel. In rushing to leave

14

Hornet accidentally touched the knob and re-tuned the radio. Across the airwaves came Wolfman Jack playing an old track from a new release. The Wolfman said it had been lost in the vaults. The steel strings of the National vibrated as the singer hit a straight C chord. He launched into a hypnotic blues based on a true story, "William Zanzinger…"

"What the hell's that crap?" Qualm screeched. Hornet was trying to drive and tune the radio at the same time. "Put on some acid-snap or zapp. Anything, but that crap." Qualm moved back and forth in his seat. His chest was rising, his anger too. "Change it. Now." He brought his right elbow forcibly into Hornet's left side, drew forward and smashed his fist into the dashboard. He hit him and the dash again. Hornet flinched as the tracked pain travelled to his chest. He held his tongue.

Qualm kicked the heater cover, three times in quick succession. The steel-on-steel sharply pinged. Veins on both sides of Qualm's neck grew like cobalt cables towards his cheeks. He had a crude bluebird tattooed below his right ear, etched on by his last cellmate, Otis Barren. When he was angry the veins enhanced the colour of the bird. Now it almost glowed. Veins on each side of his temple grew too, a dark blue. His fleshy neck flushed to a brighter shade of red. The colour spread and covered his face.

Hornet glimpsed the tattoo. He drove furiously and fumbled with the knob on the dial. He kept losing and then getting the blues song again. Finally he alighted on some raucous song that preached violence against women; something about, 'slittin' bitches.' "Turn it up. Loud. Louder," Qualm said, his buttocks bouncing to the throbbing sound. As the needle on the dial moved, the

15

strain of Zimmerman at The Gaslight died, while he delivered the original out-take of *The Lonesome Death of Hattie Carroll*.

One Hundred Years

"Hurry up. C'mon, get a move on," said Detective Sergeant Jack Jambeaux to the three defendants, Canker and Hornet and Qualm, as they dragged their feet up the steep steps of the Rochester Row Central Police Station in Feytown. They'd been arrested within a week, following a finger from an informer buying his way out of trouble. The trio were trying to huddle together to talk and walk at the same time. Given the steps and their shape, it wasn't easy as their handcuffs got in the way.

As they were entering the foyer Qualm whispered, "Don't forget, tell them nothing." Qualm put his left index finger vertically to his lips. "Nothing. You got it?"

"Yeah, Yeah," Canker said. "Yeah."

"Don't keep on. I know what to say," Hornet said.

"That's precisely the problem," Qualm said. "Just zip it."

"Whatever you say," Canker said, shook his head, sighed and closed his eyes. His peeved look spread to Hornet. They didn't want an argument with Qualm anytime, least of all now.

"I won't tell you again," Jambeaux said. "Shift yourselves. We haven't got all night. Let's get you lot signed in." His angry manner was all part of the police method of pulse-pulling, the initial preparation before the final interview. Jambeaux removed all the handcuffs. They signed in giving their personal details, but there was hardly an officer there who didn't already know them. It was a family matter. Every officer in the Station knew the defendants' fathers and family and friends. "No doubt," Jambeaux said to his colleague, Detective Constable Richard Wangford, "if we live long enough, Dick, in time we'll be arresting their children too."

"What a prospect," Wangford said. "Do we get a medal?"

"For what, patience and endurance?"

Unusually, all the defendants gave accurate details. In truth they had little choice. False details would've led to an additional charge, as they knew from experience.

"Get your clothes off," Jambeaux said.

"I never knew you were like that, Jack," Qualm said.

"Shut up, Qualm, I've had enough of you for one day. Put this on." He handed him a white paper boiler suit. "You two as well." He handed Canker and Hornet a similar suit.

"And, Qualm, it's Sergeant to you."

"Certainly, Sir." He clicked his heels and gave a salute.

"Any more cheek and you'll be on another charge."

"Why?"

"Be quiet."

"What have I done now?"

"I'll think of something. Breathing maybe."

The trio got undressed and stood in the waiting room still wearing their boots and underpants. "Have you turned the heating down, Dick?" Jambeaux asked, in an aside.

"Off," said Wangford.

"Good. We don't want these crimos having too much comfort. Or a hot head. It'll help their concentration for our questions."

"Christ, it's cold in here," Canker said.

"Cold?" said Hornet, "I've got goose-pimples on my cellulite." The trio tried hard to laugh. Jambeaux tried to hide his satisfaction. A smirk formed on his face. Wangford's too.

"All your clothes," Jambeaux said, just as Canker went to put the paper suit on. "And your boots. Socks. Pants.

Everything." He gave each of them a pair of standard black plimsolls.

"Everything, Jac-...sorry, I mean Sergeant?" Hornet asked.

"You heard. Don't look worried, we're not going to sell them. We couldn't give them away. No tramp is that desperate."

"What do you want them for? We ain't done nothing. I told you already," Canker said.

"I didn't believe you then. I don't believe you now. We're going to send them off for forensics, although by the state of them it looks like they'll travel by themselves."

"What d'you mean?" Hornet asked.

"Don't worry about it. All you lot need to know is they'll be examined for blood, mud, sweat, fingerprints, footprints and DNA. Believe me, if it's there, the forensic boys will find it." The trio asked no questions.

" So is there anything you want to tell me? We'll find it out anyway. It's up to you?" They looked at each other and then looked at Jambeaux. All he got was their customary silence and sullen stares as a barely veiled contempt. The trio changed into their paper suits. Their goose-pimples grew; cold and getting colder and still knickerless.

The arresting officers, Jambeaux and Wangford, prepared to hand the rest of the investigation on to the interviewing officers, WPC Helen Hart and DC Robert Valentine. In the briefing before the interview, Valentine asked Jambeaux, "How are the crimos? Have they made any 'admissions'?" He was hoping for some sort of confession, or an unguarded comment, at least from one of the trio.

"No chance. You'd get your leg over with the Mother

Superior sooner than you'd get an admission from them," Jambeaux said

"Not a lot to go on then?"

"You know who you're going to interview, don't you?"

"No. Just some scrote I thought. Who?"

"Well, you're right and you're wrong. It's Kevin Qualm and his mates."

"I've heard about his reputation. Thanks anyway, Jack."

Jambeaux and Wangford left their colleagues and snatched a quick cup of stewed tea and a stale iced currant bun from the canteen. Then they went out together to walk along the thin blue line again. They still had a long shift to finish.

Hart and Valentine remained in the interview room. "When I ask Qualm about the mud on his left boot, pay particular attention to his reaction. 'Cos that's the question that'll take him off-guard. Do you agree?" Valentine asked.

"Yes," Hart said. "After that I'll come in with a few questions on the diesel and the knife and the lighter. Then I'll shake him with a few on the alibi. Qualm, the others too for that matter, they'll have to say they were somewhere else. Trouble they've got is they haven't had time to get their stories straight yet. Or crooked I should say. We'll blitzkrieg – is that the word or is it zeitgeist? – it'll do, yeah, we'll blitzkrieg them." She looked to Valentine for support. He smiled and gave a knowing nod.

Hart and Valentine worked up some joint notes for the interview. He said, "I've underlined those points in red. When I ask the killer question watch that defendant's face. Don't worry about his reply. We need to catch them, any of them, on the wing. Dam the flow of their lily-livered lies. Give them something to chew on. I'll come back in on the blood in the van. We've got to get them telling three different stories so we'll set one against the other. That way, we'll smash their alibis too."

"When do I come in again?"

"I've marked an asterisk." Valentine showed her his notes. She marked her notes. "I'll quit asking questions and you take over. Our change will throw them. It's all tactics, Helen. The difference is we make the rules of the game."

"That's crisp. Let's roll."

Meanwhile the defendants were preparing for battle too. Tactics were second nature to them. The police were the enemy. After the handcuffs were removed, the booking-in completed and their clothes seized, they were banged-up together. "It seems sort of stupid to me, they go to all the trouble of putting us in separate cars so we can't make up a joint story," Canker said. "Then place us in the same cell. What's that about?"

"They've got no choice," said Qualm. "No space, no place. Same old story, too many crooks spoil the system." The defendants sat in their cell taking quick, short draws on thin roll-ups. "Anyway, don't forget what I told you. The cops can only use what we say against ourselves."

"But how strong's the evidence?" asked Hornet. They discussed evidence with the fervour of first year law students. Their criminal training was thorough.

"There's no reliable forensics, at least so far," Qualm said. "It won't get any better. Forensically, fire is our friend. It destroys everything. All they got is a pile of charcoal and a carcass. No, what they'll count on is a slip of the tongue. Or worse, one of us lying. And worser,

21

getting found out. Tripped by your own trap. That'll be your downfall. So keep it shut." He pointed at each one in turn and put his finger to his lips again.

"So what do we do?" asked Canker.

"We stonewall them," Qualm said.

"I'm with you," Hornet said.

"Me too," said Canker.

"They got nothing on us. If we all stonewall, they're shafted," Qualm said.

"Yeah," Hornet said, "but what about our alibis?"

"Shut up," Qualm said. "Keep your voice down." He pointed towards the cell door and as they listened they heard the Custody Sergeant, John James 'J.J.' O'Hara, walk along the corridor. "Forget about alibis. We'll sort them out later. Wait 'til Georgie comes. He'll tell us what to do."

All of them spoke in a near-whisper for a few minutes. Then Qualm suddenly said very loudly, "Well boys, we've got nothing to hide, we've nothing to fear, just tell the truth." Canker and Hornet looked askance at Qualm. Both were confused. As he spoke he averted his eyes towards the right hand corner of the cell. "We ain't done nothing wrong." He kept their attention by raising his voice higher, then holding the lobe of his left ear. He gripped the lobe between the thumb and index finger of his left hand and wiggled it. Still talking too loudly, he pointed to the corner. He jabbed his right index finger towards it. They scanned the ceiling, then saw it too. Canker gave a sly smile. Hornet gave a wry smile. Qualm looked as smug as a cheating politician with an expenses claim. At a certain angle the bug was reflecting a minute shaft of light from the cell window. After discovering the bug, they adopted a new approach. They spoke so loud they could certainly be heard. Their conversation changed completely from a whisper to a shrill. From them concealing the truth to revealing their habitual litany of lies.

"Will I tell them where I was, like?" Canker asked.

"Course, you do that, " Qualm said. "Why not?"

"I've got a cast-iron alibi."

"True. Or at least a brass one," said Hornet.

"You make sure you tell 'em," Qualm said and then held an invisible Bible above his head in his right hand, stood erect and announced, "I promise to tell the police the truth, the whole truth and everything but the truth." He laughed way too loud. The others joined in too readily. "Remember, we gotta cooperate."

"I always do," said Canker.

"So you do," Qualm said. "Yeah, you do." His voice trailed away.

The cops sat in the Custody Suite listening intently to the conversation hoping for a confession. Or an unguarded comment. The trio's voices were so harsh when picked up by the bug the sound crackled and jarred in the earplugs worn by Valentine and Hart. At first they strained to hear, then turned down the volume. Everything they could hear was calculated to deceive foreign ears. Far from a confession. What they had was worse than a blank tape: deep-dyed deliberate deception.

With no confession in sight the Custody Sergeant, O'Hara, shouted through the Judas hole, "You're going to be interviewed, do any of you want a solicitor?"

The answer, the opposite of what he hoped for, was a triple "Yeah."

"Who do you want?"

As to who, three voices shouted out one name, "Georgie."

"Who?" he asked, as if he didn't know who they wanted. He knew.

"Georgie Craven," Qualm said.

O'Hara went away and tried to contact the solicitor. Craven left a message on his pager. As he was in another area seeing another suspect, his message said, "I'll be delayed for about an hour and a half." O'Hara felt they wouldn't want to wait. If so, it would give the cops the first advantage as the defendants would be interviewed without an interfering lawyer.

"Mr. Craven is delayed. He won't be here for some time," O'Hara shouted through the hole.

"That's no problem," Qualm shouted back.

"He'll be at least an hour and a half, probably much longer. It's up to you, but we can't consider bail until after the interview."

"Like I said, no problem."

"Heavy traffic tonight. Do you want to be interviewed without a solicitor?"

"No," Qualm shouted.

"Any of you? Could be hours before he's here. It's raining too."

There was a triple shout: "No!"

The defendants had served their apprenticeships in crime. The P.A.C.E. Rules, which regulated the police conduct – from the Police and Criminal Evidence Act – were ingrained in them. They always had their 'human rights' uppermost in mind. That gave them the edge in their choice of lawyer. Besides, experience taught them to share the same lawyer as it made it easier to iron out the wrinkles in their similar lies and make their stories smooth.

George Craven was on his way. Craven was a chubby, sickly boy who as an only child was indulged by doting old parents. Much as a musician might be moved when he hears a beautiful melody, Craven was moved whenever money was mentioned, especially if it was coming his way. So he grew up to be greedy and money-hungry. Qualities that made him ideally suited to his role: he was born to be a lawyer.

Craven normally bought one off-the-peg suit, which he wore until it dropped off his expanding limbs. Usually it was an odd suit choice such as a brown pinstripe or green tweed. Whichever it was soon became flecked with all the detritus of daily living and dandruff. At about the age of seven he started to turn from chubby to fat. As an adolescent he didn't lose the puppy fat, it became dog fat. As an adult he kept piling on the pounds. Now he had mounds of excess flesh spilling over his trouser belt and shirt collar. His collar was always too small, so left unbuttoned at the top with the pointed tips curled over through wear and the absence of an iron. Mostly he wore the same shirt for about a week until the reek was so bad he couldn't stand his own smell. Often you couldn't tell whether the stain was part of the pattern on his frayed ties. Having divorced for the second time at the age of forty-nine, five years ago, he resolutely remained a bachelor. It wasn't hard to tell. Craven worked at being a slob.

Craven arrived wearing a well-worn, dark grey Donegal suit, a light grey shirt and brown shine-less, comfortable two-tone boating shoes. Having checked out the state of the "evidence", Craven almost hurried to the cells. He was in a good mood, feeling bouncy, even at well past midnight. In his mind he could see the money-clock silently ticking over. He greeted his clients with his practised bonhomie, "Hello boys, what brings you here?"

"Uh, huh," said Qualm. His cohorts echoed his eloquence.

"Everything okay? Any problems?" Craven asked.

"Well…. It's alright. Whatever," Qualm said. Though pleased to see him, they remained sullen. It was part act, part natural, mostly personality.

"Have you made any phone calls?" Craven was checking, knowing the cops would listen in.

"Whatchoo think?" Qualm asked. His grimace was matched in the dull, distorted faces of his accomplices.

Craven looked at his watch. He found solace by checking his mental money meter.

"I see they've taken all your clothes for forensic tests. Still they won't find anything unnatural shall we say?" Craven asked. No one answered. "Will they?"

Craven waited for a reply. Canker, Hornet and Qualm finally answered, each in turn with a single word: "No."

"Mind you, those white suits look good on you boys, brings out your complexion." His clients looked less than amused. "Anyway, what have we got here? A spot of bother?" No one answered. "So how've they been treating you?"

Still slightly sullen and sulky, they were beginning to thaw now Craven had arrived. They wouldn't be taken by surprise with him on their side. "Yeah. Alright, Georgie" – and quickly catching his angry headmaster's look – "I mean Mr. Craven," said Qualm.

Craven pursed his lips and gave him a cold crunch-eyed stare. He hated defendants being over-friendly. It was the norm in some legal circles, but Craven hated such familiarity. Otherwise in no time he knew they'd think of

26

him as their mate. For he despised the defendants he represented. He didn't want their friendship, just their funds.

As he stared at Qualm, the others affirmed they were, "Alright", with a mumbling nod.

"I expect my clients to be treated like the classy people they are, especially my favourite clients. No complaints then?"

"No, at least not yet," Canker said. Telepathic glances passed around the room. Eight eyes locked into each other in a common cause. Deception. They all understood the import of the words.

Although they were career criminals by character and choice, they were neither docile nor easy to deceive. Indeed they were hard to impress. Always they looked for and lived on the edge. Even as they faced a serious charge their minds moved towards compensation. It was always a good ploy to make a complaint against the police. Spurious or not, it gave you a wedge, right from the start.

"If it changes, be sure to say as it could lead to a civil claim," Craven said. "That would mean more compensation and costs."

Though he wouldn't recognise truth if it were fed to him gavage-style, Canker said, "They'd better not breach my rights."

"How would you know?" asked Qualm.

"Don't get stroppy," Craven said. "Keep your ears open. Listen for once. Then we'll decide what to do." No mistake, they understood what mattered for them to get the right result. They learned how to use the criminals' tools and tricks from the master, Craven. Together they used strategies as Freud used sex.

"So what's the story?" Craven asked. "What's our

version of the events? I know it must be some mistake. We'll have you out of here in no time." At once he identified with his clients. In the trade with legal aid their word was his bond.

Before any answer was given, Qualm pointed to his right ear and kept his finger there for a few seconds. Then he pointed to the corner of the ceiling. The silver spot glinted. Craven twigged immediately. His demeanour and tone changed. Qualm was thinking of himself. Craven was doing the same. He knew he had to be careful in what he said and didn't say. A loose word and the lawyer would find himself in a tight spot. At worst The Law Society would be on his trail. For in the twists and turns of their strained relationship the police were not beyond playing games with their own rules. Serendipity wasn't enough. Craven knew sometimes suspicion moved to guilt because it was proved with a police plant. They reconciled it by claiming they balanced the uneven scales of justice.

Similarly for Craven and his charges, their pattern was they spoke low when they didn't want the bug to catch their words. They talked too loud when they wanted to plant a few seedy lies in the minds of the listeners.

Craven's style was to always ask the police in advance about the state of their "evidence." That gave Craven the advantage of assessing the strength and weakness of the case to meet and the consequent choice for his clients of whether to speak or be silent during the interview. "How will it sound at the Trial?" he would wonder. He'd ask himself that split-second question, then make a swift decision. He'd be looking ahead to six months later. How will it sound in a cold, clinical courtroom? That's when words can take on a whole new meaning. When lies somehow arise from what was a seemingly innocent question.

"What's our defence?" Before any of the defendants had time to answer, Craven quickly added, "I've had a word with the Custody Sergeant. Me and old J.J., we go back a long way. He wouldn't con me. There's no ID, no worthwhile forensic, no DNA. Nothing so far, no connection, no corroboration." All the defendants leaned forward and cocked their ears. He spoke so low they had to edge closer and strain to hear.

"What about prints?" Canker asked.

"Finger or foot?" asked Craven.

"Well either," Canker said," I was just wondering like."

"Don't worry about that for the moment. We'll get an expert if and when we need one," Craven said to reassure them. Craven was happy to use words like 'forensic' and 'corroboration' to these scunners, as he called them privately. His favourite word for his favourite clients. While they only used language to lie, they knew the real meaning of those significant words. They were scientific and so technical legal hooks that if they got it wrong, by leaving evidence at the scene, they would hang on.

"So, what are we saying about this false allegation?" He scanned their three faces full of suspicion, each side wondering about proof. "It is false isn't it?" Craven having fed the line, they jumped like hungry trout.

"Nothing to do with me. I wasn't even there, like," said Hornet.

"I wasn't neither," said Canker.

"Or me," Qualm said. Their eyes shifted uneasily as each of the defendants were searching for a defence that had the penumbra of truth. It's always easier to merely bend the truth rather than try to manipulate a lie. It allows for an innocent interpretation that could be based on a mistake. Consequently they all looked towards Craven for a hint as to which direction they should follow. They also focused on the ceiling. Craven returned their questing looks with his sleek smile.

Hart and Valentine kept listening carefully to the conversation on the surveillance equipment. Each had a separate device. Occasionally they nodded, sometimes to each other, sometimes to themselves. They were trying to pick up the odd unguarded word that could be used against them in the interview. Most defendants base their lies on a true story that they then embroider. Each side then look for the same loopholes for exactly opposite reasons. Each side would seek to somehow trick the other with a soiled kind of diluted truth.

"Good," Craven said. He now had his 'Instructions' so he could see a Trial ahead and hear the jingle-jangle of money. Already he was inspired. He lowered his voice again. The four of them gathered together in a close circle. Craven was considering whether he'd feed the breadcrumbs of a defence to the suspects. He would only resort to that if it was necessary, at least that's what he told himself. The alternative was silence. That waxed the police to the core and more. It raised their blood to the boil. Given that his charges loved that result, it followed Craven did too.

"So it's definitely a trial?" Craven asked. He looked to each one in turn.

"Sure as hell," said Canker. The others nodded quicker than toy dogs from a now-cubed Cortina at a car boot sale.

"This is what we'll do. For the moment, say nothing. You know the score, you've been here before. Keep shtoom." He looked towards the ceiling being ever conscious of the pervasive bug. "After all you're only exercising your legal rights. Now you can't be criticised for doing that can you?" They all shook their heads in agreement.

"What about our alibis?" Qualm asked.

"Surely you can remember where you were?"

"Yeah."

"And who you were with?"

"Yeah".

"So what's your problem?"

"Well, put like that, there ain't one."

"What about you two? I presume you can too?"

" Oh, yeah, Mr. Craven," answered Canker.

Hornet nodded, almost winked, winced and looked confused. Though Craven knew that state was nothing new for him. "What about you, Lee?" Craven asked, looking directly at him.

"I think so," Hornet said. Craven, not convinced, kept staring at him. Hornet then said, "Yeah. No. I mean definitely. 'Course I remember where I was." He smirked. "Now."

"We're all agreed then." Craven gave them another friendly grin. His chins moved and opened his collar a bit more. He loosened his tie, putting another grease stain on the knot. Craven looked around the cell. He lowered his voice because the interviews were about to begin. Although these characters were low-lifes at heart, Craven knew they were far from stupid. He learned from his past dealings these clients had a strong survival instinct coupled with a native cunning. It ran with their blood.

Valentine was a decade older than Qualm. He and Qualm were opposites in every way possible. They were the

North and South Pole. From his well-cut black hair to his dark grey chalk-stripe suit and polished loafers, Valentine looked what he was, a professional. He exuded style. Most of his problems stemmed from 'the Job', as the police always called the Force. He was inclined to take every small point personally as if it was a principle. In equal measure he hated lawyers and their clients. It was why he practised yoga. The Job was the only job he ever had, having joined straight from school.

Helen Hart was almost twenty-nine years old. She was a fine mathematician, but having got her degree, completely lost her way. After floating in a non-stop series of Temping jobs she ended up as an accountant. Hart learned the cliché joke about it being boring wasn't funny. It was too real to be amusing. Every day she wondered how she ended up as one. For her it was worse than watching rust form. After six months off to recover from her breakdown, she trained to be a detective on the graduate programme. She had completed her two-year training period. Like Valentine she often ruminated on her future.

Valentine put three tapes in the machine to record the interviews. One was the master for the court, one copy each for the police and the defendant. The master tape was sealed and could only be opened in court with 'leave' of the trial Judge. During the first interview Hart and Valentine intended to ask questions hoping to find a hole in Qualm's story. They would use his lies against the others. After a few preliminary points, the police were introduced, the solicitor gave his name and Valentine outlined the allegation. Though he knew of Qualm's reputation, Valentine had been transferred from another Station so he hadn't dealt with him before. He judged Qualm to be a challenged recidivist. He wanted to soften him up and just when he least expected it, deliver a body blow. Before the interview they discussed the plan and their tactics. They had some secret signals as to who would ask a crucial question and when to interrupt to take advantage of Qualm's response. Both officers held their 'Notes' open as an aide-mémoire. They also hoped he would fear they had more information than they had divulged. For Craven had an outline sketch, which was all he was legally entitled to, rather than all the evidence. Qualm was cautioned.

"What's your name?

"No comment."

"What's your address?"

"No comment."

"What's your date of birth?"

"No comment."

"What's your occupation?"

"No comment."

The questions went on and on. Qualm's answers matched his mood of silent insolence. Craven's advice chimed in his mind.

Craven sat in silence, waiting, just waiting and watching the detectives. After giving his name he didn't say a word. For the moment he had no reason. Despite his appearance, everyone who dealt with Craven knew he was astute. He had a shrewd mind and never missed a beat on any point that mattered.

"We're going to send your boots off for forensic tests. Will we find anything?"

"No comment."

"We've already got your fingerprints. Will they be on the gate at Cedar Field?"

"No comment."

"Are you the owner of a green van?"

"No comment."

"Where were you last Saturday night and early Sunday morning?"

Qualm exaggerated a false yawn and during it garbled, "No comment".

"I'm going to give you a 'Special Warning'. Do you have any explanation for the mud on your boots?"

"No comment."

"It's a very distinctive colour. A streaky yellow. See?" He held the boots up in a plastic bag and pointed to both toes. "How did it get there?"

"No comment."

So it was and so it went. The whole interview continued in the same fashion. Valentine's patience was tested to his limit. He looked at Hart and with a pre-arranged signal decided to end the misery. Strained lines of furrowed skin flowed from between his eyebrows to his forehead. Valentine didn't speak as the seconds passed. He felt impotent, knowing he had failed to crack Qualm's shell and the inevitable boost that would give to Qualm's warped ego. Finally he said, "You haven't answered any questions. I must warn you that may be the subject of a comment in court by the Judge. And the Prosecution. This is your opportunity to give your side of the story. Are you going to answer any of my questions?"

Valentine was looking at his Notes. Hart was glancing at her police issue Dr. Martin boots. She feared if she looked at Qualm she would plant them in his crooked teeth and inviting crotch. Qualm didn't answer. Instead of the rapid-fire insolence, there was a short silence. Valentine thought he'd struck lucky. The heat between them was rising. Perhaps Qualm was going to change tack and go on the attack. Maybe he would deny it all, maybe lose his temper. He looked at Qualm and at once saw his concentration was elsewhere. Qualm had his right index finger so far up his left nostril he could be digging for gold. He took his time and when he had finished, Qualm stroked his finger on his sleeve. He left a snail-like film of thin snot. He then hooked up the mucus with his black nailed thumb. He examined his find. He looked at Valentine and smiled and put his thumb in his mouth and slowly sucked fellatio-style.

"You filthy, dirty, bas-..." Valentine said. Before he could finish the insult, or the truth, Craven jumped up and jumped in. Craven's whole bulk shook.

"Are you trying to intimidate my client, Officer? This interview is being tape recorded, as you well know. I may have to lodge a complaint about your conduct." It was histrionic. Craven raged on. Craven shouted because he wanted to put on a show for his client at Valentine's expense. He wanted and needed his reaction on record. He remained standing, feigning anger as dandruff fell from his shoulders to his feet. He stood there, all rumpled clothes and crumpled face, as veins rose on his red, creased forehead shooting like roots towards his balding ginger hair. He stared at Valentine and said, "Are you trying to bully Mr. Qualm? Are you trying to breach his human rights? You-..." He stopped and paused. He was going to swear for effect. Then, typically, thinking in a split-second how that would sound many months later to a sober Judge listening in a cheerless courtroom, instead he added, "Officer, I want this Complaint to be noted on the Custody Record. I'll mention it to the Custody Sergeant too." He stared at Valentine's number for a few seconds. He searched for a piece of paper. He couldn't find one. He grabbed the Charge Sheet. He checked and re-checked and slowly wrote it on the front of the Sheet. Checked his watch for the date and time of the complaint. He added those details. Craven stared at Valentine and said, "I won't forget this. Nor will you."

For Craven a complaint was a natural tactic. Most officers had to tread cautiously lest a complaint was made which would end their career. That effect was what the guilty loved about 'good old Georgie'. He'd use it during the trial to prove the officer was biased. Another angle, more compensation. It made Craven rich. For his fortune was evenly balanced by the victim's misfortune.

Their eyes locked and for a moment it seemed as if antlers would too. Time hung heavy. Seconds were suspended in space. Valentine knew, he positively knew, the solution. He was thinking, a quick knee in the bollocks would help Craven's peace of mind. He thought the same would do wonders for the well-being of his client too. Behind his fierce eyes he thought a targeted boot in each overfed face would enhance their welfare. He stood still, yoga-style, as the thoughts revolved inside his head. Now he thought, yes, that would be both the perfect answer and a real 'comment'.

All four glanced around the room, looking and searching. Valentine's nerve ends tingled. Time stood still. They were all trapped for the moment in a silent heat of their own making. To Valentine the room seemed to have shrunk. Frozen in the moment, yet boiling. Four hearts pumped in an irregular rhythm for all of thirty seconds, though to them it seemed much longer as the heat grew stronger.

Hart felt anxious for Valentine. With good reason, for she knew what he could do. She'd seen him explode before. Her anxiety started to rise when she closed her eyes. In seconds she saw the episode a year earlier, with him and herself and an abusive drunken thug, Albert Burns, who puked in his face. Valentine reacted with reflex anger. He smacked Burns so hard he fractured his jaw in two places with one punch. He followed through. She tried, but couldn't pull him off. She had to get between them before it turned into a murder. Burns landed up in Intensive Care. In the Inquiry that followed into the "unexplained injuries" of Burns, both cops claimed he fell getting into the Black Maria. The Notebooks of Hart and Valentine recording the incident, though made separately, just happened to agree on every important point. Their unchallenged evidence was they were trying to help him but "he was so inebriated he was unable to stand unaided." Fortunately for Valentine, he was not being watched [except by her] or wired for sound. There was no CCTV in that area at that time.

Hart opened her eyes. Now she could see Valentine change, his eyes narrowed, his fists clenched, his knuckles were white. He moved towards them. Eyeball to eyeball. She was sure he was poised to unleash his naked anger in an explosion of violence. She could see another Inquiry. Maybe for manslaughter this time. A double one. Or murder. Killing a solicitor was illegal. Felling a scrote too. She moved closer and gently placed her left hand on his right wrist. Hart said, "Let it go, Bobby. It's not worth it. He's not worth it."

She kept her hand there. Valentine looked at her. His eyes portrayed pain. She registered his hurt. Sweet Jesus, she thought, unsure if he was going to explode in violence or gush tears. "Shall I take over the interview?" He didn't answer. He shook his head. No. He turned away. His eyes were magnetised on Craven's again.

Before he could answer her, Craven said, "I asked you, are you trying to breach my client's rights?" He remained provocative and transpontine. He spat out the words and shouted, " Well?"

Qualm loved every sour second. Later he would sup his scrumpy and boast how they roasted Valentine alive.

Valentine was lost. He tried to regain a measure of composure. He tried to speak: no words came. Hart caught his eye. She put her hand on his left shoulder and said, "It's okay, Bobby, let's move on shall we?" He scrunched up his eyes as if they stung. His classy Pinton silver-rimmed glasses started to mist over. He removed them and wiped away the sweat. He used the time to delay his response. He wiped his eyes.

Craven glanced at his watch and thought about the money he was making.

"Of course not, Mr. Craven," Valentine slowly answered. He took a deep breath. He blew out the air. He delayed for a further few seconds and still targeting Craven's hard eyes said, "I only want to ensure he concentrates – on his rights, that is." He stared at Craven, a look that silently screamed, "legal scum." His look was tough enough. Craven understood.

"Well then," Valentine said, "let me repeat my question to your client. Are you going to answer any of my questions, um, Mr. Qualm?"

Qualm, scratched his head, switched his right hand to his groin and pulled at his goolies, then his left armpit and paused. He said, "No reply." He opened his letterbox mouth and brought up a loud belch to signify the end of the interview. On his terms. "Oh, pardon me," he said.

Craven shot him a sharp glare meaning, shut up. It had nothing to do with manners, everything to do with control.

That served to end the interview. Hart switched the machine off. She asked Qualm, "Do you want a copy of the tape?"

"No comment."

"I'll have one for him. We might need it." Craven glanced at Valentine and said, "You might too. No, you will need one."

Craven had in mind how he could use the complaint to prise open the jury's suspicion of police corruption. It didn't matter if it was true or false. A complaint had a smell of its own. It never disappeared. With time it grew more pungent.

When Qualm's interview finished he sat there looking too pleased with himself for comfort. Craven had the same self-satisfied smile forming at the corners of his mouth. Hart stared at Craven, a cold look of barely disguised disgust. Hart had a sudden feeling she just had to tie up her bootlaces. She made the movement in slow motion, timed to the second. She bent down so that her ample buttocks were facing Qualm's face. At that instant, by gut instinct, Hart let rip with a truly thunderous curry-laden fart that rumbled down and around the room and engulfed it. Hart and Valentine turned and looked ice daggers at Craven. Even Qualm stared at him. The killer feeling was only one knew who was the culprit. Craven blushed to the roots of his ginger, multi-strand comb-over.

"Whew. That cannabis next door is giving off a bit of a whiff today, Bobby," Hart said. "We'll have to destroy that exhibit when we get the verdict tomorrow."

"New shoes, Mr. Craven?" Valentine asked. "Creaking a bit. They need oiling. Or is it that door?" Valentine bounced on the balls of his feet. Craven remained red and silent. Instead, he then cleared his throat and started to sweat and smell, more than usual. Beads of sweat formed as dewdrops on his reddening, hairy nose. Both officers' faces remained deadpan.

"I'll open the window," Hart said. "It's a bit sticky in here. Do you think so, Mr. Craven? Only we don't want your client to have trouble breathing. Breach his rights, wouldn't it?"

Later Qualm would tell his cohorts about Craven's eruption, so the tale would spread as quickly as the smell.

"Right, Canker, you're next," Hart said. She had taken her jacket off because of the heat generated in the small space of the interview room.

"Mr. Canker you mean, don't you Officer?" Craven asked.

"I'm sure I do."

"By the way Officer, what's your number?"

She hooked into his eyes and moved closer to him. She pointed to the top of her left sleeve, then held the chrome number so he could read it easier. "Aren't you going to write it down?" Craven didn't bother.

"Perhaps you'd come with me, er, Sir?" She grabbed his left arm with her right hand and held his wrist tight. "This way, Mr. Canker." Canker took a lead from the body language of Qualm. He walked as if weighed down by metal diving boots. Hart squeezed his wrist, ever so gently digging in her pointed nails.

In turn-style mode Canker was wheeled in and then turfed out. His interview had the same shape as Qualm's. Hornet was last and his interview, in form and fashion, was no different. They had all exercised their strict rights by taking the time to mess the minds of Hart and Valentine.

40

Three times Valentine went through essentially the same interview. Valentine's words fell on the defendants' ears as snow on an igloo. Three times the lies by silence were deafening. He knew the criminals had the lawyer in their pocket and the power in their closed mouths. Only Valentine's training, plus the fact it was being recorded, prevented the rush of justice being delivered to what he thought were these parasites.

He wandered off to the canteen with Hart. Neither could shake off their negativity. Neither of them spoke. Unlike most criminals they interviewed, Qualm had crawled into their minds. A dark cloud covered them as they sat in silence, both feeling dispirited and dejected. Each gulped their cold coffee and both winced at the bitter taste. Hart piled more sugar in hoping she could then drink it. Valentine pushed his aside causing it to spill into the saucer and onto the table. He shifted to the next seat, opposite Hart, to her left.

"Oh, Helen, what I'd give for the old days, when a rubber hosepipe and a sock full of sand would leave a rainbow of bruises that could hardly be seen, but could surely be felt. Now we have to indulge creeps like these characters. Pure dross. Leeches and losers. All this paperwork, human rights nonsense. Where did we go wrong?"

"You tell me. Was it really so different in the past?"

"Too true. Before this human rights garbage we'd interview them and rely on the 'verbals' in court. Now these sleazy lawyers will find a way to get weak judges to throw the case out. This human right shite is a charter for crimos. For cheating lawyers like Craven too. He'd sell his soul if he could. He can't 'cos he hasn't got one. He'll throw enough shite at you knowing something will stick, even if it's only his smell." She almost laughed. He was staring at the table. His eyes fixed on the spill. He slowly looked up and directly at Hart. She thought he looked so sad. Old too. Exactly his thoughts about her. "Mind you, regardless of all that bull, do you know what really bothers me?"

"Maybe. What?"

"I wonder if I'm just too old for the Job now?" His face remained time-worn and red.

"You? Give us a break. I feel like that all the time and I'm only twenty-eight."

"I'm not alone then?"

"Alone? Most of the force feel like that Bobby. Most of us want to bring back hanging"

"You'd get my support. At least they wouldn't re-offend."

"Yeah. A real suspended sentence."

They sat in silence for about a minute. Simultaneously they caught each other's eye and suddenly burst out laughing. It was not natural laughter, closer to a hysterical fit.

"What about Craven's face," Valentine said

"That look!" Hart said. "A picture. You never know, it might end up on the Net. Someone might secretly release it. Craven loves publicity. His future clients would love it too."

They laughed uncontrollably, stopped, laughed again. They were sharing the memory of Hart's curry-fart at the end of Qualm's interview. At the time both cops had to retain a professional air. Now they laughed like loons laughing at the moon.

As their laughter finally drained away, Valentine asked, "Fancy another coffee?"

"Is that what they call it? I won't risk it. You have one.
I've got to see J.J. 'Bye."

"See you later, Helen."

Valentine and Hart still had to face the tarnished truth on
the strength of their evidence against the trio. Their prime
witness was an informer who wouldn't swear on oath
during the trial. All the defendants going 'no comment'
weakened the prosecution case. They hadn't relied on
alibis, so nothing could be checked and proved false while
they were still in custody. Even as the last laugh lingered,
nothing could erase that granite truth.

"Sign here," O'Hara said. He scowled at them, his normal
greeting for the defendants, or "dregs" as he called them,
that he dealt with daily. Each one had no doubt he
despised their very presence. However he was unbiased,
he loathed the lawyers too. He was not the kind of man
who had reason to hide his feelings. "You can write, can't
you? 'Course you can, I forgot, you forged those stolen
cheques." He pointed at the form.

"Whatever you say," Qualm said and signed. The other
two did the same.

"You're bailed until the seventh of October. See you
then, if not before. We'll be watching you."

"But that's a Sunday."

"You'll just have to give Mass a miss, won't you.
You'll have to make your Confession another day. What
about making one now?" Qualm ignored him.

"What about my boots?" Canker asked.

"What about them?" O'Hara answered.

"They're the only pair I got."

"So what?"

"Well, I need 'em."

"Like your boots, Canker, tough," O'Hara said. "We need them for forensics. Now on yer bike before I change my mind and refuse you bail. Besides, you look better in those ballet shoes. They make you look even more macho. If that's possible."

Had they been remanded in custody, O'Hara was sure at least one would have cracked. It was not to be. He was straight when it mattered regardless of who he was releasing. Blackmailer or burglar, rapist or robber, minder or murderer, he still lived the strict letter of the law in dealing with the dregs.

His decision meant the pressure was off Craven as the last defendant was bailed. As soon as they were granted bail, the trio moved faster than they had all day. The trio's thick thighs rubbed the inner fabric of their jeans as they almost ran out of the Station. They could've started a fire with the friction.

"Goodnight, Squire," Craven said to O'Hara, attempting to be amusing. It was also vaguely sarcastic, to put him in favour with his clients. O'Hara, a grizzled born-again disbeliever, ignored him. He'd have none of it. Instead he stared long and hard at Craven. Craven tried to skip quickly away. O'Hara's eyes followed him like a laser beam. Craven felt them bore into and drill through him. He looked over his shoulder, gave a short fake smile, waved and said, "See you again, J.J." O'Hara stared, with no attempt to disguise his contempt. Craven blushed again and wished he were invisible so only his smell remained, though it would anyway.

O'Hara knew Craven knew O'Hara knew he was transparent in his phoniness. All the while O'Hara remained silent. His eyes tracked Craven as if was using radar. Even when J.J.'s eyes couldn't be seen, Craven still felt his scorn cutting into him.

"Put it there, Bro," Qualm said, holding his right hand up to meet Canker's. He slapped Hornet's too. Safely outside the arms of the law, the trio gave each other a high-fives hand greeting. They climbed into Craven's silver Mercedes CLK to get a lift home. They all sat in the back in their now grubby white paper suits as if they belonged there. The trio held a post-mortem on their performance.

"Don't keep blaming me," said Canker, "you're the one who's always mouthy, Kevin.
And you can't even help yourself, Lee. I bet I've been let down by you two."

They all talked at once, anxious whether their lies were enough to deflect their guilt. Canker leaned forward from the back seat towards Craven's left shoulder and asked, "how did we do? Have they got anything to go on, Mr. Craven?"

Hornet asked Craven, "Did I, did anyone, say anything that would like, cause us problems?"

Qualm said, "They haven't got nothing. If they had anything on us we wouldn't have got bail. That's right, ain't it, Mr. Craven?"

"Yes, but listen, we need to get things sorted out quickly. We don't need a post-mortem now. You'll have to come into the office next week so we can talk about your alibis and witnesses. I'll need to see them before the police. That way I can test their memory – if you know what I mean." They knew exactly what Craven meant. He then asked, "Will that give you enough time to remember where you were at the time of the crime? The alleged crime I mean."

"What time was it supposed to have happened, like?" Hornet asked. "'Cos they didn't know about it until the next day did they?"

Craven sucked slowly, puckered his lips and refused to be drawn for the moment. His question was pregnant with guilt. Craven became conveniently deaf. He didn't want to answer Hornet's question. So far no one had mentioned anything about young Clare Springfield finding Molly the following day. "I'll check out the forensic evidence," he said and passed on seamlessly. "We'll have to cover the whole evening, before and after the event. Don't forget they've got all your clothes for forensics. And don't forget, if there's any conflict between your stories, – your version of the event, I should say – I can't represent all of you."

"Not a problem, Mr. Craven. We'll all come in together," said Qualm. "We'll have to talk to our muckers to remember where we were, like, know what I mean? Only the old cider can play tricks with your memory. We're safe. You just leave it to us."

He was happy to do so. Craven knew the gang's past and their future power. The advantage for Craven was two-fold. He would have no embarrassing Instructions as the trio's story would be the same, their faded memories would be improved after a joint discussion, all their witnesses would be primed and, of course, the friendly collusion would ensure there was no conflict between the defendants. So he could continue to represent all three. The last point was of primary importance for Craven. It meant he would get the maximum payment from public funds. He would triple his fee. That way he would protect his clients and his pension, the two being the same thing.

"In the circumstances, I suppose alibi is our, your, best

46

bet. The advantage of that defence is the prosecution will have to disprove it. All we have to do is get a witness or two to create confusion. Given that, how could the jury be sure between fact and doubt?"

"Right," Qualm said. "Thanks, George, er, sorry, Mr. Craven. Don't worry. We'll get witnesses who'll cover every single point of the prosecution case. And more."

Within a week ten defence witnesses would be found and their memories massaged. Then they would be etiquette-trained and taken through the legal hoops. A 'mock' trial would be arranged so a devil's advocate examined and cross-examined them. All the creases would be ironed out, their eventual story shaped and reserved for the jury.

"By the way, do we know where the victims live?" Craven asked.

"Why? We can find out easy enough if it helps," Qualm said.

"Well, I was thinking we might get a statement from them."

"What and frighten them so they don't turn up at the trial?"

"No, just for the background circumstances."

"Enough said, Mr. Craven." Qualm understood.

"Don't forget we'll need a diary, a note, perhaps a restaurant receipt. Something that can be checked by the police so they'll help prove our defence. Do it now while it's fresh in your mind." Craven's advice would be their code to form a defence. They knew, despite his appearance, he had a tidy mind when it mattered. "No obvious D.I.Y. John Bull outfit invoices. Or some pathetic computer receipt with a false VAT number. Do you understand? I'm counting on you, boys." He tended to

47

address them as 'boys' because, though they were in their thirties, they still behaved as perennial teenagers. The trio nodded in agreement.

"Good. Don't forget this before you go." Craven said, shoving the Legal Aid Form to each of them for a signature. "Or are you paying privately?"

"Mr. Craven, you know, you'd break our hearts, if not the bank," Canker answered, his smile wide enough to swallow a harmonica. "Our profits are right down, you know what I mean?"

"Save the violin. Just your signatures. Sign there." Each of them did so. From the moment the three signatures were on the forms, Craven was making more money. Ripping-off the taxpayers for free representation. Another scam.

He dropped all of them off at Hornet's house. "Goodnight, Mr. Craven. Thanks," they all shouted. Georgie had delivered once again.

"Goodnight boys, see you next week. Don't forget what I said. Concentrate on your alibis. We need them to be watertight."

Craven kept smiling to himself on his way home. He couldn't shake from his mind the conversation he'd just had with Canker. It lingered because he was so surprised.

All the way to Hornet's house a CD was playing quietly in the background. As they were leaving the Merc, Canker said, "By the way, Mr. Craven, that's a great sound."

Craven, taken off guard, smiled suspiciously.

Canker said, "I mean it. Seriously, you got great taste. It really rocks."

"Well, thanks Dean," Craven said. "I didn't know you liked classical music."

"Love that sound. Every time I hear it I can see the

Droogs out in force and Alex really kicking ass to that tune. I just love it, man."

"It reminds you of the Druids you say. Well I'll search my collection, see if there's any more you might like. Thinking about it, you might like Wagner too."

"As long as it rocks, Mr. Craven, I'll be happy to hear it."

"Just as a matter of interest, what sparked off your interest in classical music?"

"Oh, I've loved it for ages. Ever since I saw Alex and the boys in A Clockwork Orange."

"I see. I've not seen that musical."

Craven was confused, though he remained amused. He imagined the scrumpy was rotting Canker's brain. He pressed the CD replay. His smile spread as his shoulders shook in time with the music. A passing taxi-driver looked at him, then moved closer to the kerb and sped away, thinking he was drunk. For when the track came on Craven waved his arms and conducted the orchestra from his car seat, surrounded by the inspirational sounds of *Beethhoven's Ninth Symphony*.

Beat on the Brat

"Charles," Zogger called out his name, but he didn't respond. As ever his mobile phone was stuck to his ear. She sometimes swore that as a normal baby has a rattle he must have had a mobile phone in his cot. She heard him say something about "the 230 limit." She guessed he was speaking to his stockbroker, or more likely, his bookmaker. "Charles, I need to see you," Zogger called down the corridor.

Charles Coke-Blunt, the Senior Clerk of Credo Chambers, saw her. He smiled and waved. He mouthed, "I'll be there in a minute."

She went back to her room and slammed the door. Zowie Darrow was known by everyone, except the Clerk, as 'Zogger' since childhood. The nickname stuck when a lisp caused her to mispronounce her own name.

Almost three and half minutes later, – Zogger having checked it – Charles knocked and entered her room. "Hello, Miss Darrow, you wanted a word?"

"It's kind of you to find time in your busy schedule to see me."

"I'd always find the time for you."

"Don't ever keep me waiting again while you talk to your bookmaker. Usually when you're on that blasted phone it's one of your floozies. When I want to speak to you, it's important. Do you understand?"

"Yes." His already red face flushed redder.

"I asked you to see me yesterday evening at 5.45. Where were you?"

"Sorry about that. I didn't have time."

"Didn't have time? Do you think I'm a fool?"

"Not at all, Miss."

50

"At least we agree on something. You had enough time to go to the pub, didn't you?"

"Well I-..."

"Before you try to lie, I saw you there at 6.15."

"I was with a solicitor. I was touting for work for Chambers and you, come to that."

"With red-nosed Rupert I expect?"

"Actually, I was with Mr. Puttock. He's an important solicitor for Chambers."

"Another alcoholic."

"He likes a drink."

"What else do you have in common?"

"It's not against the law, Miss. How can I help you?"

"How? By getting rid of this rubbish." Like a crazed conductor she swept her right arm across the desk from right to left, back again and repeated it. Thwick-thwack. With that movement she swept every single brief on her desk off onto the floor.

"Oh! Zogger what the...– I'm so sorry Miss Darrow, I didn't mean to be rude. It's just, well, you...–," Charles said. He spluttered and stopped. He looked as happy as a man about to be castrated. Otherwise his chronic constipation had combusted.

"Don't say another word." She started to slightly shake. She was going to shout and swear, but checked herself. The words stayed on her tongue. She spoke slowly, measuring each word so he would remember them. "Take these miserable little briefs and give them back to those silly solicitor friends of yours. Or to one of your many, tame barristers. Someone. Anyone. Who? I really don't care as long as it's not me. Do you understand?"

"Yes, Miss. Perfectly." His voice almost cracked as he uttered the words.

"Don't dare put another brief like any of those in my pigeonhole." She pointed to the pile of papers strewn about the floor. Some red ribbons became loose as the briefs fell.

When Charles bent down his waistband cut into his beer gut. The sweat started at his nape, ran down his neck and collected in a pool in the small of his back. He stood up, hunched awkwardly, holding a dozen or so briefs in both arms. They rested on his paunch. The ribbons snaked to his crutch. Looking over the top of the briefs he said, "You'll certainly see some changes."

"Goodbye, Charles." She opened the door and ushered him out. She closed it.

About a half-hour later a rat-tat-tat on the door stirred Zogger from her daydream. Charles entered. This time he seemed to be happy, wearing his usual cheery smile. "Great brief for you, Miss," he said. Though he was only thirty-eight, with his hair loss and weight gain he looked set for an early middle-age spread. It didn't take much to keep him happy. All it needed was something to involve his second-sight, the silent clink of money. He could hear that sound in his mind as a dog would hear a distant whistle. Charles was born to Clerking.

"A real challenge this one. The solicitor asked especially for you. He said it needed someone with your 'terrier-like tenacity'. Someone who'll 'grab it and twist it and never let go', if you'll forgive the vernacular."

"Oh yes," Zogger said, the palm of her right hand almost concealing a yawn. "Parking on double yellow lines, is it? A pensioner shoplifting a can of horsemeat for her kitty?"

"This is tasty. This case needs your kind of talent.

52

Believe me Miss, he asked for you particularly for that reason. In fact, I offered him, Hugh Janus and Mr. Majewski, as I was bound to, but he just turned them down flat. I even offered him, Miss Dixoff. Professionally. He rejected her too, but for a different reason. Personal. I know you don't care for him much, but he's nobody's fool, Mr. Pharceur." He placed the brief on her desk. "Have a look at it. See what you think. There's a fat fee. Think of the bottom line."

"I always do. What else is there?" She smiled, her mixed smile pale and feigned.

She quickly untied the ribbon with an air of expectation. It was a new brief. A new life or maybe a new death. A challenge she would meet and relish the clash of heads and words. She could still imagine and sometimes feel the fingertip tingle a new brief could induce. Yet Zogger knew the odds and had the unfurled knowledge that such pages were usually just leaves of disappointment. The quiet hope always remained for her. Once that was gone, she knew there was nothing.

"I'll be off then."

As he went to leave, believing she was absorbed in the brief, she waved her right hand and barely looking up said, "Do sit down." She pointed to a hard, oak wheel-back chair in the corner. He stood there, looking awkward again, feeling the same. He didn't want to stay so he remained standing. He kept his suit jacket buttoned up.

He had a way of making his navy, well-cut, expensive three-piece suit look cheap. The trousers had never seen an iron since he bought it. Once, maybe jesting though he said it straight-faced, he told her, "It was pressed by the tailor when he made it." The serge seat shone from sitting too often on a barstool. Each hip pocket of the jacket bulged

53

with a mobile phone. The top jacket pocket drooped out of shape from the weight of an ever-present pager.

Zogger sat in the ash Captain's chair behind her American black walnut desk. She looked tired, though stylish, even cute, with her red streaked hair and black velvet suit. From the outside she looked to be the envy of all. A mind sharp and blunt, matched by the brilliance of her performance and the bourgeois rewards. She seemed to be living the life. She was simply living the lie. The ennui seeped into her and through her bones. Charles had seen the changes grow in her. He knew, though she did not share her secrets or thoughts, the changes were marked. For him they were unwelcome as his income came partly from her.

She stopped flicking through the brief. "Charles, we need to speak about my practice." She pointed at the mid-oak bookshelf. A pile of thin briefs were arranged alphabetically on the wide concave shelves. "Look at them. Some pathetic ABH, a shoplifting, a drunken affray. It's not what I expect." She paused, held her tongue as she was verging on some home truths, then added, "Or what I deserve. Perhaps you don't realise? The burglars and buggers just bore me."

"I'll happily tell the solicitors you won't do the smaller cases. I'll say you've moved on."

"I want higher quality and higher fees. It has to be one or the other – ..."

"I'll get you both. It's what you deserve." He had her interest in mind, but mainly his own. "I'll make sure you're too busy for the duff cases." He winked.

"Charles, I believed I would develop a practice where principle and justice had some meaning. These briefs-..." She waved her right hand dismissively at the shelf. "More

54

than just bore me, they somehow stifle me. They cause a rigor mortis of my spirit. I want and need to make a difference."

"Don't we all."

"I'm still not sure you understand. Do you?"

"I do. It'll change. You'll see."

"Like last time you mean." They'd had a full-blown argument a month before on the same subject. Then she demolished him, though felt rueful later. Now she caught his glazed gaze and added, "Tell me Charles, what really motivates you?"

"Money."

"No joking apart. I mean, what truly jumps your juice? What makes it all worthwhile?"

"Money, Miss. Money."

She stared at him and noticed each time he said the word "money" his eyes sparkled. "Splendid," she said. "I'll rely on you to send the right signals to those bozo solicitors."

"As good as done, Miss Darrow." He placed his left index finger at the side of his left nostril, just below his winking eye. "That's why I brought you this brief."

He caught the edge in her tone. More than before he knew it was time to leave. She sat in silence. She was reflecting about their previous heart-to-heart talk about a month earlier. She remained pensive. She asked him, "Why do you think so many counsel tread the well-worn path of promiscuity and alcohol and disillusion?"

"What's the alternative?"

She widened her eyes as his frankness caused her some surprise. "Well, I suppose you could always keel over on the job or become a judge. Is it the choice between a quick death or slow suicide through boredom?"

"You've answered your own question. You're much too good to take that route. If you became a judge you'd be dead in a week." He kept moving from one foot to the other, leaning on the bookcase, putting his hands in and out of his trouser pockets. His coins and keys rattled together. He kept touching his top pocket as if willing the pager to work. He coughed to camouflage the rumbling of his stomach. He was desperate for a cigarette. The stilted conversation didn't help. 'Bleep. Bleep.' Just then the stony silence was broken by his pager. He pressed the button to identify the caller. "I hope you don't mind, but I'd better go. I'm wanted by the Head of Chambers. He called earlier saying he wanted to speak to me urgently." Both excuses were lies. As with most Clerks, lies were as natural to him as oxygen. He'd arranged for one of the Junior Clerks, Sam, to call 'if I'm not back in 10 minutes'. "So, sorry, but I really must go. You know what Mr. Peacock's like when he's kept waiting." Charles dragged his right index finger nail across his neck in an attempt to amuse Zogger.

As he spoke she saw his finger and wished in a fleeting second it was a cut-throat razor. She immediately blanked out the bleak thought. "You'd better go now." She'd spoken to Drew Peacock earlier. She knew he was out of Chambers all day. In fact, they were to have lunch, but it was cancelled because he had to go to London.

Charles was so relieved at his release he almost danced out of the door. As he was on the point of leaving she said, "Apologise for me if I kept Mr. Peacock waiting."

"I certainly will." Her critical look was too cynical for his comfort.

"Charles, there's something I forgot." She opened the middle drawer of her desk and took out a brief. "Would you please take this to Mr. Peacock? We were discussing it earlier. He asked for my opinion on whether the Indictment should charge a separate count of Attempted Murder against each defendant or a single joint count of Conspiracy."

"What now?"

"Yes. Why, is there a problem?"

"No, not at all." His face became as plotched as a pomegranate.

"Only it's urgent. He wants to send his Advice on Evidence tomorrow. Can you also ask him to call me?"

"When?"

"After he's finished seeing you."

Charles had been ploughing through Stephen Hawking's tome on the creation of the universe. Though he was sceptical, he wished black holes did exist so he could disappear into one right now. Instead he said, "I'll, um, see Mr. Peacock and, er, ask him to call."

"Anytime, as long as it's today."

"I'd better go, Miss." His smile set as if in a mould. "Goodbye." He moved in a sluggish manner as thoughts of their pending meeting circled his brain.

"Please leave the door open, Charles. Thanks."

Charles gradually ensured Zogger had fewer and fewer briefs. He was, with her agreement, starving her. Somewhat strangely that worked to their mutual benefit. Charles passed the cases to other less competent counsel who helped to run his red BMW Series 5. Zogger took more time off to write songs and play music. Consequently the band had become much more important as the Bar became a ball and chain.

The feeling filtered into all areas of her life. Where once

she might have found the judges amusing and their childish ways endearing, now to her they were boorish bullies. While she saw them as ageing red-faced, red-robed, red-eared buffoons playing to the gallery, her patience wore as thin as blood-stained-rain.

With time she moved from subtle antagonism to open hostility. She saw the judges as stuffy overgrown schoolboys, all blubbery pink and vanity-stricken. Like politicians in drag and no less corrupt. Her eyes newly wide open, she saw most of them as raddled. Their lascivious, wandering eyes as a witness entered the court gave her the shivering creeps. She couldn't shmear them at all. Yet that was their life-blood. They needed a show of respect, however false. She knew at bottom the judges were all naked Emperors.

Recently she addressed Mr. Justice Blad on an abstruse point of law that he failed to grasp. He looked perplexed. She repeated her submission. Finally, exasperated, he said, "You have spent a half-hour making this Application. I am still none the wiser."

"No, My Lord, but better informed."

Zogger only skimmed through the brief when Charles was present. Now she was surprised to find it was from the Prosecution. That was rare. She was much in demand to defend. The hacks tended to prosecute. Initially she could see herself 'returning' it to Charles. Yet her perfunctory pose shifted as she was caught from the opening shot. She read it and was compelled to read on. Page after page told of the terror that three thugs had visited upon a tethered pony. It gripped her as she read the vet's evidence. As she read about the foal her breathing grew less controlled.

The fate of Molly gradually grew inside her. A vice

tightened on her aorta and heavy boots broke her bones. She had an image of smashed glasses and a body face down in mud and blood; the body lay prone as if dead. It was hers. The feeling was as piquant as a cocked Colt 45. Her emotions moved up a notch. All at once she knew. This is the case. She wondered aloud, "Is this my swansong?"

Zogger saw the photographs and turned them over slowly one-by-one. She stopped turning as her stomach churned. A few hard drops of rain ran down the window-pane. The temperature dropped. The light disappeared. She became cold as the chill reached her and caused a momentary shiver. She held her head in her hands and closed her eyes. After a few seconds she opened them. The image in the photograph became harder to see. Her misty eyes focused on the charred remains of Molly. She held the one showing Molly in her final moments. It hooked her heart. A single tear trickled down each cheek and exploded on the photograph.

She was due to go out that night. Too bad. She didn't even bother to cancel it. It was just some boring acne-ridden, pasty-faced solicitor who wanted her briefs. He was the son of a judge, so worth cultivating. Even so, she couldn't take spotty Sweeney seriously. He'd have to wait in the rain. Sure he'd get wet she thought, but who'd notice the difference.

Meanwhile she pored over the pages word for word. Zogger had already forgotten the first rule of practice: never get emotionally involved.

The number of lights in chambers lessened as Zogger continued to read while time sped by to the sounds in her mind. Yet she was hardly conscious of time when doors were slammed as most of the other Members left with a tired hollow, 'good night.' Abraham Zebedee, known as Abe Zee, was always last to leave. "Goodnight, Zogger," he said, from the corridor.

"Abe," she called out as she immediately recognised his voice. He had an unusual voice, gravelly but somehow easy on the ear.

"Hi, Zogger. How're you doing?" He stood in the doorway. "You're looking well." He lied. He wanted to hurry on home.

"Fine. Come on in a mo'," she said. "How are you? You're looking very well." She lied. He nodded. They exchanged weary smiles. He stepped just inside the door. He was carrying a bulging brown leather bag, stuffed to the last hole of the expanding clasp with books and briefs. He placed the bag on the carpet between his legs.

"I wanted your advice on a Conspiracy problem," she said, having just thought of the problem at that precise moment. She then raised some recondite point about joint complicity and aiding and abetting. While Zee appeared to listen, he shifted from foot-to-foot. He gave his opinion on the problem and she appeared satisfied.

"See you then, Zogger." He grabbed the handle of his bag, lifted it lightly and turned to leave.

"Abe," she raised her voice. "How long have you been at the Bar now?"

"About six years." Warily, he still hovered near the door. He put the bag down and straddled it. "Why?"

"You do crime, don't you?"

"Yes. I'm getting busier and busier. Look." He pointed at his bag.

"Tell me." She looked at him hard, but not cold. "Do you ever feel you really make a difference?"

"How?" He did a slight soft shoe shuffle in the doorway.

"Is a case special because it's done by you?"

"No, well, yes, I mean no," he said, not making sense – even to himself. "I just do the cases, you know, keep my head low, avoid the shrapnel..." He continued with a few more clichés and ended with, "I always say, 'watch out kid, whatever you did, stay away, orders from the D.A.'." He laughed, she laughed.

"Anyway, I better be off. You know what Johanna's like. She gets so stressed when I'm late-..."

Zogger sensed the rising tone of his rough voice and the nerves she'd seen so many times before. Usually it was witnesses who were stung by her scalpel tongue during cross-examination. "Abe, do you think about justice, the truth behind the issues?"

"I really have to go, Zogger. I'm already late." His voice rose to a hoarse pitch. He swallowed. He coughed. He was twenty-seven, just three years younger than her. Yet as the light caught his dark-ringed eyes, she thought he looked so old and sad. She guessed it was the sleepless nights from a new baby and two small children, plus the pressure of being a practitioner. She looked through him. As she seemed distracted, he reached behind to open the door. He tripped over his bag, causing it to fall and the clasp to burst open spilling the briefs onto the floor. He tried to stuff them back in, but couldn't close the clasp. He tried to force it. He gave up and held the bag awkwardly under his right arm. "Sorry," he said, without reason. He gripped the bag tight, forced a smile and said tetchily, "I'm going."

She got up and walked towards him. "Can I help you with those, Abe?"

Before she reached him he held his left hand up. He waved her away. "No, no. Leave me alone. Go to hell!"

61

His spiky reply pierced her. She retreated, stepping back and sat down. She connected with his eyes. "Calm down, Abe. I was only trying to help."

"Issues, making a difference, career. You're full of crap."

"Abe, are you alright?"

"'Course I'm not. Who is? Are you?"

"What's your problem?"

"Why?"

"What's wrong?"

"What do you care?"

"Tell me, please?"

"Why? What difference will you make?"

"Maybe I can help. We're friends."

As he looked at her, his face changed. His bony features grew sharp and dark. He looked haunted. He looked like a stranger. He appeared even older than before. "I lied about Johanna. When I spent night after night in Chambers – making a difference you'd call it with your high and mighty words – I didn't notice my life slipping away. Now, I'm so tired, bored, depressed. Sick at heart." He spat the words out in a rush, spraying spittle at her as he spoke. "Is that what you wanted to know?"

"How long have you felt that way? I had no idea."

"Since Johanna left me."

"I'm so sorry. I didn't know. What can I say?"

"Try nothing. I can't waste any more time on you. My mum's looking after the kids. As it happens, she's very ill. Breast cancer. Do you care? Is that enough of an issue for you?"

"Well-...I..."

"It's unlike you to be tongue-tied. The cat got it? And you're so cat-witted. I've got more important things to do than talk endless rubbish with you. Goodbye." He wrenched her door open with his left hand. In one movement he switched his hand and pulled the door hard after him as he left.

"Bye, Abe," she called after him, "take care of yourself. No one else will."

The front door slammed shut. When Abe reached his beige Volvo Estate he threw the bag in the boot. He sat in the car awhile trying to compose himself. Tears filled and flowed from both eyes. He dried his eyes so he could see to drive.

When Abe left she felt bereft, hoping she hadn't been too hard on him. Zogger spun into a vortex of pain. She read the whole brief again. Then re-read it slowly. Her mind told her it was a case she could win. Her heart told her it was a case she would win. With conflicting feelings on law and music and life she stared at the glassy Santa snow-scene souvenir, labelled 'a present from San Francisco'. Absentmindedly she turned it upside down and watched the snowflakes fall. She turned it on its base and watched the flakes fall on the reindeer's face and feet. As the thoughts swirled through her, she twirled the tape through her fingers and tied it tightly around the brief of Regina v. Kevin Qualm.

Zogger stopped reading when her eyelids grew heavy. She glanced at her automatic Oris blue moon watch and saw it was just past 9.10 p.m. She called a taxi to take her home. Normally she finished a little earlier and walked. It wasn't far, but with her mind so attuned to the case she dared not risk it. She wouldn't hear the faint footsteps following her, from someone unwanted and unknown. In the darkest recess of her memory the random thought made her flush with fear. Her mind became crowded with a myriad of unwelcome images. She tried to shake them out. Her feelings mapped her face.

While waiting, the jumbled thoughts compounded her pangs of confusion. Blessed with a second opinion, maybe she wouldn't have taken the case. 'Then again, what would it matter, whatever anyone said?' she asked herself. She knew intuitively she was dealing with something bigger than the case. She could've quit from the case somehow, but what about tomorrow and all the tomorrows after that? No, she knew, she positively knew. This is the test. She could see the angel of mortality sitting on her shoulder.

The taxi driver honked to announce his arrival. The driver was chubby and scruffy and younger than her. He wore a grubby turquoise turban. "Where to, love?" he asked.

"To the Gorge, please."

His tone only served to irritate her. Zogger was glad he didn't indulge in idle badinage. She hated the witless taxi-drivers who felt compelled to talk and worse, expected something in return. Always doing little or nothing, just driving you to a destination and then taking a tip or more for granted. All she simply wanted after a barrage of words all day was the sanctuary of silence. She closed her eyes. He said, "Tired, are we?" She murmured and ignored him, making her intention clear. She slipped her black, cross-strapped, almond-toed Church shoes off. Then she lay back in the seat and tapped her toes in time to the muffled music coming from the local radio station. Zogger listened intently to try and catch every word as Lord Buckley on Wintersett Wind played the Man in Black, growling with a perfect mind-set to match her own, *I Won't Back Down*.

64

The Bitter End

Long before the ideal of creative anarchy formed in her mind, Zogger filled her time with the case. Day after day, alone in Chambers, she fidgeted nervously with the red tape that tied the brief. She draped the tape across her left palm, then snaked it through her fingers, all the while rehearsing the contents she now knew so well. The pages curled from being turned so often.

Although she tried to stave off her true feelings, they seeped through as real as blood in a bandage. She was too hooked on the case for her own good. Her life-style was funnelled into work and music, music and work. Socialising was always a second choice. Now it became non-existent. Night after night one of the many members of Credo Chambers, leaving in a group, would invite her to join them. Tonight, Monday, shortly after six o'clock, Peter Heavy, a criminal practitioner, poked his head around the door, just enough to interrupt her. He moved his right hand to mimic the motion of drinking a pint and asked, "Are you free for a swift snifter? Drag yourself away from that desk."

Previously she would've accepted even if she was or felt under pressure. The case changed all that. Zogger looked up, her forehead framed in a permanent frown, barely forced a smile and said, "I'd really love to, but I'm a bit busy. Really busy." She opened the palms of both hands, pointed to her right and then left at the pile of papers. She shrugged, arched her eyebrows and said, "Perhaps another time? Maybe Friday evening?"

"Great idea. See you then." A social game. Both of them knew she wouldn't be there.

Heavy, Paul Pucelle, a company lawyer and fellow

drinker, Lucille Dixoff, an all-round common lawyer, and a few of the other Members seeking her, knew she was still working on the case. Time and again they'd tried to coax her to join them. Gently, but firmly she always refused. Her spent voice said it all. She wasn't merely working hard, for that was her usual approach. Early morning and into the night the case consumed her.

When Heavy left, Heather Sidebotham, a rather shy pupil barrister, wanted her advice on a case in the Magistrates' Court. She asked Zogger, "I wondered if you had time for a quick sandwich tomorrow at the new diner, the Silver Beetle?"

"Not really. I have to finish this Advice on Expert Evidence. Sorry."

"That's fine. I was only wanting a bit of a chit-chat."

"Are you sure?" Zogger sensed it was more than that. "Anything I can help you with now, Heather?"

"No, it's not important. You're busy. Just a bit of Robing Room gossip. A few were talking about the future of the Bar. I was wondering how you felt about it?"

"How long have you got?" They both guffawed with a social laugh. "You're sure that's all you wanted?"

"Yes. Just a chat." Sidebotham was troubled by, what was for her, a complex legal problem. She lied to keep Zogger sweet. She would need her when seeking a tenancy in Chambers.

"Perhaps another time?"

"Certainly. See you soon. 'Bye, Zogger." Both knew it wouldn't happen. As Sidebotham left, Zogger, alone again naturally, felt a pang of guilt.

More than any other case she had ever been in, this one she had to win.

After re-reading Regina v. Qualm, she committed complete chunks of the evidence to her memory bank for future use. The images were so vivid it was as if she'd been there. She could see the blood and smell the diesel. She shut her eyes, concentrated, winding the memory spool right back to the beginning. Each time the anger grew in her. The tentacles of her anger spread through her body and mind. She couldn't, even if she had wanted to, quell it. Her right hand formed a fist by instinct alone. Her teeth set on edge enamel-to-enamel. Even her eyes stung. She opened them. As she looked at the photos of Molly, she felt it would be easy to stick an ice pick in their hearts. She thought at least that would make some point.

Their acts flickered across her closed eyes. The images came rapidly, though she tried, she could not block them out. Sitting at her desk, she shifted the snow-scene souvenir, turning it upside down. Zogger could synaesthetically see the whole scene. She opened her eyes for seconds then closed them. She could see the trio. She knew the facts so well she could all but smell the defendants' imprint on the pages. She gained a vast knowledge about the circumstances, having spoken to the police and the solicitor from the Crown Prosecution Service. She discovered a lot about the defendants too. She knew their guilt was as indelible as a prison blue tattoo.

She read the brief again from cover to cover, the instructions, the comments, the problems, the 'unused material' and the 'sensitive' information meant only for her eyes. Some of the defendants' enemies, of whom there were many, reluctantly gave the police a bird's eye view of their tastes. Zogger hoarded all the details that would help her to harm them. She studied the police photographs of the trio. The mug shots did them justice. They looked human. The I D Parade stills captured their essence. Zogger stared at their images. She viewed the video of their arrest to interpret their body language at a time when they were potentially vulnerable. Of the three, Canker looked most alone and lost. Zogger could see it would be easy to cross-examine him. The right question from her would prick his bubble of lies.

Focusing on the two exhibit albums, Zogger locked into why she hated the trio. With her experience she had cracked the carapace of the common criminal and found Qualm under every shell. For her these three were a species of modern man: the worm in a society that was sick in its soul. She saw Qualm as the virus. Zogger kept reading. Although she loathed what the pages disclosed, she couldn't help herself. Their deeds hammered into her head and heart.

She knew the case so well she could quote page numbers and even paragraphs. She had a photographic memory anyway, so could see the words inside her closed eyes. Reading the pages, turning each one, her temperature rose higher. The dunt moved to her breast and reached her head and spread throughout her. Her stomach developed a peristalsis, as waves kept shooting pain towards her throat. Her palms began to sweat. She kept opening her clenched fists, crossing and uncrossing her legs. Whatever she did failed to bring her comfort or relief. She kept trying to smooth out the deep frown lines etched on her forehead. She could hardly turn the pages fast enough. The words became harder to read. Re-living Molly's ordeal, Zogger's eyes became filled with tears of rage.

Reading the statements again, she could see the two children, Clare and Tom Springfield, gaily wandering at will, skipping and jumping now and then in the grass. She could hear their words and share their feelings:

"Oh look, Tom. A black horse. It's a scarecrow," Clare said to her little brother. As she got closer she could see Molly's eyes. Something was wrong. She knew somehow they were real. From being excited, she became frightened. She turned away. Clare didn't want Tom to see what she'd seen. She held him back.

"What's wrong? Why can't I see the scarecrow?" he asked. She shielded Tom from the sight.

"C'mon. No, no. Let's go," she said, dragging him away. He resisted.

"C'mon," she said, pulling him along with her. "We'll tell Mum," she said. He began to softly cry. They started to run for home.

Clare Springfield, a child of seven, was with Tom, her four year old brother, walking through Cedar Field on a short-cut to St. Kliphs Church on Sunday morning. Clare found Molly and at first thought the charred carcass was a charcoal pony. Just a toy.

When Clare and Tom got home, Marie, their mother, held them tightly in her arms. Both children sobbed hard tears. Neither could speak. Marie almost cried. "Whatever's wrong? What is it, sweetheart?" Marie asked, kissing each child as their tears wet her wrists. Finally, Clare told her mother and Marie alerted the police. Her find caused Clare to skirl a few times during the following weeks.

Hanging on each word, Zogger had to keep reading. The first civilian on the scene of the investigation was a young vet, David Priest. He called Molly, "remarkable", as she had fought against such "terrible odds." He discussed his opinion with the Forensic Scientist, Alexander Knight. Priest made a passing comment and a brief note about "bestiality." The conclusions of the scientist and the vet were similar.

69

Later the police called Mark Armstrong, the senior vet, to examine Molly as a prosecution was likely. Following the initial investigation, it was discovered to be far more serious than they at first believed. So they needed to show the cause of her death. Armstrong said to the investigating officer, D.S. Barney Buckle, "The injuries were so horrific, the terror she felt couldn't be quantified. The cuts were so deep and the abuse so prolonged, it was no less than torture. No animal could survive that treatment."

Louise Rowe, the owner, was on a short walking holiday and had yet to be informed of the bad news. Lily Mernagh, her neighbour, told Buckle, "Louise loves horses and was so fond of Molly. That was her mother's name. Louise took her in after Molly was mistreated and nursed her back to health. Louise couldn't wait for the Spring."

While preparing the case, Zogger had a Conference with Armstrong. At the end she asked him, "Why did Molly hang on for so long?"

"Well, it was survival of the strongest kind," the vet said. "Molly had slowly bled and quickly burned to death. That night she was fighting for her life. Indeed, more than her life."

"In what way?"

"We found it when we examined her injuries. An embryo. She was fighting for her filly, her unborn foal."

His words, though couched in colloquial and soft scientific terms, served to harden her heart. Zogger kept focusing on the fact her foal was killed before she took her first breath.

Zogger knew many innocent people had been burned that night. She shuffled the papers together in a neat pile holding them in both hands like an open prayer book. It was an absent-minded act, as she stared out of the window into the distance; her scrambled thoughts, were now clear. She knew what had to be done. Molly's death would spread its ripple effect. Everyone would have their day in court. She thought, what more could anyone want?

She stopped staring and stood up. Her ideas sprang into life. She couldn't hold them in. "Wait, just wait. Your day will come soon enough," Zogger said aloud. She shouted, making it a promise and a threat. She then slowly tied the red ribbon in a neat bow on the thick brief. She paced across the room, back and forth. "Members of the Jury, these miscreants are cast-iron liars whose guilt is as clear as they are all murky..." She continued in the same vein. Her voice rose. "You'll have no doubt about their violence on that early Sunday morning..." She carried on, gathering pace, her voice rising with controlled anger. "You will hear how they tortured and torched a defenceless pony. At least one of them, though they acted in concert, committed."

Catching her reflection in the window, she frowned. Is that me? Am I that haggard?

So engrossed, she didn't hear someone running down the corridor. There was a loud knock on the door. Zogger heard it, but chose to ignore it. Another knock, this time a little louder. Zogger pulled it open. She looked at the Clerk, startled, as if to say, 'what do you want?' She remained silent and open-faced.

"Are you alright, Miss Darrow?" Charles asked. He was catching his breath. He was wearing his suit and overcoat. "Only I thought you were alone? It sounded like some kind of an argument."

"I am alone," she said. "There's nothing to worry about, Charles."

71

He continued to pant and pause and pant, between each breath. "It's just I heard a raised voice. A lot of shouting. It sounded like a threat."

"It was, but by me, not to me. I was rehearsing my Speech. Perhaps I got carried away."

Neither spoke for a short while. Zogger was still high. Charles looked at her. She appeared to him to be bigger and taller than she was, her stance reflecting her fire. After their recent meetings, she now seemed different. Changed. She had come alive.

"I was going home when I heard the threats. Well, the raised voice, I mean. Anyway, I'm glad you're okay." He hesitated to ask, but took a chance. "Is everything alright?"

"Yes. Why shouldn't it be?"

"The Brief I mean, Miss?"

"Yes. Fine."

"Well, all I can say is, with that much passion you're definitely going to win." He started to button up his coat. "I'll be off then. Good night, Miss."

"Charles, just before you go. You were right, this is an interesting case."

"I told you it was a challenge. I told you to trust me. It's just right for you."

"Is anyone else available to do it?"

"No. The solicitor, you remember, Mr. Pharceur, was definite in his Instructions. It's reserved for you. Otherwise he'll have it back. He'll instruct another Chambers. We don't want that, do we? He knows you're available. Why?" He could feel a thin trickle of sweat from his armpit run down his left rib to his paunch.

" No reason." She paused. "Charles, do you ever read the briefs?"

The question threw him. He looked as if a Dobermann

had just clamped its molars on his gonads. "Not in-depth. I don't really have enough time. Too busy collecting fees. Obviously I skim through them as much as I can. I have to get a feel for the weight and, of course, the fee. I know some of them are really interesting. Why?"

"Oh, I was just curious..." She hesitated and let her voice trail away. "Only a passing thought. Nothing worth worrying about. Goodnight, Charles." They both knew why she asked. She was considering returning the brief even as they spoke.

"Goodnight, Miss Darrow." He left quicker than he entered. So relieved to leave, he ran out the door before she could recall him. Once outside he bent forward, his hands pressing on his knees, puffing and panting, trying to regain his breath. In a moment he found the solution by deciding, 'I need a pint.' He walked briskly to the Queen's Retreat.

Sitting at her desk, still intense, she clamped her hands to her head. For a while she sat there, deep in thought, gripped by a pain and a passion. She re-played the scene where the police became involved after the call from Marie Springfield. One officer was still affected even some months after the event. Buckle had lost his neutrality. Closing her eyes, she reflected on what he'd told her at the Conference. "You know Zogger, I'd like nothing more than Qualm and his cohorts to rot behind bars. Knowing everyday they'd have to wake up and have a shave and a shower and a shite with a pack of prison wolves. People like them don't like it up 'em."

"You're right, Barney. You know what I'd do with them? If I were the Governor I'd put them on the prison roster as ready and willing and able catamites. Pack them in a cell with a couple of Arab shirtlifters. A better use of their talent than making toys."

"That would put the cat among the chickens," Barney said. She gave him a knowing look. Both laughed too loud, each seeking some kind of release.

Focusing on the future, Zogger could see the end game. She could see a secret sect forming, a new Molly Maguire for the 21st Century. Although she knew the law would take its true course, she had a wild justice on her mind. The same feeling in her heart. Opening the middle desk drawer, she took out one of her favourite tapes; one she found so inspirational, she kept a copy in Chambers and at home. She flipped the lid of the portable player she used to listen to police tapes of defendants' interviews. She slipped in the black-and-white cassette and tuned into a tale that reminded her of the realism of Zora Neale. Zogger played it and pressed the 'repeat' button. Turning the volume up, she was glad Yoko, in suggesting the title, had given her a reason to believe. On the third play she jumped in the air, swirled around the room and sang along to the feral, fervent voice of the ever-young O'Boogie telling his truth, *Woman is the Nigger of the World*.

Such A Night

She felt the hand reach over her shivery skin. As it slid and slithered she tried to move away, but the hand followed the contour of her body. She drew back when the clammy fingers of his right hand cupped the cusp of her left breast. As he fondled it, he felt her stiffen and freeze. He continued to hold her. "Are you alright, Zogger?" he asked, half-asleep. "What's up? Is-..."

It was almost 2.00 a.m. The early morning negative feeling bit into her. She answered Deke Rivers swiftly. Before she heard all his words, she kicked him hard with her right leg, bringing it forward, then jerking it backwards with some force on his bony shin. She repeated the action, with more force. Drowsily, she reached out with her right hand, clawed his wrist and wrenched his hand away. She shouted, "Get away, get away. Leave me alone. You bastard!"

"What the hell, Zogger, what's wrong?" Despite his usual intake of alcohol the previous night and the time, the sudden pain almost jerked him awake.

"Leave me alone."

"Why? What's wrong?"

"You."

"What're you on about? I'm tired. Go to sleep."

"Go to hell."

"What've I done now?"

"Everything. Nothing. Just let me be."

Though Deke knew she meant it, he was confused. Later he felt the same. He tried to understand, but really never could. You may as well try to live in someone else's skin. You can empathise, sympathise, but you can't feel their misery. So it was when Zogger kicked Deke out of her bed. The following night they slept together, separated by a block of ice. The next night the block grew into a wall of ice. By the end of the week they slept in separate beds in separate rooms. Within a fortnight their feelings, certainly hers, faded towards evanescence.

It started with Qualm's Case and ended in unavoidable acrimony. Their long-term relationship bled dry before his eyes. Within a month he moved out for the good of their friendship and the future of the band. Now the emotions on both sides were still raw, but for very different reasons. His remained fresh and bleeding. Her feelings withered on love's vine, her heart shut his out.

Since then it got no easier for Zogger. Reading the case resurrected so many memories she tried so hard to hide. Night after night, lying there on her own, she was an emotional volcano ready to erupt. This night was no different. Tonight those thoughts came tumbling down.

Tossing and turning time and again, no sleep would free Zogger. Throughout the long night she moved every way seeking a release through sleep that failed to come. First lying on her front and then her back and then as a half-formed embryo. Whatever she did gave no relief and made her ever more restless. At the same time she kept getting hotter and as bothered as a bird trapped inside a window-pane.

The night-time is the loneliest for lonely people. It's no surprise that most people die at night, whether naturally or not. Darkness and death are companions in the same cell. Zogger now felt that void. She started to hear the sound of cymbal-footsteps pounding inside her head. She buried her head in the wet pillow. She buried her head beneath the wet-sweat sheets. Still the escape of sleep escaped her. The void was no stranger to her.

76

Why did I agree to do this case? Was it greed? Insecurity? The 'taxi-rank' system? Why me? The early Sunday morning quivery feeling offered her neither any solace nor answer.

Every night the ghost of her past rattled his chains. The crazy stranger with teeth bared and tooled-up, ready to wreak his warped will, was always at her door and in no time inside the vestibule. The 3.00 a.m. force froze her as every sound in the night brought the fear of a burglar at her patio window. Every strange noise brought his face close to view and his hot stale breath on her neck. She drifted pinball-style between sleep and nightmares with no time for dreams or zizz.

Throughout the ceaseless tossing, she still kept questioning herself. Why did I accept this case? Why did I make that choice? Though the thoughts criss-crossed her inner voice, she knew the truth was she had no choice. Regardless of Pharceur, when the brief was sent to Chambers it was somehow name-checked for her. Naming her as his choice was only part of it. There was a certain determinism about it. When she first handled the brief, she felt the telltale tingle of cold sweat trickle down her back. It would've been so easy to turn it down, but Zogger was caught in the net of her own twisted fate.

Finally she slept fitfully for almost an hour. Then just before 4.00 a.m. the flashing images revisited her. She was running and running, but wasn't fast enough. She ran faster and faster. Her feet were pounding the pavement as her heart beat in time with the frantic rhythm of Gene Krupa. Suddenly she lost her right shoe. More than her heart in her mouth, she could feel her whole being would explode. Still she ran and ran, yet was almost standing still. She lost her left shoe. Each shoe was marooned in the rain-swept street. She was lost and barefoot. Feeling lonelier than a pregnant bride-to-be deserted at the altar.

Her shoes were cream and brown, a brogue pattern, with a low heel. She remembered, in the strange way such stray thoughts surface, how she had intended to go to the cobblers about the faulty clasp. There was a small clasp on each, holding the bar across her ankle. Now one was broken and the clasp glistened in a puddle. The other was still closed, but the heel was stuck in a drain where she hip-hopped on one leg before losing it. She turned and looked for a split-second at each shoe. Zogger loved those correspondent shoes. Pitter-patter went each foot, out-of-time with her heartbeat. Both were out of sync with her mind and pulse.

She tripped and stumbled and fell to her knees. She struggled to her feet. Both knees were skinned and bleeding. She rubbed her knees and felt the grit. Without shoes she felt small and vulnerable and the pounding sound behind got closer. The ache spread from her soles and shot through her. She had to keep moving. A silent 'Help' was trapped in her throat. The looming shadows mystery sounds terrified her. She was burning alive in this concrete desert, with not a light or soul in sight. Yet she was illuminated as a victim, her fear flashing as if a gaudy neon sign. An arrow pointing at her as an open invitation no grassant stranger could or would resist.

She could feel the rough ground beneath her soles, but her feet made no sound. All she could hear was her heart and some stranger's hard feet pounding in unison, each beat and step a mirror of her terror. The hard feet behind her were gaining. They belonged to the perennial stranger. A victim, a woman, already she was within his vulture's clutch.

Then image-on-image scattered through her. Where before she tossed and turned to find sleep, now she tossed and turned to escape it. She couldn't do so. The footsteps gathered a-pace. The force was on her back. A huge weight smashed her spine. Her knees were almost capped with the suddenness of the attack. Her body was wrenched onto the handy, nearby waste ground. The blanket darkness added to her horror. Tears streamed down both cheeks. A grubby hand that reeked of grease and nicotine clamped her mouth, causing her to bite her tongue. The stranger said quietly, "Shut up slag or you're dead. Enjoy it. Scum."

The image of those three obese girls who bullied her every day at school flashed across her fuzzy eyes. She could see their ugly, distorted, fleshy faces and smell their sweaty bodies as they punched her. Poleaxed her, kicked her, ripped a handful of hair from her head. She could still hear their harsh hatful of hate. Now she felt another kind of hatred.

She could see her mother's kind face and wished she could reach out to hold her hand once again. 'Mum! Mum! Please help me...' she screamed and screamed, but no sound came out. Her voice remained as silent as the earth beneath her.

Beautiful was the only word to describe her mother, Elizabeth. She was tall and slender with a natural way of wearing clothes that made a high-street store dress look elegant and expensive. Everything about her evoked style, her face and form reminiscent of Audrey Hepburn. She seemed ageless as even at forty-four she had long black hair and porcelain skin. Zogger, though not her natural daughter, shared her beauty when in her natural state.

She saw the dreary barrack-like hospital. She saw her

mother visiting her. Then she saw herself visiting her mother. Two deaths in a short time, both lives lost too soon; each by a surgeon's scalpel though both innocent: one dying too young and one unwanted, so killed before being born. She plunged ever deeper into a pool of pure panic.

As the shards from her smashed glasses cut into her, both eyes began to bleed. The stranger grabbed a handful of hair and pulled her head back, using his boot as a pivot. With a jerk he thrust her full-face into the mud. Zogger tried to turn. She tried to twist. She tried to resist. She screamed to the soles of her shoeless feet. Her mother's face flashed behind her eyes. She thought she would be joining her in heaven. She cried, silently, 'if there is a god where is she now?'

Dazed and defenceless, she could hear his rapid movements. Even his breathing. He delivered steely kicks to her ribs – both sides. Putting his foot on the nape of her neck, he forced her face deeper into the unforgiving, cold wet mud. Her brown corduroy jacket became browner. Her pleated suit skirt was caked in sludge. He shredded her clothes, tearing at them with a fever. With fists and feet he pounded her body and face, breaking her jaw and more ribs. The whip crack of boot on bone was repeated in the harsh darkness. Her once snow-white blouse was stained with patches of swelling, bright blood. Rolling saliva around, he gobbed it into his left palm. He dipped his index finger in the spit, rubbed it on his palm and forced both inside her. She felt his hardness on and in her body. Each orifice. Her insides nearly split wide open. Her deep groans just gurgled in the mud and died. Almost spent, he grunted, "Take that you black bush bitch. Cock-cracker."

When he got up and slunk away a few feet, she heard

the spiked tongue enter the buckle as he fastened his belt. He made to leave. He hesitated. He moved forward and turned her over. He thrust into her mouth and, almost as an afterthought, dumped all over her muddy, bloody face. He squashed her jugular with his Cuban heel, compressing her towards the grave. He kept his heel on the target. He watched her eyes bulge. Slowly, he walked away, satisfied, sure she would not survive.

As he ambled away, he mumbled, "Scrubber."

She could feel the dirt grow hard. The blood meshed with the mud to block her nostrils. She was cold and wet and motionless. She lay there for hours until a passing stranger, Betty Robbins, walking her rescued dog, Sparkin' Hopkins, found her in the desolate dawn. Sparkin', a lively young Collie pup from the Pet-Holly Sanctuary, ran across the grass to her supine body. Zogger could hear the welcome bellwether sound. "Woof! Woof!" Sparkin' barked and barked until his throat ran dry. "What's wrong now? Not another bone?" Betty called out and followed him and discovered the naked body. Betty placed her fleece over the woman. She rang 999. Betty waited until they arrived. The ambulance crew found Zogger was a-bleeding from every orifice.

The night got blacker as Zogger's head spun out of focus. "No, no, no, no, no!" she screamed as she awoke. Not for the first time, not for the last. There would be many more nights like this one. Zogger wondered, when will it end? She pleaded to some unknown spirit for a sign. But none was to come. She screamed. Flailing her arms, she knocked the clock clear off the bedside table. When it hit the ground the sound pounded through her. The moment she screamed to break the silence of the dead night, the alarm went off. As the repeating alarm split the night and shattered her skull, the reverend's daughter blasted from the two-tone cream Robin radio, telling her own tale with *Respect*.

On The Evening Train

Although Zogger's mind was focused on the case, she constantly thought about the band and their music. She continued to find strength to excel in the law through the power of their shared vision in music. Though they played fewer gigs these days, she still loved the release the energy of their music gave her. Often, when alone, as now, her thoughts strayed to the day they formed their intent and forged their dream-goals. It was at The Freefall. All of the band, Arnold Kokomo, Chrysler Kreisler, Deke Rivers, Floyd Lloyd and Zogger, were there. They met to resolve a vital issue: their name.

It was the first week of September 2009. Zogger was sitting at her desk in Chambers on Sunday afternoon, the day before the trial. She stared at the snow-scene souvenir and drifted back to a time before Qualm's Case had entered her life. A time, although it was over three years earlier, that was still fresh in her mind. A time that still reminded her of dreams and destiny.

"What about the Four Top Mops?" asked Arnold, the organist.

"But there's five of us," said Floyd, the drummer.

"Yeah. That's the joke."

"'Some joke," said Chrysler, the bass player.

"No, you don't understand. It's like the Temperance Seven and the Fruits Quartet."

"What are you talking about Arnold? This is serious," said Deke, the lead guitarist.

"Well, there were eight of them and only three, you see."

"Some joke," said Chrysler.

"What, eight in the Quartet?" Deke asked.

"No, there were only three. So it's kinda funny."

"Hysterical," Chrysler said.

At that moment Ritchie Valiant's new girlfriend, Anita Phuncello, brought the band five bubbling expressos from a gleaming Gaggia machine her father, Giovanni, imported on his last visit home to Genoa. She took the money and rang it up on a carved matt steel cash register. The Freefall was one of the first in the city to deliver the real deal in coffee. It was one of the last, if not the only one in town, to sell Zoragon. A rare brand favoured mainly by fallen angels with the early morning blues, pale riders and waifs, but appreciated by anyone whose tongue it touched.

"Look, Deke's right," said Zogger, the guitarist and vocalist. "This is serious. We have to find a name for the band. We can't keep dreaming one up just before the posters are printed and then change it for the next gig. We've been doing that for far too long. The Celibate Milkmen, The Bad Habit Nuns, Motorpsychonightmare. You know, some of those names we've used, they'll haunt us when we're rich and famous."

"If, you mean," said Floyd.

"I said what I meant, – when," Zogger said. She'd never let something important pass, even when it was meant as a joke.

"I'm with Zogger," said Deke. "Let's get down to business. Look, we all agree there are certain people, who produce something that from the start has the hallmark of success. You can't really define it, but it's more than originality or panache or style. It's as if they were bound to be a success, regardless of any obstacles, because the people involved are dedicated and determined to a rare

84

degree. No one in this band is a quitter. The only failure we recognise is failing to try. We were born to win. That's our lodestar. So our name is crucial. We need a name that rocks. You can't just call yourself, The Four Moptops, and then expect to become a force to change the world. You've got to become The Beatles, a name that resonates with chutzpah. Moreover, they coined it care of Lee Marvin and Charles Hardin and that's class. We need a name that shows we mean business. One that will instantly lodge in the listener's mind. One that when you hear it, you want to know more, you have to know more, about us. Like The Band."

They shot ideas back and forth. Even when there were some humorous asides, they remained serious. Their aim was for their name to have a nominative determinism. The conversation flowed freely as they were all open, yet on edge.

"What about Fat is a Male Issue?" asked Arnold.

"Great," said Zogger.

"I know, Rebel with Paws, they'll remember that," said Floyd.

"Yeah. For all the right reasons, no doubt," said Zogger.

"Well, what do you say? Have you got anything better?" he asked.

"That would be difficult," she said.

"'Look, let's stay with the action," said Deke. He could sense a cutting cynicism creeping in. He reminded them why they were there. "Today's the day. We're going to have our first authentic CD out soon. Liam has made the final mix. We've got to confirm the artwork with Toerag tomorrow. We have to agree on a name today. We have no choice. We gotta have a name we want and can live with. Something that really rocks."

"I've got a good idea," said Chrysler. "Just a word often works. What about Alcatraz or Veritas or even, Zoetrope?"

"They're all okay in their own way, but they don't rock," Deke said. "We need something that says it all. That sums us up and our music."

"Precisely," said Zogger.

"What about Principles and Potions?" Floyd said and added, "or Love not Fear?"

They started to laugh at his first suggestion, but stopped on his second. "Actually that's quite good," said Arnold.

"Yeah. I like it," Chrysler said. "It's what we stand for and the music flows from that. What you think, Zogger?"

"It's quite good, but it just doesn't flick my switch. It's a poetic cliché, a little fey. Prissy."

"She's right," said Deke. It's not perfect, but we're heading in the right direction. Let's have a few more imaginative ideas. Bold and spunky."

"I know," Zogger said, to ease the tension, "Bold and Spunky?"

They all laughed – genuine – and ordered a refill of the expressos. They all had a double shot. Anita brought them over, looking, as usual, neat and sweet in her black skin-tight slacks, pink sweater with a 'G' clef logo and her ponytail. Like Sandra Dee with an urge.

Some of the names bandied about were surreal or absurd and instantly rejected. Others had a superficial attraction, but when they rolled the name around their tongues there was no connection. Yet others had connotations that didn't rest easy with their beliefs. The band was of one mind. Each time someone strayed from the ideals they lived by and analysed, the others would take the rise and say, "Hey, no compromise."

At one stage their catch-phrase, 'no compromise', was thought to be good enough. It was rejected because it lacked the essence of what they wanted and were. The talking went on into the long night.

"Look, none of us want to live and die and have nothing to show for our existence, but a broken gravestone or, worse, a casket of cinders. Like, 'What did you do in the war, Daddy? Overtime, son.' Do we?" said Zogger. "My take is we have to make a difference. I don't want a dull routine life. We have to take it to the wire. If on the way you lose it all, well that's the risk you run." She paused and asked, "Who agrees?"

"I do," Floyd said. The other three nodded.

"I want to shoot a hole in the moon," said Arnold.

"I want to take it to the limit and beyond," said Chrysler.

"I do too," said Deke. "Except, I want no limits."

"After all," said Chrysler, "being different, being true is the real reason we're in a band anyway. Otherwise we might as well work in computers. I want to be alive, I don't want no nine to five."

Everyone agreed. They continued to bandy names back and forth, some simple, some silly, some you'd need a chiromancer to decipher. They suggested and rejected Rinky Dink and the Doo-Wop Dykes, The Blackboard Jangle, the Narcissistic Sociopaths, the Dying Light, Hotspot Now and Threatening Veils."

"What about Johnny and the Howling Moon Dogs?" said Arnold.

"Mmm, maybe," Deke said, when the last one was suggested. Although it was rejected, it had a certain elemental attraction for all of them.

They examined the names as they examined their own

existence. The band was not separate, but a part of their lives, the sum of their identity. As a band they were bound to each other, held by known and unspoken ties and their music as a vector for change. Their songs were not and could never be poppy, throwaway, bubble gum, 'I love you/ please be true/ otherwise I'll be blue.' There were references to Byron and Bogart and Shakespeare and Sartre. Their music filtered through the listeners' consciousness and infiltrated the soul of player and audience alike.

"Our name has to touch the band and the fans. Are we ad idem?" Zogger asked. They agreed. "Then let's home in on the fact we have no fear of failure. We want our fans to feel the same way."

"That's it, Zogger. You've hit it," said Deke.

"Let's dwell on the ultimate question, 'cos that'll tell us our name. It's that simple."

"But, Zogger, what is the 'ultimate question'?" asked Arnold.

"There's only one, what's our Room 101?" Zogger asked, "This is the acid-test question: what is your death-bed vision? What is it we really fear? If we fail, we do so on our own terms. If we lose it all, so what? What's the worst that could happen? We could lose our looks, our luck, our liberty or our lives. Tough. What else can you show me?"

Her words hit home. For all of them, there was a single answer.

"I'm only speaking for myself," said Arnold. "I'm not willing to rust away in the hope of a pension and dying in the process. I've seen too many live that life to want to be a part of it. My death-bed vision is this, for good or bad, I lived my life in the way I wanted."

"Keep rockin', Arnold," Floyd said, "rock to the grave. That's my vision."

"My take is this," said Chrysler. "I want to be alive and creative and dream and dare until death closes the final door. I intend to live so well even the undertaker will regret my passing. The one thing above all that's my creed is I'll grasp each challenge and not die before I die."

"This might help you decide," said Zogger. "My guide is the gospel of Kubler-Ross. I like you intend to live before I say goodbye. Our lodestar has always been to choose love over fear on every call, every chance, every time. If it all goes wrong there's no time for tears. Kill or cure, there'll be no scapegoats for no one else is to blame. We may all be damned or exiled." She paused. "Or dead, I guess. The worst that can happen if we do what we want to do and it all goes wrong, well we all go to hell. What's new?" Zogger waited for their reaction. "What do you feel about that?"

Magnetised by her wry smile, they all pondered her line, 'we all go to hell'. "What do I care?" Chrysler said, laughed and shouted, "Hellsucks!"

They rolled the name around, wrote it down, added words and still it stood alone. The name, pared bare, said everything about their beliefs and everything about the band. Hellsucks was their quintessence. For the five into one it was their sine qua non.

"There's nothing more to say. That's it folks," said Zogger. The other four put their thumbs up.

At that moment the voice of Eddie whooped from the grave on the Rock-Ola jukebox, joining in their minds' time to the tambourines rhyme singing, "Who cares? C'mon Everybody." A smile crept across Zogger's face. Time had been well-spent and the minutes moved slowly.

As they left The Freefall the jukebox played some sad song by a dreamer lamenting the gift from his ex-girlfriend, a pair of Clown Shoes. "We'll be on there soon," said Chrysler as he motioned to the shiny Rock-Ola. No one demurred.

Now Zogger stared at the souvenir, dwelling on the day the band found their name. A day that touched them all and offered up so much. She let the red ribbon fall. She closed her eyes for a few seconds and could see the other four move across the floor of The Freefall in time with the forty-five as she followed, feeling high on life. She was last to leave, behind Deke, looking at him through the eyes of young love. Life was so easy back then, she thought. She remembered how Deke drove the van and dropped the band off. First her then the other three. He then returned to her.

Zogger got up from her desk and walked to the window. She reached for her little wooden Roberts radio. A present from Deke. She recalled playing it that very night because some scrote had broken into the van and stolen the radio. The battery was so low they could hardly hear the song. She meant to replace it, but being so busy, had forgotten. She hadn't used it since. She remembered the last song because she loved the voice and the man. The Big 'O' was someone steeped in the tradition of no triumph, no tragedy. Zogger switched it on. She leant over it and pricked up her ears. "Wow," she said aloud. It was the same song. Zogger saw it as a portent. She looked out the window at the copper leaved trees shaking their conkers free. She concentrated on one. The green prickly case broke open so the shiny conker was revealed. As the grey afternoon sky became overcast, the battery was fading to the heartbreak falsetto sound of a universal misery she understood and shared, dum-dum-dum-dummy-do-wah, *Only the Lonely*.

God's Gonna Cut You Down

Even though it was only September, it was a dull, wintry, cathedral-mist day when Canker and Hornet and Qualm appeared at Wintersett Crown Court. Shuffling down the street, they moved along the pavement as if they owned the very stones beneath their pachyderm feet. All of them made with their best bad-boy plodding Belmondo look. The trio wanted to ensure any photographs would do them justice. Perfecting their ponce stride, the hacks skulking outside obliged and clicked their cameras into action. Photo after photo caught their mood.

The trio strutted into the building with a clichéd street-swagger. The defendants had even shaved. Their odour didn't change. Their array of friends followed and mooched around with mannered menace. All eyes were on them. Exactly what they wanted.

As their mates went through the security system check-in the alarm in the foyer buzzed non-stop. Larry Melvin, the surly guard, looked hard and asked Joseph 'Jonjo' Jaynes, "Have you any keys, mobiles, studded belt?" Jonjo curled his lip and shook his head meaning, "No". Robby Steel, the really surly guard, white-haired and as wiry as a human terrier, asked Jimmy Rushman and Amanda Kane the same question. No one answered. They each gave a hooded look and shook their spiky-haired heads in denial.

Melvin immediately saw the problem. "Remove them. Now." Melvin picked each nostril. There was so much metal riveted through Rushman's ears and eyebrows and nose, the security detectors flashed on 'red alert'.

Kane only had one bar, a ring, through her tongue. She poked it out at Steel. He said, "OK, put it away or I'll give you a French kiss you won't forget."

Melvin let them through. Seeing the display of studs and tattoos throughout the group he said, "When you gonna get a tattoo then, Robby?"

"What and look a bigger prat than I already do?"

"That'd be hard." Unusual for Steel, he gave a half-smile.

Qualm and his group made their way to the Court Café, the Habeas Corpus. They gathered in the back alcove where they joked and chain-smoked. Above Canker's head hung a graffiti-spattered 'No Smoking' sign. All the bent defendants met there to make sure they got their stories straight. This was the final rehearsal before the public saw their act.

"Alright Kevin? How are you, my man?" asked Rushman. "Give me five." Qualm raised his hand and Rushman slapped it.

"Slip me some skin, Jimmy," Qualm answered as their hands met in a repeated jive pattern.

"Areet, Bro'."

A tall, young, skinny Rastafarian looking worried as he awaited a verdict on supplying 'crack' cocaine, glanced at them. "Honkies," he muttered, almost inaudible, though loud enough for them to hear. He got up. He was about to face them down when the tannoy sounded, "Would Trane Coleman go to Court 7 immediately." He pushed his chair in their direction and shot them a look of pure pity. With more time he'd have probably sliced them with a stroke of his machete. "Bloodclots," he said as he left.

"Who's prosecuting?" asked Rushman. "I hope it's not Theodore Randy, he's vicious." Most of the group, now swollen to about a dozen, nodded. They knew of his reputation.

93

"Why, what's wrong with Randy?" Bryan Cassidy asked. He was a heroin main-liner who had just shot-up in the gents. He rarely made sense, whatever his condition. Everybody always said, "Cassidy knows nothing about nothing." The group humoured him because he was their tambourine man. From axle dust to zepp, he could supply every form of illegal delight.

"Randy makes a simple question seem like a blackmail threat," said Canker. "He'd weld you to the witness box."

"He oozes real cynicism when most briefs ooze false charm," said Rushman.

"Ah, there's Georgie boy now. I'll go and ask him," said Hornet. Craven liked his clients to know he cared. So the cost of attending the Crown Court was weighed against his primary purpose of being present. More than showing he cared, it gave him control. Everyone, lawyers and witnesses, knew who was in charge.

"Mr. Craven, who's against us?" asked Hornet. "Tell me it's not, Randy?"

"Don't worry, Lee," Craven said. "We've got some female. Probably a diesel dyke wearing a veil."

Hornet rushed back to the others and gave them the good news. Craven walked towards their table, looking his usual unkempt self. He gave them the last encouraging word before the performance began. "Be on your guard. Remember what they used to say in the war. Walls have-..."

"What, the First World War?" Qualm asked.

"Listen, just listen. You might just learn." Craven rolled his eyes. "Trust me-..."

Before he could finish they all joined in saying, "Yeah, 'cos I'm a lawyer." At least it put them in a good mood. Craven laughed and knew it was time to take his own counsel.

The tannoy crackled into life when a coarse voice ordered, "Will all parties in the case of Qualm and Others go to Court 1." The case was listed 'not before noon', so they were saved from getting up early or being late. The group moved en masse away from the café. The trio strutted towards the court with a gait only the guilty can cultivate.

Outside Court 1 Canker spoke to Kane and Terry Radstock. Both were fast friends who could be counted on, as they were crooks too.

"Mandy, you go upstairs, sit near the door." Canker motioned to the public gallery.

"Tez, go to the other side. Don't talk to each other. You're strangers. You got it?" Both nodded. "No notes, no mobiles, no shared fags. Nothing." More nods.

"Tracey, you stay inside the court, I need your support," Qualm said to his wife. "Just look as innocent as you are." Neither laughed, it was a serious business. That was why she wore her best black dress that finished about four inches above her knees. It covered her spare tyres as close as a retread. The thick, wide white belt emphasised her waist and shape, a day rather than an hourglass. Tracey Qualm had the puffy ugliness of women fat before their time with wrinkles and lines borne of past smoke-filled rooms and endless face-feeding. "If you need to leave court for a fag or a slash, don't make it obvious."

"Alright," she said. "Don't keep on."

"And don't talk to me," he said. "In or out of court."

"Why not?"

"We'll talk about it tonight."

"Yeah. Like we always do," she said. Tracey waddled into court. She sat down and found the Victorian seat reserved for the public much too tight given the size of her thighs. Moving to the end one, she spilled into the aisle.

They planted a wheen of their friends in the public gallery too. They could hear the prosecution evidence, then cut and tailor the defence evidence to suit. A nod, a gesture, even a raised eyebrow, would send the right signal. Qualm's side would know what to do and who to call. A whisper in a willing ear and the next witness was fully prepared. Or one, whose lies would easily be discovered, would be eased out and forgotten.

Zowie Darrow was tall and thin with the body of a natural athlete, though these days she would always jokingly moan, "I've worked on this sculpture. My other body is a temple." She had clear light coffee skin and long red hair. It was made redder by her mobile hairdresser who visited on Saturday morning, when the Chambers was closed. When she was scruffy on a Sunday, she was smarter than most in their Sunday best. Zogger epitomised style.

Zogger made her Opening Speech for the prosecution. Fair yet firm to her fingertips. She told the jury, "The core issue here is identification. That is a troubling and difficult evidential point to prove. Bear in mind innocent mistakes on identity can so easily be made. Indeed, a mistaken identity of the same man twice was the reason for setting up the Court of Appeal in 1907. Here, in fairness to the defendants, it's right you should know it was dark at the time and those responsible escaped before their deed was discovered. These defendants are connected to the arson by the forensic analysis. We say they all gave false alibis. Of course, we have no direct evidence because the victim is dead. There is a vital fact you will have to consider. All the other witnesses to the violence are voiceless."

Zogger opened the case to the jury, pitching it so they

neither expected too much nor had any sympathy for the defendants. She pitched it low so she could end on a high note. She referred to the photographs of Molly, holding them, but kept them in her hand to gain a greater effect when they were produced during the trial. She concentrated on the defendants' 'no comment' interviews. "What will you make of their Iscariot-like silence?" she asked the jury. "What would you do? Would you hide behind a veil of silence, hoping your guilt wouldn't be discovered? Or would you shout about your innocence from the rooftops?" She ended telling them about, "The defendants will no doubt call their friends as witnesses. Rest assured, any evidence they give will be lies in favour of false alibis. Be wary. They are here to hoodwink you. Don't be deceived by them because, like these defendants, they wear the face of falsehood like a second skin."

When she finished her Opening Speech many jurors appeared to wonder what the defence was and how they could possibly plead, 'Not Guilty'. Her strength was she spoke with a controlled passion. Zogger's conviction reached the jury. The defendants' collective guilt seemed obvious to them. Some of the jurors surreptitiously fixed their eyes on the defendants, as if they were trying to read their faces for traces of guilt.

After her 'Opening', the evidence for the prosecution was adduced. She called all the evidence she had, intending to gnaw at the defendants' security of silence. Zogger, realising she had to take every opportunity to make her case, watched and waited.

The opportunity arose on the third day, near the end of her case, when one of the jurors was concentrating on the photographs of Molly. Zogger, ever alert to the effect of the evidence, caught her reaction.

"Your Honour, I'm sorry to interrupt my Learned Friend," said Zogger. She smiled knowing she was swimming with sharks. 'Smokey' Jones, the defence counsel, was cross-examining DC Buckle. She chose that moment to break his stroke. "One of the jurors appears to be unwell," she said, looking at a middle-aged woman in white who was flushed red and looked upset. She was sitting on the far left of the back row. The well-dressed woman looked close to tears and more. Zogger thought the juror was going to faint or vomit, possibly both.

"Are you alright, Madam?" asked Judge Lionel Lipschitz. "Would you like a short break?"

"Yes, please," the woman, Alison Costello, mumbled. She held the photograph of Molly, blackened and dead, in her left-hand and looked as if she was ready to puke all over it. She closed her eyes. The man in front of her heard her almost retch. He put his hands on the crown of his shiny head.

"Well, Members of the Jury, we'll have a break. Just time enough to have a quick coffee and stretch your legs." The Judge looked at the Usher, Ron, and said, "Make sure the lady is alright, Mr. Wycherley."

"Certainly, Your Honour," Ron answered and went into the Jury Room. He was also the Jury Bailiff, so they could deliberate without distractions. He was a War baby, a retired garage mechanic, fifty years on was still a Ted. Not a man you could mess around.

The Judge stood up. Everyone stood up and bowed. The Judge left court. The defence team did too. The prosecution team remained.

"That's it. Exactly what we wanted," Zogger said. "Those photographs crystallise the cruelty. Wait until they're cross-examined. The jury will hate them."

"Almost as much as us, or at least me," said Buckle.

"This moment, the break, the photographs, the woman, they'll all stay with the jury. It's probably a talking point in the Jury Room now."

"I can't wait for the slaughter," Buckle said, "when you cross-examine them." He rubbed his hands together.

"Hold your horses, Barney. It'll be worth the wait. I'm still honing my tongue."

Before the jury returned, the Judge unexpectedly entered court. Everyone stood up and bowed.

"Mr. Jones, I'm thinking in terms of time," the Judge said. "What is the position, now the prosecution case has almost finished? Is Qualm intending to give evidence?" Lipschitz, in asking the question in the absence of the jury, gave the defence a chance to rehearse their position.

"Your Honour, I have given serious thought to that point and um, er, of course, advised the defendant as to his position. Mr. Qualm has, in all the circumstances, that is, um, and upon mature reflection, decided to exercise his legal right not to give evidence."

"Thank you, Mr. Jones. I quite understand. I have no doubt you have given proper consideration to the evidence, the position of Qualm and properly advised your client. What's the position regarding the other defendants, Hornet and Canker?"

"Your Honour, I've also considered the position of those defendants. Well, it's.. They, given the rather peculiar circumstances of this case, have decided to exercise their legal rights. So, I mean, neither defendant will personally be giving evidence, Your Honour." Smokey smiled as sincerely as a practised honest lawyer.

"Mr. Jones. I'm sure you have properly advised your

clients." The Judge's tone helped Smokey, as it was intended to, so a 'comment' from him on their silence was unlikely. A comment by the Judge on a defendant's silence was something they all feared because the simple fact they had no defence was usually the simple truth. Their silence was a shield for their lies.

The advantage for the defendants was achieved via a legal code, but the message was clear enough. Certainly to Zogger and Buckle. She was aware Lipschitz was a life-long friend of Smokey. They met at Oxford and were even at the same Lodge.

"What's the position on their antecedents, Mr. Jones? Do any of the defendants have any previous convictions?" the Judge asked.

"All of them, Your Honour." He shuffled through his papers, which were, as usual, in untidy piles and some disarray on the bench. He couldn't find the list of their convictions. "I thought I had a copy with me, Your Honour. I must have left it in Chambers."

"Fax it up, Mr. Jones?"

"It does somewhat."

"I don't suppose they're relevant. It doesn't call for a comment from me." Zogger wanted to flash their antecedents. Holding a sheet of their convictions, she went to rise, but before she uttered a word, the Judge dismissively waved his hand as if to pat her on the head. "Are there any other witnesses you will be calling?" he asked Smokey.

"Yes, Your Honour. I have several alibi witnesses and a forensic scientist."

"Very well, we'll adjourn until tomorrow. Can the Usher ensure a message is sent to the jury? It will give the lady juror an opportunity to recover." The Judge got up and left court. The defence left. Though there was more than an hour of court time left, he was giving the defence extra time to prepare their case. More time to coach their witnesses too.

The prosecution team were stunned. Zogger was being denied a shot at them. She grabbed her papers. Buckle swore loud enough to hear. He cracked his knuckles. They left court. They gathered in the basement room, where the C.P.S. had an office.

"You won't be able to question them. What a pathetic decision. That fat clown."

"Who, Smokey or the Judge?"

"Both. Though that barrister takes the biscuit. As smarmy as charmless Cameron."

"What, Our Dave?"

"What now, Zogger?"

"Well, Barney, we'll either have to suck lemons and look as ugly as Qualm or make lemonade by attacking his witnesses. That's our choice."

"I know you can do it." He added, "Is there anything I can do? Anything at all?"

"Thanks, Barney. You're fine as you are. Just provide inspiration. See you tomorrow."

Zogger burnt the midnight oil, working until the early hours, poring over the details of the defence expert's evidence. She knew, while there were no lies, he had carefully chosen what to address and what to omit in his Report. The alibi witnesses were her other target. As most of them had appeared in court more often than the average judge, it held no fear. Their lies became so second nature even they believed them. Zogger turned the snow-scene souvenir upside down. She peered at the shaken flakes. Looking for an answer that never came. She resorted to a plea: "Ah, save me," she said quietly. Though from what or who she wanted 'saving', she was not sure – perhaps herself. She studied her notes. As the words jumbled across the page, running into each other, the notes slid from her hand to the floor, as she slowly submitted to sleep.

The following day the trial continued with Zogger formally 'Closing' her case.

Smokey rose with some show, erect and stiff, looking at the jury and then the Judge. He adjusted his gown, shaking the dandruff flakes off and said, "I won't be calling my clients, Your Honour. I don't want to waste any more court time." He looked at the jury and then slyly at Zogger. "I shall move swiftly on to the alibi witnesses in respect of all three defendants. Then I shall call the forensic expert."

"Yes, thank you, Mr. Jones. Who is your first witness?"

"Your Honour, it is a young man, a Mr. Jaynes." He shouted, "Please call, Joseph Jaynes." Although the fact a defendant does not give evidence is often embarrassing during a trial, here it was so seamless it seemed part of the procedure. It flowed so naturally the jury were unaware it was usual for defendants to give evidence, especially when they relied on an alibi. Otherwise, there was a real danger the jury would think their mates had concocted a story to help them escape, because they had no defence. Exactly what Zogger had urged during her Opening Speech. The jury's scepticism was a high risk for the defence. Lipschitz had given a judicial helping hand at the most crucial stage of the trial. Before the defence began, he helped Smokey, without the jury knowing.

Instead of the defendants giving evidence personally, they called their mates as quotable lie-o-grams and rent-an-alibi. Those characters paraded like gilded pimps in the witness box. Without the benefit of a diary or a note, characters that were usually stoned and could hardly string a sentence of seven words together and make sense, deftly remembered graphic details of faces and people and places. Whenever Zogger got close to opening a chink in any of their stories, they had an automatic 'schooled' answer: "I'm not sure I can remember exactly what happened / It's a long time ago / I don't want to guess in case I'm wrong." Strangely, as part of their act, they were generally polite. It gave credence to their evidence. Whenever the story started to crack and the truth was in danger of being revealed, they opted to adopt another lie: "I swear on my babby's life." Jaynes was so used to lying he trotted that one out even though he had no children. Or at least none he would admit to or knew about.

Craven used their instinctive gift to coach them in the choreography of mendacity. He impressed upon them the value of the odd Churchillian pause. "Look, just imagine you're smoking. You're desperate for a drag. Suck on it. You'll buy time." Craven produced a cigar to emphasise the point. He held it between clenched teeth and didn't speak. The aide-mémoire was not lost on them.

"Or ask them to repeat the question. That really irritates barristers."

Using Jaynes first was a tactical move to lay the ground for the defence. The sting within Zogger's questions was less effective as he was a bozo. Rather than simply a liar, he appeared simple.

Jimmy Rushman, after giving evidence of Qualm's alibi, was cross-examined by Zogger :

"What time did you leave the pub?" she asked.

"About half-one."

"Isn't that after closing time?"

"We had a special licence, like." Zogger knew that was true.

"Who was driving?"

"I was."

"Was it your car?" She knew that car was involved in a hit-and-run a month earlier where an old lady was killed. A forensic test traced it to him. When interviewed by the police, Rushman claimed his fingerprints were found on the rear view mirror because he touched it at work. He was a valet at the Portishead Car Wash. The car was now in police custody being examined by Scenes of Crime Officers. If he agreed she could prosecute him for perjury or attempting to pervert the course of justice. More importantly, it would discredit him in front of the jury. He paused, searching for the right lie. Zogger repeated the question, "Was it your car?" He caught Kane's eye. She slowly shook her head. A balding man in a grubby, belted, beige mac had taken the outside seat. She pretended to be trying to get comfortable, as if the seat was shrinking as the clock hands ticked by. She was wedged between the arms. Kane affected to scratch her face and used her thumb and index finger to form a 'K'. Rushman had what he wanted.

"No."

"Whose was it?"

"Kevin's."

"Where was Kevin Qualm?"

"Sat in the back."

"Why didn't he drive?"

"He was too bladdered to stand up, Miss." Rushman gave a look of primitive innocence as his friends, planted in the Public Gallery, tittered. Others joined in and then a few jurors. Zogger thought she could easily press her sharpest stiletto heels on his piles and force them up straight through his throat.

"But you had been drinking too, hadn't you?"

"No Miss, I wouldn't dare."

Rushman was an alcoholic. She couldn't just let the lie, lie. If she finished at that point, he'd won. She knew of his driving record and his piss-artist status.

"You 'wouldn't dare'. What do you mean?"

"Well, I wouldn't drink and drive."

"But you were with your mate Joseph 'Jonjo' Jaynes weren't you?"

"Yeah."

"When he gave evidence in this Court this morning he said you and he were drinking all night. Is he lying?"

"No. Jonjo wouldn't lie."

"He wouldn't lie about you, would he?"

"No. Jonjo's a bit of a cret though."

"In what way?"

"Well, his memory, like. He forgets things easily."

"Why?"

"He drinks a bit, does Jonjo."

"You mean he drinks a lot, don't you?"

"Well, I suppose so, yeah."

"So what he's told us about the supposed alibi, you say he's wrong because he was too drunk to remember?"

"Yes, that's it."

"How are you any different?"

"What do you mean, Miss?" Rushman needed time to think of the right answer.

"You say Jonjo was so drunk he forgot what happened. You forgot too didn't you? Because you drink a lot too, drank a lot, didn't you?"

Rushman was confused. He struggled to answer, then stopped. He was in danger of being trapped. He faffled, "I, I like...I mean-.."

"That's two or is it three questions you've asked the witness, Miss Darrow. You're an experienced Counsel. Which one do you want him to answer?" Lipschitz asked.

"Thank you, Your Honour," she said. "Let me re-phrase it." The interruption by the Judge was intended to belittle Zogger as if she was trying to bamboozle the witness. Using her status to take advantage of him. The Judge looked at the jury, sighed and nodded. She saw him and noted their reaction.

"If Jonjo got the night mixed up, as you say, you might have made a mistake too? Isn't that right?"

"I don't really know what you mean, like?" Rushman was buying time and trying to needle her. He picked up on the Judge's attitude.

"Well he got it wrong, you say, because he drinks a lot. So do you. You drink and drive don't you?"

Rushman hesitated, squinted and pouted, thinking about his answer. He paused. Just like he'd been told. Craven's craft had raised its head. He was pretending to dredge his memory while thinking of Craven mimicking Churchill. Rushman blanked her and said, "No, Miss." He didn't rise to the bait.

"You're lying again, aren't you?"

"No. I don't think so."

"What do you mean you 'don't think so'? Surely you know whether you're lying?"

"Well. Yes. No. I'm not then. You're confusin' me again."

"You're certainly no stranger to this Court, are you?"

"No."

"You've been convicted in this very Court of being three times over the legal limit for driving, haven't you?"

"Yes. Only once though."

"You were chased by two police cars and only stopped when you crashed into one of them. An officer was seriously injured. Isn't that right?"

"Yeah."

"You've come along to give a false alibi for your best mate haven't you? You weren't even with him, were you?"

"That's two questions, Miss. But 'no' and 'yes', I was." Rushman smirked. Lipschitz laughed way too loud. Then Smokey and the jury joined him. The harsh laughter filled the court.

"How long have you been an alcoholic?"

"About seven years."

Lipschitz could sense some sticky questions were going to be aimed at Rushman "This is all very interesting, but where is it leading, Miss Darrow?" the Judge asked.

"Your Honour, I have to explore what the prosecution say is a false alibi."

"Yes, but you have to stop drilling when you're only boring. Surely?" Lipschitz mirrored Smokey's smugness.

"As it happens, I haven't many more questions anyway."

"After over an hour and all your fecund questions, so far, that's a relief. Let's get on."

"I'm grateful for Your Honour's view. Thank you for your fecund suggestion."

Lipschitz's natural frown became more pronounced. As his eyes pierced her, she turned towards Rushman.

"Let's continue where we were before His Honour's helpful intervention. Alcohol affects different people in different ways, doesn't it?"

"Yes."

"Sometimes they become a bit noisy, argumentative, even aggressive?"

"Yes."

"Sometimes they become tired, fall asleep in a corner, no trouble to anyone?"

"Yes."

"Alcoholics drink every day, don't they?"

"Yes."

"They have no choice?"

"True."

"How does alcohol affect you?"

"What'cha mean, like?"

"Well, do you become aggressive, maybe violent or just sleepy?"

"Sleepy, Miss." He smiled. "I'm not violent. I can't, like, stand blood." He lied, paused, added, "Everyone says after seven pints I sleep like a corpse."

"You wouldn't be able to drive would you?"

"I wouldn't be able to stand up."

"Jonjo is your main drinking companion?"

"Yes."

"When you and he meet, there's always a session?"

"Yes. We always try an' drink each other under the table. If we can find the table."

"That night with Jonjo, you were drunk, weren't you?"

"Yes, Miss," he said. He caught Kane's eye. She was shaking her head. "No. I mean... You're confusing me.

108

I'm not sure. I didn't break the law again, if that's what you mean."

"You lying b...." Those words sprung onto her tongue, but remained unsaid. She felt Lipschitz's cold stare. Instead she said, with a sincerity to make a celebrity jealous, "So that's your story," – she caught the Judge's eye before he could intervene – "Or evidence, I should say. No more questions. Thank you, Mr. Rackman." She sat down, feeling she'd opened a chink in the defence armour.

The defence relied on an expert. That was a shrewd move because it deflected the jury from dwelling on the absence of evidence from the defendants. Dr. Irving Landers, the forensic scientist, gave evidence of his experience, qualifications and the content and conclusion of his Report. Smarter than the average barrister, Landers sounded impressive. He was over sixty, but assured and alert to every point. His black suit with a muted red pinstripe was as bespoke as his manner. Tall and well-built with shorn silvery hair, he looked the part and played to the court. After Landers gave evidence for the defence, he was cross-examined by Zogger.

"Doctor Landers, there were footprints found on the sods near the dead pony. Did you examine those?" she asked.

"Yes."

"They matched the boots found at Kevin Qualm's home?"

"Yes."

"Isn't that evidence the owner was at the scene?"

"No."

"That he was there at some other time?"

"No."

"Someone he was with was in that field?"

"No. Not necessarily."

"Why not?"

"I understand they were size 10, Exhibit BB7. Mr. Qualm takes size 11."

"What size does Lee Hornet take?"

"10, I believe"

"And Dean Canker?"

"10, I believe. But...-"

"Just answer the question, Doctor." She knew he wanted to give some irrelevant evidence from his Report that was favourable to his clients. The Judge frowned at her, went to say something, then let it pass. His reaction didn't go unnoticed by the jury.

"You agree the footprints were fresh?"

"Yes, but those marks could've been made by any one of a thousand boots sold in this area. They are very popular, a fashion item – so I am told."

"Do you have any information on how many were sold?"

"No."

"Or how many size 10's were sold?"

"No."

"Or the number of those boots of size 10 sold in this area in the last year?"

"No. But those are my Instructions. I'm a Forensic Scientist. I rely on my solicitor to give me the information, which I consider and come to a conclusion and prepare my Report. You have a copy of it. If you have any information that's different I shall be pleased to consider it and, if necessary, alter my conclusion. Do you have any such evidence?"

110

"I ask the questions, Doctor. Thank you. You simply answer them." She scanned his Report for her next question. She was anxious to move on. "If-..."

"Just wait a minute. Hold on, Miss Darrow," the Judge said. "It's not for the defence to prove anything is it?"

"No, of course not, Your Honour."

"So, although you are right Dr. Landers should not ask questions, what's the answer? I'm sure it will help the jury."

"To what question, Your Honour?" Zogger was now trying to buy time. He knew it. She was dancing through treacle.

"Does the prosecution have any evidence to counter-act what Dr. Landers says are his Instructions?" Lipschitz kept her in his vision.

"No." She stretched the word as if she was going to say more. She looked as she sounded, embarrassed.

"That's settled that then. Let's not waste any more time."

"Before His Honour's helpful question, you were telling us about these boots being a fashion item. Many of them were sold, you claimed?"

"Yes."

"Maybe Doctor, but let's return to the fresh footprints." Zogger had to pin him down, as it was the vital link between the defendants and the arson. "Regardless of how many boots might have been sold, those footprints matched the ridges on the sole and a cut mark on the heel in every way?"

"I agree."

"There was yellow clay soil in Cedar Field in the spot where Molly was mutilated?"

"Yes."

111

"This is outrageous," Smokey said, rising to his feet. As he did so he spread his arms and knocked the carafe over, spilling water on his papers and the bench. The carafe rolled to the edge of the bench, the top lodged on the corner and water poured onto the carpet. Ron, the Usher, rushed over and put it upright. Smokey ignored it all as he thundered on in his clumsy fashion. "I object to my Learned Friend using emotional words like 'mutilated'. It has no purpose, but to promote prejudice against these defendants. I ask her to withdraw it."

"It's a very reasonable word to use. After all, it's true," Zogger said.

"That's for the jury. In any case-..." Smokey almost spluttered his words. His jowls moved and his naturally red face turned crimson and glowed with feigned anger.

"Now, now," said the Judge. He could see a little verbal bloodshed splattering across the benches, unless he intervened. He knew she'd chew Smokey up. "Perhaps it was not the best choice of word to use, Miss Darrow? Perhaps you could have used a less emotional word, a more neutral one." His words were directed at her. Cosy, yet caustic. "Now, Miss Darrow, would you like to re-phrase the question using a different word, one more appropriate for Prosecution Counsel to use? I'm sure you can find one."

"Of course, Your Honour," she said. Smokey's objection to the word, 'mutilated', was tactical and fatuous. He baited her to put her off her stroke. Lipschitz did likewise using the added authority of his judicial position.

"Dr. Landers, let's continue," she said. "There was yellow clay soil where Molly was maimed." She paused and before he could answer, added, "And burned alive."

"Yes."

"Both of the boots had yellow soil encrusted on the soles and heels and toes?"

"Yes."

Which particular defendant wore the boots was not crucial as it was a joint enterprise. "It fits the footprint as if it was a fingerprint?"

"No, it does not."

"Why do say that?"

"Well, two reasons really. There was a mark on the toe that was not in the mould I examined. Also I understand the soil was never analysed. Or was it?"

The question asked by Landers hung suspended. Her mind went into overdrive. Zogger was really sore as she had urged the CPS to analyse the soil, but they refused because the "Budget wouldn't stretch to it." They said it "Wasn't important enough." In that split-second she remembered being stung at the time by that response and turning first to Sally Saunders, the Clerk, then to Billy Fargusson, the CPS lawyer, saying in her steely best, "Listen – and listen good – I don't ever ask for information for its own sake. I never ask for anything unless it's important. The jury will want to know. Do you understand?" Fargusson had looked at the ground. That was why he was a CPS lawyer. He said nothing and as to analysing the soil, did the same.

"Is-..." Zogger ignored Landers' question and intended to continue her cross-examination.

The Judge swiftly interrupted. "Before you go on, Miss Darrow, would you help the jury with the answer? Dr. Landers raised a fundamental point. So is he right or wrong?"

"Right, Your Honour."

"He is right. Good. At least that's clarified the position. Let's get a move on. We're spending time on irrelevant matters."

"I thought, Your Honour, you believed it was a fundamental point?"

"We don't want to waste more time. Let's see if you can be a little crisper in your cross-examination." He looked at the clock, held it in his gaze, glanced at the jury, then at her and said, "Shall we?"

She tried another line of attack. "Blood found on the defendants' boots was analysed by the prosecution expert, Dr. Gilbert Green, and yourself?"

"Yes."

"And that blood was from an animal, not a human?"

"Yes, but-…"

"Just answer my question, Doctor. Is it-…"

"But it's important," Landers said. He looked towards the Judge. He raised his right hand as if to scratch an invisible itch on the left side of his neck. The Judge saw the sign. A secret architect's sign for his eyes only, Mason to Mason, passed from Landers.

"One moment, Miss Darrow," Lipschitz said. "Doctor, what did you want to add?"

"I wanted to explain about the blood."

"So the jury are not misled, I presume, Doctor?"

"Precisely, Your Honour."

"Surely you can have no objection to that, Miss Darrow?"

"Of course not, Your Honour."

"Then please go ahead, Doctor."

"I agreed with Counsel the blood was from an animal, but it's important for the jury to know the defendants work in an abattoir."

114

"Yes, thank you, Doctor. That was very helpful," Zogger said. Her tone said, don't find excuses before I even ask the question.

"The blood was from a pony?" she asked.

"Yes."

"Rather than a cow or a sheep for example?"

"Yes, that's right."

"Do the defendants slaughter ponies at their abattoir?"

"Well..."

Zogger hoped he would let slip something from his Instructions that was otherwise 'privileged'. Intuitively she believed he'd been asked to consider whether any blood from a pony could have contaminated the beasts they slaughtered. If the answer was 'no', that would definitely help the prosecution. While he paused she was running on instinct. Before he could answer she followed up with a killer question. "You're not suggesting there was any contamination of Molly's blood with other blood, are you?"

Landers, wise to her ploy, said, "I really don't know. You see, what I mean is...um, I was only asked to analyse this blood. So I, I, er, can't really help you." For the first time he seemed a little flustered. He coloured slightly, looked uncomfortable and glanced at the Judge again.

"What's the purpose of that question?" the Judge asked. "You're not asking the expert to guess, are you? It seems irrelevant. How can that help the jury?" Before she could answer, he said, "The Prosecution are not suggesting there's anything illegal about slaughtering a pony at the abattoir, are they, Miss Darrow?"

"No, of course not. My question had a different purpose."

"It was lost on me. It was lost on Dr. Landers. Probably

on the jury too." The Judge looked at them and some in both rows nodded in agreement. "I'm still confused."

"I'll certainly be willing to change that – if I can. Assuming it's possible, Your Honour."

"Get on with it." He was always, as most judges are, impatient. Now he was getting, as most judges do, ratty too. "How much longer are you going to be?"

"Not very long. Perhaps ten minutes."

"Ten minutes. I'll hold you to that." Lipschitz growled and nodded. "We've wasted enough time. This case has got to finish today." Landers had thinking time. Smokey was happy. The defendants grunted and guffawed when the Judge interrupted her. The jury were getting a bit fidgety. A young burly man, John Carr, third in on the front row, kicked the ankle of the youth next to him, Harold Jenkins. Carr mouthed something to which Jenkins raised his eyebrows. He was concerned why Zogger kept being criticised by the Judge. "Why does she keep getting things wrong?" Jenkins shrugged and yawned. On the right hand side of the back row one juror, Marilyn Rhodes, nudged her neighbour, Ellen Bookbinder, each time the Judge interrupted. The Judge's supposed confusion was spreading to them.

Zogger had a gut-tingle she had just dented Landers' charm, regardless of Lipschitz. She wanted to hit him hard. "Doctor, would you help us with this point?" She picked up his Report and pretended to read it. "Was the blood contaminated at all?"

"Yes, it was."

"Tell us, tell the jury, in what way? How?"

He coughed and hesitated, before answering. "I found semen in the stream."

"Animal or human?"

116

"Human."

Landers' right hand scratched the artificial itch again. All the jurors paid attention. Some of the jurors on each row visibly gasped. At the back opposite to Rhodes, Ritchie Penniman, nudged his older neighbour, Mary O'Brien. Both appeared pained. He whispered, "That's horrible, isn't it?" She didn't reply. An atmosphere engulfed them all and leaked around the court. At that moment truth peeped above the parapet. Mirrors of hate passed from the jurors' collective eyes to the perverts in the dock.

Zogger intended to ask another question. She only wanted to magnify the moment. "Doctor, human semen you say, just help us with this-... Well, no, you've helped us enough already. I have no more questions." She wished she could have asked the clincher as to whose semen it was, but had to refrain because the 'CPS budget' didn't cover a DNA analysis of it.

Zogger sat down and left the rest to Smokey.

As usual, he asked a few dull questions. Landers, shaken, answered them in a changed manner. The jury were not paying attention to either of them. A queasy feeling spoiled their air. Zogger believed the jury could see the defendants' lies in the guise of science. Rhodes appeared shocked. A middle-aged woman with muscular arms, wearing an old-fashioned flowered dress, she looked at Bookbinder and both grimaced. Bookbinder held her stomach, which bulged through her pink T-shirt, as if she was about to be sick. She mouthed something to Rhodes who anxiously put her left hand to her mouth.

After Landers evidence the defence 'Closed' their case. Smokey announced, "Your Honour, that is the Case for the Defence."

117

"Thank you, Mr. Jones."

The Judge caught her eye. Zogger knew what that meant. She decided to strike first. She stood up, "Your Honour, I note the time. The jury have had a long day. Perhaps it would be convenient to rise and resume tomorrow?"

"Yes, thank you, Miss Darrow."

Zogger blew a slow breath. Relaxed and relieved. The jury perked up for they believed they were going home. Each was ripe to be deceived.

The Judge directed the jury, "Members of the Jury, you have now heard all the evidence. There will be no more. You will hear a Speech from each Counsel and then I will Sum-Up the case to you. I doubt we will have time for both Speeches today. So you'll only hear the Prosecution Speech. The likelihood is the Defence will address you tomorrow. After my Summing-Up, I shall send you out to deliberate and return your verdicts." He then looked directly at her and said, "Thank you, Miss Darrow."

Lipschitz misled her. She was taken completely off-guard. As it was 4.05 p.m. on a Thursday, she assumed he would adjourn the case until the following day. At least he would ask her whether she wanted to make her speech, 'now or tomorrow'. That was the usual practice. She wanted to find the right phrase to make their guilt as transparent as she knew it was; to cast memorable lines that would hook the jurors' hearts and minds. That would take time. Now the Judge gave her no choice. It was late in the day. The jury were bored, tired and restless. They had other important matters in mind like collecting children from school, avoiding the heavy traffic and hurrying home to see the next episode of their favourite soap opera. Two were separately thinking about meeting their illicit lovers,

118

hoping they wouldn't be discovered. Two others had become an item during the trial. They were only interested in finishing early and seeking the shadows. Zogger's Speech was the last thing any of them wanted to hear.

In seconds she had to make sense of all the spindrift thoughts, scrambling around her mind. Yet the strength of the prosecution case was Zogger's Closing Speech. As expected, she delivered it with a rarely heard eloquence. Her eyes fixed upon the jury, her hard-wired words fired at them. The jury came alive. She opened with a reference to a "Moving finger that writes and moves on. Just as the writing remains, their guilt can never be erased. Their blood is on Molly's body." She continued, telling them how the defendants "Acted together that night and now hide behind the silence of their lies. Make no mistake, as the great American philosopher, Emerson, has it, 'when a crime has been committed the world is made of glass.' Their acts are latent and patent. The one thing they each can't face is their murky conscience – if they possess one – and the indelible stain of truth. They know they abused that animal and set her on fire. Together they committed that vicious act of violent vandalism. Together they took Molly's life as well as her unborn foal." She captured the jury as soon as she spoke. She never let them go.

When she mentioned Emerson several of them looked glad she mentioned their favourite organist. One of them, Pete McCullough, a very tall, ultra-skinny man with a weather-beaten face, wearing a faded black denim Wrangler jacket and jeans, sat up and paid attention. McCullough, an unemployed musician, was an ageing hippy with no hair on top, but a straggly grey mane and a beard to match, murmured seriously to his companion, Jim Starky, "Whatever happened to Lake and Palmer?" Starky,

119

small and rotund in a shiny civil servant suit, nodded sagely.

As far as she could judge, the jury were listening intently. McCullough and Starky passed notes back and forth. Who could say what they said? Zogger hoped they would feel the force of the fact, "The cruellest lies are often told in silence." She continued with that theme, emphasising why if they had "nothing to hide, they sought refuge in the final conspiracy, their Judas silence?" The jury's seeming attention to detail and firm, serious faces, even the nudges between them when she made a telling point against the defendants, gave her hope they were on her side. Many of them made notes as she spoke. Zogger prayed some of the solid points she made would stay with and sway them.

Conscious of the lateness of the day, Zogger ended her Speech within an hour. She tied the loose ends together, emphasising their guilt. "If they had a defence, why haven't we heard it from their own lips? Why are they afraid to walk the twelve steps from the dock to the witness box?" She ended with a crescendo. "Don't be bluffed by their expert. Dr. Landers is only telling you what he's been told. He wasn't there that night. The defendants were, of that you can be sure. How, if not, did their boots get covered in that yellow mud? As for their alibi witnesses, if truth ever landed on their tongues, they'd get lockjaw. Their vicarious lies shine brighter than their silence, each a beacon of their guilt. Justice is like a train that's nearly always late. I ask you today to make sure it is on time. Canker and Hornet and Qualm have paraded their friends before you for one purpose. To create a smokescreen so you are distracted and blinded by their lies. They are here to create doubt where none exists, to muddy the clear waters, to dissemble and to fool you. Yet even after all this time these defendants still smell of Molly's blood. The stink of guilt clings to them as fresh as stale Stilton. A stink that neither time nor lies can erase. Find them all, as you too must know they are, guilty!"

She finished, trusting Yevtushenko's wisdom would lodge in the jurors' minds.

As soon as she sat down, Zogger worried and wondered; thoughts rebounded across her frowning forehead. Did I hit home? Was it enough to nail those scrotes? Believe me, I hope I didn't let you down, Molly.

Zogger went home, as usual, alone. She had very little to eat as her insides were tighter than the top of a tom-tom. She knew if she did she would puke and never get to sleep. As it was, she couldn't sleep anyway. It was never any different during a trial. Question-after-question streamed into her mind about what she should have asked the witnesses. "Why didn't I trap Rushman? Why didn't I ask Landers another killer question? Why didn't I destroy the false alibi?" She tried desperately to shake the thoughts out, but they kept returning as unwelcome as a rattling skeleton in an unlocked cupboard. Hour on hour she read lazily until her eyelids drooped. 'Lonely Avenue' slipped from her hands, onto the duvet and dropped heavily to the floor. A hardback. Finally she drifted off. After a few hours sleep, she got up and, unusually, had no breakfast, except for two cups of extra strong coffee. She was tired and hungry. Her guts were still tighter than a stripper's thong. The last thing she wanted was to vomit in court, unless, she thought, it was all over Smokey.

Keith 'Smokey' Jones was a corpulent, triple-chinned

buffoon who had contacts throughout the Bar and Judiciary. His nickname originated from the only good thing about him as far as Zogger was concerned. As he was growing up he listened to Arthur Alexander, Barrett Strong and everyone else that mattered. During his university days he was crazy about Motown and sang with the Soul On Ice band. You couldn't deny he had a great voice. His speciality was Miracle songs and everybody said he sounded just like Smokey. Since then he had grown fatter and more prosperous, but two things remained: his love of music, his hatred of work. He worked closely with Craven. They worked well together because they had so much in common. Smokey was lazy and greedy. He chose to practice crime because he believed it involved little work and no academic law. He saw evidence as just disguising lies as an excuse for truth.

On Friday morning Smokey stood to address the jury. Smokey, who was barely articulate, often completely lost track of his legal argument. He relied on connections. In time he would become a judge and continue the chain of nepotism. His voice was naturally haughty and snobbish, as rich and round as he was, a plummy patrician. He boomed, "There's no evidence against any of these defendants. It's a pack of, er, um, well, just assumption and presumption. But where, I ask you, is the evidence to persuade you so you're sure, all of you? The evidence is so weak you wouldn't hang a dog on it. I mean, it's poor. Besides, these defendants weren't even there. You've heard about their alibis from a few, well several, solid witnesses." Seeing him gave every good reason to drag the court attire into the 21st. Century. He pushed his wig back as it fell forward in front of his eyes. The wig stood atop his huge helmet head like a dead badger. His gown was sprinkled with dead cigar ash. He didn't care enough to brush it off. His dark double-breasted suit, with a button missing, stretched across his massive midriff. Smokey continued, "Members of the Jury, you've had the advantage of hearing, hearing, from the expert. He, he's someone who knows about these things. There's surely a mass of doubt about who did what, or even when. I mean, you can't rely on any of the prosecution so-called evidence." As usual, he made a lacklustre Defence Speech. It was full of legalese, "In my submission to you" and "I venture to suggest", that induced and spread yawns among the jury. Some shifted in their seats, a couple secretly ate sweets, one was openly chewing gum and others seemed to be losing the threads of the evidence. They appeared neither interested nor persuaded, but merely bored. Starky grimaced like Gromit to McCullough as soon as Smokey opened his mouth. McCullough wrote a note saying, 'Lord Haw-Haw.' When Starky saw it, he put his finger across his nose like Hitler. Smokey ended by saying, "And so I invite you to come to the only decision you can on this pathetic evidence, um, though you can hardly call it that. A few vague allegations and no proof. So you must find them, not guilty. All of them."

There was almost a silent handclap before he finished; you could hear an imaginary one when he did. The joke about Smokey at the Bar was that he 'never got any applause, but he once had the clap'. Some wags suspected it was true. Most thought he was too close to the queens he represented.

Lionel Lipschitz, a confirmed bachelor, then Summed Up the case. Like all weak judges, he being a typical specimen, he'd do anything to avoid criticism by the Court of Appeal.

123

He directed the jury, "There is very little direct evidence from the prosecution in this case. The defence have called evidence to support their position. Candid young men, you might think. They say the defendants were not even present. Did the Prosecution disprove those alibis? It's true that the soil was not analysed, properly or perhaps, at all. That is something you will have to consider. Moreover, you've also heard from Dr. Irving Landers, a Forensic Scientist, called on behalf of the defence. It's a matter for you, but you might think he was an extremely impressive witness. Highly qualified, with over forty years experience. He's a well-known expert, indeed of distinction, in forensic science. You have to decide whether the Prosecution have disproved the evidence of Dr. Landers?"

As he concluded, the Judge said, "You have heard two fine Speeches from Counsel. You must base your verdict on the evidence and only the evidence you have heard in Court. You must not speculate on what evidence might have been obtained. Remember this above all: you have not heard from the defendants. Do not hold that against them. They have called witnesses who support their alibis, who have sworn they were with them at the time of the crime. If that is so, or even might be so, the Prosecution have not proved their case. The Prosecution have a heavy burden. They have to disprove the alibi. They have the burden of proving the case, of making you sure of each defendant's guilt. That is a very high standard of proof. The defendants do not have to prove anything. The burden and standard of proof, as I say, both are very high, are on the Prosecution throughout, from start to finish. They bring the case, they must prove it."

The Judge deliberately paused so the jury would realise the significance of his direction. "It is not a question of the benefit of any doubt. Before you convict any defendant you must be sure of his guilt. If you are not sure, then the Prosecution have failed to prove their case. In that event the defendants, not just one, I emphasise, but all of them, are entitled to be acquitted. That is consistent with your oath and duty."

Finally he directed them, "You must now appoint a Foreman. It can be any one of your number, a man or a woman. I can only accept a unanimous verdict. All of you must agree. You may have heard about a majority verdict, but if and when that time comes, I will direct you. For the moment you must be unanimous."

"If the Jury Bailiffs can now be sworn." He looked towards the Ushers.

Wycherley and Harry Webber each swore the Bailiffs' Oath, "I swear by Almighty God to keep the jury in some safe and secure place and not to speak to them without leave of the court unless it be to ask if they have reached a verdict." Webber led the jurors out of court followed by Wycherley. A shroud of weariness covered them.

Zogger clandestinely scanned the jurors' faces as they trooped out of Court. Arrows of poison darted from them towards the defendants. They gave little away. All she could glean from their quick movements was they wanted to leave court. As with so many others, the case had affected them.

When the bailiffs took the jury out, Zogger and the cops and the CPS clerks met in the basement office again. There was a palpable gloom in the prosecution room. Zogger tried to keep their spirits high. That was why she was such a good advocate. She couldn't and wouldn't concede defeat until a verdict was delivered.

As Zogger waited for the verdict the caffeine coursed through her veins. Whichever side you were on, waiting for the jury was always a trying time. It was impossible to consider anything important or concentrate on any other matter. No different in many ways than being on a maternity ward. While waiting, if you smoked you went out in the rain and your fingers soon became tar-stained. If you drank coffee you soon consumed proportions to rival Balzac. Either way the waiting hastened your death.

"I'll see you all shortly," Zogger said to the police and the CPS staff. "If anyone wants me, I'll be in a room just down the corridor on the second floor. I've got some prep to do." With that she politely left the basement room. When she was awaiting a verdict she needed peace and space. At the best of times she was simply not good with chit-chat and small-talk. In the empty hours before a verdict, even with her sense of diplomacy, the effort was too great. She needed to be alone. Away from the Robing Room and forced jollity, idle boasts, the odour of cigar smoke and sweat, she found a room reserved for journalists. She wandered in, discarded her wig, removed her gown, slumped into the seat and closed her eyes. She clasped her hands, joined them, without thinking, as if in prayer.

Although it was nearly an hour, what seemed like only moments later, there was a knock on the door. It was Buckle, who Zogger liked a lot. He was a professional through and through, thorough and intent on winning. They'd worked together before. They'd also been on opposite sides. There was a mutual respect.

"Oh, hello Barney. What can I do for you?" Her question was matter-of-fact.

"How long do you think they'll be out?"

"Who can say? Could be ten minutes or ten hours. How long is the line between suspicion and proof?"

"What do you think the verdicts will be?" Buckle frowned.

"I watched the jury carefully. They paid a lot of attention during my Speech. They almost fell asleep during Smokey's. His monotone was matched by Lipschitz's drone. Both of them bored the jury rigid. I think they'll pot them all." She said it confidently, telling him what she knew he wanted to hear. In her heart she was not so sure. There beat the invisible rain of doubt.

"What did you think of the Summing Up though?"

"As biased as expected. He's a judge."

"I didn't think much of that Judge. He seemed to have a downer on the prosecution."

"I wouldn't worry about that. It's always the same with him and me. The jury aren't as stupid as he seems to think. He's judging them by himself."

"So you reckon we'll get guilty verdicts across the board?"

"Well, certainly on Qualm and probably Hornet. I suppose it's less likely on Canker as it's really 'association' with his accomplices and a false alibi. But you never know which way a jury will jump. Could be the domino effect and they pot them all." She looked directly at Buckle, "Is there anything else I can help you with?"

She glanced at her Oris watch and asked in a way Buckle knew what the answer should be. "No. That was all." He slid out of the room, walking backwards, saying as he left, "I'll see if there's a question from the jury or a verdict. I'll see what's happening in court."

"Thanks, Barney. If there's anything I should know or needs my attention, do say."

127

"Don't worry, I will."

Buckle tried to look busy, but loitered in the corridor to ensure no one gave her any news before him. He waited. In no time, Buckle was back rapping on her door.

"What is it? What is it now?" she asked, startled, as she was almost meditating; plus a little angry to be disturbed again.

"I-I-I just wanted to mention something, Zogger."

"Can't it wait?"

"It's quite important."

Zogger, used to assessing witnesses, immediately understood his predicament. "Barney, I'm sorry I snapped at you. It's just I'm so tired. Like you can't imagine."

"I know. You're not alone. Have you got any matchsticks? My eyes are closing too."

"What's the problem Barney? How can I help?"

"You're not going to like it, but I think you've got to know. Where do I start?"

"Perhaps like Alice at the beginning?" He tried once or twice and then stopped when the words just wouldn't come. "You start when you're ready. There's no rush."

"Miss Rowe loved teaching, she loved the children. Didn't like people." He struggled to find the words. "She loved all her animals and fussed and fretted when they were poorly. Her vet's bill for when they were ill was enormous, but she never counted the cost. She was alright as long as they were. Just like a mother may love all her children, she may love one in a special way. Miss Rowe loved Molly above the others because she was the runt who had survived." As he related the story, Buckle jumped from point to point over the history of Molly. His emotion rose close to the surface.

"I don't know whether you know, Keiran Logan? You

might have prosecuted him or, more likely, defended him, 'cos he was usually acquitted."

"Where does he live?"

"Over on the big housing estate at Fastliffe. It's the corner house on Gristmill Avenue. Looks a bit like a breaker's yard with bits of several cars in the garden, a rusty lawnmower and a chipped sink full of weeds."

"What does he look like?"

"You might have seen him when you drove through Fastliffe on your way home. A big man, big ass, big belly, big head, balding, an aertex vest and shrivelled elastic braces holding his stained trousers that curled over his navel. A gormless Paddy, the sort the IRA would use and then rub out."

"I might have seen him, but maybe I mistook him for Elvis," Zogger said. "What's he got to do with, Molly?"

"Logan was a prolific Catholic who believed animals were provided for sport. Molly was the prize donkey he won in a poker game with a gypsy at 'The Queen's Retreat'. Logan didn't loathe or even dislike Molly. He had no feelings for her at all."

"What did he do?"

"His favourite game was to ride Molly when he was drunk. He'd dig his heels into her bony flank. His brats followed his example. They'd climb on the neighbour's shed roof and jump feet-first onto her bare back. The last time it happened one of them, Seamus, was wearing a pair of fashion boots with thick ridged soles covered in steel studs. When he jumped, he injured her so badly they thought her back was broken. Logan dumped her in a ditch. Logan and his boys crept home in the dark. Never gave Molly another thought."

"I hope I prosecuted him. What happened to, Molly?"

Buckle halted as he fought his emotion. "Molly lay in the damp ditch, unable to move, without water or food. Drinking the dew. She was there over a week before being discovered by a motorist, Willie Kursaal, who was caught short and taking a leak. She was close to starvation. Kursaal, a travelling salesman in ladies exotic underwear, heard her groan and saw her ears, slightly pricked to the sound of his hissing in the grass. He called the cops. Without Kursaal she wouldn't have survived. It's a-..."

"Take your time, Barney."

"The cops called the RSPCA, who rescued her. She somehow ended up with Louise Rowe. Truth was no one else wanted her. She was in such a sorry state. Fortunately her back wasn't broken, only fractured. Most people thought Miss Rowe cared so much for Molly because her fight mirrored her own. Louise was a fighter. She had to be because loss was part of her life. Her own mother, Mollie, died giving birth to her."

Buckle stopped. He ran out of air and words. The vacuum was filled by an awkward silence between them, each conscious the jury were still out

"You knew her quite well, didn't you, Barney?"

"Well, yes, you know, just investigating this case."

"Reading about her, she seems a lovely lady?"

"She was, just naturally caring and that. She was a shuttlecock child when she was growing up, shunted between aunts and uncles, some wanted her and some didn't – if you know what I mean."

"What about her father? Didn't he care for her?"

"He did, but the poor man couldn't cope. He was distraught after the death of his wife and slowly lost his mind. Eventually he was 'Sectioned' under the Mental Health Act. A short while later he jumped in front of the midnight milk train hurtling through Yeovil Station. All her siblings, there were three boys and two girls, were put into 'care' of one sort or another."

His voice trailed off.

"I spoke to the neighbours and some of the villagers. I know a lot more about her than I would normally know about a victim or a witness. Besides, I've always been keen on animal cases. Given different circumstances, who knows, I might have joined the ALF...." With that, especially as Buckle was such a straightforward copper, Zogger could barely believe her ears. She looked up. She gave him an old-fashioned look. When she locked into his eyes, she had no doubt. He was for real. Buckle said, "After this case I might start my own cell." He didn't smile. His straight face helped to break the tension.

He filled in more about her background and how, "Some of Hitler's pilots hounded and surrounded and shot her fiancé down in flames from the summer sky. He was older than most of them, almost twenty-one. No one replaced him. Louise found her salvation in helping the 'friends' she rescued over the passing years. Molly was her special friend. She hadn't wanted to leave her to go on holiday. She had to be persuaded she needed a rest. A few days later Molly became ill. Country folk seem to understand these things. One of them, Herbert Salt, told me Molly was pining for her surrogate mother, Louise."

Buckle continued, slowly, keen to keep Zogger's attention. "When Molly died something stirred inside Miss Rowe, she was never the same again. From being contented she was riddled with apathy. She started to rise later. Food became unimportant. Her grooming was all but forgotten. Each day the effort was too great for the reward. Everything became a chore as she became an...anorexic, hell what's the word. I ought to invest in a dictionary. Although I don't know how could I find it if I didn't know it. Anyway, apathetic, fed-up, but sort of psychological. I'm getting tired. Or put it down to premature senility. Well, maybe not premature."

"You mean anhedonia, perhaps? A touch of Bergman."

"That's it. You got it. Thanks. She started to become forgetful, neglect herself and even neglected her animals. None of it was deliberate."

Zogger openly glanced at her watch. He took the hint.

"Miss Rowe foundered. She fell ill. Her neighbours called the doctor out. He gave her pills and potions and advice. She politely accepted the pills and potions, but never took them. She put them in pots as rich nutrients for the plants. She quietly listened to the advice and likewise ignored the doctor's words. That was why, I don't know if you knew, Miss Rowe couldn't attend court?"

"No, I didn't. I assumed she couldn't face knowing the facts. Still it'd be nice to meet her. I'll see her after the verdict if she's around. I hope we've got good news for her."

"Well,...She'd intended to come, but she was rushed off to hospital. Her condition was worse than it first appeared. Louise was transferred to the Intensive Care Unit and placed on a drip."

Buckle's eyes fixed on the floor as he told her story. He fidgeted with his hair, his tie, even the ribbon on Zogger's brief. He'd tie the ribbon in a bow and then untie it, all the while stumbling through the story. He kept mumbling so she had to strain to catch the words, though she readily understood the meaning. He looked up. Catching her gaze, he said, "No medicine existed that could help Louise. For the first time in her long life she'd lost the will to fight. Finally on the twelfth day, she faded away."

Most of the time Buckle spoke, emotion in his wavering voice, she didn't want to interrupt. On mention of "faded away", Zogger stared at Buckle. "What do you mean she 'just faded away'? When? What happened? Why?"

"She passed away."

"What was the cause?"

"The cause doesn't matter too much now. It's happened. She's gone."

Buckle ended on that note. Her heart pounded and skipped some beats. She shivered and felt a stone-cold pony ride through her. Zogger had invested so much in the case. Much more than time, this case was part of her heart: part of her life. She was fighting for Molly and Louise as well as herself.

Buckle broke the uneasy feeling. "The doctor certified the cause of death was from a heart attack. Everyone in the village knew that was a formality. In their eyes there was a single cause. They knew Louise Rowe died of a broken heart."

"When, Barney?"

"Yesterday morning. I learned at 10.10 a.m. "

"That's ages ago. Why didn't you tell me earlier?"

"I didn't want to add to your burden. You had enough to deal with, what with that rude Judge and that fat twat barrister. That's why I kept bothering you. Sorry. I didn't want anyone else to tell you. You had to know. I didn't know how to, couldn't find the words."

"I understand, Barney. You're right. Thanks." Spent, she sat there with both hands covering her eyes to stop herself from crying. The news hit her as sharp as a syringe piercing an eyeball. Buckle was standing. Zogger slumped lower. The pain that passed between them was white-hot.

Buckle reached into his back pocket and pulled out a

card. He ripped it in half, then into quarters and threw it in the bin. "I won't be needing this now."

A voice on the tannoy crackled to break the silent despair: "Will all parties in the Case of Qualm go to Court 1."

"I'll see you in court, Zogger," Buckle said as he left.

"I'll be down in a minute." She picked up the pieces from the bin. She laid them out on the table and re-arranged them. Black writing on a white, silver-edged card. 'Barney Buckle is invited to celebrate the eightieth Birthday Party of Louise Rowe on 11 September 2009.' The last word was in italics: RSVP.

She scooped the card up and ripped it into smaller pieces. She dropped them into the bin. As they fell her thoughts strayed to her snow-scene souvenir.

Everyone rushed back to court. It was soon full of people looking confused, no one quite knowing the reason for the call.

"Is it a question from the jury?" Zogger asked Henry Kow, the Court Clerk. He shook his head. She breathed in and blew the air out in a slow sigh. "Is it a verdict, Henry?" she asked, her breath too quick to hide her anxiety. He nodded in assent.

"For all the defendants?"

"No, I understand it's just one."

"Which one, Henry?" Buckle asked, butting in, unable to help himself. "Do we know? Is it, Hornet? Qualm?"

"The only message from the Foreman to the Usher was they have a verdict for one defendant. You'll be alright, they'll convict them all. Did you see the way some of the women on the jury looked at the defendants? They could've lynched them in court. Especially after they saw that photo. The one of the torched horse."

Lipschitz entered. Everyone stood up. Bowed. He sat down, motioned to Wycherley, who then got the jury. They walked in, looking serious and sat in the same seats they had occupied throughout the trial. Kow asked the Foreman, Lester Read, "Have you reached a verdict in respect of any of the defendants upon which you are all agreed?"

"Yes," Read replied.

"Have you reached a verdict in respect of Kevin Qualm?"

"No."

"Have you reached a verdict in respect of Lee Hornet?"

"No."

"Have you reached a verdict in respect of Dean Canker?"

Read was already standing up, but he became more erect like an old soldier. It must have been nerves. His grey hair was lank and greasy, hanging over his collar at the back and right eyebrow at the front. His suit was a punk style, fashionable three decades ago, so he was probably married in it. He had a beer belly that made him look as if he was ten months' pregnant. The jacket had a single button fastened that strained at the opening as his belly expanded in time with his breathing.

"Yes," he answered.

Buckle looked at the Foreman. The Judge looked at his papers. The defendants looked at the floor of the dock. Smokey looked bored. Zogger looked straight ahead.

The order of the defendants in the dock reflected the Indictment so it was Qualm, Hornet and Canker. Qualm was on the right facing the Judge and nearest the jury. Canker was furthest from them.

"Will the defendant, Dean Canker, please stand?" asked Kow.

Canker rose slowly, shrugged, his eyes rooted on the floor.

Kow asked Read, "Do you find, Dean Canker, guilty or not guilty of arson?"

Buckle clasped his hands on each knee. The Judge shuffled his papers for no reason. Canker's eyes twitched. Qualm clenched his sphincter. Hornet joined him. Smokey sat there, chins wobbling as he breathed, though he never moved. Zogger had to steel herself so she didn't let out a mad scream. The tension climbed. Jennie Hershlag, a junior reporter, was red-faced and fumbling as her pen ran out the moment the verdict was delivered.

The Foreman mouthed the words before he uttered them as a tyro actor making sure he got his lines right. Then, erect and nervous and ruddy-faced, he said firmly, "Not Guilty."

Read went to sit down, relieved, when Kow asked the second question. "Not Guilty. And that is the verdict of you all?"

Before his balloon buttocks hit the seat, he rose slightly and made a muffled, "Yes."

Smokey almost jumped up. He asked, "Your Honour, may Mr. Canker be released?"

"Of course, Mr. Jones," the Judge replied. "You can go, Canker."

Zogger felt a jolt she had to restrain. It jerked through her body as a whiplash on hearing Read's first word.

Canker left the court and loitered in the corridor. All the alibi witnesses and his associates littered the place too. They exchanged whids. Their mood became meaner. People passed by as far away from them as possible.

Zogger left court, flushed and confused. Her face coloured as the blood surfaced. She tried to appear composed. Racing along the corridor, she made her way to the journalists' room again. She sat there seeking a solace that never came. A short while later there was a knock on the door. "Is it alright to come in?"

"Of course, come on in, Barney."

"How in hell did they come to that decision?"

"The key evidence was always weakest against Canker. I only put him on the Indictment in the hope he'd break and turn Queen's Evidence. Don't worry, we'll get the other two."

"Really?"

"Why not?"

"I hope you're right."

"Have faith, Barney."

"But what if they come to the same dumb decision on the other two shitehawks? That would mean no one tortured Molly to death." You could've raced toy cars on the tracks of pain that creased Buckle's forehead. "I don't know, I don't understand it. How could those creeps con them? All twelve jurors?"

"Barney, listen, we haven't lost yet. Jurors are ordinary people, just like you and me."

"You say that, but we can see through their lies. Why can't they? It's obvious they're guilty, isn't it? They're lit up with guilt. Like a bloody Christmas tree."

"Don't forget we know a lot more than the jury, Barney."

They engaged in a little light conversation. After a while, Zogger looked at her watch and said, "I hope you don't mind. I'd like a few moments on my own. Nothing personal."

"I need to stretch the old legs anyway. I'll see you back in court." He stopped, knowing he had to go, but still too troubled to remain silent. "Why are they taking so long to decide on the other two, especially Qualm? His guilt is transparent. A blind man could see it."

"Your guess is as good as mine, Barney. You can never tell what worries a jury. It could be the alibi, the forensic, the mud or the blood. It might even be just one or two of the jurors holding out. Remember we've got two things on our side, time and truth."

Meanwhile the defendants were asking their legal team exactly the same questions for precisely the opposite reason.

Something stirred in less than a half-hour. Buckle was just leaving when the tannoy alerted them again with a similar message: "Will all parties in the Case of Qualm go to Court 1." He gazed at Zogger and she gazed at him. Their eyes magnetised each other's fear. They didn't speak as they walked back together to Court 1. Their faces signalled nerves they vainly tried to hide. A slight tic caused her eyes to squint. He kept rubbing the tip of his nose. Barney and Zogger each felt too little time had passed since the last verdict. For them it was a bad sign.

You could reason it either way. The defence team equally thought it was much too soon to be good news. Only one of them could be right.

The Judge entered court. Webber brought the jury in. The ritual between Kow and Read was repeated.

"Have you reached a unanimous verdict in respect of Kevin Qualm?

"No."

"Have you reached a unanimous verdict in respect of Lee Hornet?"

"Yes."

"Will the defendant, Lee Hornet, please stand up?" asked Kow.

138

He asked Read: "Do you find, Lee Hornet, guilty or not guilty of arson?"

Buckle looked at the Foreman again. Lipschitz absent-mindedly put his right thumb and index finger in each nostril as he looked at his notebook. Hornet stood up and looked down. Zogger looked at a stray red hair caught in a paper clip on the bench. She was transfixed by it. Anything, but the unknown verdict. The Judge and Hornet and Zogger shuffled their feet, though all of them were unaware of doing so. Smokey still looked bored, only because he was.

The air grew heavier. Read coughed his habitual nervous cough and looked, with a tired half-smile, at Kow. He delivered the verdict. Just two words, "Not Guilty."

"Not Guilty. And that is the verdict of you all?" asked Kow.

"Yes."

Read sat down. Kow sat down. Smokey stood up. Without being asked the Judge said, "You can go Hornet. Is there any other Application you wish to make, Mr. Jones?"

Smokey, who never understood law let alone criminal practice and procedure, had no idea what the Judge meant. Smokey looked confident in his ignorance. Craven tugged his gown and said, as Smokey half-turned around, "Costs, Mr. Jones. Ask for costs."

"Yes. Your Honour, may Mr. Hornet have his costs?"

"Certainly."

As he was about to sit down, Craven tugged his gown again. "We need a Costs Order for Canker too."

"Your Honour, I am reminded by my Instructing Solicitor. It slipped my mind. May I also apply for the costs of Mr. Canker?"

139

"Of course, it follows the event. He was acquitted. He's entitled to his costs."

Within those few moments and words the effect for the whole prosecution team, but especially Buckle, was of a mallet meeting a peach. A sharp pain hit Zogger directly in the solar plexus. A silent pugilist pounded her guts. The gut-shoot splattered her insides. Yet she sat there, as she had to, as if the verdict was of no consequence. She held the pain inside and sat there writing, noting the second verdict on the brief. She took some time to write the words, adding a note on the Costs Order. Each stroke of the Waterman pen spiked her.

Hornet walked out as if he'd just won a title fight. He joined the others outside court. A lot of backslapping and noise followed their triumph.

After the verdict, Lipschitz said, "Members of the Jury, continue to try and reach a verdict on Qualm. Remember the Directions I gave you, particularly what I said about the burden of proof. It's on the prosecution throughout." The Judge rose and left court.

Ron took the jury out again.

Hour after hour the jury remained in their room deliberating about Qualm. The Judge was getting ever more bored as he couldn't fit in a quick round of golf with Smokey, as they had planned. After about three and a half hours, he came back into court. A message went out on the tannoy calling them into court. Everyone except the jury assembled again. The Judge wanted to put pressure on Zogger. He said, "I'm going to call the jury back in. They've had long enough to decide. Do you want me to discharge them?"

"No, Your Honour. Perhaps a little more time would be wiser?"

140

"Then what? If they still don't agree? We can't wait all day, can we?"

"No. But they've not had a Majority Direction yet. That may make a difference. As we've had two verdicts already, perhaps it would be better to wait a little while longer." She believed they were on the cusp of convicting Qualm. A compromise verdict.

"I hear what you say. Let me hear what Mr. Jones says."

"Your Honour, I agree the um,...pragmatic course would be the best one, er, so we should continue for the moment. The problem is if we discharge the jury it may result in a re-trial – depending on the view of the prosecution – which would be, er, premature. Costly too." Smokey was giving the Judge a cautionary warning in coded legal language that the next time they would have a different jury and, of course, a different Judge. Worse, much worse, he would be on trial on his own. That would result in all the evidence being aimed at Qualm alone. A bonus for the prosecution.

Lipschitz read Smokey's signal. His mood softened. "I see the sense of your proposal, Mr. Jones. If we continue there could be a further saving of costs, especially if we avoid the risk of a re-trial. I think I shall send the jury home now, a little earlier than usual and bring them back on Monday. Does either counsel disagree with that course?"

Neither counsel disagreed. Smokey had no reason. Zogger did, but what would've been the use? She wanted him to make the jury decide today. Smokey wanted more time, more doubt. If Zogger objected the Judge would have ignored her. She knew that too.

Webber and Wycherley brought the jury back into court. The Judge gave them a brief Direction. "Members

141

of the Jury we will adjourn now. You've been deliberating a long time already. You can take as much time as you need. We want to avoid a re-trial. Don't forget what I told you. Don't speak to anyone about this case, except your fellow jurors. So forget about the case until tomorrow, I mean Monday."

The Judge left court. The jury left court. People meandered in and out of court. Smokey looked happier than he had earlier. Buckle was near breaking point. Zogger looked worse, her face distressed in a series of strain-lines. She had aged a decade during the case.

The prosecution team had a restless weekend. Buckle went to the pub on his own and continued drinking at home alone. For two days he drank too much and slept too little. Zogger didn't drink or have a decent night's sleep at all.

Smokey and Lipschitz met at the Judges' Lodge on Saturday and Sunday night at the taxpayers' expense. They swapped tall tales of their many victories in the Court of Appeal, over champagne and caviar.

On Monday morning Smokey and Lipschitz looked perky when the court re-assembled.

Buckle looked lost, quite lost. Zogger shared his state, reacting as if in a trance.

The jury were then sent out to continue their deliberations.

Zogger wandered around with a rictus smile borrowed from Boris, frozen in her cocoon of confusion. Her nerve-ends jangled with a feeling she'd rarely known. She knew if the jury knew the truth, the verdict would be the right one. However, they didn't know because of the Judge's refusal of her Application, that Qualm had two previous relevant convictions: for slashing a horse and burying her while she was still alive; the other was for rape and sodomy. She kept praying Qualm would be convicted. She made a pact with some unknown numinous woman that she would change, be better, help people. Zogger tried to make a bargain with god, if she existed. Promise after promise was made. The same sort of pleas she'd made whilst lighting penny candles to pass her school exams.

She went straight from court to her temporary refuge, the journalists' room. She needed to be alone. All the reporters were in different courts covering the cases. She sat in the same room with the same feelings, but a different heart. This time it was heavier and pumped too much. Zogger was drained. She sat in the dark for almost an hour.

She opened her eyes as the sandpaper voice on the tannoy shattered her seclusion. "All parties in the Case of Qualm go to Court 1." The message burst through her solitude and eardrums. She hurried back to court. Zogger could hear the sound of her heart.

She saw Buckle trudging down the corridor to court. "What do you know, Barney?"

"I don't know if it's a verdict. Tell you the truth, after the two verdicts we've had, I don't know anything anymore." Defeat was etched on his face. It was contagious.

"What is it, Henry?" she asked the Clerk.

"No verdict yet. It's just a Note."

After some hours the jury sent a Note to the Judge saying they couldn't agree on a verdict. The Judge called them back into court and gave them a Majority Direction. "I would ask you to still try to reach a unanimous verdict. As the time has passed, I can now accept a Majority Verdict if at least ten of you agree. It can be either way, an acquittal or conviction. So please continue your deliberations."

The jury listened closely. The numbers seemed to cause some consternation. Some nodded as if it sealed their decision. Others registered a blank stare. McCullough mouthed to Starky, "What if it's nine?" After about two minutes they went out to deliberate again.

Zogger glanced at the Foreman and the other jurors to try and gauge their mood. She studied their faces trying to second-guess their thoughts. Her instinct had disappeared. Her thoughts raced through a heady mixture of optimism through pessimism and back in a trapeze of despair. She never looked at the jury when a verdict was to be delivered. She felt compelled to catch their mood without the risk of a verdict. Yet their faces gave nothing away. Her face told its own tale.

The air in and around the courtroom grew stuffy and heavy with sweat and tension. Second-hand stories and retread jokes were replayed to a bored audience of lawyers and clerks and cops. Each party, be they prosecution or defence, waited and waited while smoke-rings of time grew circles around their hands.

"Hello, Smokey. How are you?" Zogger met him in the corridor with the ever-present untipped Gauloise held between his thick lips. The fag was the same colour as his teeth.

"I'm fine. Two out and one to go? I think this is another one you've lost, Zogger."

"Let's wait and see. You never can tell."

"Hoping for solace from Chuck Berry now?" She quoted Shaw knowing it would go over his head. His knowledge of law and literature was from the same source: 50's and 60's R. & B. He continued to laugh and shake his face.

"Let's just wait for the fat lady-..." she started to say, as she left him.

"What about the fat man?" She laughed falsely at his hollow humour. She had to escape. The only company she wanted was her own.

Smokey irritated her at the best of times. Now she could have castrated him in the corridor and made the prize a prosecution exhibit. Zogger went to find sanctuary in the same room she used in the morning. As she entered the room it was full of journalists. She couldn't complain, it was their room. She went down the stairs to avoid the lifts, the cops, the CPS and anyone who might want to idly chat. She sat at the back of the Habeas Corpus Café. It was still fresh with stale smoke and sweat. The defendants and their mates gathered there because they could swap lies drowned by the sound of the rattling crockery and cutlery. Seeing her, Hornet and Canker waved and both blew a Judas kiss. They kept looking over at her, whispering and laughing. She sat there, fired eyes staring through their faces into the distance. Zogger never blinked. To her they were invisible.

The air was cut when the tannoy crackled for the fourth time: "Would all parties in the Case of Qualm go to Court 1 immediately." The message was repeated. The operator's voice was tinged with urgency.

Zogger inhaled deeply as she had learned to long ago, from the diaphragm. She sang flinty rock with Hellsucks at every opportunity. Learning how to breathe helped her to stay calm. She slowly exhaled for a good ten seconds and ended with a round 'ooohh'.

145

As she moved to get up she shook the uneven table and spilt the cold coffee in the saucer all over the cuff of her white blouse. A dark, dirty stain soiled the left cuff and small bubbles formed on her watch-strap. Zogger dabbed both, using the cheap café tissue as a blotter. The stain looked like the map of Ireland. A place she loved for the music and the craic. A place she wished she was right now. Anywhere, but here, she thought. Anywhere.

She wandered back to court in a daze. "What is it, Henry?"

"It's a verdict," said Kow. "They'd better get it right this time. Surely they can't get it wrong again?"

"Too bleedin' right mate," a voice from behind her said. "Sorry." Buckle looked frustrated and fazed and in desperate need of good news and a warm bed.

It was 4.26 p.m. After deliberating all day and minutes before the Judge was going to discharge them, a Note was sent saying they'd reached a verdict. The jury entered court, moving slowly and sat in the same seats again. There was a visible tension between them. Most of the jurors in both rows kept their eyes lowered, feigning an interest in their notes. Bookbinder looked at Rhodes and both then glanced at Qualm. They stared hard at him. Rhodes shook her head and Bookbinder rolled her eyes as if to say, "That's it?" Court 1 was packed, the well and press section and public gallery. Canker and Hornet and all of Qualm's cohorts slouched into court. As intended, you knew they were there. Their presence made the place appear a shambles. The air was pregnant with anticipation and a palpable fear of the truth. Jurors, who come in all shapes and sizes, tend to have a healthy cynicism towards the police. Sometimes the jury resemble refugees from a reality-TV programme. Those feelings plagued Zogger as the moments ticked off in her mind-clock.

Kow asked everyone to, "Please rise", as the Judge entered court. After the bowing, he asked Read, "Have the Jury all agreed on a verdict in respect of Kevin Qualm?"

"No."

Zogger turned around and whispered to Buckle, "No? I thought there was a verdict?"

"I did too. What are they playing at? What the hell's happening? I can't take much more of this."

Both could detect the nerves in their own and each other's voice. Each was raised at least an octave. Given their mutual tension, their confusion mushroomed.

Kow coughed twice and checked with the jury: "Have at least ten of you agreed on a verdict?"

"Yes."

Smokey seemed oblivious to it all. Lipschitz was calculating the date when he could draw his pension and how fat it would be. An easy task as he was often engaged with that equation. Smokey wondered whether he would be free for another game of golf with the Judge. As they'd arranged to dine that evening, each was thinking about the menu too.

Zogger looked straight ahead, struggling to keep her eyes open. The vibration sucked her into a vortex. Her mind raced. Her heart beat to the raw sound of a snare drum playing a rock 'n' roll song.

"Will the defendant, Kevin Qualm, please stand?" asked Kow. He rose slowly as his cellulite arse glued him to the seat. The scowl remained on his hostile face.

Kow asked Read, "Do you find the defendant, Kevin Qualm, guilty or not guilty of arson?"

Qualm cast a glance at the Foreman. He knew the case had gone well, but who could tell what the answer would be? If he could, Qualm would have hexed Read. He would've done anything, indeed had up to now, to escape justice. The seconds seemed suspended in time. It all depended on one word or two. The infinity of this moment would fix the fate of the protagonists in this legal chess. There were no rules in this game save for one that influenced both the queen and the pawn. Each side had to win at all costs.

Kow read out the Indictment for the third time. Count 1 charged all three defendants with arson for destroying Molly as she was just 'property' in legal terms. So killing her was merely damaging property. Count 2 related to Qualm alone. Kow asked Read the second question, "Do you find the defendant, Kevin Qualm, guilty or not guilty of Intercourse with an Animal namely a Shetland pony?"

During the magnified moments between the last word from Kow and the first word from Read, the atmosphere was charged with an AC/DC current. It was as if time had stood still and no one really wanted to hear the answer. All the months that had passed since the brief first landed on her desk led up to this one moment. Sleepless nights, the hard work, the racks, the research was now encompassed in the answer. Everything hung on two words or four. A see-saw balancing doubt and destiny. The electricity of fear felt by the prosecutor and defendant, but for opposite reasons, was enough to light up the courtroom.

For the third time the Foreman delivered the same verdict on Count 1, "Not Guilty."

Then he delivered the same verdict on Count 2, "Not Guilty."

Rhodes and Bookbinder looked at each other. They gritted their teeth and violently shook their heads. Their dissent proved why it was not a unanimous decision. Bookbinder focused on Qualm's foul felonious face and said sotto voce, "Scuzzball."

148

Rhodes nodded and said, "Scunge, pure scunge."

When Zogger heard the word "Not" drip from Read's lips, her heart banged inside her breast. Once, then twice. A spasm of defeat shot straight through her. She had lost her will, her everything. For her it was like the Cincinnati Kid staking his life on the jack of diamonds and getting the joker; putting your faith on the line for the ace and turning up a deuce; looking in a broken mirror and seeing a reflection of your own imperfection; being betrayed by your only lifetime-lover; being locked naked in Room 101; being a priest and finally having proof there was no god; staring into the crystal ball and seeing your own death.

Smokey then stood up looking smugger than a bugger with a barrel full of cabin-boys. He rose quicker than he had all week. "Your Honour, may the defendant be released?"

"Of course. Qualm you are free to go."

Craven tugged Smokey's gown. "Costs."

"Your Honour, I almost forgot. May the defendant have his costs?"

"Let me ask, Miss Darrow. I don't see that a Costs Order can be denied, do you?" asked Lipschitz, merely to embarrass her. A further twist of the still-bloody knife.

"No, Your Honour." Zogger seemed to fribble and was hardly capable of getting the words out. In the moments following the verdict she was transformed from a woman of rare beauty to looking old and shot. She smoothed the lines on her forehead; pushed her wig up onto her hair; the askew wig, normally so right, added to her frazzled appearance.

"Very well then, Mr. Jones, your client may have all his Costs." The Judge beamed at Smokey. Smokey reflected their mutual self-satisfied smile.

Qualm shouted, "Yeah. Result!" and distorted his face. He threw his clenched fist in the air in contempt and defiance. The Judge ignored the outburst. Qualm got out of the dock as quick as his bulk allowed. He squeezed his thighs threw the small exit door. He grabbed Craven, gave him a bear hug, shook his hand and hugged him again. "Thanks, Georgie. You did brilliant." Craven was uncomfortable and brushed Qualm off, but said nothing about his unwanted familiarity. Qualm knew who had delivered. He saw Smokey as a legal mouthpiece and Craven's puppet. He ignored him. Qualm quickly joined his accomplices in the lobby, where they celebrated another win for the team. The vuelta.

"Win some, lose some 'eh Zogger," Smokey said, rushing off to meet the Judge.

"'Bye Smokey, see you again," she mumbled. Her wan smile circled her hollow eyes.

In the part of her heart she had reserved for winning, it was raining. The four verdicts delivered a blow as real as a shaft of sharpened glass to her soul. There would be time enough for tears. Presently she had to wear her professional face. Zogger thanked the CPS and the police for their "Sterling effort and teamwork." She talked to the witnesses briefly, giving them some solace in the knowledge, "Don't worry they'll be back; there will be another time."

She shook Buckle's hand. "Be sure to brief me next time." He looked at her warmly, their weariness reflected in each other's eyes. "Barney, I mean it. I'd like another stab at them, especially Qualm."

"Your name's already on the brief. No one could've done more than you. Thanks for it all. It was that faggoteer judge that did it. I hope the clipdick chokes on his caviar."

"You're too kind," she said.

Buckle got in the lift. Alone, he continued to curse Lipschitz. He stared in the mirror. He moved closer. Seeing the state of his face shocked him. More wrinkles than a walnut. His smooth skin was frazzled in a week. Another reason to abuse the absent Lipschitz. When the lift stopped he quit swearing.

Zogger went to the Robing Room. She spoke to no one, changed and packed her wig and robe away. She left by the stairs.

As she was leaving court, the defendants saw her in the foyer. "My Learned Friend, Miss Darrow," shouted Qualm. She turned around. Each defendant's face spouted a gargoyle grin. The trio started to slash wildly through the air, all the while mimicking the braying of a pained pony. They swung Nazi-kicks at a prone 'body'. Qualm made a sprinkling motion, got out a red lighter and flicked it at each end of the body. Their re-enactment of killing Molly.

Zogger, was about seven metres away from them. The defendants and their friends roared with tart laughter. Their guffaws echoed around the foyer and surrounded her. She wasn't afraid, just so alone. Her heart jumped and pumped. Her head hurt more than before.

A shiver ran through her. Zogger hooked into them, staring flint-hard with no attempt to conceal her contempt. She stared at the trio for about twelve seconds. She focused on their faces. The laughter stopped. She moved closer. Without a word, she reached into her bag, pulled out a plastic bag and held it up so they could see the contents. She held their gaze. Forced them to see what she was holding. A soot-black stiletto. Burned and blackened, the covering was melted away by the flames. An exhibit.

151

The knife Qualm had plunged into and left in Molly's head, leaving her looking like a forlorn unicorn.

She held up another exhibit. It had been dropped at the scene, though it was clean of fingerprints. Qualm wiped it, but anyway he was a non-secretor. She sparked it and a blue jet flame shot vertically from the yellow beretta lighter. She captured all three faces in the feathery flame. The defendants were held fast in her eyes and the flame, unable to escape her icy smile. Having snarled them, she snapped it shut, turned and marched away.

The defendants watched as she left. They shifted uneasily, sluggish and awkward and gawky. Faces agape. Her reaction totally confused them. Women didn't act that way. They went to follow her, saw the CCTV, stopped and Canker shouted, though not too loud, "Black slag."

Hornet gave her the toad-in-the-hole.

Qualm muttered, "Slut."

In those moments the ghost of her past rattled his chains again. The noise deafened her. Yet on leaving court Zogger secretly swore Molly's silent scream somewhere in the distance would be avenged. She felt raunchy. She smiled inwardly, the pure irony of Qualm helping her to hurt him. Watch your back, honky. You'd better watch your back.

On returning to Chambers she immediately saw Charles, the Clerk, in her room. "I'll be taking some time off. I don't know when I'll be back."

"How long shall I mark you out for, Miss?"

"Oh, I don't know. Say three months," she said, then quickly added, "no, make that six months, or until I contact you."

"Very well. I'll tell people you took a long-deserved holiday."

"A sabbatical, Charles. Say a sabbatical, it sounds as if I'm going to do something useful. Some sort of assignment. Could be true too."

"As you wish, Miss."

They knew this day would come and soon. No discussion and no argument on either side. Charles would rule a line through her name in the diary. For him, now she couldn't earn him his percentage, she no longer existed.

"Are there any messages, anything urgent to deal with, Charles?"

"No, I don't think so. There's a buff letter in your pigeon-hole. I don't know if you overlooked it, only it's been there a few days. Maybe longer. I know you've been busy."

"Didn't you open it, Charles?"

"Well it had private marked on it."

"That's never stopped you before." Rather than being angry, she could now tease him.

"It somehow looked different, private, – well personal – if you know what I mean."

"I think I do." With that she collected it. He waited. She returned, shoved it in her Gladstone bag along with a few personal items, including the snow-scene souvenir. He hoped she'd open it. He burned to know her business. She had other matters on her mind.

"Oh, by the way, Miss. Perhaps you'd be good enough to ensure your finances and rent are up to date?"

"Of course."

"Before you leave, please."

Straightaway she wrote a cheque and handed it to him. As he looked at the figures his face changed towards a genuine smile. "Thank you."

"'Bye, Charles. All the best."

"Goodbye, Miss." As she left he looked at the cheque again. His smile returned. Perhaps he'd miss her after all.

Zogger left the Chambers and drove to Salisbury and then to Bristle. She stopped off at 'Under An Elvis Moon' to grab a cappuccino before going home. Listening to Blind Boy Grunt singing Pagliacci's Return in the background, she knew what she had to do.

She went to the docks car park, opened the boot of her restored pearl black Prelude and removed her Red Bag. A fierce look filled her face as she walked with a purpose to the Bridge. "I hate these," she shouted. She threw the Frisbee and watched it land near a group of swans. One went over, pecked it and tried to eat it. Finding it wasn't food the swan shook it loose from her beak. It drifted towards the reeds where a cob grabbed it and sat on it as a ready-made nest. At least the wig has some use, Zogger thought.

"'Big Issue', Miss? My last one." The question came from Chester Burnett. Not so long ago he was wealthy. After a series of personal disasters he became who and what she saw, a dishevelled, homeless man. Starving. Freezing. Looking so much older than his years.

"Here, get yourself a meal." She handed him ten quid. He handed her a curled over magazine. It was out of date. "Don't worry. You keep it. You can sell it again."

"Thanks. Thanks very much." He kept looking at the note as if he'd not seen one in a long time. Unless he thought it was counterfeit.

As she was leaving, as an afterthought, she asked, "Haven't you got a coat?"

"No. I'm alright. I'll be under the Bridge soon."

"Here have this." She handed him her Red Bag. He

reached in for the material, put it on and wrapped it around himself. He danced around the lamppost. She walked across the Bridge. She looked back. The sight of a drifter wearing the clothes she once wore looking like a cross between Batman and a Don made her happy.

She drove home in the drizzly rain, lost in thoughts of tomorrow. It amazed her how the day had turned out. From the ashes of the verdicts, she could feel her spirit grow. Zogger put her keys on the cherry davenport and was drawn to the photo of Danny Fisher. She'd had it for over twenty years. She got it on her tenth birthday. My, he sure was handsome, she thought, transported back to being seventeen again. Danny looked dark and dangerous with a blue-black Superman quiff and a DA. She felt an impulse shoot through her veins. She needed to hear something that would match her newborn mojo. His voice could always stir her soul. She rifled through the drawers of the hand-made Krenov maple sideboard and found a pile of original RCA records. Her body was already moving in rhythm. She got out the old 78's, shuffled through the pink shellac, switched the repeat lever and danced 'til her feet burned to Danny's anthem, *Trouble*.

How Dirty Girls Get Clean

"Guillotine the Queen," mused Zogger, aloud, with a feeling of reckless optimism. Wild song, wilder idea. "Make that her squirmy husband and wormy son too. Wow. What a thought. At one swift drop of the honed blade, we could be rid of those royal parasites."

It was the first night after the trial as she fought the negative thoughts that disturbed her sleep. "What a sight. Just to see the heads of those mangy monarch hypocrites roll would be worth it all." Already Zogger could see the tumbrels being wheeled away. Lying there staring at the ceiling, drowsy yet determined, she knew these early morning thoughts would soon shift from dreams to deeds. The feelings had bubbled just below the boil for far too long. They were bound to surface. Nothing could stop her will to will it. Though Qualm was not the defining cause, his perverse verdict was certainly the catalyst. A tear of fresh sweat trickled across her chest. She stretched her legs as even her toes felt tense. A slow-burn rage grew in her breast.

Wave after wave surged through her. Meanwhile, she thought, at least those stuffy, impotent judges will have to wait. Zogger mused how 'me and the judges will soon miss each other more than a prisoner misses a screw.'

No doubt on some dark future date they would meet again, but for now she had a mind-set as tight as diamond and ice. The time for tears would be after her trial, if the verdict went against her. Even then she figured "The cops will first have to catch me." Given the odds, who knew if or when that would happen. Her head was hot with sleepy adrenaline and the racy excitement of the risk. For the moment she sensed, as to "How far my ideals will take me, the jury are still out."

156

Now her feeling was more than enough to harness the naked hatred for all the animal abusers and fuel it to ignite the fervour in the boys in the band. Together they would take on the world. Her body tingled. The feeling was as rare as love and raw as truth.

Still the thoughts kept tumbling down. She knew after tonight there was no turning back. She made another silent promise, as if a marriage vow, to herself and the world: "I'll have no truck with the takers who seek solace in conscience-sleeping silence."

Zogger never had any need of such losers, let alone now. She knew what she had to do. Her thoughts were sharp even in her weary state. First the scheme had to be sold to the whole band. None of them were easy meat as Arnold and Chrysler and Floyd had a ferocious independence of mind and spirit. They couldn't be manipulated. They couldn't be bought. To the core they were their own men. Deke was a slightly different character, although no less his own man. It was just that Zogger felt Deke maybe knew too much to refuse. Alone they were all strong. Together the five were more than just a band. A joint stiff finger to the world.

Zogger had known the band a long time. With them on her side she knew she couldn't fail. Her first hurdle would be proving to the band the need for their brand of anarchy. Fighting sleep she kept kicking the thoughts around, wondering which way would convince them the time for talking was spent. For her the currency of reason was all used up. In the still darkness Zogger knew, despite the balmy belief, violence is as English as roast beef.

Her eyes opened and quickly closed. Her needle feeling became more focused following the hurt she felt over the last week. Lying there, lost in the feeling, Zogger knew this time it was different. There was an urgency caused by so many strands coming together. Several of the stray strands that blew across her fertile mind refused to disappear. The scene unfurled in colour and sounds and words. A synaesthetic spectrum. She saw the FBI repeatedly playing the sounds of rabbits being slaughtered to the fugitives at WACO to implode their minds. Then the hands of the brats who murdered the baby as they first practised their mutilation on cats and pigeons to perfect their craft. Next was the political fakers of every hue who put the farmers' profits before the animals' pain. She saw the struggling young mother being dragged to her death beneath the wheels of a lorry load of veal calves, in turn dragged across a continent and then dragged to the jagged knife and sliced to whet the appetite of the merchants of greed.

The images whisked her brain. Now the perverts had flooded the Internet with 'crush' movies. She saw a future where there were clones of clones and still the scientists would not be satisfied. Anything that could be imagined by the corporate creeps and cash-register conspirators would be done. She knew she had to adjust the figures on their balance sheet to make them a constant loss. It's time she thought for my examined life.

Amongst the debris, another random fact floated through her mind. Blake Paine had a near life sentence, if not longer, because a grumpy Lord Chancellor declared, "Robin Hood or those ardent anti-vivisectionists who remove animals from vivisection laboratories are acting dishonestly, even though they may consider themselves to be morally justified in doing what they do...." She thought it was the same hoary old story of some vain ermine-stained judge just spouting his curship mouth off again, between abusing maids and stabbing stags. Zogger believed, like old Walt, the ideal of "resisting much" and "obeying little" had a magnetic appeal. She was infused with the desperate feeling of one who dares to dream. From dreams to deeds. She'd travelled too far in her mind and heart. She was finished with building bridges. Now she'd burn them. Of all the messages being mixed in her mind, one surfaced above all. As Qualm had burst the dam, let him drown in the waterfall.

Like a Lovin' Spoonful song, the vista before her was as irresistible as an old-time movie. She could see it as she floated towards her future. Her imagination ran riot as she resisted sleep and clenched her fists. If there is a way, 'I'll find it'. Tonight the abattoir would be reduced to ashes. Tonight the laboratory would shatter and be less than a memory to all the nameless statistics of misery that died within its shell. Tonight the battery-hens would fly with wings unhinged from a human cage as nature intended. Tonight there would be a fire that would set the world alight to the animals' plight. The world would see Buckingham Palace burn, the House of Lords torched and ideas spread from mind-to-mouth and back again as a crackling bush fire. This very night a spark would cause a conflagration across the cosmos. Wheels turning wheels turning wheels.

In that hazy dream-like state, she could it forming, her passion as its source. There was some half-crazy beauty in the idea becoming an act. Zogger dipped deep into the danger, catching the excitement like it was some welcome disease. Her heart moved to a gentle rhythm and her face shone with the smile of someone who alone knows a secret. Soon the world would see flames lick the fireman's face. But Zogger alone knew the first spark in the dark

159

would spray from the match she struck. From her mind to the moment, finally, the explosive magic of it all. Nothing or no one could stop her now, save herself.

She knew that time's bullet was already in the chamber. If she died in the attempt, well, who cares? Who really cares? She hurled the words to the world as if they formed a fitting epitaph. She had too much to win to care about losing. Zogger had long since kissed her depression and ulcer goodbye. She'd been forced to quit her dream of being a singer and ended up as a lawyer, barely a notch above a politician. Her promise to herself meant this time there would be no lies or compromise.

The room was beginning to spin. Her eyelids slowly grew heavier. She had an empty-pit pain low in her stomach. It was the acid and the action, the danger and the direction, the bliss of it all. Zogger had finally rolled the bones in the crapshoot of her life.

The warm bed and the sure-fire idea seduced Zogger towards sleep. She was cocooned within the will to win. She zeroed in and was captured in the moment that gave her life a new direction. It was what she'd been waiting for, no longer to make the law, but to break it. The frown that had grown across her forehead gradually faded. Suddenly she looked as good as she felt, somehow younger. Half-asleep, keyed to her destiny, Zogger then tuned into the radio in her mind. High on life she smiled when she heard the feverish Peggy deliver the bluesy, *Is That All There Is?*

Some Humans Ain't Human

"Look, are you with me or against me?" Her voice rang
with impatience. "There's no time to waste. There's no
better time. So what's your answer? Just call it."

Zogger was standing alone and raising her voice above
the normal noise at The Freefall. This was the place to be
if music was part of your life. It was a place where real
decisions were made about love and hate and everything in
between. It was mid-September, the fifth day after the
verdicts and Zogger didn't want another sleepless night.
She had quit the law. It was her time for fearless living.

She called and spoke to all of them earlier, except Deke.
He hated the distraction of phone calls and only answered
it when it was a matter of life and death. As he couldn't
tell the urgency of any call unless he answered it, he
remained distant by choice. She left a message asking him
to meet them at The Freefall. So he'd know it was
important. The Freefall was their oasis of choice. It always
was when they had to talk turkey. She didn't want to wait
for him, so she told the band what was on her mind. They
knew it was time to lay it on the line. Knowing how
Zogger had been lately, they knew it was in the wind. She
had rehearsed her argument. She approached their meeting
as if preparing a case.

"You must've thought about it by now, surely?" She
stared at the three of them, her eyes darting from one to the
other and back again. They knew this was serious. When
they met at The Freefall, fun place though it was, the talk
always centred on their future, together or apart.

A couple of the night-time girls, sisters Annie-Mae and
Eleanora Fagan, shimmied fast to the rhythm from the
juke-box. A couple of shims did the same and clasped

161

each other. There was only one rule at The Freefall: there were no rules.

It was an important time for the band. The others knew that for Zogger wore her hurt outside her heart. Although she tried to hide it, the shilpit look told its own story. The dark semi-circles below her deadened, tired eyes told the same one. From the start they were stung by her accusative tone. "Well, it's not as simple as that Zogger," said Floyd. "This is your fight, not ours. Why should we become involved? It's your problem." She looked askance at him. Her eyes had a dim light of anger. "Well that's right, isn't it? Whose problem is it, if not yours?"

Before she could answer Chrysler joined in. "Floyd's right. We may have some sympathy for you or your cause, but in the end they're only a few miserable miscreants. What makes them special? They're hardly worth our thoughts or time." He paused, then said, "I mean, I don't mean to be unkind, but it's you who lost the case. That's the truth. So how's it our problem?"

Her eyes moved as she made an unspoken plea for support from Arnold. He said, "Besides it's not the cause of the century is it? It's only another shiteface case. Give me a break, Zogger. Let's talk about something that really matters, our music, not all this garbage. Who cares about them? What are they to me? Let's stay with our music."

Zogger had dragged her tired bones from the Court to Chambers and then home. For some long loose days she'd hidden in the darkness, doing little except fighting the pangs of her confusion. Now having almost licked her wounds dry she was ready. First she had to persuade the band to join her. She wouldn't trust anyone else. She couldn't trust anyone else. Secretly she wanted to test their loyalty too. She also wanted to know whether her future

162

lay with the band or without them. She needed Floyd and Chrysler on her side. If they were, she felt Arnold would join too. She believed Deke would always want to follow her down. She believed she knew her former lover well. She needed them. The last thing Zogger wanted was for them to know she felt that way.

"That's alright," Zogger said. She tried to temper her tone so it didn't sound too threatening. Even so, her impatience kept rising to the surface. The muscles in her face tightened with tension. "I'm not pleading with you. You all know what you want to do. It's your choice alone. I don't mind. I'll do it on my own. So what's it to be?"

"You're asking us to indulge in more than heavy-duty arson. You're asking us to do some serious GBH. Maybe more," Floyd said. "Even if they deserve it, it could be illegal."

She shook her head and sighed as if responding to an obstinate child.

She was going to whip his arse with her tongue. Though she didn't want to, she could feel she might have to cross-examine him into the ground. She thought about it, realised it would give her a fleeting satisfaction, but she'd lose the argument. Before she could say anything Arnold said, "The trouble is I'm not convinced. I don't doubt your feelings, but that don't make it right. It just doesn't seem like a very important case to me. I feel sorry for the poor old pony, but cruelty is second nature to humans. It's part of their oxygen. They get it with their mother's milk." He stopped staring at his feet, looked up and at her. "Floyd's right, you're making your problem ours. Or trying to. I really don't care, why should I?"

"You make out like this case is some big deal," Chrysler said, before she could answer. "Given it happens

163

every day in every way, why should we risk our lives? For what? So you feel better? We could all end up in the Big House." He hesitated then said, "What then? If you think I'm doing porridge for some pony, you'd better think again."

"You all say 'Who cares?' Well maybe you should. I've had enough. I'm going, but before I do just listen for two minutes." She stopped. She wouldn't begin until she had their attention. "Look, it's up to each of you. I'm not going to try and get you to do anything you don't want to. You have your own code of the road. You know what counts in this godforsaken world, now and tomorrow. You make your choice. Only you can regret it." Zogger was shrewd enough to know that would gently tweak their tails. She tried to divide them.

"If you're afraid of the risk, that's OK. I'm not going to spend time trying to change or mess up your mind. I'll tell you what though, let me give you a little history first. Then you can each decide whether you're in or not. If you're out, I'm happy. That's fair isn't it?"

Her patience, never her strong point, already thin and stretched, was becoming threadbare. She knew she had to touch and move them before she could count on them. She reached into her inside ticket pocket and took out a folded sheet. "I just happened to have this with me." She opened the paper and, looking at them, one-by-one, said, "These are not my words. Please listen. That's all I ask."

The three of them sat there impassively. None of them were really interested in hearing her. "It's a copy of the Police Report of the investigation." She read it in a slow monotone. No emotion. They barely concealed their boredom:

During the summer holidays two schoolboys decided to buy a gerbil. The boys, who were 8 and 9 years old, were cousins. They had saved and pooled their pocket money for a particular purpose. They had over £6.

Together they went to the local pet shop. Gerbils were for sale at £2 each.

They bought one and took it to the older boy's home. They had agreed in advance to kill it.

They placed it in the garden.

They got an inflammable aerosol they used as a blowtorch in trying to burn it to death. As it tried to escape, one of the boys threw a brick that struck and wounded it. Then they took it in turns to burn her with the torch at close-range until she died.

The boys then threw the body away.

The next day they went back to the pet shop. They bought another gerbil.

They took it to a nearby park and threw it into the river in an attempt to rown it. It did not die. When it was only half-drowned they dragged it out of the water. They then impaled it on a stick. They then threw her back into the river where she drowned.

The next day they went back to the pet shop. They bought another gerbil.This time they took it to the younger boy's home.

They placed it in the garden.

Then the cousins got some white spirit and poured it all it. It was then set alight. Both boys burned the animal alive.

The gerbil did not die quickly.

One of its legs was seen to still move, so they poured more white spirit over it and torched her again.

The boys then threw her charred carcass away.

They had no pocket money left.

When the matter was discovered neither boy gave any reason for their actions. The most revealing comment was that one had initially said to the other, "I feel like killing something."

"That's an outline," she said. "Canker and Qualm were the cousins."

Zogger stopped reading. She let the silence stab the air. She knew their histories. She had to reach the invisible scars. Arnold and Floyd and Chrysler sat there in stunned silence. Arnold played with his spoon, flicking it on the edge of the saucer in succession. Floyd placed his left index finger in the spilt coffee and used it to write a single word: bastards. He sighed. He blew a stream of air. Chrysler closed his eyes as the images of Qualm and Canker banged against his creased brow. They saw the reason behind Zogger's misery. Now they knew these characters were not your average animal abusers. Today they would torture an animal, tomorrow their target would be human.

She stayed silent.

"What happened to them? Were they sent to Borstal or prison?" Arnold asked.

"No. Nothing at all," said Zogger. "They got off scot-free. You see, they were too young to be prosecuted." Her words trailed off.

166

"Well I hope they got a good beating from their fathers at least," he said.

"No. They didn't, they couldn't," Zogger said. "Canker's father was in prison at the time for another assault on his wife. She refused to give evidence, but the police compelled her because it was the fifth time he'd fractured her jaw. She could hardly speak through her wired-mouth, but fortunately the slob was convicted."

"What about Qualm?"

"As for Qualm, his father was even nastier. He fell out with his neighbour, Peggy Day, over some paltry hedgerow dispute. She was an elderly lady who lived alone except for her cat, Isis. Sean Qualm squirted ammonia in Peggy's face. He then trapped Isis. He held a stun-gun to her temple and fired."

"What, he killed her?"

"No, she lost one of her nine lives. He blinded her. 'Course he blinded Peggy too."

"So was he proud of what junior had done?" Arnold asked, as his body began to heat. He could hardly get the words out. Chrysler felt skeins of tension gradually grow tighter round his shoulders and chest. He massaged the pain across his shoulders with his left hand, then with his right hand. Floyd felt the heat and tension even keener. He distractedly bent the spoon and broke off the bowl. He put his head in his hands. He crossed his fingers and joined them on his forehead. His eyes closed.

"Proud? He certainly would've been," said Zogger. "Before he could stand trial some stranger plunged a knife in his heart. Just another bar room brawl. Self-defence. No one saw anything. They didn't want to. He wasn't missed. One less statistic in an overcrowded, crimo-ridden world. I was due to prosecute Sean Qualm. So I lost the brief. He cost me money. I wrote it off as a charitable gift."

No one said anything for a while. Silence engulfed the air. Zogger let it hang. Music played in the background and washed over them. They were oblivious to everything except the assault on their senses.

Chrysler then said, "Hey hold on. Before we make a final decision, all you've told us about is Qualm and Canker. What about Hornet? It's hardly fair he should just be lumped in with his mates, is it? Those characters have a history."

"Yeah, that's right," Floyd said. "If Hornet's not involved, he simply happened to be there that Saturday night with them and the pony, that's not enough."

"Not only that-..." Arnold started to say.

Zogger could sense the mood of the moment. She had the momentum. Zogger interrupted Arnold and grasped the gauntlet, "Don't go feeling sorry for him. Hornet certainly wasn't corrupted by Canker or anyone else. He was a bastard, born and bred, evil through and through and spent his life proving it. Being nasty keeps him happy. He's horrible and mean, um, as a, as nasty as a pit of cannibal shit."

She was going to say he's meaner than Mr. Mustard, but it seemed so dumb she bit her tongue. She continued, "Listen, I've got all his details too. I just happened to have them with me. I won't put a slant on it. I'll read you a Police Summary of his first offence" She read it in the same tone:

Lee Hornet and his brother, Scott, often used to run errands for Eddie Burke, an 82 year old pensioner who lived in the village. He was a bachelor and lived alone in the bungalow where he was born. He had no electricity, no heating, no inside toilet and no money. He lived alone with his chocolate Labrador, Poteen.

Mr. Burke gave the boys some money on their birthdays and for the errands. He liked the boys. He was one of the few people in their lives who showed them kindness.

Lee and Scott got it into their heads that Mr.Burke was extremely rich. So they burgled and ransacked his bungalow. They tied him in a chair and bound his hands and feet. Then they smashed him repeatedly across the face with a pick-axe handle because he would not tell them where he kept all his money. As he protested, they hit him harder.

Both the Hornets showed Mr. Burke no mercy. [See photographs Ex. PJPRO 1-9].

Poteen was old and ailing and deaf. A friendly dog. He went to the Hornets. They brought Poteen directly in front of Mr. Burke.

When Mr. Burke still refused to give them the information, Scott held the collar so tight Poteen's mouth sprang wide open. Lee then sprayed bleach down his throat.

"Why the hell didn't he tell them? The old fool. Was he a miser?" Arnold asked. He was shouting. He couldn't control himself. His eyes lit with anger.

"He couldn't. He didn't have any information to give them. He was almost destitute," she said. "Let me continue:

169

Poteen died in agony before Mr. Burke's eyes. Both boys smashed his battery radio. They then spent the day at the Mall. Mr. Burke had a stroke and never recovered from the burglary and the assault.

He would have died except a neighbour, Justine Hawkins, called the following day when he failed to collect his pension. She found him on the floor in a pool of blood.

"What happened to the old man?" Chrysler asked.

"Mr. Burke recovered. Well, sort of. He's now in a wheelchair. He'll be in one for life."

"What happened to the spankheads?" Arnold asked. You could see him visiting Hornet, casually ripping his giblets out and using them as a garrotte. "Did they get a shilling from the Sheriff's Fund? Or were they too young to be prosecuted too?"

"No," she said. "Lee Hornet was 13 at the time. Scott, his brother, was 11. But the result wasn't much different. He had some lizard-tongued lawyer-...."

"You mean there's another kind?" Arnold shouted.

"As I said, the lawyer, he told the Youth Court Lee just needed some TLC. So they gave him a Supervision Order. Scott got a Conditional Discharge." She waited. "So it goes. Then as now. What's changed?"

Zogger stared at the three of them, each in turn. Switching from one to the other. For the moment words were spent. They knew, in a heart-burning way, the choice between acting and doing nothing was no choice at all. Zogger's pain had reached them.

Calculating her chance, Zogger asked quietly, almost inaudibly, "What's it to be? If you're with me, we have to strike now. If you're not, that's fine. I'll do it on my own.

It's your call. It's now or not at all. It won't wait, tomorrow is too late."

She spoke softly. "In or out?" She ended with a gentle emphasis on her mission. "What's it to be? Say the word."

Arnold and Chrysler and Floyd looked at each other, their fierce eyes signalling their decision. The three of them punched the air in short bursts. Arnold shouted, "Yes!" All four shook hands. The deal was sealed.

Zogger said to herself through clenched teeth, 'Yeah, yeah, yeah.' She then said it aloud, "Yeah, yeah, yeah," as she twisted her clenched fist. At that moment their four hearts beat and burned as one.

Just then Deke arrived looking horny and happy. He moved across the room in motion with the music. As soon as he saw the band he shouted, "Hi, Arnold, how you doin'? Chrysler, how you cuttin'?" Neither of them replied. He saw why as he got closer. The atmosphere was still tense, though now for a different reason. His smile soon faded when he caught their faces, bathed in frowns and way too serious. The mood was as sombre as a closed cemetery in winter. "What the hell's up?" Deke asked. "You look like you're having a picnic at a funeral and then it starts to rain." The mood stayed the same. "So what's the craic?" Deke asked. He shifted from foot to foot, rocking on his cowboy-booted heels. He arched his eyes as if to say, tell me then?

Zogger knew she had to get Deke on her side. She repeated the stories, plainly and simply. She read out the two Police Reports. She told him of their plan. Not wishing to overplay her hand, she slowly distilled what had been discussed. She impressed upon him his value to the venture. Though she pitched it low as the last thing she

171

wanted was for him to know her view. She needed him more than a priapic pope needs a mother superior.

Zogger felt his feelings for her still ran deep. How could it be otherwise when, at first hand, he'd seen her nightmares? He shared her hurt. Their history as lovers bound them together. Yet it was her history that helped to force them apart. He listened to her, didn't interrupt. Nodding often and easily. Here and there he screwed his eyes up as the story reached him. When she finished there was a certain relief. "Well, Deke, what's your take? Out or in?"

Deke was diamond-hard and just raring to go. No hesitation, no questions either. "Let's do it. All the way. No stopping us now. We were born to win."

"And born to run!" shouted Chrysler.

"Born in the purple, you mean," Arnold shouted back. All five laughed in unison.

"So what's our plan? When do we strike," Deke asked.

"Now. We're going to teach the crimos a life lesson they'll remember this side of the grave," she said. "Their time has come. Roosting chickens will crow at dawn."

Their eyes mirrored their mutual feelings. The decision was made. The trio were now the target. Everything changed about them. The decision gave the band an instant visible bond. They sashayed across the floor in time with a Nashville song about some forlorn fool who was feeling down because he was 'Cathy's Clown'. As they were leaving The Freefall they looked great. The early morning darkness had disappeared as they strolled towards the midday sun as musketeers ready to rock and run. They looked, as they were, deep and damned. Dangerous too.

Zogger kept having fugitive, negative thoughts rush through her. Why did Deke agree so easily? Is he trying to

172

win me back? Is he genuine? Why didn't he argue like he usually does, like he always does? As they invaded her she circled them and cancelled them from her mind. She knew this was not the time to pettifog.

Zogger smiled slightly so as to hide her spasmic thoughts. She remained troubled by Deke's readiness to join. She figured he's trying at least to get back into my bed and at most into my head. He should have known both were closed to him. There was no chance he could be a part of her closed heart ever again. His reaction to her secret pain told them both their only future was as members of a maverick band, not as a dove-like pair. In those rapid-fire moments she could not shake off the question as to why he was so eager to get involved. Normally he asked numerous questions and had to be persuaded to the nth. degree before being committed. Now he'd nodded and in a flash was sold on action. Something about him lit a query in her mind. Again she cancelled it out. Maybe I'm wrong, she thought, I usually am.

The five felt a pervasive strain of sadness about the Police Reports. Balanced against that they held a vision of their mission. The juke-box jangled with a new bittersweet sound. It captured the white-hot Jimmy Cagney feeling that bounced between them knowing that 'Mama we're on top of the world'. Zogger was the first of the five to arrive. She was last to leave. As they left they heard Ralph and his boys on the jukebox pleading in perfect Clinch Mountain harmony, *The Darkest Hour Is Just Before Dawn*.

Life Is A Pigsty

Deke knew immediately he had the right place when he walked into the yard. He sauntered rather than walked, with a slow pronounced slouch. His identity was important for this job. He wanted to look the part, not too dim and definitely not too smart.

Deke remembered not to shave. He dressed down to impress his future employer. He wore a pair of battered original Jack Purcell's, a dirty pair of black Wranglers and a second-hand red v-neck Levi's T-shirt. Unlike the effort made when attending most interviews, Deke tried to look rough. He aimed to show them he could easily do the job. He desperately wanted this job. In a strange, at that stage unknown way, his life depended on it.

His body language was as important as his incoherence. He had to fit in, even if the job was only temporary. For this kind of work required a particular personality: you had to enjoy cruelty as participant more than voyeur.

Lots of students had applied for a job at this abattoir, but were turned down. They were categorised as namby-pamby by Qualm, types more suited to picking hops or delivering post. The sort of job for someone with no guts, compared to this one that was all about guts. The problem for the jobseekers usually sent was they couldn't control their emotions when they saw the scenes. Black blood and gore. The sight and sound and smell of death. Instinctively they flinched. Before you know it their feelings would show. This was no place for someone like that. No room for arse pirates, as Canker called them. Hornet dismissed the students as box-shifters.

The stories of the treatment meted out to the students were

legendary. Just a week before Deke's visit Qualm asked Roderick Beswick, a polite, shy sociology undergraduate, whether he was, "A Nancy Boy as you look and sound like one." To assess how much he would enjoy the job he gave Beswick a huge, long knife. "Just hold it, grip it, like," Qualm urged him. "Hold it tight like a tennis racket. Like your girlfriend grips you. Ha-ha. Well, your boyfriend then." He handed him a huge machete that Beswick gripped in a limp-wristed way.

"No, look, like this," Qualm said, his right fist gripping Beswick's wrist.

"That's more like it, that's it," Canker said when he finally seemed to hold the knife half-right. "Now, strike, strike," Canker said, holding a struggling, squealing sow directly in front of Beswick. He just couldn't do it. Beswick tried to strike with the knife, but his hand froze. He tried again. He was almost paralysed with fear and guilt. "Cut her, cut her for Chrissake," Canker whined, "I can't hold her much longer."

With that Hornet held Beswick's hand and forced a single saw into the sow's throat. "Look, that's the way to do it," he laughed. They all laughed. They laughed a lot. Loud. All except Beswick, who was soused with a spurt of blood from her ruptured throat, all over his shirt and horn-rimmed glasses. He blenched and drew the knife back. He withdrew his body as best he could. His face changed from red to pale, he started to sway and then spewed a fountain a vomit all over her. They all laughed louder at Beswick and the dying pig. Beswick looked at the sow, she appeared to look back. Both were caught. The pig had a slow death, as his first strike was the only one struck.

"Get him out of here," Qualm said. "I hate Nancies." Beswick was not even allowed the luxury of washing off

175

the puke. They wanted him to remember them. He did. The sow stuck in Beswick's mind long after her death.

Emilline Lazarus, The Job Centre Clerk, warned Deke about the reception he was likely to receive. The feedback on the treatment of Beswick and others had become part of the Job Centre folklore. Deke knew all that, but was prepared to meet them on their terms. He was the first face-worker. The place so reeked with death it was an effort for Deke not to retch. It was a stench he'd never known before. It was not the offal bins filled beyond the brim; not the decomposing flesh rotting on the bone; it was not the blood or gore or noise or even the sounds. First it was the smell of sheer fear. Then he saw them. A group of cows and pigs were goaded and whipped by several men with blood-spattered sticks. Men with coats covered in shades of blood from pink to maroon. "Get a move on. Shift yer fat arse," shouted an acne-ridden youth, prematurely bald and double-chinned, kicking a limping pig. He kicked her so hard he almost lost balance, slipping on the spreading bloody pools. They hit the animals when they refused to move and hit them when they moved. Some of the beasts tried to bolt, but were whacked into submission by a stout stick across their snout. As the animals, lined up to die, they emitted the smell. Deke could hear their fear. "Aaah. Uuumm. Zooww." The bellows and grunts of the beasts echoed in time with the blows. Their hot fear stuck in his ears and nostrils so he remained at the gate.

He saw the three partners some distance away. He tried hard to look hard. They were playing some sort of amateurish rugby. Deke thought it was a bit strange as it was only about 11.00 a.m. Canker and Hornet and Qualm were running all around the yard holding, throwing and kicking a grubby ball. Two of them tried to stop the other one from placing the ball between two tin cans that made a makeshift goal. All the while they were laughing in an affected, childish way. Laughs without smiles. Deke sussed them as overgrown schoolboys. Perhaps, he figured, stroking his stubble, I'm being too kind.

One moment Canker had it and ran the length of the pitch. Then Qualm slid into his path, tripped him up and took the ball to head for home. With that Hornet dove for Qualm and brought him down on the hard ground. Hornet had the speed and stamina of a rhinoceros in a tutu. He wrestled the ball from Qualm and placed it between the cans. Each of them had a go at scoring. They seemed to take the game seriously. They were shouting and swearing in a mock friendly way; goading each other with a complimentary curse. Whenever anyone scored, the goal was marked with their raised fists and a waddling dance. No kissing though.

"Hey, you fat, lucky slob," Canker shouted when Hornet scored. "Get him Kev, hack him. Grab his goolies."

All the while the stench of blood and guts pervaded the air. It couldn't mask the smell of fear from the animals waiting for death. All they could do was await their fate at the abattoir gate and occasionally just kick against the pricks.

Deke stood on the sidelines. They ignored him. He didn't ignore them. Clods and sods moved as the game progressed. Hornet kicked his opponent as often as the ball. When a goal was scored or a good tackle made, Deke clapped and shouted, "Nice one. Yes." Realising he was sounding far too stiff, even mannered, he added a couple of "Yeahs" and "Good on yer." Fortunately they paid him no heed, as his image needed work. Even raising his arm he looked like he was back in the Fourth Form. He wanted to share their passion. He wanted them to know he could fit in. Seeing them he knew he had to change his persona in a matter of moments.

Although they had now noticed Deke, they continued to ignore him. He hoped his hollers didn't sound too desperate to please. Just then Qualm shouted, "C'mon, that's enough. We've got work to do." With that Hornet kicked the ball high, aiming between the cans. It was a perfect shot. It landed right in an oil drum near the fence.

Deke hesitantly walked behind them. "What d'you want?" Qualm asked, looking towards Deke. "Who sent you?" It wasn't a question, but an accusation. Almost a threat.

"I've come about the job, like," he said. He slurred his words for emphasis. He tried not to sound too plastic. "It ain't filled, is it?"

"Why? What's your problem?"

"Why? 'Cos I'm your man," Deke said. "If there's anyone else here, send 'em home." He sounded a touch bolshie. Some edge and some bottle.

"Right. Respect." Qualm motioned for him to join them as they went inside. He did so. As Deke passed through he saw a sow oozing blood, but tried hard not to register any emotion. It was neither the time nor the place.

They all sat down for an interview of sorts. Qualm was almost as articulate as a ventriloquist's dummy. The three of them asked Deke a few bland questions which he answered in the same vein. After a few minutes Hornet left and returned with a battered tray full of steaming mugs of tea. Canker shoved a mug in Deke's direction. Deke sat

178

there drinking brown sludge from a multi-chipped mug with encrusted blood on the handle. He smacked his lips to mimic their response to sipping the sludge. Hornet passed him a roll-up. Deke hated smoking. At one time he smoked as soon as he awoke, then throughout the day and up to the last thing at night. Now he positively hated smoking with all the passion of a convert. He took the matchstick-thin fag and feigned a drag on it through cupped fingers. The constant slurping and laughter was a noisy chorus that allowed him to forget about the fag. He slyly pinched the tip causing it to go out.

Hornet leaned over and asked, "You wanna light?" He flicked his Zippo gun. As it sparked Deke's eyes lit upon the colour, a vivid Canary yellow. One of a stolen job lot, he thought.

"It's pretty heavy work, mate. Are you fit?" asked Qualm, in his best interview mode, looking as fit as a corpse.

"Well, thing is I'm well fit, you know. Too right." Deke adopted the style of the average footballer trying to be a pundit or chat show host. The "umms" and "aahs" grew longer on Deke's part. Qualm was neatly matched by Deke who liberally laced his answers with "yeah" and cliché after cliché. The interview continued in the same ping-pong fashion as one stumbled over the questions and the other mumbled the answers.

"Mmm. I dunno. You look a bit thin to me," Qualm said. Canker and Hornet nodded in agreement. Feeling fatness equalled fitness the three of them shifted in their seats.

"Don't be fooled by that. It's all muscle. Feel that," Deke said, flexing his biceps. "Go on, feel it." He pulled his T-shirt up. He grabbed his stomach with both hands,

179

his fingers parted, "Punch it. Hard. Go on, hard as ya like, like. Do your worst. You'll see."

Qualm didn't take up the offer, but liked the cut of the comment. He was taken with Deke, so he asked him what was probably the most relevant question for a potential employee, "Can you sink a few mate?"

"You bet your sweet bippy," Deke said. "Always the last man standing. I can sink fourteen pints a night. More when I'm thirsty." Qualm grinned at that, so the others laughed too. The wheels of their work were being slowly oiled on each side. They saw Deke as a stooge who they could pay poorly and work to death. He saw them as three stooges he could teach a life lesson.

Deke was glad to be addressed as "mate". He felt he was making some headway. He continued with the interview. "Oh, yeah. I used to play quite a bit of rugby," he lied. "I'd like to get as fit again as I was like. I cycled here you know."

"Why are you, like, studyin' philosophy?" Qualm asked, a bit casual and throwaway, but it caught Deke off-guard. "What's the use of that stuff?"

"Well, it's just a scam, a skive while I con the taxman, you know. I get a grant. I don't pay VAT on the Indie Record Company I run. You know. I work with you guys and top up the old funds. Who knows? Who cares? Know what I mean? You're happy, I'm laughing. It's a win-win situation."

"Enough respeck." The answer appealed to Qualm. It clinched the deal. "You'll be alright here, we pay everything on the lump. No cards, no stamps and no questions. Know what I mean. Is that okay?"

"The only way. I hate the bloody taxman, you know. Bleedin' leech. My money ain't gonna be used for

180

foreigners. Breedin' like rabbits. Messin' up our country and all. No way." Deke smiled, he was beginning to enjoy the game. He felt he'd cracked it. He longed to do the same to their skulls.

"Can you start next week?"

"Yeah. Sure."

"What about Sunday? Can you come in then, like?"

"Yeah. No problem."

"Great. See you then. Don't forget it's an early start."

"Don't worry. I'll be there. Told you I was fit." Deke smiled slowly and winked. Qualm gave a short sort of snort, his kind of laugh

He passed. He would start the following week. As he was leaving he said, "Thanks for the tea mate. See ya soon." He winked again. Qualm winked in return. As Deke was walking out he saw the sow he noticed on the way in. Her belly was slit wide open. She was still alive. She was squealing in pain. He walked on.

Deke walked over to the fence to collect his bike. He glanced into the oil drum. There was the rugby ball they were kicking a half-hour ago. It had been removed from the sow's open belly. There were two other unborn piglets too. Trash. Tomorrow they would be dog food. Their mother would be a politician's breakfast.

As Deke was leaving he heard the bellow of some creature soon to become a carcass. He closed his eyes momentarily and saw the dirty pink ball they'd been kicking and pitching every which way. He opened them and saw the real thing. He unlocked his bike. He wondered whether he should toss a grenade straight through their window. It would've been so easy. His tongue brushed the inside of his upper teeth as if he was feeling for the pin.

Deke rode down the lane. He listened on his vintage

181

Walkman to the tough voice of one of his lonely heroes. He knew how badly Robeson had been treated as an actor and an attorney and an activist. In each case because of his face. Deke thought about all the ripe fruit hanging on the magnolia trees, forced to rot before their time. As he listened to the deep roar his feelings started to soar and he knew something had to change. He would make the change. He was always a rebel. Now he had a cause. Deke cycled like a madman, hot and hard, listening to the sad strain of *Strange Fruit*.

Another Place To Fall

The abattoir was open day and night seven days a week. Qualm and his partners had a good business going in the chilling and killing of any animal that ended up at their door.

"Have you got the books?" Qualm asked Hornet around late March 2006, just before the fiscal year began. They were in the front 'office' that was the hub of their business. Qualm was sat down making a phone call, arranging a new supply of amphetamines and crystal. "Only the Accountant, Nick McPherson, he'll be coming next week. You know what he's like. Snivelling creep. "

Hornet wandered off. He returned red-faced, breathing heavy. "Here they are. Phew," Hornet said, heaving three big black ledger books onto the stained table. He rested his flabby arms on the top one. "I wish you'd warned me about the weight."

"What, yours?" he said, without looking up. Hornet almost laughed. Qualm saw the books. His mood changed. "You shag pile of shite. The books. I told you McPherson is coming. What's wrong with you?"

"Whatcha mean?"

"What do I mean? You're a thicko. Twangeface." Qualm's face got redder, in tune with his anger. He screwed his eyes and showed the tip of his tongue. He went to rise out of the chair as if he was going to give Hornet a good kicking. His buttocks stuck. He did too. "Now get out of here. Talk about a boy to do a man's job."

Hornet's face got as red as Qualm's. It clicked. "You mean the red ones?"

"Yeah, obviously I mean the red ones." Hornet went to leave. Before he could, Qualm screamed, "Where do you think you're going?"

"I'm goin' to get the red books. Why?"

"Why? Why? Are you gormless or what? Get these bloody books out of here. Away. Now. You're even thicker than I thought you was. D'you understand? Anything?" He looked at Hornet and cracked his knuckles. "Shift your lard arse. Now. Or I'll shift it."

"Alright. Keep your hair on. I'm going," Hornet said as he left, looking and feeling sheepish. He carried the huge books down to the basement and placed them back in the rusty trunk. He locked it and covered it with various spoiled, bloody skins. He swore to himself. He cursed Qualm again. He went upstairs to the back 'office', a makeshift half-furnished breezeblock shell, next door to the similarly constructed, never-cleaned lavatory. Only last night's curry forced anyone to take a crap there. Or dysentery. Usually they fertilised the field, organic fashion. A few ledgers and notebooks were intentionally kept on view on the rickety pasting-table. Two were always open at random pages. The owners rarely went there as the smell of the damp books and the lavatory was as inviting as a Sunday ramble in a sewer. The office was reserved for any visiting VAT Man.

Hornet found what he was looking for and returned to the front office. Still red-faced. "Here they are, Kevin," he said, placing two red books in front of Qualm.

"That's more like it." He fingered the pages. His visible irritation lessened as he looked at the doctored figures in the ledger. The black books were for their eyes only as they held a dangerous secret: the figures told the truth.

" So, you got it now, Hornet?"

"Yeah, don't keep on."

"Then don't forget it. You know why, don't you?" Qualm held the edge of the table between his right thumb and pinky, as his three middle fingers drummed an uneven pattern.

"Yeah. I know. We've got to show McPherson the red ones 'cos he's straight."

"Too true."

"It won't happen again."

"And don't you know it." That first lesson was well learned, so every year Hornet would religiously get the red books for the inspection of one of the very few honest men they knew. The deliberate use of snowflake Tipp-ex and a liberal sprinkling of blood-stained fingerprints added to their authenticity. The inspection was always was carried out in the back office. It was over in no time.

There was an extra element to their entrepreneurial spirit as the three of them owned the slaughterhouse. They bought it from Bobbie French, the previous owner's mistress, he having died after a frisky horse within the last gasp of death kicked him in the head and ruptured his alcohol-addled brain – or at least where it would be. Mick Shaugnastie had transferred the business to Bobbie to keep her sweet and seductive. That's how he saw her. Though in truth she was as bitter as the sherbet lemons she constantly sucked. Either way they each got what they wanted. She kept it out of reach of Maggie, his ex-wife, who he loathed more than he once loved. There was gossip he had talked about taking out a contract on Maggie, but it might have been just talk. Anyway, before any deal could be done the frisky filly helped Shaugnastie towards death and justice.

As people, all of them were cut from the same avaricious pattern, yet always hungry for an angle. Cheating and conning their way to victory, Shaugnastie and French and Qualm were made for each other. So alike they deserved each other. Together they ensured the business made a killing. Whether it was an animal or artefact mattered not, only that it led to a profit.

Thereafter Qualm and his mates took over the business and it was thriving. They sometimes worked hard to build it up. They cut corners to increase the profits and used the premises as a convenient warehouse to stash stolen goods. Often the carcasses would be used to hold condoms filled with cannabis oil imported from the West Indies. Anyone and everyone who crossed their path had the offer of a greased palm. Most of the time the officials, the tax collector, a customs officer, the weigh-in operator and everyone whose ears tingled to the sound of crinkled notes were led towards temptation. Then invited through the open door.

"Is he worth approaching?" Canker and Hornet would ask Qualm about someone they had just met.

"Leave it out," he occasionally advised the others. Usually he would say, "Definitely. Go for it, he'll bite. No question." Otherwise Qualm might advise them, "leave it for the moment. In a couple of months we'll strike. He's got some heavy expenses coming up, he told me about them today." He'd lock in his memory a forthcoming wedding or holiday or divorce. He'd strike at the right time. So it was and so it went. Someone like McPherson was so rare, his true value was his presence was impressed on Hornet's memory. So in future he had to get the wrong books, that is, the right books.

Meanwhile for Qualm and his mates it was the best of all worlds. On one level they were earning vast sums in subsidies, development grants from the EEC and with all the BSE-type scares and every known precaution being taken, it was truly boom-time. These were matched by the illegal profits and yet further by the tax and VAT scams. The other level that was satisfying was they had a boost every time they stunned an animal. None of them were properly stunned as it would cost them more in electricity.

From his first day Deke had to both bite his tongue and pretend to look the other way. Everyday was the same. There was no difference between the owners and the workers in their attitude towards the animals. The owners set the bar and the workers raised it. Both types dragged them around daily by their tails, acting as legal executioners and pleased to be paid to boot.

"Hey look at this," Hornet shouted as he cursed and kicked some unwilling cow, unable to move because of a broken leg, as his boots shattered her bones. "Goal!"

"Let me at it. I'll shift the bitch," Canker said. One and two and three pile-drivers. Three times he brought his boot down, stamping on her good leg until he broke that too. He kicked her in the belly. She moved a few inches and bellowed in pain. "That's more like it."

Deke rushed over. He was split between kicking Canker so he spewed his crotch up and rescuing the cow. Before he could act, Qualm pushed Canker aside. "Hold on," Qualm said. "Let the dog see the rabbit. Watch this, Deke." He held his left arm across her throat, forcing her head back. Using his hooked knife, he carved a diamond hole in her forehead so her head bled. He slipped the chains that held her between his hands so the cow crashed to the concrete floor. She lay where she fell. The blood began to seep around her brain. "That'll do the trick. Cutting costs, 'eh Deke?" He guffawed for Qualm.

The abattoir was carefully sited away from the prying eyes of any neighbours and passing motorists. It could only be found by going down an unmarked, unmade lane. It couldn't be seen from the motorway, being carefully shielded by distance and trees. It could be found by the few welcome visitors – or else only seen by passing pilots. Everything about the abattoir was clothed in secrecy because they feared so many different kinds of unexpected visitors: the police, other criminals, the VAT Man, stray ramblers and weird eco-terrorists.

What they had not counted on was someone like Zogger getting information that was otherwise unavailable. She had all the details from the papers with the brief. She knew from the alibis put forward that there was only a skeleton-staff of the three co-owners on a Sunday night.

The place was like a fortress. It was almost burglar proof. The problem for anyone wanting to keep burglars out is an inside job is the best course in a crooked business as the knowledge is gained directly. There is also a certain solace in knowing the police are unlikely to be involved or even welcome. For then too many questions would be asked. It's why supergrasses rarely collect their pensions. Qualm and his mates guarded their loot with the same motive a starving mongrel hoards a meatless bone.

Until now everyone who visited was wanted or they were warned about in advance. Then Deke entered their lives. When Deke got a temporary job there, it was supposedly during the University vacation. Deke relied on a story about being a mature student who was studying to be a philosopher. Every moment he could he used to build up his knowledge about the abattoir and his employer: the deliveries, the deals, the meetings, the drinking, the drugs and the books. Any snippet they let slip, he noted with a nod and memorised. Meanwhile he got the details of the electric fence, the multiple-zoom lights, the burglar alarms and especially the video cameras he'd noticed on his previous visit. Deke was affable to all of them, despite his natural prickly self. When he made the effort he could be as smarmy as oleaginous Osborne. Unlike him, he made sure the mask never slipped. He was personable and capable as well as having the human touch. In a short while he was, even though only a temporary worker, given the run of the place. He struck up to a kind of friendship with Qualm who himself had pretensions towards homespun cod-philosophy. He was soon trusted to lock up when all the others had gone home. Sometimes Deke would call one of them, usually Qualm, from the front office, with a spurious enquiry about the work. It was a precaution to ensure he was not being watched.

The trust that was built up quickly was cemented in an odd way. Qualm had a quirk he liked to exercise by testing people. One Friday in late September he gave Deke a DVD to take home and told him, "Have a butcher's, Deke. See what living's all about. You'll soon want a bit of the action. If you're man enough. Know what I mean?"

"Great. Thanks Kev. I'll have a look at it tonight. It'll go down well with a couple of six-packs and some nookie." He imagined it was some pornography Qualm had probably imported. It was bound to be illegal. He'd have to watch it because he knew Qualm was testing him. There was no choice. He couldn't fake it. He had to worm his way further into his trust. Qualm would ask him about the film. Qualm had a schoolboy love for smut.

Deke watched it the same night. The film started with a picture of a fenced back garden of a terraced house on an ordinary run down estate. The neighbouring houses on either side were empty and boarded up. The fence was

189

covered in coloured spray-can graffiti. Obscene drawings and threats mixed with, 'Liz luvs Ricky Dicky'. Some children could be heard laughing and swearing in the background. Adult feet could be seen as the scene shifted. A ferocious pit-bull terrier was first shown. Something was suspended in a sack tied on a pole and held inside a swinging old tyre. The pit-bull was attached to a length of chain just long enough to reach the tyre. The dog kept jumping up, but couldn't quite grasp the tyre. An indistinct voice said, "He's not been fed." The scene moved from the dog to the garden to the sky. It was a clear sunny day. In between it went back and forth to the dog and the tyre. Gradually, as it swung, the dog grabbed the tyre. He held it and gripped it in his jaws. He shook and shook and shook it. He tore the rim of the tyre. The sack fell. The pit-bull ripped open the sack, caught the contents tight in his teeth. Catching it, he clamped his teeth tighter. Chewed and chewed. Then spat and spewed the remains. The loud laughter captured was not enough to drown out the dying screams of the kitten.

The scene moved on to the cloudless sky. Then there were several out-of-focus shots. Deke thought it was the moving hand of the operator. He was wrong. It was the airborne blood splattered on the camera lens. At the start there were five dogs. The training developed the dog's stamina and gave them a taste for blood. A failure to kill a kitten, whether as a result of time or temperament, meant they were not made of the right stuff. They were then sacrificed with a bullet. Bang. Bang. Bang. Amongst the laughter and screams, the sound of repeated shots could be heard. The camera panned the three dead pit bulls. Mouths open, tongues hanging loose and holes where their eyes used to be. Ready to be diced and served up as dog meat.

The camera then moved past a child's swing in the garden and the fence and the field beyond and onto some waste grassy land near a wood. Two pit bulls were unleashed and unmuzzled inside a small makeshift ring made of wood and steel fencing. Both dogs then attacked each other with fangs ablaze. The shaky camera started moving around the pit catching in close-up the dogs' faces; it then caught the blood-bubbled saliva and the mood of the people watching. "Come on, Caesar," someone shouted. "Get right into him Ghenghis. Chew his head off," another voice shouted. You could hear a woman's voice screeching above the noise, "Bite his bollox off, big boy. You can do it!" The encouraging shouts continued throughout the fight. Many hands, some slender others gnarled, could be seen passing huge wads of notes as the betting increased in tune with the blood. "5 on G. 25 on C." The numbers were called out in tic-tac fashion between the screams. Both dogs growled and snarled and bit and chewed each other with a fierce focus, as both their faces became a bloody mass. Chunks of flesh were chewed from each face. Blood stained both dogs' moving jaws and dripped from their bare teeth. Finally one dog expired in a pool of blood and mess, gurgling in panic towards death.

Ellie Wayman, the owner, cursed Caesar for losing. The winning dog, Ghenghis, was in such a state he too was taken into the woods. He couldn't be taken to a vet as the owner, Byron Warniak, would be traced. His swift reward for victory was a shotgun blast between his ears, at such a close range it almost blew his head off. The camera followed in a magnified close-up so the bones in Caesar's half-eaten face could be seen. Neither dog was worth burying. The film passed over the feet of the owners. It

191

then withdrew and panned a pile of blood and bones in the distance. Two carcasses were slung next to them. The camera showed some podgy young woman smiling as she waved her winnings. She had gaping nicotine teeth in a fleshy equestrian face. The repeated shots and laughter captured their own truth. As the laughter faded the shot ended on the sunlit sky and picturesque woods of an English countryside.

As the left hand of the operator motioned to a man to move, Deke noticed a ring he'd seen somewhere before. For the moment he couldn't remember where or when or on whom he'd seen it. Deke's stomach churned. He thought about switching it off. He couldn't, he knew he had to watch all the sport. Knowing Qualm, he realised the incentive was the lure of blood-lust and blood-money in his dog-eat-dog world. It was why he started hunting when it became illegal. Deke's concentration lessened. He kept thinking about the ring. He couldn't shake it off. Then the scene changed again. The film crackled and picked up a faint wave of a fire. It was grainy, a copy. He couldn't quite make it out at first. He squinted. He moved closer. As he focused it became less faint. The waves of the fire grew. Nothing to do with the dogs. It was a different incident. He saw the flames at their fiercest. Amongst them was the burning body of Molly.

The following day, Saturday, Deke steeled himself and sought out Qualm first thing. "Great video, Kev," he said. He'd rehearsed what he wanted to say. He was desperate to perfect his insincerity. "Fantastic. I've never seen anything like it. Fangs for the memory." They both laughed. "You got any more?"

"Plenty. Plenty more where that came from. You'll be

amazed, my son. Put hairs on your chest and a bit lower down." He was happy Deke liked it. He saw Deke as a kindred spirit. "Beats studying your philosophy, don't it? You free later? We'll go for a drink after work. Alright? Have a chinwag?"

"Great. Yeah. Look forward to that."

Deke was dreading the meeting all day. He hoped Qualm would forget or be too busy. He was wrong. They met and went to the Salman's Shadow as it was close and cheap. Just the two of them. After a couple of drinks Qualm said, "Let's go down the 'Treat. You got time?"

"Well, not really. I was hoping, like, to watch the DVD again."

"Don't worry about that. I'm lookin' after your education."

"Why, what've you got?"

"You'll see. I've never let you down, have I? It'll be worth it."

"You've twisted my arm."

"When you see it you'll wanna twist more than that. Believe me."

"I do. I've learned to."

Sandy Bukowski, the barmaid at the Queen's Retreat, greeted them. She knew Qualm well. Every week he supplied her rocks. As she kissed him her lips missed his unshaven cheeks. He kissed her in the same luvvie-style of second-rate celebrities. She'd met Deke twice at the abattoir. She brought them two pints of foaming scrumpy. Qualm gulped his sherbet as if his mouth was ablaze. Deke frowned, supped his sherbet, looking and feeling pensive.

" So you like a bit of sport then?" Qualm asked.

"You bet. Especially when it's as hot as that." Deke said. His frown faded. He was so enthusiastic there was a clear danger he was plainly faking it. His fixed smile formed. "The way the old pooch chewed that kitten alive, like it was an old slipper. Hey man, that was too much. The dog's bollox." Qualm burst out laughing, spraying a mouthful of scrumpy over the sticky carpet. "Amazing. All that dosh. Lotsa motza passing hands. You ever win?"

"Too true mate. I part-own all the bitches. The dogs too. So I win even if I lose."

"Anyway, thanks for the loan of the film. You'd better have it back."

"No, you keep it. Enjoy it. I've got a lorry load of 'em. Sell them for a tenner a time. The punters can't get enough. I got me contacts all over, in offices and shops and factories. Everywhere. I'll be doing mail order soon." When he stopped laughing he said, "Mind you, if you thought that was good, think again. I've got something that will even fill your pencil full of lead." Qualm snorted. He cackled. He bent forward, closer to Deke. While feigning amazement, Deke still had to move back when Qualm's halitosis hit him.

"Here, Sandy," he motioned to the barmaid. When she came closer Qualm leant over the bar and whispered in her ear. She smiled. Sandy disappeared for about twenty seconds. When she returned Qualm gave her a tenner saying, 'Have yourself a drink, sweetheart."

Sandy gave him a DVD. Deke was now sure. He recognised the silver ring on the third finger of her left hand. It had a royal blue set square design. A compass.

Qualm passed the DVD openly to Deke. "Here. Have a look at this. It'll stiffen your joystick."

"Why, what is it?" Wide-eyed, he tried hard to disguise his disgust.

"Wait and see."

194

"No. Come on Kev. What is it? Is it as good as the last one?"

"Better, much better. And that's just a taster, you know. If you thought that was good, wait 'til you see this. You'll really want to fill your boots."

"Yeah, but what is it? Gimme a hint. Is it badger-baiting, spanking? A touch of the mass horizontals, S-M, scissor sisters? Zamies?"

"I told you, better than that. You can't wait can you? It's a couple of dogs and a bitch, real one I mean, a black bitch, but with a difference. Chained. Two big, fit, furry German shepherds – and hungry too. She's shafted in every orifice. Two at a time. After a quick double-doggie position her fanny becomes dog meat. Juicy. Snuffed out." Qualm laughed his jackal cackle.

Deke held his guts and kept his mouth closed. He thought he was going to puke. "Phew," he said instead. It was all he could manage. "I'll see you in a mo'. I need a quick Jimmy." He ran to the Gents. Within seconds of entering he vomited straight into the sink. He moved over, continuing to puke in the shute. Two drunken punters looked at him as he gurgled and retched. Each punter washed down his rain of vomit. Deke splashed water on his face. He hurried back to join Qualm at the bar. He gulped his cider. It tasted worse than before. "I needed that," he said, wiping his mouth with the back of his hand. He blew a stream of air. Initially he wasn't sure if Qualm was joking. He wasn't. Deke sipped his scrumpy. He remained silent. He was thinking he might jump Qualm in the car park and pummel him to pulp so even his repulsive wife wouldn't recognise him. It seemed the best solution.

Still lost and distracted, they parted an hour later. Qualm said, "Tell me what you think about it tomorrow.

I'll look out another one for you. Full on. No cuts. I've imported it from Germany. A real snuff 'n' crush movie. No bluff. Remind me tomorrow."

"Yeah. I'm really lookin' forward to this one. " Deke had to leave. He knew if he stayed he couldn't control himself. He'd boot Qualm's guts out through his arse. "Thanks, Kev. See you."

"Take my advice, don't watch it tonight. You'll be so horny you'll never get to sleep."

Deke rode off into the night, sick and sore. His teeth locked and eyes hurt with anger, real anger. Tomorrow. He'd definitely remind him tomorrow. Deke wasn't the kind of man to break his promise.

Deke had another restless, sleepless night. It was swamped with thoughts of what he had to do. The minutes ticked by so slowly, twice he shook the clock in case it had stopped. Now there was no turning back.

It was a hot, autumn Sunday night and the trio were on duty with one other. That just happened to be Deke. He volunteered, telling them he needed the overtime to pay off his student debts. Besides, he was good company and amused them with funny, long words, odd ideas and unpronounceable foreign names. Latin too. They enjoyed pulling his pulse about philosophy.

Time was tight as the front office clock struck midnight. Deke was fascinated yet nauseated by the clock. He stared at the figures on the face. It was a beautifully made, hand-crafted clock in mahogany, with a bright painted dial and a big brass bell and steel striker. On its face was a butcher with a cleaver poised over a sheep. As the hour struck both figures moved, the butcher striking in time with the cleaver and the sheep falling at his feet. Their movements revealed a bloody pool that spread as the hours passed from one to twelve. Qualm told him he'd bought it at a country auction because "It somehow appealed to my sense of humour."

The clock struck midnight. Just after the butcher's last strike Deke de-activated the alarm, the camera and the fence. He couldn't turn the outside lights off, as it would've alerted the trio to the problem and lead to an immediate investigation. The trio had to be taken on the run; become hunters hunted. That left the telephone. As there was no one to call on Sunday night he cut the wire just after the midnight hour. Deke was due to remain until about 6.00 a.m., but the others prepared to leave.

Meanwhile, the Cochise RV, the band van, pulled up in the lane. They all got out and lay in wait. The four went to the back and unloaded and mounted their machines. Zogger waited while the other three moved to the rhythm of the night. They rode quietly up the lane, without lights, gleaming like ghost ships in the half-light of the silvery moon. Modern missionaries cruising through the countryside jungle. Each man and machine had to be seen, two-wheeled chrome cowboys gliding through the night. Avenging angels.

Canker was out first and walked casually to his car. As he was going to open the door Arnold came from behind and held him commando-style. He held a honed knife to Canker's throat. Arnold didn't say a thing. His message was clear. He put a handcuff on Canker's wrist and placed the other on his own. "What the f-...?" Canker shouted. Arnold held his hand up and kept the knife in his right hand at Canker's throat. Canker realised this was not a time for pillow talk. He usually used steel on others. This was the first time he felt its power against his strained, veined neck.

Hornet came next and almost galloped to his car. Hot thighs, he was in a hurry to get home. Rushing there on a promise. Floyd grabbed him in exactly the same fashion as Arnold had Canker. The knife at his throat kept him frightened and quiet. The handcuff kept him still and in some pain. Floyd didn't say a thing. "Hey. What're you-...?" Hornet shouted. Floyd, still silent, just pressed the knife on his Adam's apple. Hornet got the point.

Qualm came out last and strolled to his car. He was fiddling with something. He seemed a bit distant. Distrait. Both of his partners were in the shadow of the abattoir door. Canker and Hornet were silent save for their muffled, low breathing. Neither had any interest in warning Qualm, thinking only of how to save his own skin. It didn't register with him that the other cars were still there – unless he didn't see them leave. He made his way to his van. As he was nearing it, he stopped. Still fiddling. Oh no, Chrysler thought, he knows. Qualm then turned around and went back to the killing shop.

Deke was more than a little surprised to see him. He played possum while his eyes flickered with guilt. "Alright, Kev. Got a problem? Anything I can help with?"

"No. Nothing," replied Qualm. "I just wanted to tell the missus I'll be home soon." He reached for the phone. He picked it up and put it to his ear.

"Haven't you got your moby?" His voice shot up an octave. Deke felt trickles of sweat flow from his left armpit.

"Yeah, but the battery's dead. I can't get a signal.

"You should've said. Here use mine?" He took the phone from Qualm with his left hand and placed it on the cradle. He hooked it on the wrong way. At the same time he gently forced his red and white mobile on Qualm.

"Oh, thanks, Deke. Neat moby. Sweet colour."

"You like it, have it."

"You sure?"

"'Course. Least I can do for a mate. It's yours."

"Good on ya. I won't forget it."

"I nicked it."

Qualm gave a half-smile and pressed it so it lit. As he examined it again he said, "I'll have a Jimmy while I'm here." He went to the far corner lavatory and left the door open. Deke immediately turned the outside lights off, gambling it was safe to do so. He followed Qualm.

Chrysler lurked in the shadow and scanned Qualm. He moved into the abattoir and followed Deke. Qualm held the mobile in his left hand and his flaccid fang in his right. He fumbled with both bits. In his rush Qualm slashed all over his boots and jeans. No matter, for he only washed off the blood. "Oooohh!" As he zipped up he caught his Clinton and squealed like one of his slit pigs. When Qualm pulled the chain, Deke pulled the mains switch down. All the inside lights went off.

"Aaahh!" Deke let out a false scream. It was so high it sounded like a woman in trouble or a stuck pig. As the scream hit the ceiling Chrysler kicked the door closed, then wrenched it open and grabbed Qualm. He held a stiletto to his throat. Qualm could feel the cold steel on his hot jugular. Instant darkness and fear and shock. Qualm's temperature rose as he was handcuffed by and to Chrysler. In less than six seconds flat. Deke was silent. Chrysler was silent.

"Whatchoodoin'…? Who the bloody hell are you?" They didn't bother to answer Qualm's questions. The steel forced on his unshaven throat ended his questions. Qualm was taken, along with Canker and Hornet, to the middle of the adjoining field. A pool of light appeared from the three Harley-Davidsons parked there looking like patient panthers ready to pounce on a passing prey. In a way that's precisely what they were.

Arnold and Floyd and Chrysler were dressed all in black, except for a bright red beret worn atop their masks of a lamb, a pig and a pony. The masks were black and dripped with fake dark blood.

Canker was forced to lie face down. Arnold released his handcuff and clamped it on Canker's free wrist. Floyd and Chrysler did the same to Qualm and Hornet. A chain passed from the seat of the sickle onto the handcuffs holding Canker and back again. Chains held the others too. Arnold mounted and revved at full throttle without moving. Floyd and Chrysler did the same. No one save for those there could hear them. No one save for those there could see them. Now no one could save them.

The trio blubbed as their blood ran hot, hitting the walls of their arteries. Their sweat oozed through and formed map patterns on their shirts. Their matted hair dripped onto their foreheads. The smell of their fear was palpable. They infected each other when their loose bodies exuded the smell of fresh shite across the chilled air of the night. They could smell each other's death. More than that they smelt their own.

The row of H-D's glinted like diamonds in Tiffany's window. There was the Fat Boy, the Electric-Glide and the Model-V. Pure grace and power and splendour on the grass. Arnold and Chrysler and Floyd were revving like crazed delinquents. The revs soared and the band roared around the field as if they were on Thunder Road. The three clunks chained to the seats hollered in horror and screamed until their lungs could take no more. They shouted and shrieked in pain. All the while the sickles swooped as wild eagles over the hills. The trio's faces were bloody, their arms and legs were bleeding too. Their limbs were almost torn from their sockets, knee-caps bared and their hearts all but burst open with a fright right off the Richter scale.

The band didn't give them a thought. Then the sickles slowed and stopped.

The trio were released from the bikes and laid supine. Just as a prey that can take no more and openly – let alone secretly – seeks death as a pleasant release, they felt there was no more pain they could endure. All they wanted, needed, was rest. Looking at the black sky, they stared into the void seeking a release that never came. The pain barrier was passed. The numbness ate into their bodies. Canker and Hornet and Qualm lay on the hard ground, each in a different way, feeling it wouldn't matter if they were below it.

The sound of the Low Rider purred in the night silence. The lamp matched the moonlight. Zogger then came out of the shadows. So far she had just observed it all. She looked as chic as a single real red rose in a white vase. Stunning. Looking like the hangman's beautiful daughter, with hennaed hair and otherwise all in black. Cuter than Cool Hand Luke. Wearing a black velvet suit and a jazz polo plus zoot boots. Jeeze she was as sassy and sexy as a walking dobro. She wore a raspberry beret and a Lynx Lynx mask.

The no-return point had long since gone. It would have been easy to eliminate them. That escape would have been far too easy – for them. Death would be too light. For that's the precise reason the child killers run off their murderous mouths about the 'right to die'. It's also the precise reason their deluded requests are always denied.

Zogger didn't speak a word. Not to them, not to the band. Everything was done in absolute silence. Whilst noise can induce fear, the final fear is to cause a Kafkaesque-nightmare so they would never wake up, sleeping or not. All the questions were rubbing at the trio's wired nerves, yet all the answers hung in a silent hell. For years they had claimed at every opportunity their 'right to silence'. Now in their hour of need they had exactly that and more.

Zogger figured all their tomorrows would be fixed by this day. She knew the problem they had to face was they alone had sown the seeds of their own destruction. Now they would reap a feral justice. Just before the deed, Zogger silently hummed her personal mantra like the monk who sold his Ferrari, the honky tonk refrain from *Last Date*.

Danger/Blind Painter Paints It Black

"Thank Christ it's all over," Hornet whispered to Canker.

"I thought those crazy mothers were going to kill us. Did you-...", Canker said.

"Shut up, shiteheads. They might yet," Qualm said. "They're coming back. Zip it."

The trio lay there, handcuffed and helpless hoping the night would end. The interlude as they lay there supine seeking refuge in sleep was at an end. Much as a drowning man minus a raft will see his life flash by in moments, the trio scanned their lives for signs of where they went wrong. In seconds they'd see the flowers from the seeds of their sins.

Canker was first. Zogger slowly released the button and the double-bladed silver stiletto flew with a whisk as it kissed the wind. She then placed the point on each thigh, cut his sodden trousers right off, slashing leg to groin and back again. She swept across him, cold and controlled. As she did she cast a cursory glance at Canker and saw the fright register in his edgy eyes. With three swift movements, right and left and right again, she cut each side of his scrotum and slit the whole cod. "Aaaaaahh!" Canker screamed and screamed so loud it was as if he would die screaming. Who cares? Who really cares? Zogger thought. Not so much to end his misery, but simply to end hers having to listen to his howls, with a gloved hand she grabbed the severed scrotum and shoved it into his mouth. He tried to cough and splutter until his protest was cut short by her double cuff around his snotty mouth.

Hornet's imagination went haywire as he tried to deal with his fear. He failed. He was caught up in guessing whether he would be the next victim and suffer the same fate. Given what had happened, it wouldn't have mattered had she done nothing to him. He already experienced a deep pain without even feeling the blade. His head was spinning. Why be kind when you could be cruel? Zogger thought. After all that was Hornet's response to any obstacle. A kind of respect he would surely understand? Zogger kicked him in the ribs with a pointed boot and turned him over so he lay prone. She cut his greasy jeans away as he lay there arsy-versy in the gravel and grass. Then she kissed his trembling cheeks with the stiletto and slit his arse from north to south and east to west. The blade cut through his blubbery arse like a piano-wire through a stretched neck. "Eeeeee. Ooooohh!" His screams echoed so loud you'd swear you were in a Wookey Hole cave.

Zogger turned Hornet over. His mouth was wide open, fixed in fear as a chimp exhibit in a laboratory or a zoo. She grabbed a handful of stray offal from the ground and stuffed it in his gaping mouth to stifle his screams. Like Pavlov. In time the guts would reach his own and the foul taste linger much longer than this night. He could breathe through his nose. She figured, with luck, he could even choke.

Qualm was last. It's not every day you see your mate buggered by a switchblade. Qualm was in such a state, if a double-barrelled sawn-off – whether loaded or not – was placed in his mouth and the trigger pulled, it would be as if he'd got off lightly. What he'd heard and seen happen to Canker and Hornet was something of a deterrent. However, his problem was Zogger didn't share that view. She always reckoned he had no cojones. She slashed his blood-encrusted jeans and exposed his mottled fodder. He wore no knickers. With her left hand she forced his mouth open even wider. His teeth gripped her hand by instinct rather than intention. It was what she wanted. With a swoop and a swipe like a Woody Guthrie strum, she lopped off about an inch and a half from his shrivelled man muscle and shoved it in his mouth. It sat there gripped between his clenched teeth as a bleeding cigar stub. Held tight, it was certain to remind him of tonight. He always smoked too much anyway.

She turned Qualm over. Zogger then sprinkled a few drops of fuel on his bleeding buttocks. She lit it. His hairy arse gradually became a black mass. She turned him again. There was a redemptive beauty to it: she used the Prosecution Exhibits, the lighter and the stiletto; the same ones Qualm had used on Molly.

All three almost passed out at various stages. A tug-of-war between the mind and body. The trio lay there, all thinking, if she's going to kill us why not do it now? Almost as if she was a scryer, similar thoughts blew across her mind.

All in all the trio were befuddled because they couldn't calculate what sort of man – for they had no idea it was Zogger – would do this for pleasure? Or was it punishment? They racked their brains thinking who is it? What's the reason? Their crimo life-style led to so many different ideas and possible conclusions. It might've been the double-dealing on the drugs consignment or the stolen goods they falsely shipped abroad or even the pimps whose girls they muscled in on. The one thing they wouldn't or even couldn't think about was some sad sick pony living out her life in a quiet corner of a field. Molly was so unimportant to them, so insignificant, they couldn't give her a first, let alone a second thought. No one could be stupid enough to go to all this trouble for some dumb animal.

For them the pony was no different than any other creature they had mutilated. In their eyes her life counted for nothing. The funny thing was that feeling was the exact one shared by Zogger, except it was for them.

Zogger then reached in her pocket and took out what looked to them like two brass telescopes. She wanted them to see it. Their eyes followed every movement of her fingers. She extended the components, shook three tubes free and removed what appeared to be a small piece of cutlery or a tool from within. She unscrewed the apparatus and put the parts of the blowtorch together. The six eyes of the trio bulged. Their eyes fixed on the blowtorch as the flame changed colour. From blue to red to white. The colours of rebellion. Their minds raced in unified desperation. Are we going to be burnt alive? 'Save me,' all their eyes seemed to say to her. Her eyes met theirs hard on. Zogger chose to ignore their plea.

Silence hung in the air as none of the band uttered a word. It mixed with the smell of burning flesh and the trio's fresh fear that leaked out. Plus their reflex, multiple-grunts and muffled screams. The strategy of silence added to their confusion, driving the trio to their mental borderline. They kept trying to examine their lives, re-tracing past incidents. Each one was searching for the reason, the purpose behind their torture. All they could silently ask was the unanswered question: why?

Zogger then passed a photograph that had been an Exhibit in the Case across their eyes. She held it close to Canker and then to Hornet and Qualm. Each of them gazed intently at the image. Their collective confusion increased as the image etched on their eyeballs was of the charred carcass of Molly.

She played the blowtorch on the tool from the tube

making it red-hot and then white-hot. She brought the miniature branding iron to each of their foreheads in turn. She pressed on Qualm and passed to Hornet and Canker. Scream on scream came out, tripled. Before, during and after they were branded, their screams hit fever pitch. Their skin sizzled like a shrunken savloy. It was skin-deep. They were branded for the world to see the truth: ANAL.

Zogger didn't hear their screams. She was there to earn her wings.

The trio watched closely, hypnotised, as Arnold and Chrysler and Floyd began digging three holes. None of the band spoke. Each of the trio was placed in a hole. They were buried right up to their necks. Placed so they faced the abattoir. The animals had been taken to the Market on the previous Friday. The next cargo was due on Monday. Whilst the band were busy digging, Zogger drove the cattle-lorries, the fork-lift trucks and all the transporters into the centre of the warehouse. She tipped the skins in a pile. In that area at that time was all that the trio had borrowed, mostly stolen and occasionally even worked for over the years. It was the complete heap of their winnings. Everything they possessed. The eyes of the trio were focused on their future.

Zogger gained some useful knowledge from the brief. She knew the abattoir was not insured. That is, not under-insured or on a voidable contract, it was not insured at all. They kept everything secret. Hidden from anyone who might want to know. In their wildest nightmares they never dreamed it would end like this. Their eyes were trained on the abattoir doors, flung wide open and jammed with trucks and the tools of their trade. Zogger used Qualm's Zippo to light the lorry in the middle. It erupted and spread to the whole gallimaufry, causing a cauldron

207

that rapidly became a blazing furnace. Simultaneously the band torched the warehouse. The dead animals formed a pyramid. Skin upon skin piled high as an early Fawkes bonfire. The trio could see their life's work form a burning mass, scarlet flames flying towards the sky. Everything they had was taken. Every penny they possessed was destroyed and they couldn't do a thing to shift the pangs that skewered them.

Arnold and Chrysler and Floyd and Zogger caught the crossfire of each other's thoughts and then glanced at the trio. It was a beautiful sight. Each of the trio was crying. Small, silent, wasted tears rolled down their cheeks. Such a sight as to make a cat laugh. For the band their tears revealed their defeat.

Zogger was glad their life's work would soon be reduced to ashes. The events of this night would haunt their daytime nightmares every time they ate and spoke and had a shite. The silence of it all enhanced the glory. Everything about them was broken without a word being spoken.

'Yeah. Yeah.' Deke shouted to himself as the flames flew higher. Deke hid in the shadows watching from a distance with shared ecstasy. He had the feeling you get when heart and mind and soul dovetails to join ideals to deeds. It was knowing you counted for something in a world full of phonies. All five looked at Qualm and Hornet and Canker in their sabotaged state and felt nothing for them. Save for contempt.

Just then Qualm, still desperately trying to make sense of it all, saw the glint of the moon and the Harley's lamp catch the strands on Zogger's velvet collar. No, no, it just couldn't be, surely? He asked himself. His confusion increased with each question. Yet the deep red hair was unmistakable. It couldn't be, could it? Not that black bitch, that scummy lawyer? Why? What have I ever done to her? He continued to be riddled with unanswered questions. It couldn't be about some dumb animal's death. It can't be her. It just can't be. Must be some stuff I done. Maybe the E's playing tricks again. The thoughts rebounded in his mind. He wasn't sure if it was a reflection from the fire or the masked 'man' really had red hair. He wasn't sure now if it was a man. He wasn't sure anymore of his own name. His confusion circled his scarred mind.

She tilted her head and stared at the sky. As the flames flew on upwards, the fiery signals seemed somehow to say to Zogger: 'This is for you. A torch to your memory. You're not forgotten, Molly.'

Zogger and the band rode off in the wild night as heroes on Hogs across the desert sky, their sickles like shiny saxophones moving through the music of timeless dreams. They had been there and knew it. All at once they were T. E. Lawrence and Steve McQueen and Captain America and the Wild One Johnny. You could even feel the phrase tattooed on her heroine's heart as Zogger smiled secretly like a contented Buddha, thinking about Qualm and his ilk: 'You ask what's my problem? What's my beef? Well hell man, how long you got? Let's start with you!'

Tonight she had found a purpose. She had come alive. Riding behind the other three, she was listening to the voice of her own nirvana. They rode off looking like the Four Horsemen of the Apocalypse and in the strangest, most prophetic way, that is what they were. A moving message for animal abusers of the world. A kinetic streak, they rode as one back to the van. Their mood was matched by the music of their hearts and heroes. As Zogger rode towards her destiny, she clamped the cans to her ears, just in time to hear the last refrain of the acoustic version of Moondog Johnny as the *Working Class Hero*.

Goodbye-Palladium-Blues

Once Chrysler grabbed Qualm and frogmarched him from the lavatory to the outside yard, Deke took advantage of the darkness to escape. Deke snuck out of the warehouse and ran, as planned, down the lane towards the bands' Cochise RV van. He was out of harm's way and couldn't be fingered, when the time came, as a possible suspect. Before he reached the van he stopped, attracted by the sparking flames and their sounds. "Woowww!" Screened by the trees he shuffled down low, listening to the siren screams of the trio. He crept through the bushes, moving around the inside perimeter of the fence, to see it all. He saw the band still looking grand. Proud, he felt like the Fifth Horseman. He saw the three butchers he worked for, buried up to their necks in freshly-dug earth. He was not close enough to see the pain and panic in their eyes. He was content to see the lorries and the abattoir pyre as the fire climbed to brighten the black sky. Occasionally a gentle wind fanned the flames, forcing the sweet destruction. Deke was mesmerised.

Deke watched the band watching the butchers watching the flames and could hardly drag himself away. Since he was a child something about fire always fascinated him. Now he saw its power. Deke was transfixed in the bushes as he saw the blue and red and white/chrome and black electric steeds ride through the mood indigo night. The Hogs, together a picture of mechanical beauty, purred and shimmered in the moonlight. Aware of what this night meant, he wondered if he and Zogger could ever turn their own clocks back.

They all met back at the van and continued in silence with the plan. There was no time to lose or waste. As a well-oiled machine, they complemented each other's actions. Floyd lowered the ramps, Arnold and Chrysler gently pushed the Harley's up them and into the back of the van. They were placed back-to-front, two on each side and secured by chains, then covered by platforms that hung overhead.

Zogger got in the front with Deke doing the driving. The others were too hyper to concentrate on the road. They remained in the back. All of them sat there in silence, front and back, quietly breathing in the contented air. Energy flowed between them. On the side of the van as it noisily sped through the night was their legend: no compromise. As usual, Deke was driving far too fast.

"Move your hand, Jacques," Neena Wayman said, as Phrostés' fingers moved up to the top of her black police issue tights. He ignored her. As he fumbled in the dark his jagged index finger nail almost snagged them again. She grabbed his hand. "Look."

"What is it now? I'm busy." Phrosté raised his head a little from her thigh, strained his neck and looked out the window of the Vauxhall.

"That van, it's moving at some speed. Driver's probably drunk or drugged or both. Let's pull them over. Have a bit of fun."

"I thought we were."

"One of us, maybe. Anyway, we're on duty. Now get your hand off my privates, sergeant."

The marked police car raced after them down the M4. The blue lights whirred and the sirens wailed as it overtook their van on the inside. They pulled in front and Wayman switched the red sign on. It glowed 'Stop'.

"Shall I?" Deke asked, turning left to look at Zogger.

212

The first words he spoke as he drove. He gave a tired smile and gripped the wheel. His foot was poised on the pedal, ready to pump it to the floor. He tapped his toe in time.

"No, no. Just pull in. Get real. We'll deal with it," she said.

The two cops got out and walked towards the van. Zogger blew her harmonica like Little Walter. Then slipped it into her top jacket pocket. The sound was a sign for the boys in the back. As soon as they heard it they sprang into action, shifting the overhead platforms. With the platforms in position, a few cushions and magazines were carefully, carelessly scattered. Their gear was stacked against the platforms. The rest of the inside was taken up with a few old amplifiers and odd instruments.

Wayman, a road-rat cop, asked Deke a set of routine questions, where they'd been and where they were going. She asked for his licence. Deke was wise to it all. He almost charmed her.

Zogger sat there quietly trying to catch Phrosté's eye. She did. It was a sickly-sweet schoolgirl tease smile that made Phrosté think he was in with a chance. She wanted to distract him from the back of the van. Taking the bait, he asked, "Are you playing locally or do you prefer to play away?"

"Depends. We might be. What did you have in mind?"

"Now, that's a question. I'll think about an answer if you-..." His voice had the smile of a paedophile.

Wayman heard his smarmy words, the same kind he'd used on her. She interrupted his flow. "Everything in order, Sergeant?"

"We'll be off then," he said. The smile ran from his face.

WPC Wayman and DS Phrosté walked from the cab.

213

Deke and Zogger gave a side-glance to each other. They were relieved. Wayman stopped, turned around. "Just a minute. Can we have a look in the back?" she asked Zogger.

"'Course. No problem." Zogger jumped out and walked slowly to the back to the van. She jangled the keys. She fiddled to find the right one and unlocked it. Her heart beat faster than Moon on a high. She tried to remain calm as her palms began to tingle. The keys felt heavy. She twice gave an embarrassed cough, her voice locked and dry with nerves. In opening up the back, she caused some din. Deliberately. She swung the back doors wide open. The tip of her tongue touched her top lip.

The officers scanned the inside of the van. Though there was a small light on each side, both officers shone their torches. Arnold and Chrysler and Floyd were playing poker while the Bosch portable radio played some Motown memories. The band looked up, holding their hands in front of their faces, each blinded by the beam. To the inquisitive passer-by or any nosy cop they looked to be what they actually were: another band on the run.

"Sorry boys," Wayman said and moved the light to the top and back of a van. Phrosté switched his off. Seeing the amps, leads, the instruments and cases, she asked, "Where were you playing? Was it a good gig?"

Before they could lie, Zogger intervened. She had her mind on an alibi. "No, we haven't played yet. We're on our way now, officer. An All-Nighter at Oxford. That's why we were, perhaps, just above the limit. I'm not sure. Sorry about that, if we were."

"Don't you worry about it," Phrosté said. He licked his lips. He kept his tongue visible.

"Oh, thank you, Sergeant," Zogger said, still showing

her post-teenage, teasing smile. "You're too kind. I hope I wasn't going too fast."

"Thank you, Sergeant," Wayman said. She spoke in a broken glassy tone. She looked at Zogger. "We've got work to do. Are you ready, Sergeant? Good night."

"Evening all," Deke said, stood erect and saluted. The band laughed like open drains in a burst main. The cops did too. Zogger took her harmonica out and played the theme from Hot Fuzz. The nervous laughter infected them again. The cops waved and disappeared from view.

"I'll drive," Zogger said. She took the keys from Deke. He climbed into the passenger seat.

Phrosté and Wayman resumed their touch of mutual lust to kill the boredom. After their paired rocking in the Vauxhall, each made up the their Notebooks to cover the time. Both signed each other's Notebooks. Anyone inspecting either later would see they claimed they saw a band at Oxford. While they were busy searching for drugs and trying to execute a warrant. Their lies would cover their illicit tickle. By chance they would also provide an alibi for the band.

Zogger drove through the night back to the All-Nighter at the Airfield near the Charles Hardin Airport in Oxford. It was just after 3.30 a.m. when they arrived. They were still flying. The adrenaline was in full flow through their veins, their pupils were round and starry and their movements twitchy. They were hyper without trying. "Okay. You all know what to do. Make it spacy," Zogger advised them as they split up. "Mix it. I'll see you all backstage in ten."

The band played a set earlier and then zoomed down the Motorway to torch the abattoir. They had to be quick so

215

they wouldn't be missed and could set up an alibi. It had to be seamless. Being stopped by the police outside Newbury could have posed a problem. As it was their problem was solved by the lies and lust of those cops.

The band knew exactly what to do. "Put it there, my man. Put it there," said Floyd. Straightaway they slapped a few hands, grinning and gurning through the crowd; going completely over the top so everyone would remember how out-of-it they were. They mingled backstage with the liggers and made out they were out of it on every kind of junk that was on offer. The band had strong views on hard drugs and eschewed their use. On that they were as one. They knew hard drugs only served to enervate and ultimately destroy the only thing of value humans had, will.

Anyway, all in all it now suited their purpose to feign the musos stand of being unable to stand. As the unpawned painter allows dull bankers to become rich while he starves garret-style, so it is with soft musicians who fall prey to the time-honoured trap of drugs, giving carte blanche to the swindling managers and avaricious record companies to siphon off the royalties and hike up the expenses without protest from their prodigy. When the musos discover the unvarnished truth, it's always far too late. Without will they are nothing. So they are forced to veer between the twin evils of financial and mental suicide. Another route as Highway 61 crosses 49; another ride towards a self-inflicted menticide. So it goes. Another hit-and-run victim on the endless road of rock 'n' roll.

"Hey. How are you Zogger?" some wild-haired woman asked. Hair sprouting in pink curls. She was a picture, as pretty as pink purslane. From head to toe her clothes matched her hair.

216

"Oh, great man. How's about you? You look terrific. The hair. Wow."

"I'm driftin', really driftin' Zogger."

"Keen boots," Zogger said. "Tough and true. Like you, hey. Whaddaya say?"

"You think so?"

"I really do. You're too much."

"Thanks, Zogger." She looked at her muddy, pink Timberland boots and skipped off happily to spread the news. "Zogger was hip. I talked to her for ages. I don't know what she was smokin', but she was floating on some serious stuff. She was really real. Believe it. I can't wait for their next set. They'll be roarin'."

"Chrysler, you gonna play again tonight?" a fubsy, bald, drunken journalist asked. "I want to do another review. Your last set was fantastic." He looked as if he'd left his dirty mac at home.

"Yeah. We're just havin' a breather, time for a joke an' a smoke. Anything you want? Anything you'd like to hear?"

"You serious?"

"Anything at all. Name it."

"What about Pagliacci's Return? That's brilliant," he slurred. "Song of the Century."

"See what I can do, my friend. Just for you."

"What a song. Zap it, man," his mate said. He was scruffy enough to be a journalist too. A classic comb-over and tattered jeans dragging on his trainers. You could see he'd get some pleasure from entrapment though he'd make his excuses and leave before the arrest. Though he thought he was 'down with the kids', he looked old enough to be most of the fans' grandfather. Only one thing Chrysler

217

hated more than a journo, two of them. He offered Chrysler a chillum. "Have a toke? It's top stuff."

Chrysler kept up the banter, his fixed jaws starting to ache, ending with "Thanks", as he took the pipe and pretended to suck. "Hey. Heavy. Lebanese too. Tasty." He laughed. They laughed. For different reasons everyone was happy.

In turn each of the band went through the same motions for the same reason with the same desired result. The dividends would be paid when the wrong answers, were given by the fans, to the right questions from the ever-present undercover cops.

The music was always less important than the image. It was why some average pub band from Eel Pie Island were still playing decades later, using nostalgia as their pension. Another peculiar part of the music business is that if you didn't ritually destroy your mind with drink and drugs, you had to act as if you had. For if you're not odd or acting as if you're odd, you were naturally thought to be odd. A daily dose of madness proved you were sane.

Here it suited the bands' purpose. Here it gave them a camouflage as to why they were not backstage. Everyone assumed they'd been out front to score. Much more importantly, it gave them an alibi. For they had been on stage from about 10 to 11p.m. the night before and now they were back. Everyone, fans and friends and fellow musos, would presume – which in time would become nothing less than proof – that they were there all night. People who relied on their mood and memory would genuinely, albeit mistakenly, swear that the band played for three hours solid, that various members sat in with other bands and even that they shared a spliff or two with Zogger. Why, they'd swear they could even recall the colour of the Rizla leaves. Moreover, none of them had any reason to lie. At once the band had about three thousand ready-made witnesses to confirm their alibi. Time would make the fans' feelings cast-iron. The police couldn't break down their alibis. Their investigation would soon become a stalemate. The fans would've lied anyway. Now they didn't even have to as the hash-fuelled memories provided their own kind of truth.

Then what the crowd had been waiting for happened. The band took the stage again as the claps and shouts grew louder than the clamour at a debauched judges' convention. The pent-up fury of the fans and band spread across the airfield. The band looked wonderful. Like bands used to do. Slim, almost skinny, like The Beatles in their old-fashioned bathing suits at Weston-Super-Mare. Like Grace at Candlestick Park. Like Patti at Brooklyn Church. They pounded out song-after-song with fervour, the energy and belief mixed with their committed down-home blues and rock and roll. Full-on rhythm. They made and wore their music as hard-core troubadours. The first song, Snow Queen, was a driving Tex-Mex love song with a hint of Steve Earle. Deke and Zogger sang it as a duo on the chorus and she led on the verses. Up there in the spotlight they looked handsome. Their voices rang like Emmylou and Gram. Their voices melded as natural as warm summer rain and for no better reason than a shared adolescent love of the music and its roots. Having played the whole song through, they were driven by the crowd to repeat the last line of the last verse over and over again: 'I'm locked and lost in the heartbeat of your heart.' Right from the start the crowd took over the song and repeated the phrase until the signal to end came with the drummer juggling with his sticks. Floyd then twirled them through his fingers, quickly crashed the cymbals and threw them into the crowd. Such a sure touch drove the crowd crazy as they scrambled for the sticks. It was a little trick he borrowed from Jerry Allison.

Zogger gave a wry triumphant cry then burst into, Somebody Loses Somebody Wins. It was a lively acoustic song with a hidden killer plant in the middle of the last verse saying, 'it's a funny answer / when I ask you who's your loved one / you say love's a cancer'. When she wrote it, it seemed so right because sometimes that's simply the way it is. She believed there was no time to fool when love is used as a weapon. It was why she finished with Deke. She wrote the song to explain her pain. He thought it was only a song about love gone wrong. Too close to the truth to recognise it.

After that and a few fiery rockers that burned holes in the floor, where boot heels stamped like litho presses with the harmony of abandon, they sang what was to be the penultimate song, Pagliacci's Return. A well-crafted song full of irony and ideals, both black and bleak, that ended with a yearning for freedom.

The last two verses said it all.

Bring on the dancing girls and serve up my head on
   a plate
The Saturnalia's over and I've really lost a hold on
   fate
   Ah! But do I care
The Fat Lady's mirror shows the haunted effigy of
   Hermann and Rudi Hess
And the face has a trace of a crooked smile and a
   boyish wish to confess

Estragon has been waiting in vain so long he now
fades into nothingness
For the tragedy is over let the comedy begin

The shrill of the whippoorwill unfolds a tale no
tongue could quell
My heart sank lower knowing I was guilty of the
crime passionnel
Ah! But do I care
The star-kissed nightmare funeral feel unleashed a
force too strong not to reveal
And the rebel-poet's chanson spun a whirlpool
wound that will now surely never heal
And the last frame of Love Me Tender froze forever
on the broken down reel-to-reel
For the comedy is over let the tragedy begin.

Normally when Zogger sang that song, she got to the last
verse and her voice cracked with the feeling of a
cracksman who knew he had the right combination.
Tonight her vision and voice were matched by the sky as it
too cracked with a shot bolt of lightning. It was as if the
gods themselves knew this was no ordinary night. It was
something special to see the whole crowd sway with the
magic of mutual emotion from stage to floor and back
again.

As the night got blacker the songs got bolder and all
their voices spun a web of ecstasy. This night would
change lives. Some would meet for the first time and
interlock their fates. Some would be stirred into the feeling
that mediocrity is death and resolve to change their
destiny. Some would only glimpse the lightning before
death. But the band would do their utmost to make that

choice no choice at all. Everyone there knew it was special. As the lightning struck a feeling of unspoken glory passed between the band that, for the moment at least, only they could share.

With emotion running towards a natural zenith, Deke and Zogger harmonised on the last song. It was a bitter-sweet ballad called, For W, that Deke wrote for his wife when they first married. People criticised them at the time saying it wouldn't last. They were both teenagers. Much too young. They knew it was untrue. She was besotted. His love for Wanda Jillson was real. He would often see Wanda's face as all the trappings of the hospital and the surgeon's words flashed before him and cut him beyond the bone. He poured his feelings into the song. The song was a moving neo-hymn written when their love and life was young, but now was a fugue. It celebrated her early death from contaminated blood in a bungled transfusion after being hit by a drunk driver. Her fate was sealed by a foreign doctor with had an inadequate command of English. All the fans knew the story, so the message for those born to be lonely, was understood. The detractors were right on one thing though. It didn't last. She died before their third anniversary.

The song was written as a sort of poem to her for her birthday, but the words were so strong, Wanda coaxed him to add music. When he sang it he could see himself writing the poem during an all-night vigil at her hospital bed as the heartbeat jumped across the green screen. His sleeping bag at the side of her bed. He closed his eyes and could see the drunken slob who mowed her down within a few yards of her doorstep. The neighbours tried to stop him leaving the scene. When Deke sang it, the poignancy of the song caused his voice to lock as the memories seeped to the surface. He sang it with a tenderness that could make a heart gently bleed. He couldn't help himself. He constantly remembered how the driver escaped with a fine. Later, the miscreant smiled as he won his licence back on Appeal. While Deke's young wife lost her life.

After that he met Zogger, who he saw as Wanda reincarnate. She was very similar in appearance and dress and all. He wanted a mother. Zogger wanted a lover. When they met each of them had too many burdens ever to be free. When they split they had too many memories to escape. Two broken hearts that could never be mended.

"Are you going to do the next song on your own?" Zogger whispered to him.

He knew what she meant. He paused and answered, "Yes."

"Are you sure? It's okay if you don't want to."

"No. I'm fine. Let's go."

Sometimes, despite repeated requests, it was simply too painful to sing. Then he just let it be. The rest of the band knew not to push it. Tonight, the soul and spirit of singer and listener met.

Zogger moved slowly to the mike on Deke's right. She announced the singer and the song and gently strummed a D minor chord on her old battered but beautiful 1961 Stratocaster. Chrysler stood almost motionless and tapped his right foot in time with his plucking of the Hofner violin bass, running a solid rhythm as natural as a musical river. Deke opened in fine voice on the centre mike, holding his original miked-up Martin D-28 acoustic aloft like his hero, Willie Nelson. The steel strings rang true as he finger-picked a dancing clawhammer borrowed from Big Bill himself. Somehow he got through the song. Here and there his voice almost locked and disappeared. He looked to the sky as if someone up there was giving him inspiration.

On the last verse he needed help from the whole band and the audience too as by then only emotion carried him through:

I want you W, one through to two
Would be a magic, mathematical proof
If I could have you my world-dreams would come
    true
I want you more than Shakespeare wants words.

When the last word was sung he was drained, but delirious. Deke was almost spent.

Arnold let his hands rest on the Hammond and defined a soft, musical marshmallow, Billy Preston riff. He was content to look to the others in the band and soak up the unbridled feeling that flowed through them. They exchanged looks as if to say, 'we did it, man.' They appeared as happy as a cat with a goldfish in the milk.

They had intended that to be the last song. The reaction of the crowd, who clapped long and loud, made them feel proud and changed their minds. Deke was shot and could only hold the emotion and let the rhythm rock through him. Zogger smiled as if her eyes were lit from behind by a church candle. Floyd pounded out a Sandy Nelson drumbeat while the steel guitar pumped with the sound of a train almost being derailed. It was followed by the straining voices of Zogger and Chrysler, who swapped his Hofner for a Guild J-200, that he slapped with a new-found energy.

There was only one song the band could end with, their signature tune: Goodbye-Palladium-Blues. It was a quicksand, rockabilly, roller-coaster classic. They had already sung it, but it warranted a reprise. The song moved in time to the wheels of a runaway locomotion. A beat you couldn't resist, though the theme was deceptive. At first listen it sounded like a happy-go-lucky ditty, but on a deeper level the song bristled with disguised desperation. The singer sold his story in a few verses that moved from ambition and optimism to pessimism and despair.

The words carried the message that finally everyone is alone:

Hey Mr. I'm just about freezin' inside this subway in
  the rain
And the pain's so bad that I really don't have to
  feign
  How long can a poor boy wait
  For fate to unlock its gate
  Meanwhile I'm dyin' too.

On the word 'too' the music and singing ended abruptly as if cut off at its source. A knife through a heart. No sound at all. That was intentional. The result was a body-blow that released the tension as a burst of steam. The crowd stood motionless as the very word floated above their heads. When the sound sliced the air and stopped, everyone knew there was nothing left to give. The band looked at each other, at the crowd and back again. The sharp silence was part of the ritual. It hung in the air for about two minutes, then the crowd took over. They began the bolo motion like punch-drunk pugilists. Suddenly, in time with the multiple-bolos of the crowd, the clouds rolled and the sky rocked with a rhythm of reeling thunder. Lightning then spread its thin white fingers across the

225

black blanket sky. A meeting of sound and spirit and living in that moment. Magical.

The clouds opened and the rain that was threatening all day drenched the airfield, stage and all. The army of rock 'n' roll nomads didn't notice the rain. The Dead-Head feeling that transcends the music and moves between fan and artist, along a wavelength of understanding, ran deep. Like Jerry at the Bay. It was the feeling that sprung up from the beginning when Hellsucks, or whatever they were called then, played church halls and back rooms of pubs. Even the long-time fans could sense there was something special, more than mere focus. Tonight was it. You couldn't be there and be unaware. Pure.

The band stood on the stage drenched in sweat and a misty-eyed feeling. Everything became one as their birthright and the Blues fused. The roar of the crowd continued to surge in waves. No one wanted the night to end.

An aura enveloped the band as they glanced at each other and knew they had to go. Otherwise they'd be sleeping on the stage. They held their arms high and left the stage with sparkly eyes. As he left, Floyd flung the two sticks high into the arena. They went to their trailer. All five flopped down, exhausted yet hyped-up. Floyd turned on the radio and tuned into Andy Kershaw. "I'll bet the two Johns are rockin' in Heaven tonight to that one," he said as the last chorus of Teenage Kicks rammed home its message of adolescent longing and lifetime dreams. There were no words necessary, now even more than usual. The five felt moxie as only those with the freedom to feel they were doing what they were born to do could know. No excuses, no apologies. Living the Blues everyday. He introduced his friend from Venice Beach. The band

226

listened closely as all Kershaw's ramblings were knowing. You could hear the milk crate being shifted and a gloved hand brush the bronze Martin strings on his Dreadnought. "You alright, Ted? O.K. After 4. 1-2-3-4." Then Teddy Picker Hawkins, singing as he always did with head-on spunk, sounding as if his life depended on it, delivered *The Weight*.

If You Could Read My Mind

"He should've been home by now," Tracey said. "I've tried and tried to get him on his mobile and there's, there's no, like, reply. I can't understand it 'cos he's always got his phone. It's like a growth on his ear. You know." Nerves were trapped in her laugh. She gripped the phone.

"Don't worry madam," said 'JJ' O'Hara, the Custody Sergeant. "I'll send a car out. I'm sure we'll soon have it sorted out."

Qualm's worried wife phoned the police when he failed to arrive home. It wasn't unusual for him to be so late, but she sensed he might have met his nemesis. The sixth sense of a spouse. That feeling always lurked in her mind. She knew him so well. "I'd go myself," she said, "but I've got a kid to look after." Before she called, she rehearsed it in the bathroom mirror; the words and the phoney emotion. She was afraid the police might visit in her absence and find their house stacked with the fruit of his illicit labour. Tracey was happy to share in the profit from his scams. The rewards offset her anxiety.

"I understand. We'll call you when we have some news, madam" O'Hara said. "It's probably just some problem with his van. You have a good night's rest. Everything'll look different tomorrow. Good night, Mrs. Qualm." His mood reflected her act.

The cops arrived at the abattoir and found the trio in a suspended state of shock. "What happened here? You shouldn't go burying yourself like that, the tide might come in," D.S. Kenneth Tapette said. "Have you got the owner's permission to dig holes on his land?"

228

"They don't seem to be saying much, Sarge," D.C. Stanley Sheetwind said. "Do you think they're trespassers?"

The trio, buried up to their necks, stared straight ahead, their eyes blank with a cold fear. They could hear the quips of the cops, but the words sounded like muffled Morse messages to their ears. "Call the Fire Brigade, Stan. Tell them to bring a couple of shovels."

"It's not an emergency, is it, Sarge?"

"We don't want to disturb them too quickly. Besides, the soil will keep them warm."

About three-quarters of an hour later they were freed by two firemen, Maurice Cole and William Melody, then taken to the Shepton Mallet Royal Hospital. They were checked over by Dr. Sid Falco. He told each of the trio much the same thing. "We'll arrange an appointment for an operation. Meanwhile, we'll close the wounds. Be careful in your, um, daily ablutions." Thereafter, aided by Sister Fatima Smith, he gave the trio a series of sutures. After being stitched up, the trio were released, each still sore where it hurt the most.

Speculation by the trio was still rife as to who the assailants were. They felt there had to be more to it than a pony. Perhaps the pony had some pedigree and so valuable? Maybe it was owned by one of the notorious Seville Brothers or the Pills Gang? They knew it had to be something serious, if only because no one would risk their wrath just because of an ass. But what was it?

They talked about it constantly and knew it had to be something more than some dumb donkey. They concentrated instead on their numerous enemies. That appealed to them more as it meant they could exact some kind of revenge on someone for a kind of reason. If they picked the wrong one, well, who cares?

Although Qualm alone had an uneasy feeling about the attack that wouldn't disappear, for the main part they believed it was probably the henchmen of Scotty Randolph. Scotty, conceived after his mum, Yankee Madge, saw her favourite cowboy actor at the Brick Lane Ritz, was involved in every scam going from prostitution to protection, mayhem to murder and all in between. Randolph was a street thug who practised the art of violence until he became a master. He'd arranged a massive fraud on EEC subsidies. However the trio made a foolish move when they reneged on the deal. A disgruntled cop ready to retire, turned informer for Randolph because the big bung for naming Qualm added to his lump sum. So the trio knew a timely visit from Scotty's boys was bound to happen.

Tracey kept the cops at bay after Qualm's release from hospital. She still wanted him to go to them rather than them visit her. Canker and Hornet listened to her and lay low. A week later, by appointment, the police interviewed the trio.

Qualm was at the Behan Police Station, sat in the Waiting Room reserved for guests of the police rather than common criminals. It used to be bugged, but they stopped because three posh judges in the Court of Appeal disapproved of the practice. It didn't sit easily with their cricket-green rules of fairness. No doubt they never had a machete jabbed in their judicial ribs at midnight.

Canker was last to be interviewed. When he returned, Qualm directed questions at him. "You didn't say anything to them, did you? About who it might be?" Qualm switched to Hornet. "Or you?" Each shifted in their seats under his questions. "You know, we're not under arrest? We're only here helping with their enquiries. I hope you didn't?" Qualm bared his black teeth.

"No, I didn't," Hornet said.

"You?" Qualm asked, shifting his gaze. He pointed at Canker.

"I didn't either," Canker said. "After all, what do I know, except I'd prefer a daily dose of dysentery to another visit."

"I thought you had that anyway," Hornet said.

"No, I never had another visit."

"Remember," Qualm said, "like old Georgie always says, 'keep schtuum'. You got it?"

They both shook their heads. A cloud of fresh fumes rose from their bodies. All three still had a stale stench about them, of fags and fire and fear.

Qualm had all but stonewalled them. The others delivered stale stories and fresh lies. After the interviews the Notebooks of Tapette and Sheetwind remained almost blank. The trio gave them little in the way of evidence and less in the way of truth. Nevertheless they must have said something right, as they never heard from the police again on the identity of the mysterious visitors. Truth to tell the cops didn't try too hard.

Qualm didn't say anything to the police about Deke as it would have exposed his tax scam. He couldn't begin to believe some scruffy student would have the bottle to betray him, so it didn't even enter his head. In his own way he liked Deke anyway.

Deke arranged to collect his bike and be interviewed at the Behan. A week later the police interviewed him as they were interested in why he was not a victim of the violence.

"I just ran for my life. I saw the fire, heard the

explosion, the revving motorbikes and the screams," Deke said. "I just ran. It was ineffable. I've never heard screams like that before. I never want to again. Night after night, I wake up screaming, still hearing those screams." He closed his eyes. "I can hear them now." He stopped, paused, trying to find the right words. Then added, "At least I wake up. Then I can forget the screams – until the next night." He went to speak, but didn't.

"We know it's a painful memory, but help us as best you can," said Tapette.

"Well, there was a small army of Hell's Angels. Reprobate types. All beards, tattoos and studded boots. Scary and ugly, really ugly. Pruny, like old Mickey Yeager. The dead rock singer."

"He isn't dead, he just looks like that. Could you see their faces?" Tapette asked.

"I don't know, I suppose, only in the darkness. You know, like I said, they all had beards. And only in profile anyway."

"Could you identify any of them? At a Parade."

"No, not really, they were just figures in the dark. To be honest, I don't want to remember them."

"So you didn't see their faces face-on?" Sheetwind asked, feeling he ought to say something. "We could get an artist to make a sketch and show you a VIPER Parade of photos, if that'll help you. It's a new scheme. You might be able to pick one or two out?"

"I doubt it. I did a runner as soon as the lights fused. I only stopped and looked back to make sure they weren't following me. Scared. I tell you I was so scared I..I..I don't mean to be crude, but I nearly, well, to be brutally honest it wasn't nearly-…"

"Don't worry, we know," said Sheetwind "It's natural. We see, well smell, the fear all the time."

"That's why I left my bike behind. I couldn't ride it, like. I came in today to collect it."

"How many were there?" Tapette asked.

"About ten. Maybe more. There must've been from the noise."

"What do you know about ANAL?" asked Sheetwind.

"What, like, gay sex? Mucky. I'm against it. It's illegal, isn't it? If not, it ought to be. Chop it off. I'm with the Turks, but only on that."

They explained the background and the reason for their questions. Sheetwind ended with, "Of you four, the other three, your employers, were all burned on their foreheads. So you see we're a bit confused, intrigued you could say, as to why you alone wasn't branded with ANAL."

"I can't really help you on that. Like I told you, I just scarpered. When I heard that commotion, I wasn't going to hang around to find out who caused it. I mean, I wonder if it was anything to do with drugs. Maybe they were high on drugs and just chanced upon the abattoir, by good or perhaps bad luck – if you know what I mean. Them Bikers are a law unto themselves. Dangerous when they're drunk, deadly when they're drugged. Bloody anarchists, if you ask me. "

"Had you seen any bikers in the area before?"

"There's a lot of open-air raves, illegal obviously, held in the Stakewood, a couple of miles west. Some of them were used as a form of security. Smart decision."

"What, like Altamont?" Tapette asked.

"I don't know them," said Deke. "Are they English?"

"Forget it. Another time, another place," said Sheetwind. "If anything else comes to mind, give us a call. The memory plays tricks. It could suddenly come to you. You might've retained something about ANAL."

"Well, actually, as we've been talking you've triggered

off a few things." Deke then helpfully told them, "Something like ANAL or AMAL was written on a lavatory wall at a recent student dance. It was run by the Psychology Department. At the time the drugs were in full flow and I saw some dropout-types selling pills. Mostly foreigners. Naturally I assumed the tablets were ecstasy or maybe acid. I'm not really sure, but a lot of people seemed troubled until they got the pills." Both cops were paying him too much attention. He continued to embellish the false memories. "ANAL might be like E or MDMA. Could be first taken by gays. You know they love snow even if it's not Christmas. Both A's were in a circle. It could even be a new band or bebop phrase. You sure it was ANAL? Might be a terrorist group if it was AMAL."

Sheetwind was more than curious. "What do you mean? How?"

"Well it just sounds Arabic, that's all I meant. 'Cos there's lots of spicks and dagoes in the Psychology Department. Overrun with them."

"Why's that?" Tapette asked.

"Jungian I suppose. Like the Greeks really. A bunch of hatters too."

"I see," Tapette said. Though confused, he nodded as if it made sense. The cops listened carefully and closely to Deke's ideas. They had no reason to disbelieve him or even suspect him. After all, he was only passing time working at the abattoir and eking out a small grant. No different than they did and their own children would in due course. He seemed helpful enough in his own way.

"Thanks. Don't forget, if anything anal comes into your head be sure to give us a call," said Sheetwind

"You'll be the first to know, Officer," Deke said and waved goodbye.

Neither Tapette nor Sheetwind were very interested in spending time and money pursuing justice for the trio. They knew Qualm and his cohorts well. Both had arrested them more times than they cared to remember. They were every officer's albatross. The cops were ready to write off this incident as part reward and part justice.

After seeing Deke, the police visited the organisers of the raves. A couple of cocaine addicts, Paulo Surley and Marco Paderowski, had used their contacts in the City to fund the enterprise. They neither could nor wanted to help with the investigation. Their amnesia of the events was convenient yet real. Two days later the police visited Randolph at Shepton Mallet Prison. He had a good knowledge of any event that affected him or his boys. He ran his operation on the outside from the inside. He could but wouldn't help them. Scotty liked to settle scores using the only law that mattered, lex talionis.

On leaving the Prison Tapette related his story on the way back to the police station. He had good reason to remember Qualm. He'd arrested him for rape. Tapette was the first officer on the scene. He thought he'd found a corpse. Qualm had left her for dead. He phoned for an ambulance and arranged for a pathologist. "On the papers the evidence was overwhelming. Besides all the lies we could prove against him, including his supposed alibi, there was forensic evidence, DNA of his semen. As far as I was concerned the case was proved beyond the shadow of a doubt."

"You mean he pleaded not guilty? How could he?" Sheetwind asked. "Any average criminal, let alone rapist, would plead and seek a lower sentence. Then lie to his Counsel, make with some forced remorse and feign he found religion in prison. Claim he's now seeking redemption."

"Maybe. Qualm's not an average anything. A spoiled bully-boy. A one-eyed jacks." Tapette braked hard, the unmarked Civic juddered, as his driving was getting erratic. He continued, "So he fought the case at every turn, not once, but twice."

"Why twice?"

"Just listen. You'll learn." The case still affected him. "You know what that pikey is like. Qualm gambled that the victim would be too ashamed or embarrassed or afraid to give evidence. He knew enough about victims as he'd taken advantage of them all his life. From schoolboy bully, taxing the boy with the lisp or limp to a fully-fledged thug and rapist, Qualm graduated with distinction."

He faltered. Stopped the story. Tapette swerved and swore at another driver, though he was in the wrong. He took a deep breath. "Qualm thought he'd got away with it." Tapette bit his bottom lip, feeling the memory of it all. "He made his victim relive the whole ordeal so, whatever the verdict, her credibility would be smashed and her life never the same again. What made it worse was he enjoyed seeing his victim suffer. She had to suffer hostile question-after-question while the whole world was watching. He loved that. You could see it. It oozed from his every pore." Tapette sighed and kept unravelling the story. "You have to understand I was there from the first day to the last. I saw the victim parading naked in public. Qualm's eyes burned. Like I say, he loved it."

Tapette was silent for a while, lost in his own misery. His high-voltage frown spread. His ringed eyes wrinkled more than usual. The effect was floating across the lines on his face. He was forty-two, but looked so much older.

He went to say something then just stopped. Spent of words, he stared somewhere into the distance. He was driving far too fast. He gripped the wheel and hunched over. Sheetwind, was almost a decade younger than Tapette and joined the force after him, had only heard the gossip and rumour. Now he heard the unvarnished version.

"So what was the result?" asked Sheetwind "Slow down a bit, Sargeant, I can't hear with the wind." Tapette laughed and slowed down, chuckling, as he was well aware of his reputation for the deadly smell of his foggy silent farts.

"Fair play to the lady – well she was only a girl. A teenager. A schoolgirl."

"Who was the judge? Do I know him?"

"No. It wasn't tried locally. They had to move it out of town – in fairness to the defendant, they said, yeah, usual garbage – as she was from a well-known family of solicitors. Most of the jury would've known her father or at least the firm. The judges and local lawyers knew her father. Well, strictly her stepfather, I should say. They adopted her you see. They were both white. So it was moved to Winchester."

"How was she in the box?"

"I've seen some heavy-duty cross-examinations in my time, but the sort of questions she had spat at her were disgraceful. Qualm insisted on this hatchet-man counsel from London, Jonathan Bruxism, who was cynical and sneering with every question. A total slob. Not so much running to fat as having won a marathon. His double chins and red, moon-faced arrogance still stays with me. So I don't know how it affected her. He pierced her with his cold eyes as each question tore into her. He held up her dress on an Exhibit stick. With his surgical latex gloved hand he picked up and waved her torn knickers at her. He held them high, away from his nose. At arms length as he looked too long at the jury. He ripped into her." Tapette's veins began to rise. His knuckles were white.

Tapette braked, hammered on his horn at the car in front, though it was his fault again. When the passenger turned around, Tapette gave him the single finger. He swore at him through the windscreen. "Perhaps it's time for a coffee, Sarge?" Sheetwind was anxious to avoid an accident and hear the whole story.

"Good idea. I need some straight caffeine."

Tapette swerved and pulled into a side street. They were both unshaved and in plain clothes. Because of the odd furtive way they kept looking around they looked more like drug dealers than undercover detectives. They made their way to the Fat Black Pussycat, a coffee stall at the top of Bemmy, close to the centre of Bristle. Each had a boiling hot coffee in a foam cup. Just hot enough to burn your fingers and scorch the roof of your mouth. Last thing Sheetwind wanted was for Tapette to throw a tantrum. He'd drench some passing stranger and then arrest him for breach of the peace. He'd seen his Sergeant do it so often. No cause, except his temper. "Hold on Kenny, I'll get some more milk," he said, before the expected explosion. It was on hold. He returned. They leant against a lamppost staying close enough to see any action and maybe hear the odd snippet from the regulars at the stall, a mix of would-be villains and old has-beens, all in their own way looking for the next under-the-counter job.

"So what happened?" Sheetwind asked.

"Bruxism kept up the relentless questions. 'Why didn't you run?' 'Why didn't you cry out?' 'Why didn't you hit him?' 'Did you try to scratch him?' 'How much do you weigh?' 'How did he remove your knickers if you were lying on them?' 'Had you been drinking before you met him?' 'Were you a virgin?' The questions were hard-hitting. And hitting home. Designed to demolish her. Total humiliation. You had to feel for her. Everyone in Court did. Except Bruxism. And Qualm, as you'd expect."

"Didn't the Judge intervene? It's part of his duty to protect her. Surely he said something? A witness shouldn't be harassed."

"No, you know the type. Public school, a few GCSE's, top university, scraping a pass degree, the best Chambers and finally a cosy cushion of life on the bench. Followed by a fat pension. For life. A no-hoper and misogynist to boot. A complete J. Arthur. Of all the bozos in the judiciary, – and there's enough of them – we had to get Judge Leon Yeneews. A fop. Believe me, Yeneews was a disaster. But then, when's he anything else?"

"How did she stand up to the questioning? Did she break down?"

"She stood her ground. She was flustered and confused certainly. Who wouldn't be?"

"So the fat-faced twat did a good job?"

"For the defence."

"What, the counsel?"

"No, the Judge. The jury retired, stayed out the whole day. Next day as well. We were getting really worried. You know what it's like. The hours drag. Your nerve ends dance."

"So what was the verdict?"

"There wasn't one. It was a hung jury."

"Oh no! That's about the worst thing that could happen in a rape case. So Qualm got away with it. What a slop bucket."

239

"No, not quite. The prosecution had a week to consider whether they wanted a re-trial. It all depended on the girl. Whether she was willing to give evidence again or not."

"And what happened? Did she?"

"As you might imagine, Qualm, through his lawyer, engineered problems before the decision was made. He wanted to grind her down. Asking for more information, more medical records, a further examination of her school reports. All designed to pile on the pressure. She also had to contend with hate-letters from sleazos. It put a retrial in the balance. The girl you see was just seventeen, if you know what I mean."

"How did it end?"

"Qualm did something really stupid. He saw her out in the street during that week. She was alone. He called her name. When she looked around he gave her the toad-in-the-hole . The old fingers and thumb. At the same time he cackled to try to frighten her."

"What did she do?"

"Fantastic. She bawled the bastard out in the street, crossed between the moving traffic, ran after him and almost got run over. She gave him a tongue-lashing the like of which he'd never known. Something his mother should've done. In that instant she made up her mind to whip his scared arse."

"And did she?" asked Sheetwind. He was now really warming to the subject. His hands clasped the steaming ersatz cappuccino.

"And some. The case, the retrial, came before Judge Jan Rankle who's in a bad mood when he's in good mood. He's in a bad mood if he's not in a bad mood. During the Trial he was in a lousy mood."

"Is he prosecution-minded?"

240

"Is a politician honest?"

"So at least you had that advantage."

"More as it happens. You know how some judges come down heavy on subjects they hate. They may be lenient on dealers, but severe on burglars. Well Rankle hated sex offenders and loathed rapists above all. When he was a 'jungle judge' out in South Africa, some of the religious maniacs and terrorists broke into his home and raped his wife. They tortured her. She never recovered. She was confined to a wheelchair. Shortly after, following numerous failed operations, she became an alcoholic and died in an asylum."

"I thought he was just miserable. It just goes to show."

Rankle was a natural successor to Judge Jeffreys who hung the defendants at Somerset Assizes on the assumption they were guilty. Even if he was wrong, he reconciled it thinking they'd probably committed some crime anyway. Besides, Jeffreys reasoned, 'they couldn't appeal from the grave'.

"So Qualm really got his comeuppance then, I presume?"

"He did and he didn't in the nature of these things," Tapette said. "The girl was brilliant. She had the advantage of the first Trial, which was really a rehearsal. The second time she was able to field the questions better. She resolved not to break down. Nor did she. A bonus was Bruxism was on guard lest he was savaged by Rankle. Even so, believe me, he shredded her."

"What about the verdict? Was it a result?"

"The jury were out for ages and ages, but finally convicted by a majority of 10-2. Everyone was kite-high. Well, everyone except Qualm. He was as happy as a eunuch on honeymoon."

241

"Great. Great story. Even better for being true. So what did he get?"

"Qualm went down for twelve years. There were so many aggravating features and no discount for a guilty plea. He was lucky not to be charged with attempted murder. Initially he was charged with attempted murder, but after a fortnight in intensive care she slowly recovered. Rankle said Qualm was a "Danger to society and all women." The followers of WAR, you know Women Against Rape, who were in court, clapped and shouted. It was like music, to hear and see. Mind you, it was much better seeing Qualm walk down those steep steps to the cells."

"How did Qualm get on inside? He was bound to Appeal, wasn't he? He smiled and added, "At least all's well that ends well."

"Maybe, but all's not well that only ends," said Tapette. "There was an unexpected bonus in that Qualm was seen as a fat white-boy catamite and gang-raped daily by the Yardies. It seems even the Muzzies had a go at him. That was the upside or should I say backside. However the downside was exactly what you hit upon, the Appeal. Qualm found grounds on some technical point of admissibility of the evidence. I can't remember what it was about now, but you know how those obscure points somehow appeal to those curious characters in the Court of Appeal who don't live in the real world. Their idea of a calamity is when their butler dies. They criticised Rankle, quashed the conviction and refused to order a retrial."

"So he finally got away with it after all?"

"Qualm and Bruxism were cock-a-hoop. Those two had a lot in common. I promise you, I was so angry if I'd had a sawn-off I'd have splattered their guts all over the long corridors of the Court of Appeal. I fumed. I was furious. I still am. It's got no better with time. What I'd give to meet him one dark night. It'll happen."

"So he slipped the net once again," said Sheetwind. "This investigation isn't going very far. I'm not going to spend taxpayers' money finding someone who's only done society a favour. They shouldn't have stopped short. They should have burned the bastard alive when they had the chance." He ripped the pages from his Notebook. He crumpled his notes into a rough ball. He flicked his disposable Bic, lit a taper, and watched the flames fly and die. He stamped it underfoot, seeing Qualm's face in the burnt ball. He then asked somewhat sadly, "What happened to the girl?"

"She didn't fare too well. She retreated into herself; became a recluse. Didn't go out at all. She failed her exams and was forced to give up her music studies at the Royal Academy. Her emotions affected her voice you see. At one point she went mute. For almost a year. Finally it came to a head and she had a nervous breakdown."

"That crapbrain! What happened, what about her career? Her singing?"

"She gave up singing as a career. Her voice was shot. She slowly recovered and decided to follow the lead of the family firm. I think she had a sense of duty too. Her mother shared her trauma and never really recovered. The family disintegrated and her mother died shortly after. I don't know if it was related or not. There was, there always is, a lot of talk. I only knew because I had to keep in touch because of the two trials and the Court of Appeal. The whole investigation, you know, took over two years. Anyway, she trained to be a lawyer, but decided to be a barrister. The paraphernalia was useful as it helped provide anonymity. In fact she's very good."

"What do you mean the 'paraphernalia'?"

"All the archaic guff. The wig and gown and 'Learned Friend' bull. She could hide behind that to gain more authority."

"When was this?"

"About ten years ago. Maybe more, you know how time passes." He looked as if he was going to say something, but fell silent. The seconds stretched.

Sheetwind asked, "What's she like?"

"The irony is she became a brilliant lawyer. Though I understand she's kept up her singing as a sideline. She's a good Prosecutor, very effective. Firm, but fair. Her cross-examination is cold steel."

"We need more like that. Not the usual lily-livered ejits the CPS send us."

"Make no mistake, this lady eats defendants alive and doesn't even stop for breath or to belch," Tapette said. Both laughed, seeking a relief. "It's a joy to hear her politely ask a question and then clamp her teeth around the crimo's testicles – figuratively I mean."

"Where does she practice? Do I know her?"

"She practises just outside World's End. She's the meteor of Credo Chambers. I'm sure you must know her. You'd remember her."

"What's she look like? What did you say her name was?"

"Long red hair, slim as a flamingo and foxy. Black girl, well half-caste really. Her name is Zowie Darrow. Mean anything to you?"

"Mmm. I think so. I'm not sure. I'll certainly look out for her now."

Tapette was always fixated, even when he seemed relaxed. Right now, charged with high emotion, it wouldn't have taken much for him to lose it all. Sheetwind was changed by what he had learned. He already had a jaundiced eye. Now it was illuminated by animus. Tapette looked lost, not unusual for him these days. Sheetwind glanced at him and wondered how he got through the day. He looked to him like a living cadaver.

A group of five weighty schoolgirls passed, eating chunky chocolate bars, doo-wopping to the sound from their heavy ghetto blaster. Tapette scanned them and hoped they could be saved. He could see a future mirroring their mothers' past. "I think I've had enough," Tapette said to the wind, unheard, as intended, by anyone else. His face had turned red and sad, bitten by his thoughts and the wind. Tapette became even sadder when he heard the sound from the blaster of the oxymoronic, *Young Hearts Run Free*.

Freefalling

Monday morning found the band bleary-eyed, but mentally wide-awake. They sat facing the steaming windows of their favourite after-gig meeting place. The band always tried to find each other in the Freefall Café. It was a noisy, raucous place just off the M4, down a dirt track that looks like a dirt track. Most of the creatures of the night gathered there when the gig was over. Dickie Pride, the 'Sheik of Shake', called in after his last gig, in every sense. It was run by Ritchie who once played rhythm guitar with Mickey Jupp and that was credibility of a high order.

The Freefall was open all day, every day. Music seeped from the pores of the floors and ceilings as well as its subterranean inhabitants. It sprang from Ritchie who once sang in The White Milk Bar on Canvey Island with Lee Brilleaux in the legendary Teenage Tarantulas.

No one caused trouble or found it. It was a place where a schoolgirl might paint her face in the neon light, hoping to find romance and maybe lose something in the night. There was an original Rock-Ola jukebox that played classic tracks all day and all night. Just like John Lee Hooker, this was hip.

Now it was different, especially for Zogger, because of the night before. Easy like a Sunday. Now it was a manic Monday. The morning-after was not unlike the pill you take to forget the night before, so pregnancy is staved off and the activity becomes a distant memory. Their dancing red eyes proved they felt the pure rush from their first brush with the law, made all the sweeter by the winning.

Zogger realised this was only the first strike. She'd changed radically since the Trial. She had less patience with analysis and moved towards instinct. Time was so precious, it was more important to just do it. Talking towards dawn was irrelevant now.

"So what's next?" asked Zogger. "Where do we strike and when?"

"We've got to rehearse and prepare for the next gigs obviously. We're playing Winchester, Cheltenham and Cardiff soon, and Bristol this weekend," said Deke. "It'll be good to be home."

"Terrific. The Cardiff gig will be great. The Welsh fans are brilliant. They just love the life. You can see their faces lit by lighters like their forefather's with their dim lamps and coughing canaries," Arnold said. He laughed.

"Yeah, yeah, yeah," shouted Floyd and Chrysler in mock baby-boomer fashion, fists raised a-bolo. Everyone laughed in a chain-reaction, loudly, everyone except Zogger. She could barely raise her puckered lips. Even then it resembled a pout.

Ritchie looked over, just catching their eyes, saying nothing, but saying everything. A mock, withering glare. Easily understood. They kept the noise down.

Maybe it was the overcast morning or just her mood, but Zogger could feel her body getting hot. An ache began to gnaw inside her head. She often had that feeling when a testy judge was too crass to understand a simple submission of law. Then, as now, it caused her mind and heart to collide. She said, as low-key as she could, "You lot don't understand do you? I thought you characters had beliefs, had ideas, had direction."

"We have. What do you mean?" Deke asked.

"I asked where we're going to strike next. I've yet to hear an answer." She paused. "I thought you had guts. Vision. I guess I was wrong."

247

"We've got to build on the dream, haven't we? The music-..." said Deke.

"You don't understand, do you?" she said. "Floyd, how do you feel? I have to know."

"Well, yes, the music is the method isn't it?" Floyd said.

"What about you, Chrysler?" Zogger asked.

"I'm not sure where you're at. I'm not sure I want to go there, anyway," said Chrysler. "The music is the life and the life is the music. That's the way it's always been for us. What else is there? Now more than ever with you having quit the law."

Zogger looked down; eyes cast to the floor. Their reaction irritated her to the core. Zogger never wasted words or time. Now the course of her history was held like sand in the palms of their hands. She had to make sure they wouldn't spread their fingers.

"What do you think was the purpose of last night?" she asked Deke. If she had him on her side, she felt the others would be likely to follow. He was always the doubter. The one who'd argue the most and accept no easy answer. He usually enjoyed the joust.

"Those scab arses burned Molly. We just burned them in return," he said.

"No, that was the reason. What was the purpose of last night?"

"To teach the creeps a lesson. And to support you, I suppose."

"No, that's still the reason. What was the purpose?" An edge crept into her voice. It rose on her irritation scale. "Do you get it at all, Deke? Do any of you get it?"

Chrysler intervened. "Hey, lighten up, Zogger. What are you on about? Purpose, reason, this is not a discourse

248

on Descartes, you know. We're only talking about a band that burned a couple of cruel quims. It was just a trip, man. What's with you? What's the deal? Who d'you think you are? Who d'you think we are?"

"That's right," said Arnold. "We've already wasted more than enough time on those tossers. Perhaps we should've just wasted them..." His words trailed off to a loose end. He added, "Let's get serious. We've got a tour to think about."

Her edginess was spreading to them. She sensed it was spreading too fast. Unless checked it would become like a slanging-match at kindergarten or worse, a bunch of braying clowns like Cameron and Brown in the Commons.

"Listen, for once and once only. I won't repeat it," she said. "We started this band, why? Because we decided the world needed something to replace The Band musically and combine it with the philosophy of animal rights. I remember the long late-night verbal rambles that stretched towards daybreak. I remember when you scavenged at night for half-eaten pizzas. I remember when we held audition after audition to find the right people. We rejected numerous fine musicians because they didn't have the feisty live-or-die feeling we needed and demanded. We struggled rather than compromise. What's changed? We never considered surrender. We were special. We had principles you couldn't buy. So what's changed? Nothing!"

"I was at the auditions too remember," said Deke. "We asked what they felt about music being the only priority, who their favourite philosopher was, what was their take on Robert Johnson, what they felt about Salt and a whole bunch of stuff about music and metaphysics. My mind ain't changed."

"I remember too," Arnold said. "Someone, maybe you, asked me how you pronounce the Christian name of Leadbelly. I didn't know then, I don't know now. Isn't the music and the passion enough?"

"That's so right," said Floyd. "We were interested in the person, not just ability. Talent alone is never enough. There are a million musos out there who border on brilliance, but are alkies and strung-out junkies, no use to themselves or anyone else. We know that, we know them. We don't need them. Dollars can't buy you dreams."

"Or love," Deke said.

Zogger said, "You're right, but only partly right. Sure we intended to set the world alight with our music. We wanted to bring the feel of Marion Keisker hearing for the first time a shy nineteen year old white youth singing the blues for his mother's birthday; we wanted to revive the soul of Hank Williams; we wanted to be busy being born not busy dying; we wanted to hold the ashes of Tom Joad; we wanted to be Paine; we wanted to be Blake. But the crux is we all wanted more. We wanted to use our voice to shout for those who can't. We wanted to say, whatever else went down, when it mattered we did some serious stuff. We sure as hell really rocked. I still do, do you?"

She paused. She caught them in her honed vision. "We wanted danger, excitement and, yeah, risk. We wanted to live through our music. We wanted music to be our life. We dared to be different. We dared to be a Daniel. We hardly had to try 'cos we had a font full of faith. More than dreams and love, money can't buy you truth. We dared to be true. I'm still willing, are you?"

"I guess so, yes," said Deke. "It's always been that way." The others agreed.

Zogger cast a glance around the table. She caught their

250

eyes rabbit-and-headlight style making them look into hers, before slowly turning away. She said, "It's one thing to be the best in the world at anything. It doesn't matter whether it's a bricklayer or poker player. Just look at The Mirage Messiahs, they were unquestionably the best. Never before or since equalled or rivalled. At most a few Johnny-come-lately types who then sank without trace, as they deserved."

"What about Mufti Fatwas, they were revolutionary?" said Floyd.

"Save me. Are you serious?" asked Zogger. "If that's your best shot, I might as well shut up and go home now. Those bunch of Zimmer-ridden geriatrics. Just like I Ran Away. Totally unoriginal, carbon copies of whatever was happening. I've heard a crowd of camels being castrated sound better. Best thing they could've done was cover the complete stage in a veil so you couldn't see them. Then turn the amps off. They're about as original as this year's Oasis with even less talent, if that's possible."

Her rapid-fire comments challenged Floyd and cut the others. The balance between her faults and their foibles was tough at the best of times. The tension in their tightrope grew. Floyd was stung. He was once a roadie for the Muftis. He said, "Anyway what's all this about? Where's this taking us? I'm hungry."

"You're always bloody hungry!" she said. "This is more serious than your guts. Instead of always talking about your guts, you'd be better off showing some. If that dumb comment is the best you can make, you may as well let your guts rumble in future. Instead of letting your tongue ramble. At least it would make more sense."

"Ah, shut up. Scut," he mumbled. She let it pass. They all did. A short stifled silence followed. No one quite knew how to break it, but Zogger felt sure she had to take a grip or it would slip right through her fingers.

"Look," Zogger said, "this is my position. When The Mirage Messiahs became what they were meant to be, that wasn't enough. That's why they went to Katmandu, why they experimented with useless quirky religions and drugs. Why they broke up. Our position is different. We know their truth. We must use it to prove our own. That's the raison d'etre of the band. That's our hunger. If you don't see that, then we haven't the same vision splendid. We have no future. Together." Her anger was mixed with a sad seriousness. She scrunched both eyes tighter. Her crow's feet showed white against her reddening face. "No future, as a band or at all."

"But wasn't last night exactly that?" asked Deke. "We were tighter than tight as people and as a band."

"You're right, it was, but that was only the first step. We have to move on. We can change the world by our music and spirit. We proved a million Molly's didn't die in vain. You know our song, 'The Vivisector's Nightmare' – well you co-wrote it so you must know it – that's what we preach. It should be what we practise. You didn't write the song in a vacuum, did you?" She stopped short to meet and catch Deke's eyes, then shifted from him to the others. At that moment an unspoken honesty passed from her to them and back again.

"When we formed the band only two things in the world mattered to us. Above all the normal sell-out jokes like pensions and security and family, we faced the selfish fact we were motivated by animal liberation and music. We pledged to fuse those two in the blues and make it our mission to shift the world off its axis. Have you lost that lovin' feeling?"

252

She smiled gently at the unintended cliché. A heavy awkward silence fell as they examined themselves. They knew their ideals were on the line. They were each asking a powerful question: am I getting too old to force the change? Zogger's face changed again as she appeared more relaxed. It was part act, part resignation. She said, "You're with me or against me. You're being tried and tested by your own standards. Your future is in your own hands. Your choice, your chance, but it may be the end of the band."

At that moment there was nothing more to say by anyone. The words were spent. The moments became minutes. All the expressos were drained. Each of the band, save for her, were searching for an honest courage. Zogger knew she shouldn't break the unwelcome silence. She let it hang. A swift self-examination flowed. Time hung suspended.

Arnold was the first to speak. He was a brilliant organist, though he could play many instruments. From the age of fourteen he was a semi-pro. He was the most intelligent and intellectual of the band. His childhood was straight out of the 'Day of the Jago' and scarred him forever. Yet he fought it all and won. He gained a Scholarship to London University where the study of law and philosophy proved to be his salvation. Arnold was a gifted musician, but equally a wonderful wordsmith, whose lyrics were so potent they jumped off the page and hurt your eyes.

Before he spoke Arnold had a childhood 'flashback' again. Like an involuntary spasm it was impossible to avoid, the thoughts often choked him. He knew he'd never be free of those shackles. "I'm with you, Zogger. I never wanted to be in an average band. I never wanted to be an average anything. I never wanted to see animal cruelty and adopt an ostrich-stance. I knew this day would come and I'm ready. I want to be a monumental failure or a magnificent success. I want nothing in-between. Leave losing to losers." He gulped as his words flowed too fast. "Let me live on my own terms and not die on someone else's."

Floyd, a terrific drummer, versed in all forms of rhythm, had learned the rudiments in the Cadets and played by instinct. He wasn't necessarily quiet, but only said something when it was necessary or useful. Like when he was stung by Zogger's nasty response. He was widely read and would scan anything to hand, be it a cornflake packet or a jumble sale leaflet. On one occasion he spent an hour at the dentist for a routine check-up because he got so engrossed in an article in a two year old edition of Readers' Digest. His parents divorced when he was around twelve years old. It hit him hard. Each parent used him to hurt the other one. Both in turn hurt him. He locked himself in his room, night after night. He retreated into himself, wounded and aching. The turning point for him was reading Animals' Rights, Salt's classic work, which led him to delve into Kant and Spira and Regan and Ryder and Descartes and Spinoza and More and more. He never bothered going to college. His knowledge was gained from reading all day and drumming all night. He read the good and the bad, the soppy and the sentimental, the philosophical and plainly nonsensical. Whether for or against, he imbibed it all. When he had all the material he analysed the position in terms of natural justice. He concluded that humans were involved in a conspiracy where we assume we have absolute and arbitrary rights over animals.

Weighing his words, Floyd said slowly, "I'm up for it. Whatever it takes, you can count me in. I'm not ready to roll over and curl up and die. Let's do it. Let's risk it all."

He could hardly speak, his voice cracked with emotion. He looked directly at her. Now he knew he was right too. "If I don't try, I'm just like all the other butchers and the hunters and the experimenters. By my silence I'll be one of society's executioners. So let me die trying. Roll away the stone."

Chrysler was a fantastic bass player, influenced by everyone from Black to Macca. At heart a pure rock 'n' roller. At face value he was the most balanced of the band having had a middle-class upbringing in Reading. Though face value is as reliable as a hall of mirrors with Janus on each side. His father was a respectable senior civil servant on the outside; on the inside he had a penchant for pornography. In the way of such sick-at-heart characters, he didn't just look at sordid books. As they always do, he graduated to practising his perversions on Chrysler, whose young body and mind were quickly soiled. He locked the dark secrets deep in his troubled soul. At the first opportunity he left home on the cusp of a dream at seventeen. The first thing he did was to change his name. Like one of his heroes, Johnnie Mellors, he dumped his history. He adopted the name of his favourite car and musician. Later, through his prodigious musical talent, he gained a wild card place at the Royal Academy. He supported himself by countless gigs in city bars and clubs throughout London, up West and each side of the River.

When he met Zogger, she helped him to rid himself of the guilt. She'd seen it so many times and the result was always the same. The guilt is shed by the pervert-in-denial and becomes a greater burden for the child. Zogger knew

255

the perverts crossed every class and position. She knew about the Sixties musician, the Tory politician and the Plymouth judge. He would've been a different man without her. She used her knowledge and experience to show Chrysler the secret of survival. Zogger proved to him he was wanted and that's a rare feeling. Chrysler felt close to Zogger. She made him lose and find himself in the music of Hellsucks. As the bass player he was the backbone of the band.

Chrysler almost shouted, "I'm with Zogger all the way. There's been too much talking and where's it got us? I've had enough. There's nothing left to say. Now's the time to act. This is our day, let's take it. Let's give real power to the powerless." He raised his clenched fist, Black Panther-style, as if he was about to receive an Olympian gold medal. Shades of Cleaver.

That left Deke. A great axe man, following in the footsteps Link and Wry, he could make his box talk. He was no pushover. A problem child who became a problem adult. His natural disposition combined a perspicuity with a defined immaturity. Being a man was hardly an excuse.

From an early age he saw all the various experts one-by-one including social workers, a doctor, psychiatrist and psychologist who finally diagnosed him as needing 'special' treatment. He was placed in a Home where all the other inmates were similarly disturbed in different ways. Deke quickly became a persistent problem child. Punishment or bribery had no effect. A truce of sorts was found when it was discovered Deke found solace caring for a feral cat. When the cat had kittens he shared the mothering with their real mother. Jack O' Driscoll, one of those teachers who every child, especially a troubled one, needs, noticed his attitude. He worked on it and brought out the latent love buried deep in Deke, so deep there was a danger it was already dead. Fortunately he responded.

Gradually the staff noticed a change in him. Nevertheless, just below the surface he had a time bomb instead of a heart. A single incident was a portent for his future. One day Deke went to the barn to feed the feral cat and found her missing. He called out her name, "Cat". She was named after some musician whose song, But I Might Die Tonight, had real appeal for him. Again and again he called, "Cat, Cat." He searched everywhere. Upstairs, downstairs, in cupboards, under the stairs, in the shed and the garage, but she was nowhere to be found. He ran across the field and into the old disused barn. He stumbled upon her. She was pegged out by each paw and peppered with air-gun pellets. Her claws were broken and bloody. There was a bloody mass at her nose and her bottom jaw hung loose, having been dislodged by something blunt like a boot or a rifle-butt. A dirty striped handkerchief was tied tightly around her neck.

Deke knew that Camrin Al-Klinker, a big goonda, had an air rifle and was the sort of stooge to satisfy his curiosity by killing a cat. He went in search of Klinker. In a nearby field, he found him. Klinker held the kitten and stubbed out her last flicker of life. The other three were already drowned. Their bodies, lodged in the moss and weeds, looked like glove puppets.

"I didn't do anything. Pleeease-..." Klinker said, immediately he saw Deke. Deke ignored him. He hated lies. The food he'd been fed all his life. "Believe me, Rivers. It wasn't me." Deke ignored him. "It's not what you think. I was only-..." Deke looked at him, eyes lit with hate. "Honest, Rivers, I just found it. It's nothing to do with me. I..I-..."

257

"Shut up. Shut up. Shut up! You fat wanker! You're dead!" Deke screamed at him. Deke grabbed him, in a frenzy of anger he ripped Klinker's shirt off, then used part as a gag. Tying his hands with the shirt, he took Klinker into the same barn where he found Cat. The same barn where she gave birth to her kittens. The same barn where she died.

Deke forced Klinker on to a wooden milk stool and tied him to the cow post. In a flurry he raced to Klinker's room where he found his acoustic guitar. The same one Klinker often strangled Hey Joe on. Twisting the machine head, Deke removed the third, bronze medium wound, 0.66 mm string. Breathless, his heart pumping through his chest wall, he raced back to the barn. He strung the string around the over-head cow-post and around Klinker's fleshy neck. Deke removed the gag. Klinker's eyes bulged, barely staying in their sockets. The wire was so sharp and steel-strong, it cut neatly into his flesh so he couldn't shout or croak. The more he struggled the more his neck bled. Deke kicked the stool away as if it was a rusty can. He removed the rag from Klinker's wrists. As the wire sliced through his neck, Deke walked away, whistling his version of Air on a G-String.

When Klinker was discovered the staff thought it was just another suicide or some bizarre sex act that had gone wrong. There were at least half a dozen every year. It didn't warrant too much attention or investigation. They knew he was a paedophile. Al-Klinker was written-off as just another confused, queer youth whose attempt at masochism failed.

Nothing ever came of it. No one at the Home wanted an investigation as it could affect any future grants. Funny thing was, after that episode, Deke never had anyone mistreat his animals again.

Deke was potentially the best ally for Zogger. Yet he was also her worst enemy. For his knowledge of the whole subject of rights, human and animal, was profound. He was expected to speak first. Instead he waited until Arnold, Chrysler and Floyd had their say. They had shown their hand and given her their support. Deke said, "Hey, hold on, what are you really saying?" He waited until he held her gaze. Staring stony, he said, "Surely we did what we had to do last night, isn't that enough? We did it for you. It's over. Otherwise you're in danger of taking action against every form of animal abuse. There'd be no discrimination between angling and halal slaughter and vivisection. They're not only legal, more importantly, where would it end?"

"There's no difference between the kind of cruelty," said Zogger. "Whether it's legal or not is not the question. Whether it's badger-culling or boar-hunting, dog-fighting or experiments, the result is the same. The blood that drains from the animal is the same colour be it for lust or money. Their pain is balanced by our profit and always outweighed. The scales of justice are tilted towards us by us."

"Yes, but-..." Deke said.

"Hold on. Cruelty knows no division or limit. It continues forever. So our fight never ends. Let's get real. This is nothing less than war. And in war law takes second-place to justice."

"Oh, come on, that's garbage. And you know it. If you're right, we're no better than the Basques or the IRA or no different than any other Middle East terrorist. We're no different than the corrupt Muslim bombers you despise. We'd end up slaughtering the innocent too. We'd be like the towel-heads."

259

"You're wrong. That's crap and crass – and you know it," she said. "There's one clear difference. The Basques, IRA, Taliban, all had the means of peaceful protest to change the policy, but chose to disregard it. That's the difference between Gandhi and King and Mandela. Mandela knew that, regrettable though it may be, sometimes violence is the only way. Don't you remember when Nelson told them candidly, 'I believed we had no choice, but to turn to violence'? Then, despite the opposition, he and his vigilantes took the 'fateful step'. Does that mean nothing to you?"

"But-..." said Deke.

Before he could interrupt her flow, she said, "Do you think slavery would have been abolished without a war? Would Wilberforce have achieved anything if the slaves refused to revolt? Would women have got the vote without violence? Would the Civil Rights movement have made progress without bloodshed? Did Rosa Parks stand up to a white bus driver and refuse to stand up, for nothing? Did Medger Evers die in vain? Why was Alice in chains?"

"Fine words and all very fancy," said Deke, "but anger breeds anger. Violence begets violence. What you're suggesting makes us part of the problem not the solution. You don't persuade by force. You're talking like a Nazi."

Zogger knew, despite their commitment, the others were waiting and watching in the wings. There was a danger they might have niggling doubts too. "Good point, but it misses an essential difference. Would the South African Government have had talks with the ANC without the violence they were forced to use? What was the ANC's weapon of negotiation? Violence is the language of politics and war. Our silence now will lead to more violence forever. No one will listen unless the noise is so

260

loud they can't ignore the roar. Without us, the animals have no one. Chrysler's right, we are the power of the powerless."

"But they were fighting apartheid."

"So are we."

Deke wouldn't let her wriggle free so easily. "You're always talking about Mandela, yet he actually renounced violence. So where does that leave your fancy Utopian notions? False, ain't they?"

"It's true he renounced violence, but only after he was released from prison. Until then, he wouldn't even agree to being released early by renouncing violence. The question for you to consider is why he was forced to resort to violence in the first place? If he hadn't found power by going underground, would apartheid have been abolished? Would he have been lauded, as he is now, or remain, as he was, a bail bandit and a fugitive and a scapegoat? What power did he have before he became a rebel with a pistol? Remember he was reluctant to renounce violence because the 'armed struggle', as he termed it, forced the government to take them seriously. So don't misunderstand his position. At one point he threatened De Clerk with a revival. Nelson had a passion, a raw passion. Without it you can't get anything done. We have too." She spread her arms to include the other three. "How about you?"

"What about the turban terrorists?" Deke asked. "The ingrates. We'd be no different than them. We'd destroy our own democracy. How could that possibly help animals? Now or in the future."

"You've got it wrong. Look, no one asked the dishcloth-turbaned Arabs to come here. They brought their fight to us. To the world. They could've changed the system from within. They could protest. They could be elected. Instead they're content to kill us. So don't bore me with talk of those hypocrites. They made their choice. Animals have no choice. Animals can't do anything."

"Yeah, but what about Wilberforce. He changed the lives of slaves. Couldn't we do the same? Within the law?"

"You're missing the point. Slaves were free to escape. To seek recourse to the law. To write. To speak. To seek help. I accept it was limited, but they could do something to ignite a revolution. Why were the goondas gonna use strychnine to kill thousands of stray dogs? Because they can. Animals have no choice or voice. All they have is you."

"But what about the anti-whalers?" he asked. "Don't they prove your point is fallacious? They're making a legitimate protest. And getting results."

" No. It's the exact opposite. In fact they've proved the principle is sound. Why did they board the ships? Why did they use the acid? Why did they chain themselves to the rail? Their action forced Australia to get involved."

"Maybe, but only because Komura said, 'violence shouldn't be used to try to force through one's opinion'. You just don't like the Japs."

"You're wrong and right. If they hadn't used violence even more whales would be killed. The Japs keep blowing their insides out with explosive harpoons while the world idly watches. As for the Nips, I'm with Churchill."

"But surely you're not denying that peaceful protest has a purpose? That's the essence of democracy. It's the quintessence of the evolution of common law. Why we have stability. Why change is slow. Why we avoid revolutions that cripple these backward countries."

"I wouldn't say Russia was backward."

"Don't go off on a tangent. We're talking about democracy."

"You mean a kakistocracy, at least where animals are concerned."

"Look, Zogger, your ideas are quixotic, they're naive. Millions are made from breeding and killing millions of animals. How could it be otherwise?"

"True enough. But you're using the same lame arguments that were used to prove the value of slavery. Lies dressed up as logic. If you can sell goods that will kill people, through cancer or cirrhosis, then what's so wrong about selling cruelty in the guise of progress? You've proved the folly of your own argument. You're relying on lies to prove your truth. Deke, money not love makes the world go round."

Deke's face was a map of troubled confusion. He kept juggling unformed thoughts. He knew she knew he was caught on the conflicting horns of conscience and law. Civil disobedience had a magnetic appeal for him. It was the root of any legal system because of the struggle between morality and law. He wrote his Jurisprudence Thesis on the power of protest as a means of change. Neither anarchy nor democracy provided the answer to his question: if there is a collision, do you act according to conscience or law? His thesis had come alive. For years he talked about action being the only way to change a bad law. Now he was face-to-face with his own ideals. Thoughts were scrambled behind his heated brow. Words were trapped on his tongue. Finally Deke asked, "Are you really suggesting we engage in a war? If so, where will it end? Have you thought about that? Are you willing to pay the price your deeds demand?"

"I've thought about nothing else. You've got the luxury

of thinking about anarchy and democracy. Idle ideas. Valueless compared to action. Democracy means nothing to animals. A motley crew of placard-waving, well-meaning, shaven-headed rainbow-plaited, rent-a-protest anoraks, woolly-minded, sociologically inclined do-gooders means nothing to animal liberation. All animal welfare means is bigger cages and more time to suffer after an experiment or during their export. They're still caged and killed and eaten. Cruelty disguised as kindness. Is that what you want?"

Deke went to speak then stopped.

Zogger continued, "Remember what Morrisey said at Oxford the day after we played there: 'if you agree with vivisection, go and be vivisected upon yourself'. He warned those working on the laboratory, 'We'll get you.' In fact do you remember he said he supported 'The efforts of the Animal Rights Militia in England'? He said the reason the animal abusers are 'Repaid with violence – it is because they deal in violence and it's the only language they understand.' Remember what Lincoln said, 'If A can prove, however conclusively, that he may, of right, enslave B why may not B snatch the same argument, and prove equally, that he may enslave A?' Lincoln and Morrisey are right. Kindness to a slave does nothing to abolish slavery. It's a fake solution as a salve for an anxious conscience. All it does is allow politicians to fool us forever."

She lowered her tone. She spoke slower. "The thing is, Deke, the animals plight will be changed by arms not arguments. You know more than me, law is law because behind its power is a gun."

Deke held her eyes fast to his, still listening hard. He remained quiet. Her words washed over him with the force

264

of a Niagara. But he had no raft. "And as to where and when it will end, it will end when the war is won. Do you remember in the Animals' Film someone said a cruel professor could be shot dead on his doorstep? You have to realise that day may come. Until then, let us make a difference. Until then, let there be no compromise. Ask yourself this one question, Deke, why did we call the band Hellsucks?"

He smiled inwardly. His eyes crinkled. The name trapped him. There was something about what the name meant that reached him. It was the danger, energy, feeling, passion and death. It was the stuff of life. The stuff of dreams. The stuff of love. The stuff of magic. The answer to every question. Deke was hooked. The mood and music and all of it had seeped under his skin. It was part of him. He announced with a weary conviction and a sense of fate meeting destiny, "Okay, I'm with you. Let's live a little. No compromise, Hellsucks."

Zogger had a vague, gnawing thought about his conviction, but let it pass. She wondered how genuine it was, but then cancelled the thought from her mind. "Terrific. So what do you say, you guys and me – no, all of us as one – against the world?" They all nodded and laughed at Zogger's declaration, except for Deke whose face was fixed with a frozen smile. She looked at him and slowly looked away. Whatever he said, he still harboured a rolling resentment from being kicked out of her bed. She saw the cogs inside his head.

They all got up and trooped out together as five Horsemen ready to wreak havoc on an unforgiving world. As they were leaving The Freefall the music followed their boot heels. One of the roadies, Jack Heath, whose late uncle Fred became Johnny Kidd, walked over to the Rock-

Ola. Jack had tattoos on each hand, borrowed from Bob Mitchum as the mad preacher, saying 'heat' and 'kool'. He used the index finger of his right hand, tattooed 'h', to press A5 on the jukebox. The band left to the sound of the song they banned in Russia, *Something in the Air*.

All My Trials

"Do you really think we'll make a difference?" asked Arnold. "I want to, I don't want it to be just words any more."

It was Friday night in late October just after 9.10 p.m. He and Zogger were in the Hungry-I near Oxford waiting for the rest of the band. She knew they'd still be talking about the decision they'd made at The Freefall. One that would test their spirit to the limit. Arnold sipped his double expresso and pushed one towards her.

She took a swallow and said, "This is how it is. There comes a time in every great movement when the talking has to stop. Three stages. It moves through ridicule, when the ignorant find fault with things they can't understand, then wider discussion and finally acceptance and adoption by the men with the means. Though all the stages are important, the first and second are not decisive. Steps on the long road. The real issue is the final one because we're here talking about a revolution."

Zogger's delivery was measured. As with the last time, she was intense. She kept him in her vision, speaking low and slow. As it was one-to-one, his concentration was total. His eyebrows knitted even closer as he strained to hear and understand every word. She wanted Arnold's support so he could pass on his strength of purpose to the others. He sat and stared at her, didn't interrupt, murmured and nodded as her words flowed between them. She continued, "There's a time in a revolution when the cause is on course and even death can't stop it. It's the shared mind-vision of those involved that pushes the idea beyond wish-fulfilment. Their dream becomes a reality because the group feeling moves between each other and back again, making their vision a vector. Then the motivation and momentum feeds off and on itself. Finally it becomes a force too strong to resist. Remember that French philosopher who said the one thing stronger than all the armies in the world is an idea whose time has come."

"I think it was Bardot, or was it Brel?" Arnold asked.

"Probably, though I think she was Belgian." Zogger felt a surge flow through her as she told him about it.

Her words induced an urge in him. A shared sparkle-eyed excitement as she talked. He asked, "But where are we at now? When do we act?"

"When? We're a band of crusaders. Our Freefall meeting proved it's time to walk the talk or abandon the notion. You can't have commitment without action. There's no path in our direction. We'll make our own trail. We're so much more than a brilliant band. We mix the Band of Mercy with the Monkeywrenchers. We're the clanking ghost of the future. You ask when? We're Hellsucks, so the time is now."

"I'm fired-up, ready for action. When do we start? Who do we attack?"

"Like I told you, the when is now and the who is everyone. We're mod samurai. We're 21st. Century crusaders. Our hair-trigger aim is on the abusers. We'll use economic sabotage to make sure their businesses don't survive. The dealers in death treat animals as commodities, no different than a tin of beans. Well let them sell beans instead. Or they'll have nothing left to sell. Bankruptcy or change. Their choice, they can make it or take it."

"But you don't mean the corner shop, do you?"

"No. I mean the big-time businessmen, the merchants, the gun runners who trade skins for profit, always providing it's not their own."

"What about the public? Most of them are shareholders, aren't they?"

"That's true, but think of the veal-calf protests. There were pregnant women, perennial students, schoolgirls, OAP's, whistle-blowers and everyone in between. Those people put their lives on the line. They still do. Economic sabotage won't alienate the public too much, yet will cause maximum damage to the red-braced executives' morale and profits. But let's get real, that's a short-term view. I'm not here to con you. A revolution has to lead, not follow public opinion. Where would Nelson Mandela be if he cared about public opinion? Or Rosa Parks? Or Hannah More?" Or Alice Morgan Wright?

Just then Floyd and Chrysler and Deke arrived together. They could sense the easy feeling that flowed between Arnold and Zogger. After their last meeting, when Zogger had raised the stakes, there was an uneasy truce that hung in the air.

"What about More?" Chrysler asked. "Is it Thomas or Hannah?"

"We're proud to be following in her shadow, walking the same long road. That's all," said Arnold. He looked like someone who was satisfied he knew the answer. They sat around for a while, swapping stories and trading dreams. They were making a joint effort to keep the action alive.

Their philosophy became their practice. During the few weeks after the meeting in the Hungry-I, the band carried out some sabotage to wake the politicians from their slumber.

Their conquests were varied, but all to the same end. Every town they visited they also found an animal factory

269

or a hunting lodge or a laboratory to visit. When they were at Oxford they travelled to Everyman's Farm in Yewbury Sods. Dressed to kill, they cut through the wire. The birds were set free from the chains of their man-made cages. Some birds were so affected by being in such unnatural conditions for so long, they wandered around aimlessly. They had never seen daylight. Most of them jumped and flew and scattered over the night sky as if their lives depended on it. With their wings a-flapping, they disappeared into the distance, whooping like escaped prisoners.

'Bert' Rahman, the owner, lived some distance from the dark factory farm as the stench made him ill. The noise too was too much for him to bear.

Zogger got out the welding kit she normally used for soldering the band's equipment and cut out four letters in each steel barn door: ANAL. The light it let in would affect the birds and reduce the profits. The lack of light in the barn was to make the birds passive and docile. They were born with that feeling in their genes. They would die that way too. They had no value alive except as multiple-laying machines. Then when their laying days were over, they were handy pigswill.

The fervid five stood in a straight line in front of the barn doors with Zogger in the middle, mesmerised by the sight of a thousand birds fluttering unchained in the night sky. A line from the poem, Sympathy, written by the son of two slaves, floated into her mind: I Know Why the Caged Bird Sings.

Zogger used the torch to light the barn and in an instant the complete factory illuminated the sky. They rode off into the night. Down the road they stopped in their tracks to glance back and saw the huge ANAL sign hung, almost suspended, against a curtain of black. Her eyes were embers. She drank in the beauty of the night.

The next day when the merchants came they cursed and complained, but all in vain. By then it was another town and another gig and another arson and another alibi. Another day for the band on the lam.

Each day there was more damage and destruction and, for the band and animals, death or escape. The band fed off the daily danger as they rapidly began to love the risk. It might have continued in the same vein until the band split or were jailed or became burnt out or burned alive. Then something happened that changed them forever. The band had heard gossip and rumours about what went on at Blackfriars, but they didn't know what was exaggeration and prejudice rather than truth. The tales were horrific, but they remained suspicious as so much was fuelled by those naturally fixed with bias. Doubt was always their talisman. As they were due to play near Exeter they had the chance to go and see for themselves.

After playing the Doc Pomus Ballroom just outside Slough, they met near Reading and gathered at The Freefall. "Are you up for paying a little visit to Blackfriars?" Floyd asked. Though he made it sound casual, they knew what the name meant. It had a resonance all its own.

"Sure, why not?" Arnold said. "What do we have to lose?"

"Only our lives," said Deke.

"Then how can we not go?" Chrysler said. "Blackfriars is what it's all about, isn't it?"

"Remember, you never swim in the same river twice. The chance won't come again. Are you up to it?" Zogger asked. The others nodded in agreement. They knew they

271

had to go. It was too late to stop now. Their wheel was still spinning.

"Make sure you go on a Friday night. All the staff, save for a few research students, leave early afternoon. There's only one guard in the gatehouse. There's no one on guard at the South West Field. That's the way in, 'cos there's a river at the border so they can't use an electric fence," Wally Bagshot said. "Still a tight time scale, mind." His head moved as if held on by elastic. His eyes darted around The Freefall, focusing on the band as well. He was checking everything. He pulled up his shirt. Pointed to each of the band and gestured for them to do the same. Four of them did. Twisting his index finger, motioned for them to turn around. "Okay. You too," he said to Zogger. She pulled up her navy polo neck jumper to reveal bare skin and a saxe blue bra. He looked a little too long.

"I'm not sure how much you know or understand about Blackfriars? Any of you been there?" They all shook their heads. "I hope you haven't got weak hearts – or stomachs, come to that."

"Have they got an electric fence in all the other fields?" Zogger asked.

"Yes," Wally said. "Take this. You'll need it." He gave her a key.

"Why's there no fence where the river is then?" she asked.

"It could harm the animals." He laughed. She frowned. Arnold stopped drinking his expresso midway. Both thought he was being flippant. "It's true," Wally said. When they realised he wasn't joking, they all laughed. "Health and Safety too. It might electrocute a few ramblers straying off their route." He was scruffy, nervy, with wrinkled skin pulled tight over his skeletal features. Very edgy, looking around constantly as if he feared he was about to be arrested. Or maybe merely pierced with a poisoned-tipped umbrella. It was difficult to gauge Bagshot's age. He looked to be somewhere in his mid-forties, but could've been much younger. Some past strain had aged him, perhaps prematurely.

"So listen carefully, this is the way to go." Bagshot then explained it all in detail.

Wally Bagshot, who used to work at Blackfriars, told them all about the poor security. He drew a plan showing the best way in, the way out and noted the time it took to do it. It was detailed. Bagshot explained the limited security was both economic and deliberate to avoid interest from unwelcome visitors and prying eyes. No one except the higher scientific staff was privy to its purpose. Even the security and administrative staff didn't know what happened in the black stoned Block inside Red Wing. Blackfriars was carefully constructed to look just like an ordinary office block. There was nothing about the buildings that would make any passing motorist, Sunday scrambler or lost rambler give it a second glance. The only information about the place spread from the whistle-blowers who used to work there. Their claims couldn't be officially investigated as they were subject to the Official Secrets Act. Legal action would ensure an injunction would follow if they breathed a word or tried to tell the truth. They were also prosecuted, ending up with a criminal record and a prison sentence. There was the deterrence of another sentence if they re-offended. So what happened inside the walls of Red Wing remained unknown to the outside world.

"Don't spend too long there," Bagshot said. Chrysler

leant forward and mouthed as if to ask 'why?' but Bagshot brushed him aside. "Don't ask. Take my word for it. I used to work there. For far too long."

"How come you got a key?"

"When I left they forgot about me. They wanted to. I was expendable. It was as if I didn't exist. I still don't except in the High Court as a nameless defendant prevented from telling my secrets. I could end up inside for talking to you. Maybe I will." His eyes darted around the Freefall again. "When I woke up in the Psychiatric Ward – on the last occasion – I found the key in my fob pocket. Just like me, they forgot about the key."

"Wally, is Blackfriars the worst place?" Arnold asked. "In your experience?"

"Blackfriars is bad, really bad. It's an animals' Auschwitz."

"The worst?"

"I've been to them all in this area. There's only place I know that's worse than Red Wing, the St. Cloud Annexe. They only operate on a Monday and a Wednesday. None of the staff are based there. They come in, perform and leave. Back to Blackfriars. It's all short-term. Otherwise they become disaffected. The staff turnover is phenomenal. No animal gets out of there alive."

"What's so bad about it?"

"It's an animals' Treblinka." He hesitated, screwed his eyes hard. When he opened them, he seemed locked in pain. He looked older than before. Unspoken gargoyle rage.

"But what do they do there?"

"That's all I'm going to say."

"Why are you doing this?"

"This is payback time."

"What's the best day to pay it a visit?" Zogger asked.

"Sunday."

"Why?" His eyes were flint hard. The pain was growing. She recognised his hurt.

"They can't carry out borderline experiments on Sunday."

"What do you mean 'borderline'?"

"Illegal."

"Surely, you can give us a hint? Why's the Annexe so bad, what happens there?" Floyd asked.

"That's it. No more questions."

Zogger sliced her right hand through the air. The band knew there was nothing left to ask or add. It was the time for silence.

Bagshot had worked at Blackfriars as a top scientist for almost a decade. Gradually he became disillusioned as the "happenings", as he called them, became more frequent and horrific. He was so affected by the "happenings" he wouldn't discuss them with anyone. Like Tommy Atkins. All he would say to anyone that asked was what he said to the band, "If you want to know what happens there, you go and find out." During his tenure he visited St. Cloud. Near the end of his time, he changed. Initially he was off sick. He returned after a few weeks. It was too early. Then his health suffered more than before. The same pattern was repeated. In the end it was a straight choice between his pension and his soul. His soul won.

A week after talking to Bagshot the band was in Exeter. It was a Friday night in early November when they arrived. They were all adrenaline-lined as this was the penultimate gig of the tour. The band was in harmony on and off stage.

275

Deke drove the van up to a small lay-by on the edge of the woods bordering Blackfriars. He parked in the dark hidden from the road. The doors opened and down came the ramp. The band opened up the cupboards to reveal the gleaming Harleys. They mounted the Hogs and rode up the lane in a single line, slowly, their lights off. They followed the perimeter fence. There were no lights on outside the Block, only one at the small gatehouse. They were surprised at the lax security as, with a snip here and a snip there, they slipped through the shadows and into the grounds. Everything Bagshot had told them was true. Nearby in the gatehouse, a single overweight guard dozed and snored. His black plastic hat slid forward over his forehead. He had a porn magazine open on his lap. His belt was unbuckled. The CCTV panned the Block. The TV screen flickered with a re-run of a Big Brother-type programme presented by Grand and Gross. Little wonder he was fast asleep.

Arnold scaled the drainpipe and filled the CCTV with dollops of fast-setting liquid foam. Floyd squirted super glue in the lock, down the door opening and around the window frames. By the time the guard woke up the band would be in and out. He'd have enough time to break the window, cut his arm, claim it was the burglars and in his panic, think up some acceptable lies. A hero in the making.

Bagshot's directions and plan were accurate, his memory proved surprisingly good. The band swept through the grounds silent and swift. They met outside the Block. Zogger used Bagshot's key to slip into Red Wing. Until now their belief was based on hearsay. The band peered into the first room. There were about twenty kittens all with their eyes stitched closed. They wandered about without curiosity. They kept bumping into each other like doting drunks around a lamppost. Zogger knew this type of experiment had been carried out for over three decades to discover 'the sixth sense of visually-impaired people'. The kittens were ten days old. When they're about six months old they're useless to the experimenters. Then they will be killed, never having had their eyes open since birth. Just like their mothers before them.

The band moved on. In the next room they saw a row of beagles. They were strapped in boxes with muzzled masks and forced to chain-smoke cocaine and heroin. She knew beagles were chosen because of their docile nature. They were easily manipulated towards addiction and death. She thought how the grant cheques continue to flutter so the research lives on while another beagle dies.

The band moved on. In the next room they saw a Steppenwolf arena where monkeys were injected every day with the Aids virus. The monkeys writhed in visible agony, their bodies covered in blisters and spots proving they are dying of a human poison.

"What do you reckon of that?" Zogger whispered as the band stared at the monkeys, confined by tubes hanging from each head and body, strung across uncovered wounds. She didn't really expect an answer. She wasn't disappointed.

None of them could take it all in. They'd seen the smuggled photographs from foreign laboratories in East Europe and Russia, depicting the horror, the terror. This was beyond what they'd been led to believe. Arnold looked as if any moment he might faint or vomit, if not both. "Let's get the hell out of here." He added quietly, "I've seen all I need to see." He gulped. His pale green face told its own tale.

"I've had enough. Let's go," Chrysler whispered. "This is sick, sick." Normally he was ruddy faced. He looked pallid, then grey and whey-faced. Within a half-hour he'd gained a prison pallor.

"You're right," Floyd said. "Why don't we vivisect the vivisectors? That'd make more sense. At least it'd stop us feeling bad."

They'd seen enough. They were angry and ready to do some damage. "Let's just have a look in that room on the left and we'll call it quits. As we're here we might as well. Okay?" Zogger asked. The rest all nodded. Each one was getting closer to the edge.

The band moved on. They heard sounds from within the room. There was a constant 'crack', 'crack', followed by a weird scream. Each of them inched slowly towards the room, keeping hidden from whoever was in there. They saw it. There were seven pigs held in devices making it impossible for them to move their legs or bodies. Two scientists monitored four marksmen who shot the pigs at close range in the head and near the heart. They were wounded and squealing with pain, deliberately kept alive, just on the point of death. "Eeek. Eeek. Yeeehh." As their wounds were prodded and probed by the scientists' fingers, their squeals got louder. No anaesthetic for any of the seven pigs. The object was to simulate the pain of soldiers in war, who caught a sniper's bullet in the body or brain. The bullets were fired so they lodged a centimetre from the heart or stayed close to the brain. The pigs' pink flesh was spattered with pus and blood. Research tools used to recreate war in the laboratory. Chrysler wondered how long the pigs had been there?

In that moment, the images crowded her mind. Zogger turned to Chrysler and said, "This can't continue. All the

278

banners and marches have continued for over a century, for what? Still the legislator butchers slaughter millions in the guise of medical and scientific progress. It won't continue." His face was fixed on hers, a mutual intent magnetised in their eyes. The thoughts reverberated through her. She could see the skin behind the skull.

The band moved on. They crept silently down the long corridor and turned left. Room after room was filled with sights worse than the stories they'd heard. Nothing had prepared them for the sights they'd seen: animals were buried alive, burned alive, drowned, knifed, shot, scalded, wounded and electrocuted. All kinds of creatures from cat to goat, from dog to foal were wired and wounded. One group was force-fed with whisky, another force-fed with acid. Every animal that could move was restrained and poked and manipulated. Every creature that had a mind that could be bent, a heart that could bleed and a body that could be spent, was destroyed. An endless process. Zogger wiped her eyes.

Blackfriars had long been condemned as an animal-hell within the animal rights movement. Bagshot described it as "an animals' Auschwitz." The band moved on. From room to room. They peered glassy-eyed and became tongue-tied by what they witnessed. They had read the literature and seen the photographs. This was something else. Arnold wanted it to end. He looked at Zogger and mouthed, "I'm off." Floyd kept shaking his head in disbelief. Zogger's head was quietly exploding. Crazy thoughts kept hammering her brain. She said to Arnold, "These creeps are no different than the ones I saw in the dock. That's where they ought to be." He looked at her, said nothing, though his pained face said everything. She said, "They have to be stopped. They're gonna be."

The band moved on. They saw creature-after-creature who were blinded and deafened and poisoned and tormented. Animals were deliberately set upon by predators and ripped apart for some scientific aim. Chrysler couldn't control himself, "What's the fec-..."

"Keep your voice down," she whispered.

"What's with all these rubbishy experiments? They're total shite."

"I know. There's no purpose," she said. "And even if there was, well so-bloody-what?
I don't suppose you've got a spare Kalashnikov?" Chrysler winced. Zogger couldn't cancel out her thoughts. Anger clouded her mind. "You know if anyone outside this Lab, this theatre of cruelty, committed these acts they'd be prosecuted."

"But why can they do it?" he asked. "And Zogger, keep your voice down." He half-smiled. He moved closer to her, bent his head and strained to hear.

"Why? I'll tell you why these experiments continue. Because the scientists are blinded by the grants, the shareholders are blinded by the profits, the politicians are blinded by the votes, the public are blinded by the politicians and the animals are blinded by the law."

The band moved on. Zogger motioned to the others to leave. "Look, quick look," said Floyd. Their collective eyes scanned something they could scarcely believe. They'd heard about such things, but dismissed it as apocryphal or pure propaganda. There it was. Positive proof. A chimera: some strange animal with an ungulates head, an equine body and legs that crossed a foal with a goat. It was motionless, with wires flowing from every orifice. It looked almost stuffed, standing there with a cold, emotionless stare. It was Einstein meets

Frankenstein. It was not the future, but now. All five froze in confusion.

Seconds passed into minutes. Everything they suspected yet feared was now too real to deny.

"C'mon. I've seen more than enough. Let's split," Zogger said. "Where's Chrysler?"

"He was here a moment ago," Arnold said. "He was outside the room where the pigs were shot."

"There he is," said Floyd. "What's wrong with him?" Chrysler was slumped against the wall, head in his hands and sobbing.

"What's up?" asked Zogger. Chrysler didn't answer. "Come on. We've got to go. What's wrong?"

"Nothing," he sniffed between the sobs. Snivelling.

"Be quiet. They'll hear us. Look, there's no shame in crying. We've all been affected. This is gruesome, I know. We all do." She put her arm around him. She kept asking, "What's wrong? Tell me."

"Brownie." He started to sob again.

"Brownie, what do you mean?"

"Brownie McGhee," he said. Tears muffled his words.

"Yes. A great blues player, but what's that got to do with anything? Chrysler, this is no time for jokes. Don't play games." Her teeth locked.

"Brownie," he said. He sniffed, wiped his nose with his right hand and then his eyes. Huge blobs still fell from each eye until he blotted them with his cuff.

"Chrysler, for Christsake make some sense, what's wrong?" Downcast, his eyes dull with hurt. "What is it?"

Chrysler just cried. No words came. They walked towards the exit door. "Be quiet," she said, as his sobs grew louder.

"Zogger, you don't understand," said Deke. "Brownie

McGhee was his old Collie. He'd had her for years, since she was a pup. The original owner died young. He got it from a Sanctuary. They were inseparable."

"Well, yeah. So what?"

"She was stolen from his back garden sometime back," Deke said.

"That's sad and all, but what's that got to do with anything, Chrysler?" she asked. To her he looked so lost and vulnerable and young.

"Brownie, she was-...," he said, then cried harder than hailstones through rain.

"What? Tell me. C'mon. But, be quiet."

"In the room, with the wires and all..." he gulped. His throat locked. "She, she, she was on the table-..." Tears gushed from his red eyes. "Her eyes were full of blood."

"Oh, Chrysler. I'm so sorry," she said. "I really didn't know. I didn't realise..." She held him, huddled closer, feeling the pain shudder through his body. She'd never seen a man cry since her father wept at her mother's funeral. It instantly brought the image back. She mumbled, "The bastards, the feck-faced feckers. They're fecked. Their time has truly come. They'd better feckin' believe it."

The band – save for Deke who seemed distant and troubled in his own way – was angry and anguished as they left Blackfriars. Their lives would never be the same again. The band crept out and found the lane that ran around the side of the South West Field just like Bagshot said. No lights. As they passed the gatehouse the guard was still deep in sleep. Trousers loose, belt undone. The magazine had fallen to the floor. The darkness hid the deeds of those inside and outside the Block. A pervasive sadness cloaked the band.

They rode slowly back to the van in silence. Once in there, there was still little talk amongst the band. The night's events had opened their eyes too wide for them ever to close. The thoughts circled each of their minds in a broken loop. Blackfriars had catalysed them. Now there was so much to do and time was on no one's side. A parallel history of Merseybeat and Grunge was on the radio as Zogger drove through the countryside towards the motorway. The Big Three sounded as good as ever. Angelina Sparrow then spun the raw sounds and spirit of unleashed youth. The night ended with the vitriolic voice of Kurt, before the shotgun blast cut short any future anthem, telling them to *Come As You Are*.

Jesus On The Moon

"Let's go," Zogger said, nodded and strode onto the stage from the right, followed by Arnold.

"Wow. Look at the crowd," Deke mouthed to her. He came from the left followed by Chrysler.

Floyd entered from the back, between the curtains. The whole stage was jet-black save for the curtains that had a picture of J. R. Cash and a background hologram of small stars circling the Man and glowing diamond white. As he sat down he switched one of the two drumsticks in his right hand to his left. Floyd juggled and twirled the sticks as if they were an extension of his fingers. When the others heard the clicks of the sticks, though tense, they inwardly smiled. Floyd kicked the pedal, 1-2-3-4. The place erupted.

"Hi Bristle! It's good to be home. So let's rock!" Right from the opening words Zogger bawled and the plangent chord she struck on her Strat, she knew the night was special. All the lights sparked into life and the stage was bathed in a misty lipstick red. It might have been the crowd or their hometown or that it was the last leg of the tour. Whatever the reason, it was a special night. The crowd went crazy. A true demented reaction. Not that imbecilic I'm-in-with-the-in-crowd embarrassing applause, where all the losers light lighters and effectively clap each other. This was genuine, the royal flush and jokers wild.

"Come on, Come on, Yield to the Night. Ooohh!" she began and Deke joined in with a heart-rending harmony. Like Roy and Cady. Their voices dovetailed in a song about first love that captured its longing and loss. Whatever thoughts he had concealed, Deke gave the song his all. From the opening notes he played and sang as if it was his last ever gig.

Zogger and the band traded glances. A connected wavelength and a mutual mirr. At that moment each knew why they were in music in the first place. The night was flying by. After the barest of introductions, song after song was pounded out with energy and exuberance. No stage patter. No time except for the music. They played their hearts out and ended as intended with Goodbye-Palladium-Blues. The last line, 'Meanwhile I'm dyin' too', finished with a run of D, D7sus4, D, Em7, D (add9) and a chunky, echoing D chord. The fans would not let it end. They took that line, repeated it again and again, so the sound shot all around the room and ricocheted from wall-to-wall and floor-to-ceiling. All the straif boys, whang-wang girls and a swarm of 'hellsuckers' ran their voices hoarse. Their fans were so natural and hip they adopted a potential slur, hellsuckers, as their password. It was an affectionate nod to Jerry the Great.

They'd played at the University before. That night was good, very good, but not life-shattering. Tonight was different. There was a spirit in the night.

It was the kind of night most bands only dream about. A meeting of minds as the music reached everyone, audience and players uniting as one. An encore was beyond question as the bands' hands were almost a-bleedin' as they too clapped to the insistent beat. The lights flickered on and off and then the stage went dark, except for the stars. They shone teal blue. Five right arms rose as one to the crowd. A triumph. The band waved and left the stage, exhausted and exhilarated. Zogger left last. The crowd clapped until they could clap no more. There would be other nights, but not like this. It was as if the blood flowed through the adrenaline, rather than the other way round.

"Hey, what a night," Chrysler said, when they left the

stage and strolled through the corridor. "Where do we go from here, the Moon?"

In the dressing room they all sat around dogged, but shot-through with the sweetest feeling. An axis of bliss. All that mattered in those moments was their music. They savoured the feeling knowing they would never pass this way again.

"When you played that riff on Love Let Me Down Lightly, the whole place went quiet. Magical. Like we were in a church," Floyd said. "That acoustic version was stunning."

"Thanks," Deke said. "It felt fine. It really did. Especially as they went wild after it."

"What about the beat on Here comes the Heat? Terrific," Zogger said. "And you matched it with that fantastic bass line. Pure Motown."

"I felt like Ringo on Rain," Floyd said.

"I almost lost the beat, almost stopped playing in awe of that rhythm," Arnold said.

The shared feelings flowed. "What a way to end," Chrysler said. "Maybe we should make it our last gig." They laughed until they realised he was serious.

Finally Arnold said, "No, this is only the beginning." They laughed again. Even Deke was delirious.

"Enough of this ego-massage," Zogger said. "But what a night. We made our mark."

Everyone nodded, said nothing, each lost in their own thoughts. Nerves began to kick in. After a while they collected their thoughts and things. It was time to go. Each one said nothing, just got up, knowing what had to be done. Although it was about one and a half hours later than the band had intended, the roads would be deserted in the early hours of Sunday. Besides, the night was ever young with the blood jumping through their veins quicker than a sparking crackerjack.

"See you back at the Shuman," Chrysler called to the roadies. The others shouted something similar. All false. They went through the motions for the benefit of eavesdroppers and quidnuncs. Later those liggers would swear they were with the band at the premier rock hotel. Already the alibi was in train.

The band travelled separately until they almost reached Blackfriars. Then they rode single-file, triumphant like tigers, prowling and sleek. Aligned as one. Shades of Shane.

Repeating their previous pattern, they followed the fence to find the Block. A snip here, a snip there and the wires were bent to allow access. As they entered Blackfriars, this time they mentally prepared for what they would meet. They stole in from the shadows. A nervous acid formed in the pit of her stomach, but Zogger knew that was how it was meant to be. She never felt it was worthwhile doing something unless she had it. She never coasted. The others were hyped up in their own way.

They snuck past the guard. The same one. He hadn't changed his shape or position. By the aroma, nor his clothes. Only the snores were louder this time. Arnold used the foam and the glue again. He made the system inactive. As the CCTV was blank and silent, the guard could snooze a little longer. They hit upon a building on its own in the corner of Red Wing where they'd seen the macaques. They crept inside, unnoticed and unknown. The lighting was low as the illumination affected the animals and could distort the data. They saw two monkeys and two scientists. The scientists were facing the monkeys who were facing the band. The scientists kept pulling various levers on a steel machine. As the levers moved the monkeys began to grin and showed piano-teeth. Zogger stared at their teeth. She'd seen similar photographs from a Slovenian lab in the Elves Journal. One of the scientists pressed an orange button that lit up and flashed 'on' and 'off' repeatedly. As it flashed both animals visibly seemed to screech and were convulsed, though the band couldn't hear any sound they made. Electrodes sprung from each of their skulls. On one, the smaller macaque, her forehead was shaved and the word 'dummy' was scrawled in black indelible ink; the bigger one had the word 'crap' badly burned, as if by a solder iron, above his eyes. Each time the monkeys seemed to scream, both scientists kept pulling the levers, turning switches and pressing buttons. While the buttons flashed both scientists stared at the macaques.

Chrysler's right hand formed a fist. He went to shout, "The-..." Having seen him mouth the word, Zogger said, "Shush. Hold tight." She held him back with her left arm on his chest. He was on a short fuse. He was there on Brownie McGhee's behalf too.

Floyd whispered, "What're they up to? Let's take them out. Now."

She held her hand up. "No. Wait," Zogger said. She had read about this precise experiment.

One of the scientists, a gross, fleshy, balding, man of indeterminate age, – the type that's born old – got the smaller monkey and strapped her in a leather harness, leaving only her arms exposed. His name was on a tag pinned to his breast pocket, William Lynch. He twisted the knobs that seemed to send signals through her shivering body. The monkey started to pant and pant. She was artificially on heat. Then they brought the bigger monkey up to her. Chrsyler read the scientist's lips. "Look at that," Lynch said. "He's big." His colleague raised her eyebrows.

The scientists continued with their experiment. Anchor squirted a huge dollop of some white substance on the small monkey's anus. The other scientist, a greasy-haired, very skinny, short, young woman looked at the bottle. Her name-tag read, P. R. Schatt. The monkey jerked to and fro, seeming to be stung as the white oil bit into her. No anaesthetic was used. That was intentional. The monkey's eyes were weirdly wide and bulging as joke-eyes without springs. Her screams were so loud the smallest echo shot through the walls. The band felt impelled to burst in, but impatiently waited and waited. They moved forward. Zogger turned around, held her arms out and said, "Get ready."

Schatt got the big monkey and dragged him feet-first inches from his smaller mate. "Come on, come," she said. She then twisted the knobs to send signals that caused the second monkey to pant heavily. Schatt smiled, licked her lips and glanced in the direction of Lynch. With a knowing look and a nod – this must have been a repeat performance – together they pressed 'crap' into 'dummy', forcing him into the screeching creature. Neither monkey could move of their own accord. Schatt then pressed a green button that made 'crap' continue piston-like, unable to stop. Crap was controlled by the scientists.

These were conventional scientists who published research Papers and appeared at Conferences at home and abroad. It was not some perverse offshoot by two bent experimenters. It was legal. Zogger knew it was an integral part of the experiment. They would then write a

289

thesis on the 'Evaluation of the Effects of Anal Rape on a Female Macaque by a Male Stranger'. Later each would gain a doctorate and become a professor. Next year they would supervise students who would duplicate the same experiments with the same results. They would try to alter the age or numbers or sex or weight or some other such insignificant matter to justify the procedure and gain the golden egg, the grant.

Zogger knew all about those archetypes. She put her arms down and turned around. Criss-cross lines formed on her forehead. Zogger looked at the monkeys, at the band and then back again. "Ready?" she asked. A fierce look was fixed on her face. Her eyes flickered with anger. She thought the difference between Lynch and Qualm was only a label and a degree. Her thoughts dwelt on the line she'd sung earlier that night in Goodbye-Palladium-Blues, 'Since I learned that the thief is just a judge in another robe'.

The monkeys' teeth and faces and bodies shivered and shook. In and out of time. Zogger was straining at the leash, her patience at breaking point. Zogger gave a sharp shake of her head, down and up, and whooped, "Now. Go, go, go!" Five burst through the door. They almost removed the frame. Their emotions were riding high on a helter-skelter of straight-no-chaser hatred.

"Get them. Get the feckers!" Floyd screamed at the top of his voice. A massive roar went up as the doors jolted on its hinges and flew open as the band released their pent-in tension. Everyone, band and scientists, screamed in unison with the monkeys. The room rebounded with the sounds of the band's unleashed fury. They grabbed Lynch and Schatt. The sudden smell of fear oozed through the pores of the scientists, instant and strong. Stains appeared on their white nylon trousers as the smell wafted around the room.

Chrysler freed the two monkeys. Each was on the verge of death. Scarred and wasted. Both had been mutilated so much and so often they would never recover. Chrysler filled a hypodermic needle. He knocked the tip, squirted a few globules into the air and then gave them a lethal injection. He laid the lifeless bodies on the floor in the corner of the room.

The scientists, stricken with fear, opened their mouths, but no sound came out. The others held and restrained them. One on each arm. With the speed of mechanics at a racetrack, they pummelled the scientists, ripped their garments apart and stripped them bare. Naked head-to-toe. Their mottled bodies exposed as exhibits in their own experiment. Chrysler joined the others. Floyd branded both scientists on their foreheads with ANAL. The band manhandled the scientists into exactly the same position they had placed the monkeys. A human mortise and tenon. Schatt took the place of dummy and Lynch became crap.

The scientists screamed and screamed. No one cared. No one else could hear. Chrysler moved the two macaques, carefully placing them so Lynch and Schatt could see them. Their fear increased until they reached a pitch where their mouths froze wide-open; they couldn't shut them or even scream. Meanwhile the machine was pumping, piston-fashion, both scientists busy being buggers.

The band stood back and admired the night's work. "Let's go," Zogger said. "This place stinks."

The last image the scientists had tattooed on their eyeballs while waiting for release was the sight of dummy and crap.

291

All five stood near their Harleys. "We rocked tonight boys," Zogger shouted. Both hands with full fists were raised high towards the sky. "Yeah, we really rocked tonight."

Arnold, Floyd and Chrysler shouted back, "Yeah, yeah, yeah" and shook their hair just like the Liverpool lads who shook the world. Each held their right arm outstretched above their heads, nieves hard and tough. Deke held his fist curled as limp as a crook. All five walked away, Deke moving faster than the others. He was out in front, eager to leave.

Zogger had one last look before leaving. The sight lit her soul. She stood alone, watching, wishing to drink in the pleasure of the night. She was transfixed. For perhaps the first time in her life she felt she really had nothing left to lose. Zogger started to sing a line from one of her favourite songs, "At the age of 37…" Now she understood her place in the world. The image in her mind was conjured from the Countess's daughter and Shel's broken-hearted epic, *The Ballad Of Lucy Jordan*.

Only The Truth

"Just stop at the top, Deke. Thanks," Zogger said.

"Where, here?" he asked.

"That's fine."

"I thought we were going back to the Shuman first. Then another rehearsal. We need to nail that new song, Snow In Her Blood. We've got a sound check too. It's our last night. We've got a lot to live up to." He snapped and was beginning to sound nasty again.

"Just stop the van," she said. "What's with you?"

The four of them got out to stretch their legs and catch the view from the Suspension Bridge across the Bristle skyline. Deke stayed in the driver's seat.

"This really is it," she said. Zogger thought about her future as she looked down on the Gorge. She could see the first signs shoot across that night sky as a beacon. She could see the flaming flag unfurled to the world. People who saw it would know what it meant, others would learn about it. Those still unborn would suckle the maverick-milk into their genes. She knew all about the history of Bristle and Somerset and its roots in rebellion. From Quakers to Portishead, she knew something had pulled her to this place at this time. As she scanned the early evening sky, she could feel the magnetic grip of Bristle. Their spiritual home, for the music and the action. Witness Massive Attack declaim the truth to the myopic City Fathers so they had to face the unpalatable dish of plated-slavery. This is Banksy's city, she mused. The folk here don't care for any religion, except rock 'n' roll.

"Just think," said Arnold, "Tom Stoppard probably stood on these very steps."

"And Julie Burchill," Zogger laughed, "So two reasons to be proud."

"That clap. A zit on the arse of Avon. She brightened Bristle by leaving it," said Floyd. "If only Cicceroni would do the same." Everyone was in good form, except Deke. He stayed in the driver's seat, clothed in a sulky silence.

After sharing a few jokes Zogger said, "Let's split." They got into the van and Deke drove through the steep back streets. Down the windy, cobbled stones past the Clifton Village morgue. He was driving way too fast. "Maybe we could pick up a bit of speed? Only my teeth are still intact," she said. As he was already rattled, he put his foot down firmer on the pedal. His mood was still sombre when the band arrived at The Mortimer Shuman Hotel. It was a lovely old hotel just near the docks and behind the gas works. The water lapped gently all night and helped the innocent and guilty alike struggle to find sleep.

The band especially liked the Shuman because most of the staff were Irish. It gave them an edge because of their history. The staff were wary of the English, but wore a welcome smile, asked no personal questions and tendered no false bonhomie. They wouldn't trust the nosiness of strangers or succumb to the curiosity of the police. "Oh, I can't help you there, Officer," or "I didn't notice anything odd, I'm bound to say," they would offer as a reflex answer to any one of a hundred questions. It was always offered in a seemingly helpful way: "I wish I could help Officer, but I'm not sure I was even on duty. And when I'm not, I like the odd drink, so I'm usually too out of it to remember anything, even my own name." The cops couldn't question their co-operation. The band liked the spirit of the staff and their kin. On every level they lived the life. They stayed up late and swapped stories with the musos. Later they were stricken with convenient amnesia and forgot who it was and what was said. Being with them made the band feel good. For the Irish loved the music, the songs, the pipes and most of all the craic.

The band could identify with and respect the Irish because they'd been betrayed so many times by the English. Throughout their history they were conned by Cromwell and Boycott and the Black and Tans. It was part of the English ethos that landladies everywhere added the greeting below the Vacancies sign, 'No Blacks. No Irish. No dogs'.

The band checked in quickly. They dumped their bags and baggage, grabbed a coffee on the hoof and gulped it down. Their minds were on the music.

They got to the University early to ensure there was time for a second sound check as well as a way out and in without being seen. Two support acts were on before them. That allowed them to buy time. The band would adopt their usual method. They would sneak out, sneak in, mix with the fans and set the wheels in motion for the audience to provide an unassailable alibi. It proved successful in the past so, unlike their music, there was no reason to change. Zogger was the one, the only one, who had the full details of the bands' nocturnal plans. Whilst the outline plans were discussed, she always kept the final details locked in her mind. She could change the plan at the last moment if the circumstances changed. That strategy protected the band too. For the others couldn't tell others what they didn't know. Though no tactic could counter-act it completely, it lessened betrayal from within. Undercover cops and collaborators were always on their mind, especially hers.

Betrayal was a constant worry as outsiders could easily

infiltrate the band as roadies and technicians. Occasionally one of the band, usually Chrysler, would ask anxiously, "Who's that new roadie?" or "Where did the sound man come from? Who recommended him?" If the checks, or more likely gut instinct, revealed anything that caused the slightest concern, they were quietly, but quickly replaced. An alert keen-eyed agent provocateur would notice the bands' absence at the wrong right time or overhear the odd provocative comment pass between them. The band was always circumspect and tended to mix as a group. However, there were always the tell-tale signs: like taking a too-keen interest in the TV News following one of their arson attacks; or ripping an article out of a newspaper about how they poured brown sugar into the tanks of a fleet of hunters' vehicles.

Of late Zogger had an uneasy feeling about Deke. He was naturally disputatious. But that was of no account, indeed welcome. It added to the adventure and honed their reasons for taking action. Zogger always welcomed challenging questions as that ensured matters didn't fester and each one had a voice.

She took her chance during the rehearsal. Deke was busy practising with his new bottleneck on his old Telecaster. She could hear some fine runs courtesy of Lowell G. coupled with an Otha McD riff, coming from a dark corner behind the stage. As usual he went to a corner of the corridor. Typically he wanted to get it right and wanted no distractions. He'd return when he was ready.

"Chrysler, have you noticed anything lately about Deke?" she asked.

"Not really. Like what?"

"I can't put my finger on it. It's just a feeling.

Something's hassling him. I know it. But you haven't noticed?"

"No. At least no more than usual. He's a natural born curmudgeon."

"What about you two?" she asked, looking towards Arnold and Floyd. "What about his attitude?"

"No," they each said in turn. Arnold added, "He's just his usual miserable self."

"What I mean is, it's like he's not part of the team anymore," she said. "He's finding fault with things that don't matter. Too much attitude. Like when we were up at the Gorge, he couldn't even be bothered to get out of van."

"I wouldn't worry about that," Chrysler said. "He's always moody, you know that better than anyone. It's the price of his genius. He's a grumpy old sod. He'd make Van the Man seem happy as a clam." They laughed to try and ease the tension. Zogger tried a half-wry smile and let it pass.

All in all the rehearsal and sound check was fine. The one strand that bound them together remained. Their love for the music still meant they cut it when it mattered. After a few verses of Pagliacci's Return, they rehearsed another new song, Here Comes The Heat. Adjustments were made to the volume and their voices to enhance their harmonies. Floyd came in on the bass line, accentuating it with a 5/4 beat on the snare and a 9/8 on the boom. Even in rehearsal it rocked. Deke's voice was soulful and strong on one of their best new anti-drug songs, Snow In Her Blood. It had an inherent power because it was based on a true story, the victim being his sister who sold her soul for a shot of smack and bought death in disguise.

Deke drove the band back to the Shuman. On arrival they

gathered together in the lounge. The chairs were arranged in a closed circle. Other guests were deliberately excluded by the body language of the band. After a few exchanges and the odd joke between them, Zogger casually said, "Arnold, how are you and the boys getting on with that other new song? Only we need to finish it for tomorrow."

"What new song?" he asked.

"That one you were working on with Floyd and Chrysler. Was it, Broke In, Broke Out, Broke Up, Broke Down? Something like that?"

"I don't recall that one. Are you sure?"

"I might have the title wrong. But weren't you working on a song?" She looked at him and raised her eyebrows. He immediately understood. The others did too. She wanted to talk turkey with Deke.

"Oh, yeah. I didn't know which one you meant. We call it Broke Wind, you know like Ham and Eggs. We're working on one or two great new songs actually. I hadn't realised we were going to showcase it tomorrow."

"I'd like to. A great way to end. It's the last gig of the tour."

"True. Well, we'd better make tracks. See you guys." He got up and the three of them left together. They walked too slow, trying to look natural.

When the others left, there was a defined silence between Deke and Zogger. They made nervous coughs in a relay. Like a newly ordained priest waiting to deliver his first sermon, they kept clearing their throats from non-existent frogs. She wondered what to say. He wondered what she was going to say. The feeling was unsettled and the atmosphere knife-cut. Before the others left, he'd not contributed to any of the badinage.

298

She leant forward to engage him, but kept her voice low and a distance between them. She asked, "What's up, Deke?"

"What d'you mean?"

"You know what I mean. What's your problem?"

"I ain't got one."

"Don't pussyfoot. I haven't got the time or inclination."

"I told you. Nothing's wrong."

"I don't believe you. You've been a complete asshole for ages. I know that's nothing new, but this time it's different. So spit it out. I'm waiting. Spill it."

He crossed his legs then uncrossed them. He leant back then sat upright. An odd ache was forming in both shoulders. He squirmed in his chair and moved both buttocks uneasily. He went to speak, stopped then quietly said, "Alright. I'll tell you what's troubling me. If you really want to know?"

"I'm listening."

"You."

"I'm listening. Tell me more."

"You've changed. Where once you were fun, now you're burning with some kind of idiotic anarchy. You used to detest violence, now you revel in it. No one's safe from you, including yourself. What happens if, at our next arson target, we meet a night watchman? He's innocent and likely as not poorly paid, just scratching a living and probably with a family too. What about him? Where does he figure in your anarchic plan? You going to kill him?"

"We don't intend to harm any night watchman at any time. Merely get him out of the lab or the farm. That's our style. We don't intend to harm any of the animals, so why would we want to harm any innocent humans? We didn't harm the guard at Blackfriars. We could have."

299

"Maybe. But you don't take that view on the experimenters, who are humans too. Do you?" Deke stared hard at her. His face became patchy and red. The veins at his temples grew blue.

"There's a difference. They're doing useless research. Animals count for nothing in their eyes. They're full of excuses, always asking for more grants. Warped and greedy. There's always an alternative and even if there isn't, they should find one. They don't try hard enough. They never have. They don't care. They all stand in the shadow of Bernard and Magendie. Two more French clowns. Animals are available and expendable."

"Though I don't agree, you might have a point if you're right. And if you're wrong? What if there is no alternative? On your reckoning people are likely to die."

"If it happens, it happens. Why are you looking at it as selfishly as the scientists? They're deliberately destroying innocent lives to advance their own careers. They're dishonest and lazy. Morrissey is right. The fact the power-maniacs despise the activists is evidence of their guilt. What side of the line do you stand on? If animals weren't around, they'd have to find another way. Well let them find it now."

Deke's throat was as dry as an AA Meeting. He coughed into the thumb and index finger of his loosely curled right fist. "I can't believe I'm hearing this. On your reasoning the day will come when you'll kill all the scientists and then what? Will that make you happy? Or will you just find some other crusade?"

"And then what? Well, so what? Do they deserve to live? Do they deserve to die? Can they continue from now until forever aimlessly killing millions of animals for the sake of a spurious career in the world of fake science?"

"They've found cures for multiple diseases," Deke said. "So what if you have to sacrifice a few animals? You're a pathetic rebel searching for a cause. You don't understand, don't realise what you're saying. You can't, you can't mean it. You're playing God." He flushed, squinted his eyes. The lines at the corners of each eye cracked into deep crow's-feet. Pain tracked his face. Words wouldn't come. His eyes met hers, cold and cynical.

She wanted to keep the momentum rolling. "The day will come when, for our fellow humans, we poison prisoners and perverts in a trade-off against their sentence. The day will come when we experiment on addicts who have willingly committed the acts leading to their own destruction. For good measure, no doubt the day will come when a scientist has a crater blown in his head instead of the pig. Well, let it be. I for one will have no regrets. I'll say no prayers for the parasites." She kept him in her vision, holding his gaze fast. "You're always talking about Donald Watson-..."

"That's right because he was a great bloke. After all he coined the word 'vegan'. But what's that got to do with anything?" Deke asked. "He wasn't violent. He was anti-violence. A sweet-natured man. He was always good to me."

"Listen and learn. When he was ninety-five years old he said, 'If I was an animal in a laboratory cage I would thank the animal activist who broke in and let me out...I have a great respect for these people who are willing to risk ten years in prison to break a lock on a laboratory door...' Well what would your hero think of you?"

"I can't believe you." Deke shook his head in despair. "You're, you're not the same person I once knew. Don was talking about a burglary. A bit of vandalism. I'd be

301

happy with that myself. You're completely distorting it. You talk about putting a bullet in the brain of a scientist and you think that's some kind of sick joke?"

"What a loss that would be. The world would be a better place without them. Save the frogs, eliminate the Frogs. What's your answer, honky? What can you show me, except surrender?"

"Don't call me a honky. Slag."

"Exhausted mind 'eh honky?"

Her eyes penetrated his, leaving him feeling exposed. He knew something now he'd ignored for many months. Whatever it was that united them was gone. It had disappeared as if it was oral smoke. Her eyes told him what he'd been unwilling to see.

"Your problem is like all you phoney feminists, you only see things from your own side. One moment it's equality for women, then equality for blacks, now you're demanding equality for bleeding animals. What's next, Free the Fruit? You used to believe in civil disobedience. Now you try to prove your view with violence. If that don't work you'll toss a grenade through a window. I know you would. I know you. You're corrupt, blinded by your vanity."

"We're finally getting there. Let's have it all." Her anger bubbled closer to the surface.

"Well, since you ask, I'll tell you. Your type makes me want to puke. You self-seeking piccaninnies are all the same. Screw the system. Always on the take. Never give an inch. You got a chip on each shoulder for balance."

"So that's how you really feel? I was right all along. Just another honky bigot."

"And what about you? Just another bitter nigger." He held her in his vision, steel on steel. He brought his right hand up quickly, formed as a gun, his fingers as the barrel and trigger. Aiming at her, his thumb cocked, he pulled the trigger and said, "Pow."

Her mind exploded. Thirty years of insults burst through her brain. She sprung from her chair and hovered over him.

Smack! Thwack! Whack!

As "nigger" tripped from his tongue, she hit him so hard on his left cheek an imprint of her four fingers etched his face. She swung her hand back and hit his right cheek. She kept the pendulum force and hit him again on the left cheek.

His face changed from pink to red to a glowing coal. He instinctively brought his right arm back, fist clenched, moved it towards her and stopped. He held his fire in check. Deke sat there for about ten seconds. He sprang to his feet, kicked the table towards her. Two sugar lumps dropped onto her shoe. The bone china cup fell off the saucer and rolled onto the Wilton. The dainty handle snapped clean off.

He strode, almost ran, to the lift. As he reached the doors, he decided to use the stairs. Deke took them two steps at a time.

Zogger picked up the handle and placed it on the tray. She could barely breathe because of the atmosphere. Though Deke disappeared, that remained.

The doors to the lounge were still swinging downstairs as he reached his room. He went in, confused and full of sull. He glanced in the bathroom mirror. The marks of her fingers scarred his face. Deke stayed in his room and lay on the bed. The dark waterfall thoughts came tumbling down. Confusion gushed through him, then tears. He wasn't sure what to do, but knew he had to do something.

Deke was noodling on his Martin. About an hour later he heard the others in the band go to their rooms. They heard from Zogger what had happened, though only her version of the event. She exaggerated his mood and forgot about her assault. No one disturbed Deke. When passing his door, Arnold heard him play some mean slide like Ryland.

They thought he'd be his old self in the morning. They let him sleep on it. That was the one thing he couldn't do. When some hours had passed and he guessed they were all fast asleep, he slipped out into the shadows.

He left the Shuman and went to the dark end of the street. He used the public phone outside the post office. He called A6.

"Hello. I want to speak to DS Kite."

"Hello. What's your name?" asked WPC Maggie Hyra.

"It doesn't matter. I need to speak to Kite. It's urgent."

"Hold on. I'll transfer you." Hyra mouthed to Kite, "It's for you."

"Hurry up or I'll put the phone down."

"It's Alvin Kite. Who am I talking to?"

"Just listen because what I have to say is important."

"I'm all ears. How can I help?"

"Don't interrupt. Time is short and lives are at stake. I won't talk for long. I know you're already tracing this call."

Deke quickly reeled off a few facts so Kite would know it wasn't a hoax call. He blurted out brief details about the plans of the band.

"It's tomorrow. After midnight. After the gig. At the Cliffs, somewhere near the Mendips. I think at The Gorge.

304

That's it. That's all I know. You'd better be there."

"Wait a minute. Who? How many? What time will-...?" Kite asked, hoping for more information as Deke was vague in the extreme. "That's typical, he's hung up."

He motioned to Hyra to tap the line. "Trace the call. Send a Scenes of Crime Officer over, get some prints off the phone, get some saliva for DNA. If necessary get some skin flakes. And hair. Don't forget the shoes. The crimos always do."

"Okay, Alvin," Hyra said. "It's as good as done."

"Now I mean, not tomorrow," he said, holding up the telephone. "Now." The line was still live with the last call. Her fingers danced as numbers clicked rapidly on the screen.

"He mentioned a 'gig'. Can you check that, Maggie?"

"Sarge, there's about a thousand bands in Bristle. How can we tell which one it is, where they're playing and when by tomorrow?"

"Good question. I'd prefer a good answer. Get on with it."

A6 was a very small unit recently set up by the Government. It was introduced as a result of pressure from shareholders in drug companies who saw their profits slashed as the attacks escalated. Barely a week passed without their profits being affected. Their staff were hassled and harassed. A6 specifically targeted the animal rights activists. There were only three cells with three cops in each cell. Everyone in the movement knew of them. Some of the more radical magazines published photographs of the police arresting saboteurs, who were their friends. That helped the sabs identify them at the next demo. Both sides, the hunters and the hunted, were alive to undercover operations. Fast Eddie Abbey, the editor of the Angel of Death, cheekily sent Kite a Christmas card showing a Cinderella scene with a turkey carving a cop with the caption, 'Is it true the police have the biggest balls?'

The Unit remained small and secretive as they too suffered from the same danger of betrayal. Surprisingly some officers, as Zogger found with Barney Buckle, supported the animal activists. So the more who knew, the more who could inform and warn the animal liberators. It was a legal cat-and-mouse game.

Though Kite felt frustrated by the lack of information, he knew this could be the breakthrough. He and his two colleagues, Patsy Birkett and Norman Hastings, had been trying for over nine months to get the smallest lead. Now Kite had the best evidence from the most reliable source: a stool pigeon.

Deke called from a public telephone so he couldn't be traced too quickly. He wore latex gloves, covered the mouthpiece with cellophane and used a cleaned coin so nothing was left for forensics, except the stale smell of his sweaty betrayal. Smarter than the average cop, he covered his Docs in plastic bags like a modern estate agent and burglar. When he returned to the Shuman, Deke burned the plastic trappings in the ashtray. He lit a joss stick and watched the red glow throw its scent around the room. By the time the call was traced Deke was lying uncomfortably in bed, hot and anxiously seeking a vanishing sleep.

His mistake was to forget earprints are no different forensically than fingerprints.

Deke fretted and fidgeted, turning every which way in a vain effort to find sleep. A troubled mind and a turncoat conscience were uneasy bedfellows. He kept fiddling with the dial of the hotel radio desperately seeking some decent music to help him find a kind of peace. He lay awake for hours and dozed in and out of a restless sleep. At about 5.00 a.m. he chanced upon Ratlife and Simba at SXSW. His eyes closed just as a story about Bobby's mysterious death ended on his swansong, *I Fought The Law*.

Way Over Yonder In A Minor Key

"You sure this is the right place?" D.S. Patsy Birkett asked and switched off and over. He was in his red series 3 BMW. After twenty years in the force he was happy to have a motor usually used by villains. Stolen to order as a choice getaway car so they could outrun a Golf.

"That's what Alvin said, definitely," D.S. Norman Hastings answered on the car radio. He was sat in his green Golf.

"Who's the source?"

"We're not sure."

"Was it a nark?"

"We're not sure. The information seemed reliable according to Alvin."

"Who's his trainer?"

"He didn't have one."

"What's his name?"

"He didn't leave one."

"What do we know about him?"

"Not much."

"Mmm. Perhaps he was just flying a kite," Birkett said.

"Shall we go?"

"Let's give it another quarter of an hour, half-hour max. You never know?"

"You reckon? But no longer."

Each officer, almost in harmony, though unseen by the other, idly poured out the last dregs of treacly tar that started out as coffee from a mini Thermos.

Birkett and Hastings had staked out each end of Cheddar Gorge. There was no way in and no way out without being seen, unless they had wings. The detectives waited and waited. They had waited for over two and a half hours. So far there was no action. They would have to wait much longer for two reasons. The gig had gone so well the band were delayed by about two hours. The other, not entirely Plod-like reason, was they had the wrong Gorge.

When Deke garbled the message he said, "I guess they'll attack a lab near the Gorge." Kite believed he meant the one at Cheddar. He couldn't know Deke didn't know it was the one at Clevedon. Zogger only told them the exact location once they were on their way. By then nothing could stop their holy motion.

The band had chosen it because though Blackfriars was an animals' Auschwitz, the Annexe was the hole of its hell. Wally Bagshot knew all too well the secrets that lurked there. The "happenings" had caused his breakdown. What others only suspected, he knew. The notorious trials were so severe that animals were never kept there after vivisection. The reason was simple. After every experiment they were already dead or killed and incinerated. All that remained was their ashes. It was why the band wanted to strike at the heart of the dark science.

The band stopped at a lay-by just past Lulsgate Airport. "I've thought about this one for a long time. Even before we visited Blackfriars," Zogger said. They gathered around her. "We left a calling card at Blackfriars. The Annexe holds all the data from experiments for the last sixty years. It was built after the War to experiment on German PoW's. The equipment is technically sophisticated. It cost millions. The initial cost was so high it's irreplaceable now. There's a bonus. A real bonus. A Chinese consortium is buying the Annexe." She paused. An advocate to the end. "The contract is signed. We're going to raze it to the ground. While the ink is drying, we'll stop the blood flow. So let's go."

Zogger only confirmed the location when they were on their way to indulge in a spot of arson and mayhem. That was usual. No one, but the band would know their target. Moreover, there were so many animal factories throughout the green and unpleasant English countryside, even an inspired guess would be pure chance. By then Deke was on his Harley anyway with no way to inform the Heat.

Equally A6 were on guard from the inside and outside. Each team consisted of only two experienced officers who were trained in martial arts and guerrilla tactics, plus one backup for liaison. Paperwork was kept to a bare minimum and destroyed when the 'action' was taken. The three in each cell were self-contained and comrades-in-arms. Birkett and Hastings and Kite were close and during the expiscation kept their knowledge within the cell. Their families didn't know the nature of their work. They didn't share information with any other team until the operation was over. No names were attached to 'Notes', which came anonymously from a central point. The approach was in effect the counterpoint of their enemies, so each single cell was a self-regulated unit. Consequently they couldn't betray other cops or identify an underground cop even if he was in the same room.

The risk was so high and the cost of a mistake so great they had to know too little rather than too much. Knowing too much could cost them their lives and, more importantly for the politicians, they'd find the survival odds too low and refuse to go. There was no shortage of volunteers because the authorities kept the officers in a state of suspended ignorance. After a stint of duty they got promotion, providing they were still alive. If promotion was denied, they had a nice ceremony. Coupled with that, given the mindless, ass-numbing boredom of routine patrol, the element of risk had the lure of glory.

"Is he of the right stuff?" Will Orson-Carte, a Tory politician, asked the new Chief Constable, Phillip De Quanacre. "There's going to be some Questions in the House about the latest raids. It's highly sensitive, as you know."

"I do," Quanacre said. "There's no problem. I've known Bert Robespierre for years. He's a man without fear or favour. One of the best cops on my team."

"But is he bent?"

"No."

"Is he straight?"

"Yes."

The conversation was the same whenever they sought to recruit new members for A6. The secret 'soundings' were taken. They had to be honest and not gay, although being promiscuous was okay. They couldn't object to that as it was a password for politicians. Each potential recruit was then vetted by Z42. Only when it was clear they were beyond corruption, would they be approached. Few could or would resist the invitation to join A6. It was for the elite risk-takers. No coasting. No cruising.

Risk and reputation were, in different ways, the twin attractions for the police and the liberators. Infiltration was always in the mind of those on each side. Strangely both the cops and activists attracted the same sort of character. All-or-nothing types. You needed a zeal beyond the call of duty. You had to be in love with the romance of death.

At the right Gorge the band rode up the hill with Zogger leading. There was no guard to worry about as they took him out on the way in. Chrysler injected him with

311

bullshypzl, so he was now deep in the sleep of the unjust. He'd remain that way for the next half a day. His memory would be shot too. True to her word, he wasn't harmed. Bagshot was right. The area was deserted. No people, no life. The next batch was due to be delivered on Monday. When the band arrived the place was in total darkness. Each of the band circled the brick and steel and wood building. They removed their bandanas and sprinkled them with petrol. The Annexe was doused in petrol. As Arnold lit the fuse at the back door, Floyd lit one at the front. Chrysler lit the bandana tail at the side so it would go in unison. Deke loitered at the other side. In a blur of motion, Zogger climbed onto the low adjoining roof and tossed a home-made Molotov through the skylight window. The Molson Molotov smashed and spread. Four of the band stared at the burning building, happy to see it become a memory.

She got the umbrella contraption from the Hog and put it up. She planted it right in front of the Annexe and torched it. As it burned it spelt out their message: ANAL.

"What a beautiful sight. Burn on babe," Chrysler shouted.

Deke kept urging them to leave. "Surely you've seen enough?" No one paid him any attention. "Look it's only a fire. Big deal." They ignored him. They lingered, taking a last long look knowing it was a night to remember. He urged them. "C'mon. Let's go. It's getting late." Still they loitered with intent.

Sweat formed on Deke's forehead. His shirt stuck to his armpits. Small pools gathered in his palms, making his gloves stretch. "We've got to get out of this place. We gotta split. They'll be here soon." Though his hoarse voice rang with desperation, his words were lost in the wind. All minds, save his, were on the carnage. Deke shouted the same message again. It didn't register as they were all exhilarated, entranced by the flames flying sky-high and what it meant. Deke shouted louder and revved his Hog hard to attract their attention. "Come on, come on. Move."

"What is it? What's wrong with you?" Zogger asked. "Soak it in, man. Tonight we torched Treblinka. What could be better than that?"

"We've got to go."

"Hold your Hog," she shouted back. She laughed.

"We've got to go," he shouted, as loud as his voice would allow. "They'll be here soon." His hot face glowed with guilt.

She heard his words. Zogger knew that look. She saw he was serious. It sobered her from the excitement of the fire. Her wild eyes hooked into his. "Who?"

While the fire illuminated his face, Deke's body shivered with icy fear. Sweat ran across and down his chest. Drops gathered near his coccyx. Betrayed by his face. She'd seen that look so many times before, in and out of Court. It always spelt guilt. "Who? What have you done now?"

It wasn't a question, but an accusation. A curse. Just like a lawyer. Deke, caught off-guard, stuttered and uttered, "The Heat. They're on their way. I warned them."

"Why? You miserable little bloodclot."

"I had no choice. You're crazy. You're declaring war on the whole bloody world. I'm trying to save you from yourself."

"Judas," she screamed. "You babyfecker."

The others were startled. They heard the last part of Deke's angry exchange with Zogger. A jolt of joint anger jerked through them. Deke sat there as scared as a schoolboy on a vicar's lap. All four stared at him, looking meaner with each moment. She asked, "So how much silver did you get to sell your friends down the river?"

"Let's lynch him," Chrysler shouted. He and Floyd and Arnold went towards him. "I got a better idea. Let's toss the tosser into the fire."

"Or over the Cliff," said Floyd.

"Yeah," said Arnold, "feed him to the fishes."

They surrounded him. As they were about to grab him, Zogger shouted, "Let him be. Leave him – for me."

"You sure?" Arnold asked

"You'd better believe it," she said. Her body flared and eyes fire-flaught. She was incandescent. Inflammable with rage. Serious. They knew it. "Go, go, go! Now!"

Arnold got on his Hog and rode off listening to his hero, Arthur, extolling the virtues of Fire. Floyd sat astride his Electra-Glide and joined him. He turned his headphones to the Motown sound of Burn-Baby-Burn. Chrysler joined them as they rode magnificently through the cold night air. He revved the chrome Model V while singing with Jason, Sitting on Fire.

When they were arguing, Deke took the chance to escape. He nudged away, gradually revving and zoomed off towards the cliffs. "Wait. I've got something for you," she shouted and laughed hysterically. She followed him. Deke hammered his Heritage Softtail down, moving around the cliff tops. She revved the Low Rider and closed the gap. At that time, in that place, the wind howled so it was hardly safe to walk. Below them chopped a cruel sea. They drove like twin-demented demons, moving their Hogs apace. They went up and down on the narrow tops with their hearts and lights blazing.

Meanwhile, the cops having waited in vain for so long, decided to call it a night. On their way back to base, separately, they saw plumes of sparkling red flames curl skywards. They had agreed to meet in Portishead. Instead, Birkett radioed Hastings as he was worried it might be a home-fire with the occupants deep in sleep. So the BMW and the Golf raced towards the smoke. They fired through the back lanes of Cheddar towards Churchill. It took them no time to get to Clevedon. The traffic was as light as music at a Madonna concert.

Birkett and Hastings could barely believe their eyes. They saw a huge burning crucifix with ANAL lit within the flames. The building behind it was a furnace. They looked at each other through their windscreens. Amazed. Confused. Both shook their heads. While gaping at it they were distracted by two moving maniacs. Deke and Zogger were speeding up and down the narrow lanes like newly-released lunatics. One moment the cops could see them, next moment they were gone. Then they'd reappear, though the sound was drowned by the wind, the speed could be seen. The cops were more amazed.

"What in hell's happening?" Birkett radioed, looking through the windscreen.

"I've no idea," Hastings replied, his palms upturned and his shoulders shrugged, reflecting his confusion. "Joy riders? Chicken racers? Chasing a villain?"

"Who knows, but someone's going to get hurt," Birkett said. "Only one thing for it, stormy Norm, we've got to move. I'd guess it's one of our boys. You up for it?"

"I'm ahead of you, Patsy," said Hastings. The radio crackled as he added, "We'll cut him off at the cliff top. That way he'll have nowhere to go unless that bike's got water wings."

Both officers could see and sense the danger. The best

thing to do was seek reinforcements. There was a simple problem: they didn't know who was chasing whom. They assumed the obvious. They assumed it was a crimo being chased and presumed it was by another cop. Could even be from A6, Hastings thought. That they were wrong on every count gave them no immediate cause for concern.

"Patsy, you go left, I'll take the right lane. We'll meet on the brow."

"Got it. I'm off."

Hastings motioned to Birkett, they'd travel in different directions to cut the villain off. Birkett clambered slowly around the steep lanes, far too slowly. He hadn't realised how steep the lanes were or how fast the maniacs were moving. He anticipated being at the corner first and blocking the villain's path. The rest would be easy and result in a commendation. Birkett could almost write the Judge's words for him. There would be a suitable mention of "risk" and "duty" and "a brave police officer serving the citizens of Bristol." He could see promotion and another stripe. In the blink of an eye he could see a passing out parade and the Queen's Medal. The rest would be him repeating the story time after time over a pint, recalling the thrill of it all and ending with a quiet chuckle saying, "Danger is my middle name." He'd tell his tale in the Police Club, at the Annual Ball and at the Federation's Convention.

Birkett's fame and fate was affected by a reverse serendipity. He was wrong on three important points: he lacked the speed to be there first; it was Deke not Zogger being chased; at the very corner he chose there was a sheer drop.

As both climbed, Birkett and Deke came to the same corner at precisely the same time. The relative force and speed and surprise as they met each other's eyes caused them to panic and lose control. The heavy Harley caused the Beamer to move closer to the edge. So much closer it didn't stay on the edge of the ledge. Travelling too fast, the power of the bike carried it on its own path. Newtonian bliss in action. Both went in separate, but similar directions, down in a hail of sparks and screams. On the way the Beamer hit the rocks and exploded in a ball of fire. His seatbelt split. Birkett shot headfirst through the screen towards Deke. The Harley went on its own trajectory, going into an arc and gliding through the moonlight towards a huge pile of jagged boulders. As the Harley met the boulders a mushroom of metal and bodies grew and flew and died.

Within perhaps twenty seconds of their pupils meeting each other for the first time in their lives, they were lying with both pairs of eyes closed forever. Deke and Birkett landed between the giant rocks, very close to each other. His head, ballooned with the plasma spreading by his body trying to lower his temperature, met the size twelve boots of Birkett.

The two charred bodies formed a perfect 'V'. But only the grave had the victory.

As they frizzled, the Golf came roaring round the cliff top. Zogger's flight-and-fright syndrome kept her juices flowing. She raced ahead in a fury and circled through the ramblers' route. Hastings was hot on her tail. The darkness was a killer. It strained their eyes, watching for the edge, now lit sporadically by the sparks from the double-death. Zogger re-appeared behind the Golf. She then flew close to his exhaust pipe. So close she could see the colour of Hastings' eyes in his rear-view mirror. He saw her. When he saw the rider's eyes for the first time, he realised it was

317

a woman. She was taking him for a ride. Given that his friend had fried, the fact it was a woman didn't amuse him.

Zogger knew the lanes from her reconnaissance for the arson attack on the Annexe. In case she needed an escape route. She twisted and teased the accelerator, all the while refusing to hide her half-smile. It changed from a chase to a duel. The reversal of the roles, hunted and hunter, appealed to her. Hastings' armpits became wet with matted sweat. It trickled down past both elbows, onto his palms.

Zogger took her helmet off, tossed it over the top, it sparked on the rocks, bobbed in the sea and then sunk. She pointed at Hastings and motioned the helmet's path and then pointed at him again. "You're next," she mouthed. The crimson bandana hung loose around her neck and mingled with her scarlet hair. She made a quick turn and then disappeared from Hastings view. She climbed up the steep dirt track, wheels shuddering and over the other side. Going down she was smack-bang in the line of vision of Hastings.

Zogger zig-zagged from side-to-side, slower and slower as she approached the Golf. Hastings was getting hotter as the seconds passed. Save for their lights it was pitch black, so they were moving to their senses. Hastings foot moved, down-up, throttle-happy and angry. He kept his right boot perched on the pedal ready to push the metal and drive her into the sea's eternity. He moved it on and off the pedal. He undid his seatbelt. His knuckles turned white, his fists clenched on the wheel. As his anger mounted, his mind lost out to instinct.

Gauging his mood she turned and accelerated and raced on ahead. He was trying to figure what was on her mind. He figured he might as well follow and mow her down. Hastings wondered if she'd taken flight, so he gingerly

318

followed her path. The darkness and fear and frustration and seeping sweat rolling across his chest unsettled him. Before he could act, she stopped on a short stretch and turned wheelie to face him. As he came around the corner she was lying in wait. Their eyes reflected a mix of respect and hate. No longer a duel. It was a joust to the death.

She continued to taunt and tease with a twist of the throttle, ready to pounce on her black and chrome panther. Hastings toed and heeled the accelerator. He'd been in many dangerous situations before, but never one quite like this. No one knew where he was except Birkett and he was now kissing the angels. Normally calm and detached, now he discarded all his experience and his cop's whispering conscience. In a split-second he became the shadow of the misogynistic racist street-thug he usually arrested and despised. "OK, you black bitch," he said, aloud through clenched teeth. "You want it, you got it. See how you like this up you." She locked on his lips and read what he said. Hastings held his right hand up, thumb angled out, moved his four fingers quickly towards his palm and mouthed, "Come on, come on." He moved closer towards her. He was wishing her towards her death.

She didn't move, daring him to win-or-lose. Her eyes tightened and heart kicked causing her to gently blow a calming funnel of breath. Something she learned at yoga. It gave her focus. She sure as hell needed that now.

The Golf slowly moved towards the Harley. Zogger throttled, getting ready for the absolute moment. Too early and she would go under his wheels. Too late and she would be mown down. Zogger switched her lights off. She could still see him. He couldn't see her eyes. He moved closer. Foot-by-foot. She moved closer. Wheels barely turning. A cliff-hanger. When she judged the right distance between them, she hammered her horn so hard it shattered the night like gelignite. The sound so sudden and loud completely threw Hastings. The sound pounded through his brain. His white fear dissolved into pure panic. The Harley's horn split the shadows and Hastings' head. At that moment she switched her main beam on to dazzle, to blind him. She wound the throttle back. Held the brake hard. Let it loose. She revved and rode the front wheel onto the bumper and mounted the bonnet and raced across the roof, still starry-eyed and laughing with her horn and heart on fire. The old Low Rider climbed down the boot and jumped straight on the ledge. Zogger revved hard and turned a wheelie again to face Hastings. She and the Low Rider stood poised and proud, her bandana blowing in the wind, each looking like a feral mare.

Hastings had no idea the place Zogger had chosen for the joust was right on the edge. The Golf started spinning madly in the mid-blue moonlight. Relying on his training school advice to 'turn into a spin', he pushed the steering wheel through his sweaty palms. He tried to reverse the direction of the wheels. Losing his concentration, losing control. His path was formed and final. Straight over the top. His face so fixed with fear he looked like Crap, the macaque. Having seen his parents die slowly and in agony, his mother from MS and father from lung cancer, Hastings always said he wanted a quick clean death. The Golf swirled and whirled onto rock after rock and landed in the swishing, surfing waves. With that the car exploded and sizzled on the sad sick sea. As he wished, he had a clean death. Hastings was even saved the expense of a coffin.

Meanwhile the others in the band arrived back at the Shuman. "Zogger, are you coming down to the party?"

Floyd called down the corridor to a non-existent musician. "Right, you'll be down in a minute. See you then."

"Can you check you've got the passports, Zogger?" Arnold asked. They both said it loud enough for the porters and cleaners and other hotel guests to hear. Of course, she was nowhere near, but the pretence was part of the plan. They were arranging her alibi.

"Here's a copy of that CD you asked me for, Zogger," Chrysler said as he walked towards her empty room.

Arnold and Chrysler and Floyd slipped into the post-gig party at the Shuman that was still in full swing. They mixed with the liggers and loons, making constant references to Zogger as if she was there too. If, or more likely when, the police happened to ask any questions at any time, the answers would provide another ready-made alibi. The answers would be genuine though false as the drink and drugs mixed reality in their minds. Similarly even the staff would satisfy the police, as for them, just as blacks do to white people, all untamed musos look the same. The most honest chambermaid would claim to have seen Zogger, indeed spoken to her, convincing both herself and any curious cop.

Zogger turned heel and thundered down the road to the Shuman. Slipping in the back exit, she went to her room. Shortly thereafter she went downstairs. She joined the party as if she was there all night.

"Zogger, how are you?" asked Nettie Moore, a guest and struggling songwriter.

"Terrific. How're you? You're looking great."

"Really good. I've just signed a new contract. I got a higher royalty and more control."

"That's great news. You deserve it, Nettie. It's been a long time coming."

321

"Too true. I was looking for you earlier. Where've you been?"

"I was upstairs rehearsing a new song with Arnold."

"Fantastic. Great. What's it called?"

"It's a spoof tribute to the Coke Porters singer, Cydney Gryphon. She's phenomenal. It's called Now That I'm A Rock 'n' Roll Star. Do you want to hear it?"

"'Course I do. When?"

"Now."

"Sure."

"I'll just see Floyd, then you can have a listen."

"Fine. I'll get another drink. Did you want one?"

"Yeah, please. I'll have two fingers of the malt. It'll lubricate the tubes."

Zogger saw Floyd and mingled with the others to secure her alibi, if it was needed. She then sought Nettie out and gave her the first listen to their new song. Again the real reason was the alibi. Nettie would recall, if asked, that they were together for ages. Most of the night. Zogger then joined her back at the party until just before 4.00 a.m. She and Nettie were still flying. When Zogger left the party she was still in high spirits. Not ready for sleep. She tuned in to the ex-copper, whispering Unkle Roberto. Far from drowsy, she listened to the radio interview with Jim, or was it Roger, McGuinn. He explained the origin of one of her talisman songs, *I Wasn't Born To Follow*.

Angel Flying Too Close To The Ground

Sometimes someone's whole life can turn upside down upon a word. Depending on who says it and when, there is a power within a word, whether it's a compliment or a curse. The word can make or mar a day or a decade. Or a life. Long after the conversation or argument has become nothing more than a froth-filled vacuum, the gaping mouth from which it sprung become a home for worms, the word is still scalpel-sharp in the memory.

"Is that the best you can do, Jago?" asks any Art teacher of a snivelling child and the ambition to be a future Rembrandt is aborted.

"That dovetail joint is sloppy, Doggett. Do it again," a Woodwork teacher barks and the shy child quietly cries as his idea of being another Hepplewhite quickly dies.

Words are so strong the use of one that is right or wrong can serve to build or destroy. A respect for language gave Zogger strength when she used emotion as logic to reach a chary jury. For her, words were the bridge between morality and law. It was why she wanted rights over welfare. The second gave bigger cages, the first guaranteed freedom.

Zogger was alone in the Shuman getting ready to leave for the West Coast. Her eyes fixed on the letter in her left hand. She gave it a cursory glance when she found it in her pigeon-hole on her last day in Chambers. As with so many busy people, she didn't open it there and then. Having just finished Qualm's trial, her mind was elsewhere and she was thinking about her future. The following few weeks flew by in a blur. Now her past clashed with her future. All the thoughts she held at bay kept returning.

Just before she quit the Chambers she visited her friendly GP. She wanted to be sure she was healthy on tour. "Zowie," Dr. James Alexander said, "I don't want to give an opinion now because it could be wrong. It's just that the initial test shows a blip – it could be nothing – and I'd like a specialist to look at it. Just as a matter of caution, you understand?"

"Sure, but what's the worst scenario?"

Alexander told her in his best bedside manner and reassured her as only he could.

"Yes, that's fine, Jim," she said. "In fact I feel better now than I have for long time."

"Well that's good, really good to hear. I'm so pleased."

Zogger knew this was something of a social charade as he never called her Zowie unless it was important. She claimed she just wanted a check-up, but deliberately kept from him how she felt so fatigued so early of late. Even carrying her Strat – she wouldn't allow anyone else to touch it – was tough these days. After a while she could feel the weight.

"We should have the results in a few weeks," he said. "If you're passing any time, do drop in. You don't have to make an appointment. Come after Court if you wish. I have a late night surgery on Tuesday and Thursday."

"Yes. Good idea, Jim. I'll do that. See you soon. Thanks."

"'Bye, Zowie. Take care," said the doctor.

Dr. Alexander had treated her for over two decades. Since before she suffered her trauma. He'd not seen her much recently, but he always sensed some fragility below her steely surface. He knew what she had coped with and ostensibly won.

He wrote to her twice. He sent the first letter to her

home. It never arrived. An alien postman stole it and used it to obtain a false passport and steal another identity. He sent the second one, marked 'Private', to her Chambers. She ignored it. He left a short message on her answer phone. She ignored it. It wasn't like her to do so. Usually she was careful to answer any letter and certainly one from Jim Alexander, whom she saw as a friend more than merely her doctor. He was there when her black dog days barked. She knew, without his help she wouldn't have pulled through. Especially after her mother became unwell. She thought then it couldn't get any worse. She was wrong. Her father fell ill. Zogger owed such a lot to her doctor. Certainly her sanity, perhaps even her life.

She was so busy preparing for the trial against the killers of Molly, she had little time for anyone or anything else. She somehow knew she was ending one way of life and starting another.

Charles normally opened all the letters that arrived in Chambers, whether personal or professional. When a plainly personal one was opened by "mistake", he claimed it was not clearly marked or he was too busy to notice. She knew he was too lazy and nosy. The letter for Zogger was obviously personal, so Charles reluctantly put it in her pigeon-hole. He watched her closely, hoping she'd open it. As with all Clerks, he ached to know other people's business.

After the trial Zogger was in a dazed haze from the defeat. She shoved it in her Glastonbury bag, where it remained. She was reeling from the verdicts; raging from the defendants' insults in the Court foyer. She stayed that way for some time. The letter, still unopened, curled at the edges. When she saw it, whilst shuffling other papers, she refrained from opening it. She couldn't afford to be distracted. Her mind was filled beyond the brim. The verdicts had changed her. There was no time to lose. After visiting Qualm's abattoir, she was caught up in the tour. During that time she practised her craft at the factory farms, the fur shops, the halal butchers and the vivisection laboratories. Now the tour was over, it was time to conquer America. Next stop the world. The letter like heaven could wait.

The morning after the night before when Deke met his death, she casually opened the letter. Her bleary eyes caught the first couple of lines and she read them, but hardly understood the words. She was not really in the mood. Her thoughts were on Heathrow and the silver bird and Marin County. Half-formed ideas floated through her mind, then scattered like scared crows. She thought about how far she'd come from when she was just seventeen and on the threshold of a dream. The letter got a little blurry as a tear came to her right eye. She continued to read slowly. As she did, the incident flooded her vision. She remembered how he attacked her, stole her mind and almost her life. When telling her parents she toned down the truth. For years and years she suffered in silence unable to tell anyone, except Dr. Alexander, of her true feelings. Her assailant had given her a life sentence. As she read on, she could hardly make out the words through her tears.

She remembered how, Giles Osbourne, the Consultant, told her, "There's something you have to know. You'll never be able to have children. The damage is too extensive." Time and again that sentence had surfaced throughout the years. When thoughts about the broken bottle and the "damage" and her loss appeared, her eyes automatically scrunched tight in an attempt to lock them out. It never worked, then or now. Anytime, day or night. The more she tried to block them out, the quicker her feelings formed.

Many a night she met his image. Many a night she awoke drenched in sweat, as wet as an otter's pocket. When she woke she came face-to-face with him. His visage, uglier than a burst ulcer, haunted her days. Then as now.

She remembered the questions, the examination for sexually transmitted diseases, the Aids test, the wires in her jaw and the strict liquid diet. All the counselling and operations and therapy as her broken body and mind struggled to survive. At one stage she nearly gave up. The pain engulfed her. There was so much for so long it passed the threshold. Her breakdown proved a blessing. It gave her respite, an escape from herself. All that kept her attached to the invisible thread of life was her will. Her thoughts of Helen Keller helped her to hang on.

It now seemed so recent and real, it was part of her make-up which time couldn't heal or she conceal. "Hello mum. Yes, I'm OK. Thanks for coming." Zogger could see herself back in the hospital. She knew how important her mother's visits were to her recovery.

"You look really well. You've improved since yesterday," she would say day-after-day and, despite the truth, would mean it as only a mother could.

"Where's Dad?"

"He'll be here soon. Don't worry. He's got some work to finish." Her father would visit too. Together they threw the lifeline she needed. As a family they pulled her through.

She held the letter lightly, the words blurrier, their meaning unclear. Her eyes kept going to a previous sentence. Odd snippets strayed through her mind. She thought of animals in agony, being injected with cocaine and gonorrhoea and heroin and syphilis and Aids, just so some junkie or pervert could destroy himself. She was pulled up with a start when she realised she was tested for Aids, yet totally innocent. Confused, yet empathetic for those genuine victims. Recognising why their hurt was her hurt too.

There are no truths save for these two: life is suffering and heart and home are one. When one becomes too much the other is destroyed. Zogger barely recovered some stability in her life when she was shaken to her roots. Without warning her mother became enervated and grew pale by the day.

"Hi, Mum. How are you? You're looking better." It was now Zogger's turn to lie to her. "Are you taking care of yourself?"

"Yes, Mum. Of course I am. Don't worry about me, it's you we want to get well. We need you back home."

Dr. Susan Ballion, the surgeon, told the family, "Elizabeth has pancreatic cancer." She explained, it was "Borne of stress from worrying about her daughter."

Zogger looked at her mother with wires and tubes and bags springing from her arms and chest. Her face was racked with pain and a honeycomb of wrinkles formed on her forehead and circled her dark, tired eyes. In less than six months she had aged a decade. Throughout the next six weeks Zogger visited every day. "Stay strong, Mum," she urged, as her mother in turn had urged her. "We need you. We really do."

"I'm feeling better," said Elizabeth, lying again. "I'll see you tomorrow."

"I won't be able to come tomorrow because I've got to attend a week-end course in London. But Dad will come on Sunday. Is that alright?"

"Yes. No problem, honey," Elizabeth said. "Goodbye, Zowie. I'll see you soon."

"Alright, Mum. I'll be back on Monday." She leant over and kissed her goodbye, praying her mother would be better soon. In a small way she seemed to be improving.

When Zogger saw her again she was lying flat, her eyes closed, in a mahogany box with shiny brass handles. She looked so young and beautiful. The way Zogger would always remember her. Her father, though ruthless in business, fell apart before her young eyes. As time passed he sought solace in one too many bottles. Although he staggered on for a few months, he was dead inside since the only woman he ever loved, died. It wasn't so much simply losing his will. He died of a shattered heart.

With each word the letter got harder to read. The words jumped and jumbled on the page like the snow in her souvenir. The doctor's signature, written in black ink, smudged with the falling mist she wiped from her right eye. Her left eye filled too. She fixed on the final word of the penultimate sentence. It was a cold clinical word that in context had the exact opposite meaning to that intended. She read it and repeated it to herself, first silently then aloud. For her the result of the test was the most negative word in the world: positive.

Qualm's bad seed had borne fruit. How long have I got left? The question she'd asked Doctor Alexander bounced around her brain. Last time she spoke to him he said, "As it has lain dormant for so long, if it's positive it will be rampant. It will be aggressive and accelerate throughout your body. Then there's nothing we can do for you. So you'll have, probably, six months left. At most a year. It's likely to be less."

She reflected on how Qualm had in effect killed her mother, her father and in a perverse way, Deke. He'd given her a life sentence. She shook herself free from those thoughts. She clenched her right fist, raised it to heaven and shouted, her voice as loud as a bullhorn, "I'm glad, so glad, I castrated you, you miserable bastard! Babyfecker!" Zogger whirled around the room, caught her reflection in the hotel window and laughed, her voice tinged with hysteria. She laughed and laughed and could barely stop. When she did, she cried. More than before.

Disturbed and distracted by the letter, she turned on the television. That act spelled out her state for Zogger hated television. She despised the clowns who appeared on it, with second-hand emotion and third-rate jokes. She loathed political programmes. She saw TV as prozac for the proletariat. The screen lit up with some jowl-jawed journalist asking an arrogant Chief Constable about the arson at the Annexe. "I understand there was a meeting at Whitehall early this morning concerning the three people killed at Clevedon. Have any arrests been made?" Stefan Phryski asked.

"It's too early to say. The forensic experts are out there now," Max Feibelman said.

"Who was killed?"

"Two very fine officers. Dedicated. They died doing their duty. I can't release their names until they're positively identified and their families have been informed."

"I thought three people were killed. Who was the third?"

"You're right. It was some musician from a punk-type rock group, I understand. I can't help you as to his name until we check the dental records. And inform his next of kin."

"But what are you doing about arresting the culprits? Surely you've got some leads?"

"We're doing everything we can. The problem is they strike without warning, leave no trace and simply disappear into the night."

"What about forensics, DNA, undercover or informers? Haven't you got anything?"

"We're still working on the case. These things take time. We've tried it all, but so far there's nothing," he lied, as usual. "These characters are professionals. They know where to go, how to get in and out, then fade as if they never existed. There's something will-o'-the-wisp about their plans and how they operate."

The police had some forensic from the anonymous phone call. It was saliva that had seeped through to the mouthpiece and an earprint. Feibelman wanted to keep that ace up his sleeve. He believed that was shrewd. It was valueless. If and when they were traced, the band would write Deke off as an imitation James Dean-like deranged character, stricken with a morbid sense of failure and a huge ego. They'd say he rode over the cliff to commit to his suicide ideation. As the police couldn't be sure of the precise time of death, they wouldn't be able to prove otherwise.

"What about this insignia, the logo they use, ANAL. What does that mean?"

"They leave that in some form everywhere they burgle.

331

Everything they come into contact with or everyone is branded with it. We think it's something to do with an anarchist organisation. A sort of voodoo vandalism induced by drugs. I understand a similar sort of logo was seen at an illegal music festival. A 'rave' I believe it's called." He'd been suckered by Deke's false explanation at the abattoir, which was passed on down the line. "It was also used by the eco-terrorists who vandalised the planes at Abbey Airport. They call themselves The Elves."

"But Chief Constable, this has been going on for ages and no one's even been arrested, let alone convicted. Surely the public deserve better, given your resources? What's all this cost?"

"Well, it's-..."

"Isn't it time for heads to roll? Perhaps your own?"

Zogger wasn't paying much attention to it. Aural wallpaper. The intellectual content of a Woss interview. As it washed over her she remained dry. She saw on the screen the faces of journo and cop, phonies whose mouths moved in a rhythm of calculated deceit. So ugly she thought there ought to be a law against them appearing in public. At least, unmuzzled. She watched and heard the sounds without meaning, "blah-blah-blah."

Then, "Bang!"

She raised her right cowboy-booted foot and smashed her pointed toe Best-style into the screen. Bang went the tube, the gas escaped around the room, then hung suspended around the ceiling rose. The questions posed were never answered. She figured it was a shoo-in anyway.

She guessed she'd better leave as the smoke without fire could raise a suspicion.

Her ideals didn't alter with the news. Zogger was still

armipotent. She vowed to grab the hot coals from the fire before she was blessed with the Tombstone Blues. She knew the view of Camus on the limits of life was true.

Zogger held the letter loosely. It fell from her fingers and fluttered to the floor. The radio DJ, Albie Breed, played a request for, "Marie Springfield, a wonderful wife and mother who is fifty years old today." The song sounded so good even though the singer was the writer. Zogger knew she would never make it to her half a century. She grabbed her bag and strode to the door. She stopped, closed her eyes for a few seconds, then hummed to the gentle harmonica and sang along with the chorus of *Forever Young*.

"Early twenties. Tall. About six feet two inches. Male. White. Red baseball cap with a logo on the front. The peak covering his eyes. Wearing sunglasses. Enters the Park. Nods to first suspect. In conversation with first suspect. Walks through Park with first suspect. Walks to nearby car. Second suspect appears. Nods to first suspect and tall male. Have you got all this, Helen?" DC Robert Valentine asked WPC Hart.

"Yes," Hart replied. "Who is it? Do we know him?"

"No. Just another junkie."

"What's happening?"

"The tall male follows the second suspect. They appear to know each other. They're leaving the Park. Entering Britannia Place. Into Dharma Row. Both stopped near a Jaguar, an S-type. Second suspect gets in driver's seat. Tall male gets in rear seat."

"Behind the driver?"

"No. Passenger."

"What colour?"

"Sort of dark blue. I can't read the number. It's F U something."

"Which way's it pointing?"

"Towards this building, towards us. Second suspect reaches down, under the seat. He's handing something to the tall male. A bag. Tall male wets his finger and dips into the bag. Dabs his finger on his tongue. Nods his head. "

"What colour?"

"He's white. I told you."

"No, the bag."

"I can't see it clearly. I can only make out movements. Tall male's nodding again. He's passing something to the driver. Driver flicks it, counting something. Looks like money. A wad. Second suspect reaches under the seat. Passes a package to the tall male. They shake hands. Tall male leaves the car. Second suspect stays in the driver's seat." Valentine sneezes as the builders' dust gets up his nose.

"Have you got it all on the Log?" he asked.

"Yes."

"Anything you didn't get?"

"No. We can check it together later. When we sign it."

"What time is it?"

"11.59."

"How long are we going to stay?"

"Have we got enough?"

"This one makes an even dozen in the last hour. Surely that's enough to prove they're dealing?"

"Let's give it 'til 1.00 p.m. We might get it up to a score."

"A score to score."

"An own goal."

Valentine and Hart were keeping the two suspects under surveillance. Valentine was in an upstairs room of a 'safe' house over looking Dart Park, the meeting place for addicts to find their dealers and score their daily fix. It was notorious in the area and a place to avoid for the public. Britannia Park was re-named because parents and children would find bloody needles, discarded 'darts', near the swings. The lavatories were littered with French ticklers and broken hypodermics. Even if you had dysentery it was never safe to visit, as punks and junkies jostled for space. The crooks were ever eager to find the next victim to pay for their fix and their fun.

Hart was downstairs in the same building keeping the Log. She had a makeshift studio so she could accurately record the details Valentine fed her. She was recording what he was seeing. Timing it too for accuracy. Both would later sign the Log to prove its truth in court. It would be an Exhibit. It would become an aide-mémoire. It would be used to identify the dealers and users. It would be used to lean on the little fish to help the police catch the Mr. Big's, the ones who otherwise always got away. If any of them denied being there, the Log would be used to crush their false alibis.

As Valentine called out the descriptions, the actions and the results, Hart inscribed it. A tape recording was made of the details so it was contemporary, legally a running log. Hart in turn relayed the information on to the six other officers stationed out in the street. All undercover. Studiously nervous and scruffy and young. They became part of the scenery. Just like junkies. Valentine continued looking, Hart continued listening. The descriptions were interchangeable: Young. Old. Dirty. Odd. Baseball cap. Long hair. Short hair. No hair. A beard. Unshaved. A ponytail. Male. Female. All shapes, all sizes. The customers came and went. Each one recorded as each crime was monitored as they mounted and multiplied. The tally had reached eighteen.

The junkies were stopped as they left Dart Park and given the option of a Plea and possibly prison or cooperation with the police. They always chose to sell the information and save their own skin.

"Skinny. Very skinny. Emaciated. Long, frizzled blonde hair with black roots. Small. About five feet two. About seven stone maybe less. Black leggings. Light T-shirt. She's a half-caste," Valentine said. "Alter that, put mixed-race. We'll be chewed up in Court."

336

"Do you recognise her?"

"No. Could be Janie Crudup or Paula Greenfield. She keeps moving, looking around, jerking her head. Obviously a mainliner."

"The description sounds like Carmel Goffin."

"Could be. Couldn't say for sure. She looks really cold. Keeps moving."

"Why are junkies always so cold?"

"The blood's thinned by the snow."

"What's she doing?"

"Same as before. Same moves. First suspect is in the bushes. Can't see second suspect. She's going back into the Park. She's shooting up. In broad daylight on open view. Desperate."

"Shall I alert Barney Buckle and Louie Berry? They're covering each end of the Park. We'll catch her in the act."

"Don't worry. Let her have her fun. It'll be her last fix for some time. Her next meal is porridge. Buckle can pull her when she leaves the Park. We'll take a blood sample at the station. See how much horse is in her veins. You wait, she'll turn turtle."

"What time do you make it?"

"12.43."

"Spot-on. The Log can be used to corroborate the forensics."

"Good. One more and we'll strike. Wait-...Holy Moses!" Valentine shouted.

"What is it? What's wrong?"

"Oh, no. Jesus wept. No, no, no."

"What's up, Sarge? What's gone down?"

"She pressed the plunger, then just dropped to the ground."

"What's she doing now?"

337

"She's on the ground, legs akimbo, flicflac, the bleedin' dart's still hooked in her arm. There's snow in her blood. She's O.D'd. Get an ambulance. Do it. Now!" His voice croaked an octave higher.

"I'm on it." She kept the Tape running. She pressed her mobile for a direct line to the station. J.J. O'Hara arranged for an ambulance. He said it would take eight minutes. It would probably take fifteen, but the record would show eight anyway. Government statistics.

"Where are the suspects? They're facing murder," Hart said.

"One's getting in the car. The other's walking to the Park."

"Do you have any idea who they are yet? Can you recognise either of them?"

"This is sweet. You'll like this."

"Why? Who is it?"

"I can see the first suspect clearly now. I'd recognise him anywhere. It's Dean Canker."

"How about that."

"I can see the driver. He's looking over the roof. It's your friend and mine, Lee Hornet."

"Those winker-stinkers have just run out of luck."

"Wait. Canker's run to another punter. Hornet's in the Jag. I'll see you downstairs. Get the motor running. They ain't going nowhere, except inside."

Canker saw the half-caste woman fall as if she'd been poleaxed. His face changed from a friendly grin, fixed for the punter, to a look of pure panic. He ran over to her.

"What about my horse?" the other punter shouted. His face was frozen in panic for a completely different reason. He couldn't live without another fix. He ignored the

338

woman. Canker ignored him. Canker went to see the skinny woman who couldn't live with one. Canker stared at her. He didn't like what he saw. He'd seen that look too often. Friends had flaked out in his arms, their arms a dartboard of heroin pricks. He knew she wouldn't survive. He didn't want to be around when she was found.

Hart rushed downstairs and was in the driver's seat of the black Jaguar X-type. The engine was already hot as Valentine raced up to her and climbed into the passenger seat. Neither bothered with seat belts.

"Move it, Helen. They're at the end of Dharma Row. They got nowhere to go. It's a cul-de-sac." Valentine panted, his chest heaved as he blew rapid breaths.

"I'll block them in. Have you got the cuffs? "

"Mmm," he said, nodded as he felt the tell-tale bump on his belt.

"Will they be tooled up?"

"No. Not their style. They'd have shot themselves by now. Or each other. Mind you, they might have a machete." Valentine wasn't fussed. He could handle their kind of trash. He anger was rising. "Can't you step on it? We're hardly moving."

"It's busy, Bobby. Look at the traffic. Shall I put the lights on? I didn't want to alert them."

"Put them on. They'll be gone when we get there. Put the horns on too. Put 'em on max. Blast the bastards."

The blue lights spun and whirred. The banshee siren wailed through the noonday air. The traffic spread each side in waves as Hart's car sliced through them. Those coming towards Hart stopped in confusion as the drivers tried to avoid the speeding X-type. Hart cut through the traffic in no time and arrived at the mouth of Dharma Row.

Canker jumped into Hornet's S-type. He was out of breath. He looked ashen.

"What's wrong, Dean? What's happened? You look like you seen a bloody ghost."

"Don't ask questions. Just go!" He shouted, panting hard, trying to catch his breath.

"Why?" Canker asked. "What's up?"

"Don't ask. Just drive. This is deep, deep shite." Canker panted, "That black bird. You know, you've just seen, the one with the massive hair like Hendrix." Hornet looked puzzled. "You just sold her a 10 bag?" Canker was always angry. It was natural, part of his charm. Hornet frowned, still puzzled. Canker asked, "What's with you?"

"I know who you mean. What about her?"

"She's just O.D'd! That's what."

"Feck me gently in the back of a Bentley. You sure?"

"As sure as your shite smells and mine don't. Now go!" Hornet hammered on the pedal, jolted and shot away. The wheels rocked, the tyres screeched.

Hart saw the S-type and drove straight in front of it. Hornet couldn't pass. Valentine went to get out, but stopped. Hornet reversed down the Row. Hart followed, swung the car through 90 degrees and jammed her brakes full on. She was in front of Hornet, side-on. Anchored. He had nowhere to go except through her. Valentine turned to her, "Sweet driving, sister." He smiled. She smiled.

"Thanks," she said. "It's nothing. You should see what I do on a sixpence." She looked around Valentine at Hornet. Her smile vanished.

"Pump it, Lee. Pump her," Canker said. "Jump the pig."

Hornet gritted his teeth, looked at Hart and revved, aiming straight at her. As he sped towards Hart he swung

340

the wheel to the right at the last moment, braked slightly, accelerated hard and caught the rear with the full force of his front nearside. The S-type smashed into the X-type. Jaguar pounced on Jaguar. Rubber burned. Glass and metal shattered and scattered across the road. The whiplash force spun the X-type through another 90 degrees so Hart was facing down the Row. The sharp pain shot through her. Across her shoulders and down her spine. "Ooohh," Valentine shrieked. His back arched as the whiplash ended. Hart and Valentine clasped their hands and held the back of their necks as the pain tracked down their backs.

Once the sound of crashing glass and metal stopped, you could hear Hornet laughing. He was hot and high, having chased the dragon moments before Canker's return with the news about the "black bird." Sampling the merchandise. Canker had snorted some smack seconds before she collapsed.

Hornet sped down the Row and swung into the heavy traffic of Desolation Avenue. Without warning, he mounted the pavement, went through two red lights, overtook slower vehicles, hit the kerb and the odd parking meter. Driver after driver moved to avoid an accident. Many of them shook their heads, followed by one or two waving fingers. Horns were pressed to no effect. Passengers wound their windows down and joined in with the drivers' curses. Hornet's speed increased to more than double the limit. He overtook a slow van turning right. His wing hit a bollard that smashed across the road. Bits flew everywhere and a flying shard hit a child who burst out crying. Blood poured from her head. His mother shook her fist at Hornet and swore as he raced down the Avenue. "Bollards," he shouted, laughing with a jackdaw cackle.

Hart pulled out of the Row and into the Avenue. Between their laughter, Canker kept looking behind. He squinted. He saw Hart gaining. He could see the blazing lights and hear the blaring horns. "They're making space, Lee. Lose them."

"I'll lose them alright. Watch this." He quickly slowed down. Hart gained on him. When Hart was about twenty metres behind him, Hornet stopped dead.

"Helen! What's that mad wank doing now?"

"He's crazy. We've gotta get out of this place," she said. Before she could react, Hornet reversed and rammed them. He pulled forward a few metres and rammed them again. Hornet's boot smashed Hart's lights and bent the grill into the radiator. Water spouted from the grill. Both wings were bent in towards the tyres.

Hornet pressing the pedal to the floor, raced away. He glanced in his rear-view mirror. Valentine and Hart looked as if they were sitting on something extra. "They don't like it up 'em, Dean."

"Follow that twat," Valentine said. "I've radioed Buckle and Berry. They'll cut him off at the Johnson Crossroads."

"He's going to kill someone."

"He's got nowhere to go after the Crossroads."

Hornet accelerated and raced towards the Junction. Just before it there was a pedestrian crossing. An overweight man with a young Akita started to cross, without looking. Hornet approached on his blind side. It wouldn't have helped if he looked, as he was blind drunk. Hart's car was limping behind Hornet. Her siren was screaming at maximum volume. Her tyres screeched. Her lights whirled around like a ballroom mirror-ball. All the other cars stopped. The only ones moving were the X-type and the S-type. The black and blue Jaguars. The lights and sounds from their cars split the mid-day autumn sun.

Buckle and Berry were at the Crossroads.

As Hornet crossed the white line, the noise and lights spooked the Akita. She was young and powerful and turned back, pulling the man as she darted away. He tried to hold on to her chain, but because she was so strong it slipped from his grip. The Akita almost pulled him to the ground as she ran off in blind panic, down the Avenue. Hornet looked in the rear-view mirror and was surprised Hart was behind. Ahead he saw the cop cars, two big red Mercedes, blocking his route at the Crossroads. Nose-to-nose. As the dog yelped, the man groaned, then staggered and swayed on the crossing. Hornet, distracted by the sight and sound, ploughed into him. He flew into the air, landed on the roof, bounced off onto the bonnet and rolled off on to the road. On coming to rest his legs were splayed and bent and broken at the knees. His arms were out-stretched, both broken at the elbows. His face was a bloody pulp, his body a jackknife. As Hornet raced on, Hart screeched to a halt. The front offside tyre came to rest just gently crushing his skull. He lay prone on the tarmac road as lifeless as a string-less puppet.

Hornet looked at Canker and arched his eyebrows as if to say, shall I? Canker formed his right hand into a fist and flashed his stained teeth. Holding his bicep with his left hand firm around his flabby muscle, he brought his right arm up at ninety degrees. He pumped his arm down and up, pivoted at his elbow. "Rock it, Lee. Rock it!"

Hornet sped towards the two cop cars. Buckle dovetailed into the determined eyes of Hornet. Fixing on Hornet's eyes, Buckle positively knew. He'd seen those eyes before. Buckle looked at Berry and mouthed through the windscreen, "He ain't gonna stop." Berry mouthed back in a silent scream, "Nor am I!" He slid towards the passenger door. Simultaneously Buckle and Berry jumped out and scampered over to the grassy picnic area. About six seconds later Hornet smashed directly into the middle of both cars. Metal on metal meshed in the almighty crash. The impact forced the two cars apart, but trapped the Jaguar so it lodged between them. The noise stopped and an eerie silence gathered for about two seconds. Whoosh. A sudden whoosh as the Jaguar became a massive fireball. A mushroom of fire and glass and metal and rubber and smoke soared as all three cars burned. Canker and Hornet were locked between the two Kompressors. No one could reach them. Though no one tried. All that reached them was the fire as their flesh melted fast on their bones. Their open-mouth shouts appeared to be, "Whoo-whoop."

Hart reversed slowly from the crossing. She drew up as close as she could and both got out. Valentine and Hart saw the sheet of heat and kept staring as Canker and Hornet became blackened corpses.

"So dreams do come true," she said.

"We'd better get another ambulance, Helen."

"An ambulance? It's a bit late for that, isn't it?"

"Not for them. All they need is an undertaker. I mean for the man with the dog. Well, without the dog. Call the fire brigade too."

Hart and Valentine went back to check the condition of the drunken pedestrian. His face was unrecognisable, covered in blood and ballooned in size. Part of the right side was caved in. Alcohol fumes filled the air. He looked at the man and said, "Cancel the ambulance. Just get the police surgeon. Tell him to bring a certifying Form. He's already DOA."

Hart looked at the man's profile closely. She walked around him, studied him, concentrating on the remains of his face. Then she muttered to herself, "No."

"Someone you know?" Valentine asked.

"Don't think so. I thought I might, it was just the tattoos. Judging by the state of his face we'll need the dental records to verify the ID. What's happened to the dog? Maybe he's got a disc or a chip."

"He ran off like a hound from hell. I don't suppose we'll ever see him again. Did you see those teeth, that coat? Around here, someone's probably already snatched him. He'll be in a backyard right now being lined up for a fight tonight."

"I'll take the Jag back to the Station. You staying here?"

"Yes. I'll get the traffic moving. Besides the ambulance and the fire brigade, send for a couple of tow trucks."

"I'll be off then."

"'Bye, Helen. By the way, don't drive too fast. Accidents can happen." Valentine laughed, relieved he was still alive. Hart laughed, glad to be in one piece, at least physically.

Hart drove the X-type back to the Station, well within the speed limit, by compulsion rather than choice. For the battered Jag had oil dripping, water leaking, wires poking from the grill and the boot, plus black holes where once there were flashy lights. It trundled along with all the style of a second-hand tractor. As the internal electrics were damaged she couldn't use the intercom to call in or receive messages or listen to the radio. She was travelling on an automatic pilot. She reached into her inside jacket pocket and put the old pink Walkman on the passenger seat. She pressed the button and selected a universal Irish song. It sounded sweet after so much sourness to hear the gorgeous brogue of Bat the man asking the unanswerable question, *Who Wants To Go To Heaven?*

All She Wants To Do Is Rock

Only animals and lawyers and rock stars are appreciated when they are dead. Or at least two of them. It's the turn of the worm in two senses that makes the feeling appear. Each one has a value only visible by death. Zogger was consumed by such thoughts. The feeling that consoled her was she had done the right thing. Given the choice she'd do it all over again. Reflecting on the doctor's letter, she vowed to act the same way for all her borrowed tomorrows.

Zogger decided not to tell the band about her little local difficulty. Her problem was irrelevant to the big picture. What mattered was the band's vision. At breakfast time all the band – except Deke that is – were cock-a-hoop. The Tour had been a resounding success. They had struck the first heavy-duty blow. They held the keys to Bristle and unsettled the City Fathers. The politicians were now forced to accept ANAL was truly in their face.

The band barely spoke to each other at breakfast. That was not unusual when a tour ended as the excitement and weariness bit into their bones. However there was one stark difference between past tours and this one. Normally it ended, they'd go their separate ways for a month or more before meeting at The Freefall. Now it was not the end, but the beginning. Deke's demise had cemented rather than destroyed the band's relationships. They were stronger than before. For when an idea has come, it has its own momentum. So it was for them. Like Mandela they felt they were fighting for freedom.

They pored over the daily newspapers. They passed them round. No one made any direct comment as you never could tell how a throwaway line would come back to haunt you. Here it would seal their fate. It was not the time to relive the glory or gloat. When Zogger said, "Deke's late then, that's unusual for him," no one blinked, but just carried on chewing their croissants. The murmurs and nods captured their mood.

"Ah, here he is now," she said. The others joined in, using the ruse. "Hi, Deke. Come and join us," she said as Warren Blackstone II appeared and sat down. Later a waiter would swear Deke was at breakfast with them.

"That's an interesting story about the railway strike," said Arnold, passing The Guardian to Zogger and pointing to the article below it. An article about another arson.

"Yes," she said. "Have you seen the interview with Chrissie Hynde on her new album and Shirley Manson's cover of The Smiths?" She passed The Independent and pointed to the other page.

"Listen," Floyd said, "there's going to be new series on BBC4 on the history of PETA. That should be informative. It's all about nutrition." He deliberately mispronounced it as if it was a bird or bread. Decoded by the band, they knew there was an article in The Times about their raid at the Annexe.

The papers carried some sensational details. They speculated on the meaning of the branding. The tabloids printed false, fuzzy photos of a different fire. The band listened cautiously to the radio bulletins. They were subject to a 'M' Notice so they couldn't stray outside strict legal limits or risk prosecution. Besides, the last thing they wanted to do was convey the contagion of fear within the scientific community. That would come soon enough. Each bulletin allowed a spokesman for the vivisectionists to spout about the true cost in hindering research. They never, however, mentioned the Silver Spring Monkeys.

348

Zogger had her bag and checked out of The Shuman quietly, straight from breakfast. The Reception was busy. Another smile another statistic. She kept it low-key hoping to be unnoticed. Just another muso on the road to Hell. The band got ready, checked out and the whole entourage made their way to Heathrow Airport. The band travelled separately so as not to arouse suspicion and, should it prove necessary, could provide mutual alibis.

Meanwhile the police were tight-lipped. The subject-matter and the investigation was so secret and sensitive that no 'spokesman' could offer information. On one level that was true. On another level it was because they had no evidence, no understanding of the cause and no way to trace the guerrillas.

At the Airport the stream-conscious ideas flowed through Zogger. All those scattered thoughts that filtered through her mind on many a sleepless night. Her feelings grew sharper after the Trial. Lost in her thoughts. She felt relaxed as she pondered her future.

Suddenly her name came over the Airport tannoy. "Would Zowie Darrow please come to the Information Desk?" She froze to the spot. The message was repeated. Her heartbeat raced and outpaced her breathing. Palpitations began as her palms became clammy. She wondered what to do, whether to run and, if so, where to and would she be caught? What do I do? Learning a lesson from many a former client she figured she would brazen it out. Breathing heavy, she tried to compose herself. She walked as calmly as she could towards the Information Desk. "It's not a problem," she told herself, "I've got a reason to be here." The rest of the band could vouch for her. She had an alibi for last night. She thought she could surely bluff a couple of plain-clothes plods.

349

As she approached the Information Desk she saw two uniformed officers. Each was holding a small machine gun. Fear flowed through her veins. Her legs began to buckle; they wobbled and shook seeming to have either no life or a life of their own. Her heart hammered against her chest. Her composure disappeared. So unexpected. Her mind was turning to mush. She couldn't believe it. How could they have got on to me so soon? Where did I go wrong? Save me, Mum?

She took some deep, deep breaths and walked ever so slowly to the Desk. She went to the side opposite the cops so she could see their reaction. Buy her time. She said to the receptionist, "Hello, I heard the tannoy, I'm I-I'm…"

As she stammered and almost announced herself, someone shouted, "Zogger, Zogger." She turned around. It was a sight to make a sinner see the light. She saw Chrysler. He walked to her and said, "Sorry. I was delayed. I forgot my passport." Breathlessly, he said, "Forgot my mobile. Almost ran out of petrol. You know me. Always the same. I had to rush back, make sure you didn't go without me. Rode so fast I could see my own ghost. I pushed a ton on the Motorway. Have I held you up? Hope you're not sore. Sorry."

Zogger laughed like a moonstruck loon and hugged him and rained a helter-skelter of kisses on his confused red face. She laughed and laughed and a tiny tear trickled down her relieved face.

"Wow. I'll be late in future if that's the treatment I get."

"I'm so glad to see you," she said, "I really am." Her eyes were sparkly and wet. She swung her arm around his shoulder. "Let's sit down. I need to catch my breath."

They sat down on the bucket seats. "Zogger, there's something I wanted to ask you. I've been meaning to for some time."

"Anything. Anything at all."

"I feel foolish asking, mind. What does ANAL mean? I'm sure the others know, but I just joined in. When you branded those creeps after the trial I thought it was a one-off. Something personal. I kept meaning to ask you, but we've been so busy."

"Strangely, it was Deke who coined it. Were you at the SXSW then?"

"Maybe. I was in West Texas around the time of your trial. On tour with Kick Against The Pricks."

"Like all the best ideas, it's very simple. It encompasses our whole philosophy. We use it so it'll become a public phrase. Think about it. The scientists kill them in our name. The sportsmen whip and kill them for our fun. The farmers treat them cruelly so we can eat them cheaply. Religion uses them with our support as food in a disguised ritual and as sacrifices and scapegoats. We take advantage of them for pleasure or profit for no other reason than we can. You and me conveniently forget that animals have feelings."

"True. But where does ANAL fit in all that?"

"It's a harsh reminder of an unpalatable truth. We bask in a false sense of identity that protects us from our own lies. We know in our pitch-black hearts we are guilty. The last thing we want to do is admit the last thing we are is A Nation of Animal Lovers."

"Oh, that's raunchy. Really. I'm with you," he said. "How long do we go on for?"

"As long as it takes to win. When the caged bird is flying free and singing on the wing. It'll probably take my lifetime. But what could I do that's better? It's the straight wire."

"Then let's take it to the wire."

"You see we're disciples of the only religion worth following: freedom. You can only gain it if you're willing to lose it. So like you say, to the wire."

Arnold and Floyd and Warren Blackstone II, a former roadie, arrived together. The band met, swapped greetings and gathered ready to board the plane. Arnold and Floyd couldn't understand why Zogger was so elated. The nerves and the tension faded. She knew this was the trip of her life.

The trip would take them through America. The boys in the band were rebel-poets, seeking neither glory nor fame.

Deke had been erased from their memories with a swish of Orwellian bliss. He was replaced overnight by Warren, a skinny Amazonian with a golden arm and a tongue to match. Warren was an ex-attorney who followed the trail led by Carmichael and Mercer and swapped a dull law practice for the once-only chance to write songs that matter. Songs that could cause a cause to burn and reach a soul and never let the flame die.

Warren, an avid fan of Blake and Greenleaf, was going home. He'd followed the sounds in his mind since he shook a rattle to the rhythm of Odetta as his mother, Marjorie, rocked around the kitchen. A roadie for Hellsucks, he was trusted on every level. The trip was an ordeal as he left the Bay Area almost two decades before. He'd seen what remained of his father, Alfred Blackstone, after returning with a purple heart. After Vietnam had stolen Alf's mind, it stole his body too. With time he became a cripple and an addict. One hard rain day Alf murdered Marjorie. He then put both barrels in his mouth and blew his brains out. The only witness to the double killing was Warren.

Warren visited the White House using forged papers. He broke into the Presidential Suite and desecrated the Office. He burnt the Stars and Stripes on the famous desk and left a human visiting card as a symbol. A hot turd. He felt it was the sort of message a politician would understand.

Later he qualified as an attorney, studying in the best environment: San Quentin.

The flight through the night seemed shorter than it might have because of the two films they showed. The Hustler and The Trial were movies Zogger loved for their style. Near the end of the journey the airhostess gave her a local newspaper. Zogger flicked through The San Francisco Chronicle. She read about a concert in Candlestick Park and a few obituaries. As she went to fold it, her eyes were drawn to a photograph. Spread across the page was a story about three thugs who had cornered a pet goat. Using her as a moving target, they pumped bullet-after-bullet into her. Her white coat had turned bloody scarlet. The colour photo brought her death to life. When Nancy, the goat, was found the owners were distraught. Byron Junior, eleven years old, who had Nancy since she was born, was so traumatised he needed psychiatric treatment. Zogger closed her eyes. She clasped her hands. A thin line of blood creased her left hand where she dug her right nails in hard.

The locked-in thoughts drew a tight circle around Zogger's heart. She had faced her own fear of being a victim, a woman and the wrong colour in a white man's world. She knew she could never go home again. She placed the paper in her bag near the only two books she ever took on her travels, Tolstoy's Diaries and The Trial of

Socrates. Closing her eyes she saw why she identified with the underdog. Animals and her kind were the unspoken token niggers of the world. The plane flew high above the cloudless sky as it neared San Francisco. "Yes," she said, "this is the first day of the Infinity Tour."

"I'm sorry, did you say something?" asked Camille Javal, an American tourist returning to California, sitting next to her.

"No. I was only talking to myself. At least then someone agrees with me."

"I see. Would you like this?" Camille offered her a newspaper. "It's today's."

"Oh, thanks." Zogger scanned the pink edition of the Telegraph. She casually turned the pages. On page seven her eyes strayed across a byline. She scanned it, then again. She couldn't take her eyes away. Two drug dealers were killed during a police chase. It ended when their car exploded. A pedestrian was hit and killed by the speeding drug dealers trying to escape. She was mesmerised by the story. She squinted, riveted to the page. Her eyes focused on two words. The pedestrian's name jumped off the page and stabbed her eyes: Kevin Qualm.

"Listen! Listen!" Arnold shouted to the others, unable to contain his emotion. He pointed to his cans.

All their ears pricked up almost in unison. They looked at each other with eyes lit as bright as a Steiff teddy bear. The news came over their headphones of the new number one on the Highway 61 radio station. It was a double A-sided record that went to the top with a bullet. Their look of dazed happiness said it all. Each gripped the seat to feel the rush as a yelp of joy pushed from them as the sound hit the airwaves. It was Hellsucks with an anniversary record bridging the past to the future. For the moment Zogger found solace in knowing the good times would keep on rolling. For all she wanted to do was rock to the grave. She heard the gruff-voiced DJ, Lizzie Cotten, say the first side was Here Comes The Heat and the second was the new seven-minute single, *Guillotine the Queen*.

Acknowledgements

I owe a debt to Henry Salt that is yet to be repaid. His classic, *Animals' Rights*, opened the door for me with a skeleton key. His wisdom and compassion was and is so far ahead of his time, I still struggle to grasp the purity of his prescience.

I remain in awe of his vision and life-style. His work has provided a map and a signpost.

J. M. Coetzee's brilliant novella, *The Lives of Animals*, was a finger-pointing book that helped to shape my ideas and hone my blunt ideals.

There were many others whose arguments and polemics I filtered into the crowded house of an untidy mind. I read those in favour and those against the concept of rights for animals. There were others who rubbished the notion of animals even having a status in society and rested their case on crapaudine Cartesian logic.

Even though the main theme and acts of my novel are borne of a fertile imagination, I am indebted to the pure truth of Singer. For Isaac knew what we all know, but prefer to look the other way. His history was a mirror to all our Nazi hearts.

I remember being taken aback when reading about Araminta Ross, the heroic vigilante who rescued slaves from their self-ordained masters. I was struck by how a black politician described her and others as *"unbending idealists."* He concluded that though he disagreed with the views of the antiabortion activist who pickets the town hall or the animal rights activist who raids a laboratory, he was *"robbed even of the certainty of uncertainty – for sometimes absolute truths may well be absolute."* That politician is now the President of the United States.

Grateful acknowledgement is given for permission by Leone E. Cynews to quote from *Pagliacci's Return, Goodbye Palladium Blues* and *For W* © 2000 Drowning Man Music and *Somebody Loses Somebody Wins* © 2005 Sough Sounds.

The pace was governed by the legacy of Blind Willie McTell and Brel as their raw sounds floated around my briefs and wound their way through my veins.

Thanks to Wendy and Molly for the rare gift.

Author

Noël Sweeney is a criminal lawyer. As well as practising crime, he specialises in human and animal rights. He also lectures and writes on those subjects. Sweeney has written *Animals and Cruelty and Law*..